PRAISE FOR THE NOVELS OF
#1 NEW YORK TIMES BESTSELLING AUTHOR
BARBARA FREETHY

"Golden Lies is an absolute treasure, a fabulous, page-turning combination of romance and intrigue. Fans of Nora Roberts and Elizabeth Lowell will love Golden Lies."

-- ***Kristin Hannah***

"Freethy's smooth prose, spirited storytelling and engaging characters, are sure to send readers on a treasure hunt for the author's backlist books."

-- ***Publishers Weekly***
on Golden Lies

"In Golden Lies, a priceless Chinese artifact, an ancient curse, and a decades-old betrayal set the stage for this gripping story. Multidimensional characters, realistic and sometimes funny dialog, and a well-constructed plot that Freethy unwraps with such consummate skill that the conclusion is at once surprising and totally logical result in a rich and compelling tale."

-- ***Library Journal***

"Ms. Freethy follows her superb SILENT RUN with this excellent sequel SILENT FALL. The storyline of a man and woman on the run is absorbing and the pacing is fast and furious. A chilling conclusion that will shock and surprise readers."

-- ***Fresh Fiction Reviews***

"Freethy hits the ground running as she kicks off another winning romantic suspense series with Silent Run...a superb combo of engaging characters and gripping plot."

-- ***Publishers' Weekly***

"If you love nail-biting suspense and heartbreaking emotion, Silent Run belongs on the top of your to-be-bought list. I could not turn the pages fast enough."

-- ***Mariah Stewart***

"Freethy has a gift for creating complex characters."

-- ***Library Journal***

"Hooked me from the start and kept me turning pages throughout all the twists and turns. Silent Run is powerful romantic intrigue at its best."

-- ***JoAnn Ross***

"In the tradition of LaVyrle Spencer, gifted author Barbara Freethy creates an irresistible tale of family secrets, riveting adventure and heart- touching romance."

-- *NYT Bestselling Author* ***Susan Wiggs***
on Summer Secrets

"This book has it all: heart, community, and characters who will remain with you long after the book has ended. A wonderful story."

-- *NYT Bestselling Author* ***Debbie Macomber***
on Suddenly One Summer

"Freethy's skillful plotting and gift for creating sympathetic characters will ensure that few dry eyes will be left at the end of the story."

-- ***Publishers Weekly***
on The Way Back Home

"Freethy skillfully keeps the reader on the hook, and her tantalizing and believable tale has it all– romance, adventure, and mystery."

-- ***Booklist***
on Summer Secrets

"Powerful and absorbing...sheer hold-your-breath suspense."

-- *NYT Bestselling Author* ***Karen Robards***
on Don't Say A Word

"A page-turner that engages your mind while it tugs at your heartstrings...Don't Say A Word has made me a Barbara Freethy fan for life!"

-- *NYT Bestselling Author* ***Diane Chamberlain***
on Don't Say a Word

"I adore *The Callaways*, a family we'd all love to have. Each new book is a deft combination of emotion, suspense and family dynamics. A remarkable, compelling series!"

-- *USA Today Bestselling Author* ***Barbara O'Neal***

Also By Barbara Freethy

The Callaway Series
On A Night Like This (#1)
So This Is Love (#2)
Falling For A Stranger (#3)
Between Now and Forever (#4)
Nobody But You (Callaway Wedding Novella)
All A Heart Needs (#5)
That Summer Night (#6)
When Shadows Fall (#7)
Somewhere Only We Know (#8)
If I Didn't Know Better (#9)
Tender is the Night (#10) *Coming soon!*

Lightning Strikes Trilogy
Beautiful Storm (#1)
Lightning Lingers (#2) *Coming soon!*
Summer Rain (#3) *Coming soon!*

The Wish Series
A Secret Wish
Just A Wish Away
When Wishes Collide

Standalone Novels
Almost Home
All She Ever Wanted
Ask Mariah
Daniel's Gift
Don't Say A Word
Golden Lies
Just The Way You Are
Love Will Find A Way
One True Love
Ryan's Return
Some Kind of Wonderful
Summer Secrets
The Sweetest Thing

The Sanders Brothers Series
Silent Run
Silent Fall

GOLDEN LIES

BARBARA FREETHY

HYDE STREET PRESS
Published by Hyde Street Press
1325 Howard Avenue, #321, Burlingame, California 94010

Silent Fall is a work of fiction. All incidents, dialogue and all characters are products of the author's imagination and are not to be construed as real. Any resemblance to persons living or dead is entirely coincidental.

Printed in the United States of America

Cover design by Damonza.com

ISBN: 978-0-9969464-8-3

Prologue

San Francisco-1952

The fire started easily, a small spark, a whisper of breath, and the tiny flame leaped and crackled. It slid quickly down the length of rope, growing in size and beauty with each inch it consumed. It wasn't too late to stop it, to have second thoughts. A fire extinguisher was nearby. It would take just a second to grab it and douse the small flames. But the fire was so beautiful, mesmerizing -- gold, red, orange, black -- the colors of the dragons that had promised so much: prosperity, love, good health, a second chance, a new start.

The fire began to pop, the small sounds lost in the constant boom of firecrackers going off in the streets of San Francisco in celebration of the Chinese New Year. No one would notice another noise, another spark of light, until it was too late. In the confusion of the smoke and the crowds, the dragons and the box they guarded would disappear. No one would ever know what had really happened.

The flame reached the end of the gasoline-soaked rope and suddenly burst forth in a flash of intense, deadly heat. More explosions followed as the fire caught the cardboard boxes holding precious inventory and jumped toward the basement ceiling. A questioning cry came from somewhere, followed by the sound of footsteps running down the halls of the building that had once been their sanctuary, their dream for the future, where the treasures of the past were turned into cold, hard cash.

The cost of betrayal would be high. They would be brothers no more. But then, their ties had never been of blood, only of friendship -- a friendship that some would think had died this night of fire, but in truth had died much earlier.

There was only one thing left to do, grab the dragons and their box of secrets. The back door offered an escape route. The wall of fire would prevent anyone from seeing the truth. No one would ever know who was responsible.

The crate where the dragons were stored beckoned like the welcoming wave of an old friend. It took but a moment to pry off the lid. Eye-watering smoke and intense heat made it difficult to see what was inside, but it was impossible not to realize that something was missing.

Only one dragon was inside! The other dragon was gone, as was the box. How could it be? Where were they? The three pieces were never to be separated. They all knew the importance of keeping them together.

There was no time to search further. A door on the opposite side of the basement was flung open. A man holding a red fire extinguisher shot a small, helpless stream of chemicals at what was now a raging inferno.

The fire could not be stopped, nor the future. It was done. For better or worse, the dragons would never dance together again.

Chapter One

San Francisco -- Today

"They say that dragons bring good luck to their owners," Nan Delaney said.

Riley McAllister studied the dark bronze statue in his grandmother's hands. Ten inches tall, it appeared to be a dragon, although the figure looked more like a monster with its serpent body and dirty scales. Its brilliant green eyes blazed like real stones, but those eyes couldn't possibly be jade. Nor could the golden stripe that ran around its neck really be gold. As for luck, Riley had never believed in it before, and he didn't intend to start now. "If that dragon were lucky, we'd be at the front of this line," he grumbled.

He cast a frustrated look at the people around them, at least a hundred he estimated. When he'd agreed to help his grandmother clear out her attic, he'd never imagined he'd be standing in the parking lot at the Cow Palace Arena in San Francisco early Monday morning with a bunch of people who wanted to have their trash appraised by a traveling antiques show.

"Patience, Riley." Nan's voice still held a touch of her native Irish brogue even though she'd lived in California for sixty years.

He frowned at his grandmother's perky smile, wondering where she got her energy. She was seventy-three years old, for God's sake. But then, she'd always been a pint-sized dynamo. Pretty, too, with her stark white hair that had been the same shade for as long as he could remember, and her pale blue eyes that always seemed to see straight into his soul.

"Good things come to those who wait," she reminded him.

Not in his experience. Good things came to those who sweated blood, pulled out all the stops, sacrificed everything, and never let sentiment cloud reason. "Why don't you let me sell this stuff on the Internet?" he suggested for the twentieth time.

"And let someone take advantage of me? I don't think so."

"What makes you think these people won't take advantage of you?"

"Because *Antiques on the Road* is on television," she said with simple logic. "They can't lie in front of millions of people. Besides, this will be fun, a new experience. And you're a peach to come with me. The perfect grandson."

"Yeah, I'm a peach, and you can stop the buttering up, because I'm already here."

His grandmother smiled and set the dragon gently on top of the other treasures in the red Radio Flyer wagon she'd also found in the attic. She was convinced that somewhere in her pile of pottery, dolls, baseball cards and old books was a rare find. He thought she'd be lucky to get five dollars for everything in the wagon.

A loud clattering noise drew his head around. "What the hell is that?" he asked in amazement as a tall man dressed in full armor lumbered toward the front of the line.

"He looks like a knight in shining armor."

"More like the tin man in need of a brain."

"He probably thinks he has a better chance of getting on the show if he wears the armor. I wonder if we have anything interesting we could wear." She squatted next to the wagon and began digging through the pile.

"Forget about it. I'm not wearing anything but what I have on." Riley pulled up the zipper on his black leather jacket, feeling like the only sane person in the middle of a freak show.

"What about this?" she asked, handing him a baseball cap.

"Why did you bring that? It's not an antique."

"It was signed by Willie Mays. It says so right there."

Riley checked out the signature scrawled across the bill of the cap. He hadn't seen the cap in a very long time, but he distinctly remembered writing on it. "Uh, Grandma, I hate to tell you this, but I'm Willie Mays. I was planning to sell that hat to Jimmy O'Hurley, but somebody tipped him off."

She frowned. "You were a very bad boy, Riley."

"I tried."

The busty redhead standing in front of them turned her head at his comment, giving him a long, sexy look. "I like bad boys," she said with a purr that matched her cat's eyes.

The old man standing next to her tapped his cane impatiently on the ground. "What did you say, Lucy?" he asked, adjusting his hearing aid.

The redhead cast Riley a wistful look, then turned back to the stooped, old buzzard who had probably put the two-carat ring on her third finger. "I said, I love you, honey."

"That's just sick," Nan whispered to Riley. "She's young enough to be his granddaughter. It goes to show that men can always get younger women."

"If they have enough money," Riley agreed.

"I hate that you're so cynical."

"Realistic, Grandma. And I don't think you'd be happy if I was walking around San Francisco in armor, pretending to be a knight. So be glad I have a job. The line is moving," he added with relief, as the crowd began to shift toward the front doors of the arena.

The Cow Palace, once known for its livestock shows, had been divided into several sections, the first an initial screening area where experts scoured the items brought in. When it was their turn, the first screener riffled quickly through Nan's stash, pausing when she came to the statue. She told them to continue to the next screening area with the dragon only. The second screener had the same reaction and called over another appraiser to confer.

"I think we might get on the show," his grandmother whispered. "Now I wish I'd had my hair done." Nan patted her head self-consciously. "How do I look?"

"Perfect."

"And you're lying, but I love you for it." Nan stiffened as the two experts broke apart. "Here they come."

"This is a very interesting piece," one of the men said. "We'd like to put it on the show."

"You mean it's worth something?" Nan asked.

"Definitely," the man replied with a gleam in his eyes. "Our Asian art expert will be able to tell you much more, but we feel this piece may date back to an ancient dynasty."

"A dynasty?" Nan murmured in wonder. "Imagine that. Riley, did you hear him? Our dragon came from a dynasty."

"Yeah, I heard him, but I don't believe it. Where did you get that statue, anyway?"

"I have no idea. Your grandpa must have picked it up somewhere," she said as they made their way across the arena. "This is exciting. I'm so glad you came with me."

"Just don't get your heart broken," he cautioned in the face of her growing enthusiasm. "It could still be worth nothing."

"Or maybe it's worth a million dollars. Maybe they'll want to put it in a museum."

"Well, it is ugly enough for a museum."

"We're ready for you, Mrs. Delaney," a smiling young woman said as she ushered them onto the set, which was cluttered with lights and cameras.

An older man of Asian descent greeted them. After inspecting the dragon, he told them the statue had probably been crafted during the Zhou dynasty. "A rare find," he added, launching into a detailed explanation of the materials used, including the jade that made up the eyes, and the twenty-four karat gold strip that encircled the dragon's neck.

Riley wondered if he could possibly be hearing the man correctly. It appeared that this very odd-looking dragon had some important place in Chinese history and quite possibly had belonged in the private collection of an emperor. The expert estimated that the dragon might be worth thousands of dollars, maybe hundreds of thousands.

When their segment ended and they were escorted off the set, they were immediately swamped by appraisers and other experts, who handed them business cards and shook their hands. Riley kept a tight grip on the dragon as well as his grandmother's arm. The dragon was like a prime steak tossed into a pack of hungry wolves. He'd never seen such covetous looks, such outright greed and hunger.

His grandmother wanted to stop and chat, but he forcibly propelled her through the crowd, not relaxing until they were in his car with the doors locked. He let out a breath. "That was insane. Those people are crazy."

"Just excited, I think," Nan said, looking at the statue in his hands. "Can you believe this thing is thousands of years old?"

For a brief second he almost could. There seemed to be an intense heat radiating from the dragon, burning his hands. Oh, hell, it was probably just his imagination. Whether it was a year old or several thousand years old, it was still just a piece of bronze, nothing to get worked up over. He set the statue on the console between them, more relieved than he cared to admit to have it out of his hands.

"And it was in our attic," Nan continued, a dreamy note in her voice. "Imagine that. It's like a fairy tale."

"Or a nightmare."

Nan ignored him as she flipped through the pile of business cards she'd received. "Oh, my goodness. The House of Hathaway. Look." She held up the simple, engraved card naming San Francisco's most famous and elegant store. "They want me to call as soon as possible. I have a very good feeling about this."

"Do you? Because I have a very bad feeling."

"You worry too much. Don't think about the problems -- think about the possibilities. This could be the beginning of something amazing."

"Is it possible that this dragon was actually crafted during the Zhou dynasty?" Paige Hathaway asked her father, David, as she froze the frame on the videotape one of their scouts had sent over from *Antiques on the Road.* If anyone could date the piece, it was her father, the head buyer for the House of Hathaway and their resident expert on Chinese art.

"It's possible," he said, a note of excitement in his voice and a glitter of anticipation in his eyes as he moved closer to the screen. "I wish I could see it better. That man keeps getting in my way. They really should make the object clearly visible to the camera."

The man her father was referring to was a tall, ruggedly built guy in a black leather jacket, who had started out looking uncomfortable in front of the camera and now appeared completely amazed and very, very skeptical. He was a striking contrast to the sweet, sparkling old lady he called Grandma, who seemed more than a little thrilled at the thought of her good fortune. And it might be incredibly good fortune if her father was right about the age of the object.

"Why hasn't she called us?" her father asked in irritation. "Are you sure you told her it was imperative we speak with her today?"

"On both messages that I left," Paige reassured him. "I'm sure she'll call back." Although, as Paige checked her watch, she realized it was almost six o'clock. "Maybe not until tomorrow."

"This can't wait until tomorrow. I must have that dragon."

David paced restlessly around Paige's fifth-floor office. The room was decorated with simple, beautiful

Chinese furnishings that were meant to relax and inspire. The calming atmosphere was obviously having no such effect on her father.

"Do you realize what a find this could be?" he continued. "The Zhou dynasty is estimated to have begun around the year 1050 B.C. This could be a very early bronze. That dragon must have an incredible story to tell."

"I can't wait to hear you tell it," she murmured. She liked her father the most at moments like these, when there was passion in his eyes, in his voice, in his heart.

"I can't tell the story until I see that dragon, until I hold it in my hand, measure its weight, listen to its voice, feel its magic." David walked over to the window that overlooked Union Square. Paige doubted he was looking at the city lights. He was caught up in the pursuit of a new acquisition. When that happened, nothing else mattered to him. He was completely focused on his goal.

And, for the first time, he'd included her. Usually, acquisitions went through preliminary calls made by his assistant buyers, depending on the type of piece and area of expertise. If they deemed the object of interest, they would call in her father. But this time, he'd come straight to her, asking her to call Mrs. Delaney. She couldn't help wondering why, but she wasn't inclined to ask. If he wanted her involved, then she'd be involved.

She smiled as he ran a restless hand through his wavy brown hair, messing it up. It drove her mother, Victoria, crazy that her husband often looked as creased as the dollar bills he stuffed into his pockets, instead of in the expensive wallet she'd given him for his fifty-fifth birthday several months earlier. But that was David Hathaway, a little bit rumpled, often impulsive, and always interesting. Sometimes Paige wished she was more like him. But, despite having inherited her father's dark brown eyes, she was more her mother's daughter. Maybe if he'd spent more time at home, if he'd taught her the things he knew instead of leaving her education up to her mother, if he'd loved her as much as he'd loved China...

No, she wouldn't go there. She wouldn't be jealous of an entire country. That was ridiculous, and Hathaways were never ridiculous or anything else that was less than perfect.

Her grandfather and her mother had instructed her every day of her life to sit up straight, be responsible, never show emotion, never lose control. The lessons of a lifetime still ran through her head like an irritating song, one she couldn't ignore. Her impeccably neat office reflected those lessons, replicating the atmosphere in which she had grown up, one of sophistication, money, culture, and coldness. Even now, she felt a chill run down her arms that had nothing to do with the cool February weather and everything to do with her family.

Maybe if her sister, Elizabeth, had lived, things would have been different. She wouldn't have had to bear the burden of expectations, especially those of her mother and her grandfather, who looked to her as the only Hathaway heir upon whom all responsibilities would one day fall. Paige felt guilty at the thought, because there were a million reasons why her older sister should be alive and none of them had anything to do with making Paige's life easier.

"She found it in her attic," David said abruptly, turning back to her. "That's what the old woman said, right?"

"Yes, that's what she said on the show." Paige forced herself to focus on the present.

"You need to call her again, Paige, right now."

The strange gleam in his eyes increased her uneasiness. "Why is this so important, Dad?"

"That's a good question." The voice came from the doorway.

Paige turned to see her mother, Victoria, enter the room. A tall, rail-thin blonde, Victoria was a picture of sophistication, the ultimate feminine executive. There was intelligence in her sharp blue eyes, impatience in her voice, and a hint of ruthlessness in her face. Dressed in a black power suit; Victoria was too intimidating to be truly beautiful, but no one who met her ever forgot her.

"I asked you a question, David," Victoria repeated. "Why are you stirring up the staff, asking Martin and Paige and God knows who else to find this Delaney woman? Is the dragon worth that much?"

"It could be priceless."

She uttered a short, cynical laugh. "Everything has a price, darling."

"Not everything."

"Have you seen something like this dragon before in one of your books? Or perhaps you've heard a story, a fairy tale? We know how much you love fairy tales, especially ones coming from China. You know everything there is to know about that country and its people." Victoria spit out the word people as if it had left a bad taste in her mouth. "Don't you?"

"Why do you care, Vicky?" he asked, deliberately using the nickname she hated. "It's not as if actual art holds any interest for you."

"Its value certainly does."

Paige sighed as her parents exchanged a glance of mutual dislike. Her father was right, though. Her mother rarely even looked at the inventory in the store. She was the financial wizard, the company spokesperson. David was the passionate art expert, the one for whom each piece told a special story. And Paige, well, no one had figured out her place at Hathaway's yet, least of all herself.

"Oh, I almost forgot." David reached into his pocket and pulled out a velvet pouch. "I bought this for Elizabeth's birthday, to add to her collection."

Paige watched as he slipped out a small, exquisitely carved jade dragon that had probably been designed to fit on the top of a sword. "It's perfect. It will go nicely with the others," she said as her mother turned away. Victoria had never been comfortable talking about Elizabeth or acknowledging the tokens that David continued to buy each year in honor of his oldest daughter's love of dragons. "Do you want to leave that with me now?" she asked.

Her father returned the dragon to its pouch. "No, I'll keep it until we go to the cemetery next week."

"Really, David, these ridiculous birthday parties of yours. They're so distasteful," Victoria said with a frustrated shake of her head. "It's been twenty-two years. Don't you think--"

"No, I don't think," David said, cutting her off. "If you don't want to go to the cemetery, then Paige and I will go on our own. Right, Paige?"

Paige looked from one to the other, feeling very much like a wishbone. But she couldn't say no to her father. Elizabeth's annual birthday party was one of the few occasions they always spent together. "Of course."

The phone on her desk rang. Paige pushed the button for the intercom, grateful for the distraction.

"Mrs. Delaney is on line one," her secretary said.

"Thanks, Monica." She put the phone on speaker. "Hello, Mrs. Delaney. I'm glad you called. We'd love to talk to you about your dragon."

"I'm so excited," Nan said. "It's been such an incredible day. I can't tell you."

Paige smiled at the enthusiasm in the older woman's voice. "I'm sure it has been. We're hoping we might persuade you to bring the dragon down to the store tomorrow so we can take a look at it. Maybe first thing in the morning?"

"The morning is out, I'm afraid. Riley can't drive me until tomorrow afternoon."

"That will be fine. In fact, we have a wonderful tea. I don't know if you've heard of it, but--"

"Oh, yes, yes, I have heard of it," Nan said. "I've heard it's fantastic."

"Good, because we'd like to treat you and a friend or a family member to tea and a private appraisal. What do you say?"

"That sounds terrific," Nan replied.

"Good, why don't we--"

"Just a second," Nan said. There was a rustling, then a male voice came over the speaker.

"Miss Hathaway, I'm Riley McAllister, Mrs. Delaney's grandson. We'll be entertaining offers from numerous dealers, you understand," he said in a brusque voice.

"Of course, but I hope you'll give us a chance to make you an offer after we verify the authenticity of your piece."

"Since your store has had people calling my grandmother all day long, I'm fairly certain we have the real thing. But we will not be making any decisions without doing considerable research into the company making the offer. The House of Hathaway isn't the only game in town. And I will not allow my grandmother to be taken advantage of."

Paige frowned, not caring for the implication. The House of Hathaway had an impeccable reputation, certainly not one of taking advantage of little old ladies.

"My grandmother will bring the dragon in tomorrow," Mr. McAllister continued. "She'll be coming with a friend and myself. We'll be there at three o'clock."

"That sounds--" The dial tone cut off her reply. "Well, that was rude," she said, pressing the button to disconnect the call.

"Why did you suggest the tea?" her father asked, irritated. "That's not until the afternoon."

"She said she couldn't do it in the morning."

"I just hope that doesn't mean she's taking the dragon somewhere else. I want that dragon, whatever it costs," he said.

"Don't be absurd, David," Victoria replied. "We don't have an unlimited budget. Need I remind you of that?"

"Need I remind you that I make the buying decisions?" David looked Victoria straight in the eye. "Don't get in my way, Vicky, not on this." And with that, he turned on his heel and exited the room, leaving Paige alone with her mother.

"Always so dramatic," Victoria murmured.

"Why do you think this dragon is so important to Dad?" Paige asked.

"I have no idea. What's important to your father has been a mystery to me for some time." She paused. "Keep me informed about the dragon, won't you?"

"Why?"

"Because I run the company."

"I've never known you to care about an old statue."

"I care about everything that concerns this store, especially things that make your father believe he has a blank check."

Paige frowned as her mother left the office, shutting the door behind her. It had been a long time since both her parents had been interested in the same thing. That couldn't possibly be good.

Chapter Two

Riley could feel the hairs on the back of his neck standing up. They matched the goose bumps that ran down his arms as his every instinct told him that someone was watching them. He'd had the feeling the night before when he'd stayed at his grandmother's house because he hadn't wanted to leave her alone with a potentially valuable art object that had just been seen on national television. And he had the feeling now as he pulled his car into the underground garage at Union Square. Although it was the middle of the afternoon, and the garage was fairly well lit, his uneasiness grew as he debated his options.

"Aren't we getting out?" Nan asked, a curious note in her voice as he flipped the automatic car locks back down.

"In a minute." He scanned the area with a practiced eye. Running his grandfather's security business for the past four years had made him appreciate details. He looked for something out of place. Someone sitting in a car. A broken light. A shadow that didn't belong. Everything appeared normal.

"What are you looking for?" Millie Crenshaw asked, sitting forward in the backseat.

His grandmother's best friend and next-door neighbor had come along for the tea and, like Nan, seemed more interested in what type of food might be served than whether they should actually consider selling the dragon to the House of Hathaway. Riley would have preferred more time to research the company as well as some of the other companies that had contacted them. But his grandmother had refused to talk to anyone else until after she'd had the tea that everyone in San Francisco raved about.

"He's looking for bad guys," Nan whispered to Millie. "He thinks someone might try to steal the dragon from me."

"I just think you should be careful," Riley said. "Despite the fact that the thing is ugly as sin, quite a few people seem to want it."

"Isn't it amazing that it was sitting in your attic all these years?" Millie said. "I went down to the basement yesterday and looked through all our things. I'm going to make Howard take me to the show the next time it comes to town. You just never know what you have."

"That's true." Nan cradled the dragon in her lap like it was a precious baby. "I don't think I ever saw this until a few days ago. The attic was Ned's place. He was always puttering around up there." She looked at her watch. "We're going to be late, Riley. I think we should go."

"I'll carry the dragon, just in case."

"Just in case what, honey?"

"Whatever," he said cryptically, not wanting to worry his grandmother. Despite the fact that everything looked okay, his instincts told him something was off. He hoped he wasn't making a huge mistake by not following those instincts. He got out and walked around the car so he could open the door for his grandmother. As the women exited, Riley perused the garage, acutely aware of every sound.

A car came around the corner, its tires squealing on the cement. He immediately threw himself in front of Nan, blocking her with his body. As the car sped by, he saw two teenagers in the front seat; they barely gave him a glance.

"Good heavens, Riley," Nan said, straightening her dress. "You're strung so tight you'll snap if you're not careful. Maybe I should hold the dragon," she added, as he slipped it into a heavy canvas bag.

"I'll take it. Let's go." He'd feel better when they were out on the sidewalk.

Nan and Millie hurried along in front of him. They were both breathless when they reached the elevator that whisked them up to Union Square and the blessed sunshine.

"Everything okay now?" Nan asked as they paused to get their bearings.

"I wish you'd let me handle this on my own." He continued to look around as they made their way across the square.

"And miss the tea? Not a chance." Nan smiled at him and stopped walking. "Now, tell me, how do I look? Any lipstick on my teeth?" She flashed him a perfect set of white teeth.

"Beautiful," he replied. Nan was dressed in what she called her Sunday best, a navy blue dress, nylons, and low heels. Millie was a taller, more colorful version of his grandmother, dressed in hot pink pants and matching top, her bright red hair flaming in the afternoon sunshine. "You could both pass for at least sixty."

"Oh, you're such a charmer," Millie said with a wave of her heavily ringed hand. "I don't know why you're still single."

"Neither do I," Nan said. "I keep telling him I want to see some great-grandchildren, but he always pretends to be hard of hearing at crucial times. Isn't that right, Riley?"

"What did you say?"

"See," Nan said, exchanging a laugh with Millie.

"Let's go." Riley led them around the corner, past Saks, Neiman Marcus, and the St. Francis Hotel with its glass elevators that ran up the outside of the building. They walked past the cable car stop, where a group of tourists was snapping photographs of one another. The House of Hathaway stood proudly on the east corner of the square. At six stories, it was nowhere near the most imposing building in a city of tightly knit skyscrapers, but its Roman columns and ornate gold carvings over the front doors were impressive.

Riley held open one of the large glass doors, then followed Millie and his grandmother inside.

Nan paused, putting a hand to her heart. "Oh, my, isn't this grand? I haven't been here in years. I'd forgotten."

Riley wasn't a shopper, but he had to admit the store was amazing. It was cool, quiet, and well lit, with paintings on the walls, wide aisles between glass display cases filled with art objects, a thick carpet beneath his feet, and a magnificent central ceiling that reached up six storeys and was capped by a stained-glass skylight. He felt as if he'd stepped into another world, one of money and culture, one in which he didn't feel particularly comfortable. .

"Look at this dollhouse," Millie said, moving toward a nearby display case. "It has miniature people and everything. And it costs..." Her eyes widened. "Three thousand dollars. Can you imagine? I think we sold my daughter's dollhouse in a garage sale for two dollars."

"It's amazing what some people will pay for junk," Riley commented.

"Hush, now," Nan said. "One person's trash is another person's treasure."

"I guess that's why we're here." Riley was beginning to wonder just what his grandmother's dragon was worth.

"Mrs. Delaney?"

Riley turned and caught his breath as a beautiful young woman approached them. Her hair was long and blond, held back with an ornate clip at the base of her neck, her eyes a dark chocolate brown. She was dressed in a silk turquoise dress that clung to her breasts and hit just above her knees, showing off a nice pair of legs. He'd thought he'd lost the ability to feel sucker punched by an attractive woman, but apparently not. His breath seemed to be trapped in his chest, and he had the terrible feeling that his jaw had dropped low enough to hit the floor. He cleared his throat and forced in some air as his grandmother shook hands with the woman.

"And you must be Mr. McAllister." She offered him a much cooler smile than she'd given his grandmother. "I'm Paige Hathaway."

He should have figured that by the expensive jewelry and the hint of perfume that probably cost more than a month's rent on his apartment. Well, he'd always wanted what he couldn't have. Why should this be any different? "Miss Hathaway," he said curtly.

"Will you follow me? My father is waiting for us in the lab." She led them to a bank of elevators nearby. "We're so glad you could come," she said as they waited. "Have you been in the store before?"

"Not for some time," Nan replied. "It's a bit beyond my means, you know. But it looks lovely."

"I'd be happy to show you around before you leave. We offer a variety of items in our emporium on the third floor that are quite reasonably priced."

"That would be wonderful. I've heard so much about the tea. It's the talk of San Francisco, you know," Nan added as they stepped on to the elevator.

Riley was bothered by his grandmother's eagerness. She was soaking up Miss Hathaway's charm like a dry sponge desperate for water. He supposed it was understandable; his grandmother's life had been difficult in recent years. He couldn't remember the last time he'd taken her out shopping or when they'd shared a meal that hadn't been at her house or at the cafeteria in the hospital his grandfather had been in and out of so frequently. He'd neglected her. He hadn't meant to, but he'd done it all the same. He'd have to do better in the future.

The elevator opened on the fifth floor. A set of glass doors labeled Executive Offices faced them, but Paige turned toward the right, leading them down a long hallway. Riley couldn't help noticing the discreet cameras in the hallways. There had been one in the elevator as well. Security seemed to be in good shape at the House of Hathaway. Paige punched in a code on the pad next to the door, then turned the knob. They stepped into an office with a desk and several chairs. The far wall was glass and looked into a lab area where two men were scrutinizing a vase. Riley noted a more sophisticated electronic keypad on this door.

Paige tapped on the window, and one of the men turned. He had Paige's brown eyes -- or maybe she had his. Riley didn't need an introduction to know this man was a relative and more than likely her father. A moment later, the door buzzed, and the dark-haired man walked out.

"This is my father, David Hathaway," Paige said, offering introductions.

Handshakes were exchanged as David greeted them with a charming smile. But there was a distance in his eyes when he looked at Riley that showed his distraction, or perhaps his focus, which was on the canvas bag in Riley's hand.

"May I see the dragon?" he asked.

Riley began to reach into the bag, but David stopped him

"I'm sure you've handled it a great deal, but from here on out, I'd like to limit the number of hands that touch the piece."

Riley watched as David pulled a pair of thin latex gloves from his pocket and slipped them over his hands.

"We will be examining your dragon in what we call a clean room, an environment that we keep as sterile as possible to protect the art pieces," David said. "Our initial appraisal will run about one hour. Paige will take you to tea while you're waiting, and we'll meet after that."

"I think I'll stay and watch." Riley felt slightly annoyed by the look of relief that flashed in Paige's eyes. She would obviously be happy to get rid of him.

David didn't look nearly as pleased. "There's really nothing to see. We can't allow you in the clean room, and most of our work will not be visible from the window."

"Why can't I go inside?"

"Insurance, liability, you understand," he said with a vague wave of his hand. "Please enjoy the tea. It will be an experience you will not forget."

"Oh, come with us, Riley," Nan said. "I want to share this with you."

His grandmother slipped her hand through his arm, taking any idea of further argument out of his head. Before he knew it, the lovely Miss Hathaway was leading them back into the elevator and up to the top floor, where the tearoom was located.

When they stepped inside, Riley felt as if they'd just crossed the Pacific Ocean and landed in Beijing. The tearoom was filled with expensive mahogany tables, glass display cases showing ornate teacups and pots, paintings on the wall depicting scenes from the Far East. This dining room was a far cry from the restaurants where he got take-out potstickers and Mongolian beef.

A woman in an Oriental silk dress ushered them to a table in a corner surrounded on three sides by ornate screens painted with flowers, fruit, and birds. She disappeared as quietly as she had arrived, leaving them to seat themselves at the marble and carved wood table.

"Mr. Lo will be with us shortly," Paige said "He's a Chinese tea master, and he'll conduct a tea ceremony for you."

"There's such a thing as a tea master?" Riley asked.

"Absolutely. Although the Japanese tea ceremony called chanoyu is better known, the Chinese also have their own ceremony. Since your dragon is believed to have come from China, we thought you might enjoy the Chinese version."

Riley leaned forward. "We've already dropped the dragon off with your father; you don't have to give us the dog and pony show."

Paige bit down on her lip. Judging by the slightly chapped look of those beautiful pink lips, he suspected he'd just noticed another important detail. Paige Hathaway didn't always find it easy to say the right thing at the right time.

"According to legend," Paige said, turning her attention to Nan and Millie, "in the year 2737 B.C., an emperor named Shen Nung was boiling some hot water while he rested under a wild tea tree. Some tea leaves dropped into his pot, and when he drank the hot water, he found to his surprise that he felt rejuvenated. He believed the leaves were responsible for this feeling of well-being, which then triggered further experimentation. This was the beginning of tea drinking in China. Today there are more than fifteen hundred types of tea to choose from. While more than twenty-five countries cultivate tea, China is still the main producer."

"Really?" Nan said. "I never knew that. Did you know that, Riley?"

"I had no idea. Sounds like quite a coincidence, those tea leaves dropping into the pot."

"There are other stories to explain the origin of tea drinking, but that's the most popular one," Paige added. "What's important to understand is that tea still plays an important role in Chinese culture. It's part of daily life. Tea is believed to have benefits that affect the physical, mental, and emotional well-being of those who drink it."

"I better switch from coffee," Millie said with a laugh.

"What kind of tea are we going to have?" Nan asked. "I've heard of green tea, but I know there must be lots of others."

"Lots," Paige agreed with a smile, "but I'll let Mr. Lo explain them to you." She looked up as a stooped, old man with thick black glasses and only a single tuft of gray hair on his balding head sat down at the table with them. "Mr. Lo. May I present Nan Delaney, her grandson, Riley McAllister, and her friend, Millie Crenshaw."

"Welcome. I am Yuan Lo." He set down a tray upon

which there were several items -- a shallow lacquered box, four small cups shaped like spools of thread, and four additional drinking cups. A moment later a waitress entered with a pot of tea that she set on a decorative hot plate. More small cups were also placed on the table.

Everything was so miniature that Riley felt as if he'd entered a child's tea party. He squirmed uncomfortably on the narrow chair, which was also too small. He tugged at the tie that his grandmother had insisted he wear and wished he was anywhere but here. He should have stayed in the lab. At least then he could have been bored in more manly surroundings. And he could have kept an eye on the dragon, maybe gotten some insight on how much it was really worth. Instead he was about to partake in some ceremonious, sanctimonious, hyped-up tea party.

"Relax, Riley," his grandmother said softly, as if she'd read his mind

"This has no purpose," he muttered.

"Of course it doesn't. Not everything in life has to have a purpose. Sometimes it's just about a little fun!"

Riley McAllister didn't like their tea, Paige decided. He'd stopped listening completely about the time Mr. Lo had begun discussing the differences among black tea, green tea, and oolong. While he obediently sniffed the scent of the tea leaves, and tasted at appropriate times, he didn't appear to be at all affected by the sensuous experience. She, on the other hand, was feeling warm, and a little dizzy. From the hot tea, she told herself, not from sitting next to Riley.

She had to admit he was an attractive man, with his raven black hair that was curly and thick and a little longer than it should be. His blue eyes blazed against his tanned cheeks, and there was a hint of a dark beard along the jawline. He wasn't the sophisticated executive she was used to seeing, but the rugged, extremely physical, very masculine sort of man that she almost never encountered. The kind of man who didn't tend to frequent high-scale gift and antique emporiums or museums, two places where she spent most of her time. Which was probably why she felt a little rattled around Mr. McAllister.

It was annoyance, irritation with his impatience, that made her feel hot and bothered, nothing more, certainly not attraction. Even if she were attracted, he obviously was not. He hadn't spared her more than a few disgusted glances in the last twenty minutes. It was clear that he wanted this over and done with, so he could get on with his life. She felt exactly the same way. She didn't need his condescension, his disinterest. She'd gone out of her way to entertain his grandmother, and she was sure her father would be making a more than generous offer to Riley and his grandmother in very short order. She didn't have a damn thing to apologize for, and she would not let him make her feel uncomfortable.

She straightened in her chair as the waitress brought over plates of food for them to sample. This was a lovely tea, and she was going to ignore Riley and enjoy it. At least Nan and Millie were fun. They chattered on, never seeming to notice the tension between Riley and Paige, which grew with each passing moment. She almost wished he'd talk. His silence, his unreadable expression bothered her. She was used to men who spoke about themselves, about their work, about everything they were interested in. She knew how to handle such men. Actually, you just had to listen, and she'd always been a good listener. If she hadn't been, she never would have gotten her father's attention. He was a great storyteller, and everyone knew that a great storyteller needed a great audience. That's what she'd been -- her father's audience.

What was she now? The annoying question entered her mind again. Each day it seemed to come back louder than before, more insistent, more demanding of an answer. And it wasn't just about her father, but about her mother and her grandfather and her role in the company. She was restless, itching to do something more important at Hathaway's than plan parties and museum events. But with her grandfather at the helm of the company, her father as head buyer, her mother in charge of operations, and long time family friend Martin Bennett overseeing the retail division, there was nowhere for Paige to go. The company ran smoothly without her. No one really needed her -- except they did, because the irony was that she was the heir, the only heir. The company could never belong to Victoria, because she wasn't a blood Hathaway. David didn't want to do anything but buy art objects, and Martin wasn't a blood relative. Which meant it would all one day belong to Paige.

But what was she supposed to do in the meantime? Just wait for her turn? That's what they all seemed to want. A sigh escaped her lips as her thoughts led her down a familiar, wearying maze from which there was no way out. She was relieved when Riley cleared his throat and made a point of checking his watch. At least his irritation distracted her from her thoughts.

"This is all very fascinating, but how much longer do you think your father will be?" he asked. "It's been over an hour."

"I'm sure he'll be here soon."

Mr. Lo stood up and bowed to them. "Thank you very much for your attention."

"Thank you for the delightful presentation. I learned a great deal," Nan said.

"I am glad you were pleased."

"Thank you, Mr. Lo," Paige said as he left the table.

"Now then, Miss Hathaway," Riley said. "Let's talk about my grandmother's dragon."

"Before we do that, I need to use the ladies' room," Nan interrupted, getting to her feet.

"Out that door to the right," Paige told her.

"I'll go with you," Millie said. "I drank so much tea I'm about to float away."

As soon as they left, Paige wished she'd gone with them. Riley had the sharpest, bluest eyes she'd ever seen, and right now his gaze was fixed on her. She shifted in her chair, not used to such a close, deliberate appraisal. She wondered what he saw, and she practically had to sit on her hands to prevent herself from reaching up to make sure her hair was still in place.

"You look nervous," Riley commented. "Why is that? Is there something about this ugly dragon I should know?"

At least he thought the dragon was making her nervous and not him. That was a relief. "I'm just distracted. I have a lot of work to do."

"So do I. Yet here we are, having tea."

"What kind of work do you do, Mr. McAllister?"

"I run a security company."

"What does that entail? Bodyguards? Computer security? Burglar alarms?"

"All of the above, whatever the customer needs. Who does the security for this store? Do you know?"

"Of course I know. It's Wellington Systems."

He nodded. "I thought I recognized some of their work, but they're not the best anymore. Bret Wellington spends more time on the golf course than he does on keeping up with the latest security systems."

"Mr. Wellington is a good friend of my grandfather."

"That explains it, then."

"I suppose you think your company is better."

"I suppose I do," he replied, a small smile on his lips.

She played with the napkin in her lap, wishing the ladies would come back because Riley made her nervous.

"So, why is my grandmother's dragon so popular?" Riley asked. "Frankly, when I first saw it, I thought we should toss it in the trash."

"It's good you didn't. If it's truly a bronze from the Zhou period, then it's quite old. Besides its age, dragons are revered in Chinese culture. They are believed to be divine mythical creatures that bring with them prosperity and good fortune. The Chinese dragons are the angels of the Orient. They are loved and worshipped for their power and excellence, boldness, and heroism. I don't know what story your dragon has to tell, but I suspect it will be fascinating."

"You think that dragon is going to talk to you?"

"No, but I think my father will be able to tell us something interesting about it."

"Speaking of your father, maybe we should go find him."

"It takes time to do an accurate appraisal. I'm sure you want him to be accurate."

Riley rested his elbows on the table and leaned forward. "There are quite a few places interested in the dragon -- Sotheby's, Butterfields, Christie's, not to mention an incredible number of smaller dealers. That makes me wonder if it might be better if we worked with one of the auction houses. If everyone wants the dragon, they can bid on it."

"While that certainly is an option for you, I believe we can make you an excellent offer. The House of Hathaway is secondary to no one, Mr. McAllister." It was a phrase her grandfather, Wallace Hathaway, had said on a thousand occasions. She was surprised at how easily the words crossed her lips, and somewhat annoyed, too. Her grandfather usually sounded like a pompous ass when he said those words, and she had a feeling she'd just presented herself in exactly the same way.

"We'll see about that," Riley replied.

"See about what?" Nan asked as she and Millie returned to the table.

"We were just discussing the dragon's value," Riley told her.

"I can't wait to find out what your father thinks," Nan said. "And I want to thank you again for tea. It was fabulous."

"It was my pleasure. I enjoyed myself, too."

As Paige finished speaking, her father entered the tearoom, his hands noticeably empty.

Riley stood up abruptly. "Where's the dragon?"

"In safekeeping, I assure you," David said smoothly. He then directed his attention to Nan. "I'd like to keep the dragon overnight, if I may. I know an appraiser who won't be available until tomorrow, but I'd very much like him to look at it. While the piece appears to be very promising, there are many fakes in today's market. And I want to be absolutely sure the piece is truly an antiquity. We'll need to run numerous tests."

"That sounds fine," Nan replied.

"Wait a second. Why don't we bring the dragon back in the morning?" Riley suggested.

"I'd like to study it further this evening," David replied. "We have excellent security, Mr. McAllister, if that's what you're concerned about. Your piece will be very safe in our hands, I promise you, and it will be insured as is every other piece in the store. I've taken the liberty of writing up a receipt." He handed a piece of paper to Nan.

"I'm not worried at all," Nan stated.

"Grandmother--"

"Riley, this is the House of Hathaway. They have an impeccable reputation. I trust them completely." She turned back to David. "I'd be happy to leave the dragon here until tomorrow."

"Thank you. If you'll give Paige a call tomorrow afternoon, we'll set up a meeting." He extended his hand to Nan. "On behalf of the House of Hathaway, I want you to know how very much we appreciate the opportunity to evaluate your dragon, Mrs. Delaney.

"Oh, it's my pleasure," Nan said, stuttering somewhat under David's charming smile.

David departed, leaving Paige to say the good-byes. She walked the ladies to the door and was not surprised when Riley lagged behind.

"Is this really necessary?" he asked her.

"My father thinks it is." She didn't know the appraiser her father was referring to but he was the expert, and if he felt they needed a third party's judgment, then that's what they needed. "You can trust us, Mr. McAllister."

He gave her a cynical smile. "Nothing personal, Miss Hathaway, but I don't trust anyone. If anything happens to that dragon, I'll hold you responsible."

"Nothing will happen, I assure you."

"Then neither one of us has anything to worry about."

Chapter Three

Wednesday afternoon had come too quickly, David Hathaway thought as he walked purposefully across town, the strap of the heavy canvas bag clenched tightly in one hand. There was still much to do, but the hour was growing late. The air had cooled, the traffic had grown noisy with the early evening commute, and the sun was falling lower in the sky, sometimes completely blocked by the tall skyscrapers of San Francisco. It was almost four o'clock. Mrs. Delaney and her grandson would be arriving at the House of Hathaway in one short hour. They would expect to receive the dragon or an offer of purchase. While he might be able to stall Mrs. Delaney, her grandson was another story.

David paused on the corner, wondering if he shouldn't have put off this visit until after they'd purchased the dragon. But he had to show Jasmine -- to be sure. He would have liked to come earlier, but Jasmine had been out all day. When he had finally reached her, she had told him not to come, but she always said that. And this was too important.

Crossing the street, he walked under the concrete foo dogs guarding Chinatown's main gate and past a red-faced deity protecting a local herbal shop from atop a rosewood shrine. He was only a few blocks from San Francisco's financial district, but the atmosphere, the neighborhood, had completely changed. Leaving Grant Avenue, the main thoroughfare through Chinatown, David headed down a narrow side street, past Salt Fish Alley, where the odors of fish and shrimp being cured in large vats of salt was overwhelming, past Ross Alley, once notorious for gambling, and past the Golden Gate Fortune Cookie Factory, where women still filled hot cookies with Chinese fortunes.

This wasn't his Chinatown, this tourist-attraction that played to the interests of tourists and locals who wanted to experience a little of the Orient in their hometown. His Chinatown was a continent away, in the streets of Shanghai. Veering away from the commercial avenues, he entered a residential neighborhood where apartment buildings were crowded together, one after another, hugging each other as tightly as the large, close-knit families that lived inside the small rooms. Jasmine's building was at the end of a lane. He used the back stairs leading up from the garden to her apartment. Three short knocks, and he waited.

For a moment he thought she wouldn't answer. His uncertainty was uncomfortable, unthinkable, an emotion he didn't know how to handle. Jasmine would come. She would let him in; she always had before. She had loved him like no one else. She had said she always would.

He hadn't treated her well. He knew that deep in his soul, in a place he never chose to visit. There were too many painful emotions there, feelings he kept hidden away. Sometimes he wished he could change, but as

Jasmine once told him, it was easier to move a mountain than to change a person's character. For better or worse, he was who he was. It was too late for regrets. In his hand was something special. A thrill of excitement ran through him as he considered the possibilities.

The door slowly opened. Jasmine stood in the doorway, looking far older than her forty-eight years. She wore a black dress that was but a variation of her usual black pants. He remembered a time when she had dressed in colors as bright as those she used in her paintings, when her face had lit up with joy and wonder. Now there was nothing but darkness -- in her eyes, her face, her voice, her apartment. The heavy incense she burned made it difficult to breathe. He sometimes wondered what she was mourning, but he had a feeling he already knew. So he didn't ask questions, and she didn't offer explanations.

"You shouldn't have come. I asked you not to," she said in a somewhat hoarse voice. He wondered how often she spoke to anyone. Had her voice grown raspy from disuse? A twinge of guilt stabbed his soul. Had he done this to her? If they had never met, would she have ended up here?

"I had to come," he said slowly, forcing himself to focus on the subject at hand.

"It is always this way in the week before Elizabeth's birthday. That is when you seek me out. But I can no longer comfort you. It isn't fair of you to ask."

Her words put a knife through his already bleeding heart. "This isn't about Elizabeth."

"It has always been about her. You must leave now."

He ignored the anger in her eyes. "I have a dragon that looks very much like the one in your painting, Jasmine."

Her eyes widened. "What did you say?"

"You heard me."

"It doesn't exist. You know that. It was something I saw in a dream."

"I think it does exist. Let me come in. Let me show you."

Jasmine hesitated. "If this is an excuse--"

"It's not." He glanced over his shoulder, not seeing anyone but feeling as if they were being watched. There were many eyes behind the thick curtains that covered the nearby windows. "Let me in before someone sees me."

"Just for a moment," she said, allowing him to step inside. "Then you must go before Alyssa comes."

"I will go," he promised, "after you look at this." He pulled the dragon out of the canvas bag and watched her reaction.

Her gasp of disbelief told him everything he needed to know.

Riley McAllister pedaled harder, the street in front of him rising at an impossibly steep angle. Even the cars were parked horizontally to protect from accidental runaways. Most people were content to ride their bikes along the bay or through Golden Gate Park, but Riley loved the challenge of the hills that made up San Francisco.

He could feel the muscles in his legs burning as he pumped harder, the incline working against him. He switched speeds on his mountain bike, but it didn't help. This wasn't about the bike; it was about him, what he was capable of doing. It didn't matter that he'd conquered this hill a week ago. He had to do it again. He had to prove it wasn't a fluke.

His chest tightened as his breath came faster. He was halfway up the hill. He raised his body on the bike, practically standing as he forced the pedals down one after the other, over and over again. It was slow going. He felt as if he was barely moving. A car passed him, and a teenage boy stuck his head out the window and yelled, "Hey, dude, get a car."

Riley would have yelled back, but he couldn't afford to waste a precious breath. Nor could he afford to stop pedaling. Otherwise, he'd go flying backward down the hill a lot faster than he'd come up. He pressed on, telling himself this was what it was all about, pushing the limits, forcing the issue, achieving the impossible. He was only a few feet away from the top of the hill now.

Damn, he was tired. He felt light-headed, almost dizzy. But he wouldn't quit. He'd faced bigger challenges than this. He couldn't give in. Quitting was what his mother would have wanted him to do, what she'd told him to do many times. *If you can't do it, just quit, Riley. You're just not that good at things. You're not smart. You're not artistic. You're not very musical, but you can't help it. You take after your father.* Whoever the hell he was. Aside from his name, Paul McAllister, Riley knew absolutely nothing about his father.

The funny thing was the more his mother told him he couldn't do something, the more he wanted to prove her wrong. That feeling had driven him through boot camp and a stint in the marines, and it was still driving him today. Maybe he was as big a fool as his grandmother, believing that his mother might actually care that he'd ridden up the steepest hill in San Francisco today.

Forget about her. He heard his grandfather's stern, booming voice in his head now. This isn't about your mother; it's about you. No one else can fight your battles for you. In the end we all stand alone. So when it comes your time to stand front and center, raise your chin high, look everyone straight in the eye, and know in your heart that you're up to the challenge.

The words sent him over the top of the hill.

Pumping a fist in the air, he coasted across the intersection. In front of him was one of the best views in the world, the San Francisco Bay and the Golden Gate Bridge. He could see sailboats bouncing along the bumpy water. Alcatraz was in the distance, a ferry boat pulling up to the famous old island prison. Angel Island lay beyond, Marin County, the rest of Northern California. The world was literally at his feet. At least his small part of the world. And it felt good. Damn good.

He flew down the next hill, loving the wind in his face. His cheeks began to cool, his heart slowed to a more comfortable beat, and his breathing came much easier. This was supposed to be the best part. But in truth, the best part had been those last few seconds before he hit the top, the moments when he wasn't sure he could do it. Now he knew. But he also knew that the good feeling would only last until tomorrow. Then he'd have to find some other hill to climb.

He let out a sigh and began to pedal as he reached a flat area. A quick glance at his watch told him he needed to get back to the office, wrap up a few loose ends, then pick up his grandmother and meet the Hathaways. He had to admit he was curious about the value of his grandmother's dragon. Finding a treasure in a pile of junk seemed too good to be true. But if it wasn't valuable, he doubted the Hathaways and all the other dealers in the country would be so hot to get their hands on it. In this case, his grandmother's dragon might just put a dent in his comfortably cynical approach to life.

Forty minutes later, Riley strode through the front door of his office and greeted the lobby receptionist with a warm smile, then headed down the hall. His secretary, Carey Miller, sat at a desk in a cubicle next to his office. The distinct smell of nail polish wiped the smile off his face, which was followed by a frown when he saw her bare feet propped up on her desk, little foam pads stuck between her toes.

"I hope I'm not interrupting you," he said sarcastically.

She shrugged. "You're not. How was the bike ride? You must have stopped off at home and taken a shower. You don't smell as bad as you normally do."

"Speaking of smells, do you have to put the paint on here?"

"If you paid me more, I could afford to get a pedicure."

"If you worked harder, you might actually earn more money."

He strode into his office, knowing she'd follow. It took her a few extra minutes, as she walked through the door on her heels, carefully keeping her toes from hitting the carpet. "So, did you accomplish anything besides the perfect shade of red?" he asked her.

"Did you accomplish anything besides a near heart attack?"

"Exercise is good for you. You should try it sometime."

"Please. If I'm going to work out, I prefer to do it in the bedroom." She gave him a mischievous grin. "Don't you remember?"

"I remember throwing out my back."

"That's because you did it wrong. You were on position seven when I was on six. The book said you needed to do it in order."

"Why I ever agreed to try anything in that book, I'll never know." He sat down in the leather chair behind his desk that had served his grandfather so well for so many years.

Carey flopped down in the armchair in front of his desk. "I've got another book now. You'd be surprised at some of the things in there. You should read it."

"I'll wait for the movie." With a pleased smile he surveyed the stack of papers on his desk, the half-filled coffee cup, the afternoon's sports page. His grandfather's office was beginning to feel more like his own, a place where everything was under his control. He picked up a small plastic basketball on his desk and sent it swishing through the hoop mounted on the opposite wall. "Any messages?"

"Nothing I couldn't handle." Carey popped a chunk of gum in her mouth.

"Do you have to do that?"

"It beats smoking. You know I'm trying to quit." Carey hooked her jean-clad leg over one arm of the chair. An ex-stripper, ex-smoker, ex-drinker, and ex-girlfriend, she was now his right-hand man, make that *woman*. While she hadn't been a particularly good stripper, smoker, drinker, or girlfriend, she was a good assistant, even with the painted toenails.

"What else has been going on around here?" he asked.

"As you requested, I got the goods on Paige Hathaway." She tapped the file folder in her hand.

His heart skipped a beat. "What did you learn?"

"Well, it's all incredibly..." She tilted her head to one

side. "What's the word I'm looking for? Oh, I know. Boring. It's incredibly boring."

"Excuse me?"

"Boring, dull, put-you-to-sleep kind of reading. I can give it to you in a nutshell. Paige Hathaway grew up in a fancy mansion in Pacific Heights with her parents, Victoria and David Hathaway, and her grandfather Wallace Hathaway. Apparently, the grandmother died before she was born. There was a whole slew of housekeepers, maids, gardeners, and chauffeurs over the years, but apparently they were paid well, because no one has had anything negative to say." Carey popped her gum. "Paige moved out a few years ago. She lives in an apartment in one of those high-rise buildings with a view of the bay. David Hathaway spends most of his time in China. And Victoria Hathaway and the old man, Wallace Hathaway, spend most of their time at the store."

Riley opened the folder she handed him and read through the facts Carey had just recited. "What else?" he asked, looking back at her.

"The family is a pillar of society. They support many nonprofit organizations, especially those connected to the arts, the ballet, the symphony, the opera. They're hosting an exhibit on Chinese art at the Asian Art Museum in a few weeks. They're on the A-list for parties. Oh, and get this -- Paige Hathaway was actually a debutante. Can you believe they still have debutantes? Not that she isn't pretty. There's a photo in the file." Carey sent him a knowing look. "But you already knew that, didn't you?"

"She's not my type."

"She sure isn't," Carey agreed.

He felt annoyed by her assessment. "Why? Am I too blue-collar?"

"Yes, as a matter of fact. Because Paige Hathaway is

not blue-collar. She is blue blood. If San Francisco had a royal family, Paige would be the princess."

"What did you learn about the rest of the family?"

"Victoria Hathaway is the queen. She's the CFO of the company. Wallace Hathaway, the old man, retains the CEO title despite the fact that he's eighty-something. He apparently still comes into the store every morning to review the profit and loss reports or perform surprise inspections in unsuspecting departments. David Hathaway is the main buyer for the store, and quite the jet-setter. He spends more time in China than he does here. Paige seems to be drifting through the company right now. She plans a lot of parties. I'm not sure what else she does. Those are the main family players. Although..." She paused. "I'm not sure if you want to know this or not, but there was a small tidbit in one of the gossip columns that Paige is engaged to Martin Bennett. He's a vice president at Hathaway's and another blue blood. A match made in Tiffany's no doubt."

"No doubt."

So Paige was engaged, huh? As he recalled, she didn't have a ring on her finger. He wondered why not. Probably couldn't find a stone big enough. He tossed the folder onto the desk. He'd read the rest of it later -- if he bothered to read it at all. If the Hathaways made his grandmother a respectable offer, he'd encourage her to take it and be done with the whole thing. "Did you call my grandmother and tell her I'll pick her up?"

"She said she couldn't leave. You should go on your own, and she trusts you to make the best deal for her."

"What?" he asked in surprise. "Why doesn't she want to go? Is she sick?"

"You're not going to like it."

"Just tell me."

"She said the phone rang and there was no one there, just the sound of breathing, but then she heard someone clear their throat, and she thought it might be a woman." Carey paused. "She thought it might be your mother."

"Goddammit. She can't keep doing this every time someone calls the wrong number. It's been fifteen years since my mother walked out the door. She's probably dead." He jumped out of his chair, pacing restlessly in front of the window.

Carey stood up. "What do you want me to do?"

"Call my grandmother and tell her that she's coming with me. She's the legal owner of the dragon, and she's the one who needs to sell it."

"What about –"

"Tell her I'll be there in twenty minutes, and she better be ready." He was relieved to hear the door shut as Carey left. His chest was tight again, but this time it had nothing to do with exercise but with the past.

It had not been his mother on the phone -- he knew that. There was no reason to think otherwise. None at all. But despite the ruthless affirmations, deep down inside there was a part of himself that still wondered where she was, and if she was ever coming back.

An hour later, Riley was less concerned about his mother's whereabouts and more interested in when David Hathaway would show up with his grandmother's dragon. They'd been cooling their heels in the executive offices of Hathaway's for fifteen minutes and there was no sign of David or his daughter, Paige.

"This is ridiculous," he said with irritation. He'd never been good at waiting, but he especially didn't like waiting for what belonged to him.

Nan worked her knitting needles with quiet, competent hands. He had no doubt that by his April birthday he'd have another sweater to put in his closet.

"Relax, Riley," she said. "I'm sure they'll be with us at any moment."

"It's after five. We should take our dragon and leave. There are plenty of other potential buyers out there. We don't need Hathaway's."

"Why don't we wait and see what they have to say? They gave us that lovely tea yesterday, and Paige is such a sweetheart. Pretty, too, don't you think?"

He frowned as he stretched out his long legs. "I didn't notice."

"Blind now, too, as well as hard of hearing," she teased.

Riley ignored that and jumped to his feet when the receptionist said, "Miss Hathaway will see you now."

Paige met them at the door to her office. She wore a blue suit with a lacy white see-through blouse that offered just enough cleavage to distract him. But he wouldn't be distracted, not today, not by someone he had no intention of ever seeing again.

"I'm sorry to have kept you waiting--" she began.

He cut her off. "Where's the dragon?"

"Why don't you come in?"

Riley followed her into her office, his grandmother close behind. He'd hoped to see David Hathaway, or at the very least, the ugly dragon statue, but neither was there. Paige looked decidedly nervous as she stood behind her desk, motioning for them to sit down in the chairs in front of her desk. Nan did as suggested. Riley decided he preferred to stand.

"Well?" he asked.

"My father has been delayed."

"Where's the statue?"

"He'll be here very soon, I'm sure." She offered him a tentative smile. "Can I get you some of that strong coffee you like so much?"

"No."

"Mrs. Delaney?"

"I'm fine, dear." Nan pulled out her knitting and sat back in her chair, content to wait. During the past year, Nan had spent a lot of time waiting for doctors to come back and tell her what was happening with her husband. She didn't deserve to have to wait for this, too.

"Miss Hathaway," he began again.

"I know. I'm very sorry. My father probably lost track of time. He does that sometimes. He doesn't mean to make anyone feel as if they're unimportant. He just gets caught up in the moment."

"I used to know someone like that," Nan said, a sad note in her voice. She glanced over at Riley, but he looked away.

She was talking about his mother, and he didn't want to go down that road. "This is ridiculous." He waved an impatient hand as he glared at Paige. "You're running a business here, aren't you?"

"Yes, but I can assure you that everything will be fine. This is just a small delay. If you'd rather come back tomorrow--"

"Absolutely not. I don't know what kind of scam you're running, but I'm not putting up with it."

She stiffened, her conciliatory smile turning angry. "I'm not running a scam. My father is simply late."

Riley's instincts told him that something was wrong, the same instincts that had been raising goose bumps along his arms since they'd discovered the damn dragon might be worth something. He leaned forward, rapping his knuckles on the top of Paige's mahogany desk. "I don't give a damn about whether or not your father is late for our meeting. I want the dragon."

"I can't conjure it up out of thin air."

"Why don't you have someone bring it up here? Isn't it in one of the vaults or a clean room of some sort?" He didn't like the way she avoided his gaze. "Isn't it?"

"The dragon doesn't appear to be in the lab. My father must have already retrieved it."

"And where is he?"

"I'm not exactly sure."

"Are you saying your father took the dragon out of the store? I don't believe we gave him permission to do that."

"I don't believe I said that he left the store. I just haven't been able to track him down."

"What the hell are you up to?"

"Look. I appreciate the fact that you're angry, but there's nothing going on here. I can assure you of that. Hathaway's has never lost a piece of art, and we're not starting with yours. I'm truly sorry for the inconvenience."

"Inconvenience, my ass!"

"Riley, I don't like it when you swear," Nan chided. "Now stop yelling at Miss Hathaway. There's nothing she can do about the delay. I'm sure Mr. Hathaway will have a reasonable explanation when he returns."

"I'm sure he will," Paige said.

The door behind them opened. Riley turned, expecting to see David, not another nervous young woman.

"I'm sorry for interrupting you, Miss Hathaway," she said.

"It's all right, Monica. Did you find my father?"

"That's the thing. He doesn't seem to be in the store." She paused, darting a worried look at Riley. "And the dragon isn't here, either."

Chapter Four

Victoria Hathaway sat down in front of the mirror on her dressing room table and began to brush her hair. It was a pre-bedtime ritual that she'd followed every night since she was a little girl, living in a small two-bedroom apartment with her drunk of a mother and her two older sisters. Her mother had used one bedroom, her sisters the other. She'd had the couch, the bumpy, lumpy, bright red couch that her mother thought was so pretty.

Her surroundings now were quite different. Her elegant four-poster bed could be seen through the gold-edged mirror that David had bought her for their fifth wedding anniversary. As she pulled the brush through her smooth blond hair, she remembered a time when David had actually brushed her hair. She could almost see his reflection now in the glass, his dark hair rumpled, his brown eyes warm and caring.

It was foolish to turn her head, to see nothing but blank air. She knew he wasn't there. She couldn't remember the last time he'd been in her bedroom. David had moved out a few years earlier, because he was a night owl and she was an early bird, because he liked to read in bed, and she liked to get up early and do her hundred sit-ups in the privacy of her own room. God forbid anyone should know how hard she worked to keep her size-six figure. But those were only the reasons he said out loud, not the real reasons, not the ones that had isolated them in their own very private and personal hells for too many years to count.

She glanced back at the mirror and sighed. She could keep her body lean and trim, but not even the most expensive creams in the world or BOTOX treatments were managing to keep the wrinkles at bay. Already she could see the tiny lines around her eyes and lips. She could cover them in the daytime, but with her makeup removed, they were clearly visible. Perhaps some women would have turned away, but she forced herself to look, to examine, to be critical. It was the only way she knew to be.

When she was a young girl, she had made herself look at her life, her family, the way they lived and the manner in which they behaved. She remembered cutting out pictures from magazines of big houses and fancy restaurants. She'd made a list of how to get what she wanted, and she had followed that list to the letter. She'd gotten an education when many of her friends had dropped out, taken ugly, messy jobs in order to make enough money to go to college, always keeping her eye on the prize. Putting herself in a position to meet David at a party, marrying him, making her way into the Hathaway business had all been steps in the plan. She was no longer Vicky Siminski; she was Victoria Hathaway, and no one could ever take that away from her. She would not allow her life to be tarnished in any way.

Which brought David again to her mind. He'd

postponed a trip to China when that old woman had discovered the dragon statue in her attic. David never postponed trips to China, which meant the dragon was special. She didn't know why it was different from any other artifact that had come to light, but something about it had filled him with barely restrained energy. He knew something about that dragon, something he had not seen fit to share with her and she didn't like it. Nor did she like the fact that he'd been out of the office all day.

A knock at her bedroom door cut into her thoughts. For a moment, the quiet tap reminded her of other times when the loneliness had grown too keen, and David had come to the door. A shiver ran down her straight, stiff spine. What would she say if he'd come to her tonight?

The knock came again, followed by a voice. "Mother? Are you awake?"

Paige. The disappointment was not as annoying as the anger Victoria felt at herself. She didn't need David. She had everything she wanted in life.

"Come in," she said. "What are you doing here so late on a Wednesday night?" she added as Paige came into the room wearing running shoes, tight-fitting navy blue leggings, and a short matching warm-up jacket. "What on earth do you have on?"

"I came from my gym," Paige replied. "I'm sorry it's so late, but I need to speak to you."

"Why? What's wrong? And you know you can work out here in the house. The gym downstairs is state of the art and completely private."

"I like to be around other people when I exercise. It's inspiring."

"It's unsanitary. All that sweat on the machines after people use them. Heaven only knows what you might catch."

"I wipe the machines down with a towel, but that's not what I came to talk to you about." Paige sat down on the chaise next to the bed. "Have you seen Dad today or tonight?"

"No." Victoria picked up her brush and ran it through her hair, watching Paige through the glass. Her daughter was biting her nails, a nasty little habit Victoria had never been able to break her of. She remembered when she'd painted Paige's hands with a bad-tasting black polish just to make her aware of how many times she put her fingers in her mouth. It had worked for a while, but apparently the fix had not been permanent. Why was she surprised? Paige had a lot of her father in her.

"Dad didn't show up for an important meeting this afternoon," Paige said. "He's also not answering his cell phone, and no one seems to know where he is, not even Georgia."

Victoria's lips tightened. She hated the fact that David's secretary was more up-to-date on his whereabouts than she was, but she didn't particularly want to waste her time keeping track of him, so she'd allowed that to slide.

"I can't imagine where he is," Paige muttered.

Victoria heard the worried note in Paige's voice and tried not to let it concern her. Paige was a natural-born worrier. David's unexplained absence meant nothing, absolutely nothing. He was always missing. She'd spent too many hours to count waiting for David to show his face, to be where he'd promised to be, to support her when times got tough. All that had gotten her were more lines on her face. "He'll turn up. He always does -- sooner or later."

"This isn't just about Dad. The dragon is missing, too."

Victoria's hand paused in mid stroke. "The dragon he

was so eager to acquire?"

"Yes, but he never made an evaluation or an offer. He must have taken it somewhere for some reason. Mrs. Delaney is being incredibly patient. Her grandson is another matter. If Dad doesn't bring that dragon back to the store tomorrow, Mr. McAllister will be a huge problem."

That would be bad publicity for the store. Damn David. He never thought before he acted.

"Do you have any idea where he might be?" Paige asked.

Victoria had a terrible idea, one she didn't care to contemplate, one she couldn't possibly speak to her daughter about. "I'll see if I can find him." She set down the brush and got to her feet. "Why don't you go home and let me worry about your father?"

Paige rose, hesitating. "Do you think I should speak to Grandfather?"

"Good heavens, no. Why on earth would you want to do that?"

"Maybe he and Dad--"

"No, absolutely not. Your father doesn't confide in your grandfather. You know that. And let's not borrow trouble. Your father will turn up, he always does. There's no reason to upset Wallace." Her father-in-law was hard enough to please as it was, always looking for reasons to keep her in her place, to remind her that she could never run the store as well as he could.

"I guess you're right," Paige said slowly.

"Is there something else?"

"I just wonder--"

"Don't wonder, Paige. It's pointless where your father is concerned."

"Don't you ever worry about him?"

"Does he ever worry about us?" She knew her words hurt Paige, and she wished she could take them back. Hurting her daughter was never her intention, but sometimes it seemed inevitable. Paige had been disappointed by her father time and time again, yet she never seemed to see him for who he really was.

"You're right," Paige said.

"Well, he does worry about you," Victoria amended. "You're very important to him. And to me. Since you're here, there's something else I wanted to talk to you about."

Paige's expression turned wary. "What's that?"

"Martin. His mother tells me he's falling madly in love with you."

"Martin doesn't do anything madly. And we've known each other for years."

"But things have changed between you in recent months, isn't that true?"

"We've gone out together a few times," she said with a shrug. "The six-year age gap between us doesn't seem so big anymore, but that doesn't mean--"

"Six years is nothing. And I shouldn't have to remind you that you're not getting any younger. All your friends are married or about to be. Cynthia McAuley's wedding is in two weeks. Isn't that the fifth or sixth wedding you've been a bridesmaid in?"

"Tenth, but who's counting?"

"Don't be flippant, Paige. This is not a joking matter. The fact that Cynthia McAuley, who has the IQ of a lamp shade, is getting married before you is just ridiculous."

"She's a sweet girl. I'm happy for her."

"Of course you are. We all are. But we're not talking about her -- we're talking about you. Martin is an excellent candidate for a husband. He's very successful and extremely smart."

"You make it sound like he's running for office."

"You should make a pro and con list, Paige. You'll see that Martin is right for you. It's important for you to marry someone who can work in the business with us. After all, the store will be your responsibility someday, and a husband who can help you shoulder that burden would be very good."

"Because you don't think I can handle it?"

"I didn't say that. You're so sensitive, Paige." She felt a twinge of remorse, but she forced it aside. "This isn't personal. It's business."

"I'm your daughter. That's personal. Getting married is even more personal. I have to go. Tell Dad to call me." Paige shut the door behind her.

Victoria let out a frustrated sigh and a muttered curse as she stared at herself in the mirror. Why couldn't the people she loved do what she wanted them to do? If she told Paige to walk, her daughter would run. If she told David to go out, he would stay home. It was as if they took perverse joy in making her life difficult. Paige needed to get married. And David -- well, the list of what David needed to do was very long. Right now she'd settle for him coming home and bringing that damn dragon with him. He better have a good reason for taking a valuable artifact out of the store without the customer's permission. He knew better than that. A surge of uneasiness swept through her body. Had something happened to him? Or was this just another one of his famous disappearing acts?

Victoria walked across the room and looked out the window. A bright moon illuminated San Francisco Bay just a few miles from her home in Pacific Heights. All was quiet and peaceful in this part of town. Too quiet and peaceful for David. She knew where he'd gone, where he always went when he was on the mainland, as he called it. He'd gone to Chinatown. And she had a terrible feeling she knew exactly who he had gone to see.

She should have known better than to visit her mother. She'd accomplished nothing. Paige tried to slam the front door behind her, but it was so damn heavy and expensively made that it merely swung shut with a quiet thud. So much for venting her anger. She stopped at the bottom of the steps and drew in a deep breath. She tried counting to ten, but she was still feeling angry when she got to twenty.

Something was wrong. She knew it. She could feel it. But she had no facts, nothing to go on but instinct. She crossed the graveled drive, got into her Mercedes, and buckled her seat belt. There was nothing more to accomplish here. She might as well go home. Halfway down the street, she realized she didn't want to go home, didn't want to sit in her quiet, empty, lonely apartment -- whoa, where had that *lonely* come from? She wasn't lonely. She liked living on her own. She didn't need a man in her life, even one that was as good a candidate for marriage as Martin was.

Her mouth turned down at the thought of her mother's suggestion to make a pro and con list. Marriage was supposed to be about love, lust, breathlessness, recklessness, falling head over heels; it wasn't supposed to be about IQ, credit rating, college degrees, family connections, business mergers -- was it? How would she know anyway? Her mother and father were hardly a shining example of passionate love. Still, they'd been married for thirty-one years. Maybe they'd had all that earlier on, and she just hadn't been old enough to see it.

She hit the brake as the traffic light in front of her changed to red. She should turn right. It was the fastest route home. But she didn't want to go home. She wanted to talk to someone who would understand.

Unfortunately, as her mother had pointed out, all of her friends were married or about to be. Besides that, it was almost nine o'clock on a Wednesday night. She couldn't just drop in on anyone, especially not her married friends. Something happened once a woman walked down a rose-strewn aisle toward the man she loved; she changed, became one of a pair, half of a couple, someone you didn't stop by to see without a reason.

And, to be completely honest, most of her friends hadn't been all that close to her before marriage; they'd been girls she'd gone to private school with, college friends, or fellow debutantes. They were women she had lunch with, not women she confided in, at least not confidences that were more serious than the chocolate she'd sneaked after a Pilates workout. She wasn't in the habit of sharing personal information with anyone. The Hathaways had always been targets of gossipmongers. No matter how close the friendships were supposed to be, confidences always seemed to leak out.

Making a quick decision, she turned left at the green light and drove across town to the neighborhood known as the Avenues. She found a parking spot just down the street from a popular neighborhood bar. It wasn't the kind of bar a Hathaway was supposed to be caught dead in but she wasn't dead yet, she thought with a smile as she got out of the car and walked down the street.

Fast Willy's was a cozy sports bar with photographs of athletes in every available space, some signed to the owner, Willy Bartholomew, a third-generation Willy from what she understood and a former minor league baseball player. There were four television sets, one placed at each corner of the room, with small tables crowded together on what was sometimes used as an impromptu dance floor. On the weekends, the bar overflowed with customers, but tonight there was a quiet after-work crowd, content to talk and listen to the jukebox.

She avoided the tables and headed to an empty stool at the long bar.

"What's an uptown babe like you doing in a joint like this?" the red-haired bartender asked her as he set down a napkin.

"Looking for a friend," she replied.

"Aren't we all? Just how good a friend are you looking for?" he asked with a wicked grin. "Because I can be pretty damn good, you know what I mean?"

"A monkey would know what you mean. Does that line work on intelligent women?"

"Did I say intelligence was a requirement?" He gave her an exaggerated wink.

"My mistake," she said with a laugh.

"What do you want, the usual chardonnay in a pretty glass?"

"I'd like a vodka gimlet."

"You don't drink vodka."

"I do tonight. In fact, forget the gimlet part and just get me the vodka."

"Oh, my God!" He clapped a dramatic hand to his forehead. "You went to see your mother. Why on earth would you do that?"

"It was a last resort, believe me."

"Paige, Paige, when will you learn?"

"Shut up, Jerry. I didn't come here for a lecture. I came here to get drunk."

"You don't get drunk." Jerry Scanlon pulled out a bottle of mineral water, poured it into an ice-filled glass, and handed it to her. "Try this."

"There better be some vodka in there."

"Then I'd have to hold your hair while you threw up. I'm not going to do that again."

She tried to frown, but ended up smiling instead. Jerry was the closest thing she had to a brother. The son of one of their housekeepers, Ruth Scanlon, Jerry and his mother had moved into the apartment over the garage when Paige was eleven years old. At thirteen, Jerry had been a tormenting pest, an irritating big brother, and a best friend. He'd saved her from lonely isolation, and their friendship had nourished for five years, until his mother had gotten fired during one of Victoria Hathaway's annual servant purgings.

Paige could still remember the sixteen-year-old angst she'd felt when Jerry and his mom had moved away to San Diego. Seven years later, Jerry had come back to San Francisco, and they'd found each other again. They'd kept in touch over the years, an odd but close friendship between a red-haired, freckle-faced pro athlete wannabe turned bartender and a sophisticated, blond debutante. She hated to think of herself in those terms, but she knew most of Jerry's friends thought of her in exactly that way. Not that they mingled with friends much. They moved in different circles except when they were together, which wasn't as often as she would have liked. Paige felt guilty about that, but Jerry understood how often she was torn between what she was supposed to do and what she wanted to do.

"My mother wants me to marry Martin," Paige said, reminded of what she was supposed to do now. "If I make a pro and con list, I will see that he's perfect for me."

"Martin Bennett? You can do better." Jerry wiped down the bar with a damp towel. "Is that all that's bugging you?"

She shook her head. "My father is nowhere to be found."

"What else is new?"

"It's different this time. He took a valuable artifact from the store. The owners are very upset. I managed to stall them until tomorrow, but I haven't been able to find my dad. He doesn't answer his cell phone. He's not at the store. He's not at home. I'm worried."

"He'll show up. He always does. You know what you need?"

"I have a feeling you're going to tell me."

"A game of pool. Or, as you Hathaways call it -- billiards," he said in a mocking British accent.

"I don't think so," she replied with a shake of her head.

"Come on. When was the last time you played?"

"Probably the last time you talked me into it."

"I've got a break coming up." He set his towel down on the bar. "Let's rack 'em up."

"Why do I let you talk me into these things?"

Jerry grinned. "Because you love me."

Paige Hathaway got off the bar stool and followed the bartender through a door leading into a back room. Riley frowned, wondering what the hell she was up to. He hadn't been surprised when she'd gone to the gym or even to her mother's house, but this latest stop didn't make sense at all. This wasn't the kind of upscale bar she would frequent. These people weren't her crowd. And who was the bartender she'd been talking to for the past few minutes? Their conversation had looked more than friendly. Riley could hardly believe that Paige Hathaway, the princess of San Francisco's royal family, would be friends with a bartender.

Maybe this stop had something to do with the dragon, a back room deal. It was a reach, he knew it. She certainly didn't have the dragon with her, but it was possible she knew more about its whereabouts than she'd let on earlier. His grandmother might be content to wait until morning to get her dragon back, but he wasn't. In fact, his impatience had been growing since he'd left Hathaway's a few hours earlier. Something was wrong. He could feel it in his gut. David Hathaway had taken the dragon out of the store and missed their meeting. Paige had been concerned despite her best efforts to appear calm. That's why he'd decided to follow her.

Deciding to risk his cover, he walked into the bar. He needed to know what Paige was doing in the back room.

Five minutes later he couldn't quite believe what he was seeing.

Pool! She was playing pool. Paige's sweet ass was all he could see as she bent over the table, her attention focused on the cue stick between her fingers and the ball she was about to hit. It was a good shot, better than good, and she cleared the last two balls from the table. A murmur of appreciation from three old guys watching the action echoed his own thoughts. But he suspected they'd been watching her more than the game.

Paige exchanged a bouncing high five with the bartender. "Who's the best?" she demanded.

"That was a lucky shot," the guy replied.

"Luck had nothing to do with it. So tell me who's the best. Come on, you can say it."

"You're the best," he grumbled. "And not a pretty winner, by the way. Do you want to play again?"

"Do you feel like another butt-kicking?"

"Cocky, aren't you?"

"I could take you with my eyes closed."

"What about me?" Riley interrupted. "Could you take me with your eyes closed?"

Paige whirled around in surprise, her jaw dropping when she saw him. "What are you doing here? Oh, my God, did you follow me?"

Ignoring her questions, he said, "How about a game?"

"I don't think so." As she spoke, she stiffened, and there was no sign left of the unrestrained, laughing young woman he'd watched from the doorway. Her face went to stone. Her lips tightened. Her chin lifted in the air. Despite her casual clothes, she now looked exactly like the elegant, reserved businesswoman he'd met hours earlier -- untouchable, unreadable, and unlikely to spend more than five minutes in conversation with him. He didn't care for the transformation.

"I have to go," she added.

"So, you're afraid you can't beat me," he drawled. "I can understand that."

"I am not afraid of losing. Tell him I'm not afraid, Jerry."

The bartender laughed. "Why don't you show him, Paige? You like a challenge."

"I'm tired."

"Scared." Riley smiled as a spark of anger flickered in her eyes. He had the urge to provoke her, to do anything to bring down the wall she'd put up when he entered the room.

"Fine. You want a game, I'll give you a game."

"I want a game, Miss Hathaway."

"I should have my head examined," she muttered as she moved to collect the balls.

"What did you say?"

"She said she should have her head examined," Jerry said helpfully, a big grin on his face. "I take it you two know each other."

"Yes," Riley replied.

"Barely," Paige corrected. "Don't be nice to him, Jerry. I think he followed me here."

"You're stalking her?" Jerry asked, his smile vanishing. "Maybe you should get the hell out of my bar, then."

"No, no," Paige said quickly. "It's not that way. It's not personal."

"She's right. It's not at all personal. It's business."

"Mr. McAllister's grandmother is selling a statue to us," Paige added.

"*Maybe* selling a statue, if it ever shows up again." He gave her a pointed look.

"It will."

"I hope so."

Jerry moved toward the door. "All right then. I'm not getting in the middle of this. But I'm warning you, dude. You mess with her, you mess with me. Let me know if you need anything," Jerry added to Paige.

"Good friend of yours?" Riley asked as Jerry left.

"Yes, he is, as a matter of fact."

"I'm surprised. I didn't figure you for a Fast Willy's kind of girl."

"I don't think you know me well enough to make any assumptions about me. Not that that will stop you. Stereotyping is hardly confined to the rich, is it?"

"At least you admit you're rich."

"It's hardly a secret that my family is wealthy, but

believe it or not, I'm nowhere near as rich as they are."

"Maybe not now, but I'll bet there are some hefty inheritances in your future."

"Not that it's any of your business."

"Until you return my grandmother's missing dragon, everything about you is my business."

"It's not exactly missing. It's just unaccounted for at the moment."

"Splitting hairs, don't you think? Why did your father take the dragon out of the store, anyway? I thought you had state-of-the-art testing equipment on the premises. Isn't that what your brochure says?"

"You've read our brochure?"

"I've read a great deal about your company in the past twenty-four hours."

"Then you shouldn't be worried."

"Maybe I wouldn't be -- if you weren't worried. But you are, aren't you, Miss Hathaway? This isn't standard operating procedure. This isn't the way things normally go down." She glanced away from him, guiltily he thought. "I can't help wondering what's coming next."

"Nothing is coming next. You just need to be patient."

"I'm not a patient man."

"I can see that." She paused. "Do you actually want to play pool?" She waved her hand toward the table.

"Do you really know how to play, or did the red-haired guy give you a break?"

"Jerry give me a break? Not in this lifetime. And, yes, I do know how to play pool. Although at our house we refer to the game as billiards." An impulsive smile broke across her face as she said the word. "Or, as Jerry calls it, billiards." She added a British accent and a laugh that broke the tension between them. "My grandfather always refers to it as that."

God, she was beautiful all loosened up again, her long blond hair falling out of its ponytail, her slender body encased in tight-fitting sweats, a pair of running shoes on her feet. Looking like this, he could almost forget she was the princess of San Francisco and way out of his league. He could almost forget that this was business.

She cleared her throat. "You're staring." She tucked a strand of hair behind her ear. "I look a mess. My mother would have a fit if she knew I was out in public looking like this."

"I like it."

"You do?" she asked, amazement in her voice. "It's not at all appropriate."

"Who cares about appropriate?"

"I always have to be careful what I wear, because with my luck some photographer desperate for a photo to fill tomorrow's empty slot will snap me in my sweats and suggest that maybe Hathaway's is losing money, and the incident will be blown completely out of proportion."

"Gone a few rounds with the press, have you?"

"More than a few."

"Well, there's no paparazzi here. And I don't have a camera. Although I wish I did, because you don't look anything like the woman I saw earlier today. In fact, since you've been in this room, you've undergone several transformations. You remind me of a lizard I used to have as a kid."

"A lizard? I remind you of a lizard? That's quite a compliment."

He laughed at her look of outrage. "A chameleon. The kind of lizard that changes colors to fit its environment. That's what you do. And it was a compliment. I don't know many women who can be comfortable in the back room of Fast Willy's and the next day go to work in the executive offices of Hathaway's."

She frowned at him. "I still think you could do better than lizard if you're looking to give a compliment. It's no wonder why you had nothing better to do tonight than follow me around. That's what you've been doing, isn't it? I should call the cops."

"I don't think you want to call the police, not with my grandmother's dragon missing."

"I told you before--"

"I know what you told me before. But my instincts tell me something else is going on. Have you spoken to your father since we met earlier?"

"Since you've been following me, you know that I haven't."

"I thought he might have called you."

"He didn't."

"Is that unusual? Not hearing from your father when he has a valuable artifact out of your store?"

"Potentially valuable," she corrected.

"Oh, come on. If it was a fake, it would have been returned to us hours ago."

"There's nothing to worry about, Mr. McAllister."

"Riley," he corrected. "And I am worried, because as I said before -- you're nervous."

"Maybe I'm nervous because you've been following me around." She paused as her cell phone rang. She hesitated, then pulled out of her purse to answer. "Hello."

"Hello?"

Riley watched the color drain from her face. "Wh-what did you say?" she stuttered. "Where? When? Yes, I'll come right away."

"What's wrong?" he asked as she ended the call.

"My father," she said, her eyes dazed, frightened. "Where is he?"

"He's in the hospital. He was attacked in an alley in Chinatown. He's in critical condition."

Chapter Five

Paige found her mother in the waiting room on the fourth floor of St. Mary's Hospital. Next to Victoria was her closest friend, Joanne Bennett, another well-to-do socialite in her fifties, and Joanne's son, Martin, the object of their earlier discussion. A tall, lean man in his mid-thirties with perfectly styled dark blond hair, Martin was still wearing the charcoal gray Armani suit he'd had on at work earlier that day. While sometimes his never-a-hair-out-of-place demeanor annoyed Paige, right now she found it reassuring. Things couldn't be that bad if Martin looked so calm

Martin got up to greet her, putting his arms around her in a comforting hug. "It will be all right, Paige."

She wanted to linger. It felt good to let someone take care of her, but she knew she couldn't hide in Martin's arms. She had to see her mother's face, look into her eyes, and then she would know the truth. She pulled away and said, "Mother?"

Victoria's face was white. There were tight lines around her eyes and mouth. She'd come out of the house without touching up her lipstick, without wearing hose, for God's sake. In fact, she had on a blue skirt and a yellow sweater that didn't match, all the little details her mother took such pride in. It was bad. It had to be bad.

"How is Daddy?" she forced herself to ask.

"They don't know yet. He's unconscious. He has a bad gash in his head, maybe a skull fracture." Victoria cleared her throat as the words came out choked and emotional.

"But he's going to be all right? He'll recover?"

"I'm sure he will," Victoria replied, but there was no strength in her voice, no confidence, just fear. "The doctor said it may be awhile before we know anything."

"I don't understand what happened. Was he robbed? What was he doing in Chinatown?" The questions tumbled out of her mouth. "Did they find the person who did this to him?"

"Paige, slow down," Joanne chided gently. "There's time to know everything."

"Is there time? Are you sure there's time?" Paige asked, meeting her mother's gaze.

"I hope so," Victoria muttered.

"This is a private conversation. Do you mind?" Martin said.

Paige turned to see Martin bearing down on Riley, who had stopped a discreet distance away. She'd forgotten he was there, forgotten he'd given her a ride to the hospital.

"Are you with the press?" Martin demanded.

"He brought me here," Paige answered. "Riley McAllister, Martin Bennett." She turned to her mother, leaving the two men to shake hands or not. "Have you spoken to the police?"

"Just for a few moments. They don't know anything.

Or at least they're not saying what they know. Someone found your father lying in an alley in Chinatown." Victoria put her head on her hand. "God. An alley, of all places."

Her mother's words created a vivid picture in Paige's mind, one of her father defenseless and in pain, maybe crying out for help, for family. Paige felt nauseous at the thought. "I don't understand how this could happen--"

"Paige, I know you're terrified, and you want answers," Joanne cut in with a compassionate smile, "but your mother is also upset, and she doesn't know anything more than she's already told you."

"Except that he was in Chinatown," Victoria said a bitter note creeping into her voice as she exchanged a pointed look with her friend. "Probably with that damn woman."

"Dad was with another woman?" It was too much to take in. Paige started to sway.

Riley was suddenly behind her. He caught her by the arm, and she sank back against his solid chest. His arm came around her waist. "Hang on," he said, leading her to a nearby chair. She sat down, and he pushed her head down between her knees. "Breathe."

"I'm okay." She sat back up. "I'm okay," she repeated, looking into Riley's skeptical eyes. "I just felt dizzy for a second."

"What can I do to help?" Martin asked, drawing her attention back to him.

She didn't know how to reply to that. What could anyone do to help except make her father be all right again? But Martin wanted to do something. "Maybe some water."

"I'll get it right away."

Riley took one of her hands in his and gave it a

squeeze. "The hardest part is the waiting."

"You sound like you know something about it."

"I've done this a few times."

His compassionate gaze completely undid her. Was this the same man who had stormed into her office yesterday? Who had followed her all over San Francisco tonight and practically accused her and her family of lying and stealing? Because he wasn't acting like that man right now. He was acting more like a friend. And they weren't friends. She couldn't start thinking they were. He'd given her a ride because she'd been too frantic to get her keys in the lock of her car door, and he'd insisted she go with him. Why had he insisted? Probably to find out whether the dragon had come in with her father.

"You don't have to stay. I can get a ride home," she said. "This is a family matter." Paige dropped her voice down a notch. "As soon as my mother gets her bearings, she'll be horrified that you've witnessed such a private moment. And she doesn't need that right now. I'll find out about the dragon as soon as I can. I know that's your main concern."

"I do hope your father is all right."

Her eyes misted. "So do I. He's not the best dad," she whispered, "but he's the only one I've got."

Riley squeezed her hand once again. "Keep the faith."

His words brought back memories from the last time someone had said that to her, the night before Elizabeth died. She had been only six years old, but those words were forever burned in her memory.

Keeping the faith then hadn't stopped the worst from happening. And now it was happening again. Why? Was it a random attack? A mugging gone bad? Or something else?

He'd been in Chinatown -- maybe with another

woman. An affair? God, she didn't want to go there.

"Here's your water." Martin handed her a bottled water.

"Thank you."

"Are you a friend of Paige's?" Martin asked Riley as he got to his feet.

"His grandmother is the owner of the dragon we're interested in acquiring," Paige explained, as the two men sized each other up. They were night and day, she thought. Riley was midnight with his black hair, olive skin, and light blue eyes. Martin was sunlight -- blond, clean, a golden boy. They were both good-looking men, but they didn't seem to care for each other at all. Their matching frowns showed wariness and distrust, maybe a bit of rivalry. Which was completely idiotic, because Riley was a customer and Martin was -- well, she didn't know exactly what he was, but this little display of showmanship was the last thing she needed. "Riley was just leaving," she added, breaking the tension.

"I'll talk to you tomorrow." Riley tipped his head in her direction, then strode off down the hall.

"What were you doing with him, Paige? It's after ten o'clock." Martin sat down in the chair next to her, looking decidedly put out.

"It's a long story."

"I think we have time."

She sighed. Sometimes Martin was like a dog with a bone. "I wasn't out on a date, if that's what you're thinking. Mr. McAllister's dragon has gone missing. I think my father took it from the store."

Martin looked surprised. "That doesn't make sense at all."

"No, it doesn't. But right now it's the least of my worries. Where's Grandfather?" she asked abruptly. "Does he know what happened?"

"Yes, of course. He's upstairs with the chief of staff, Dr. Havenhurst. They're making sure the best doctors are on the case. He'll be down shortly."

She tapped her fingers against her legs. "What's taking so long? Damn, I hate this. And where are the police? Why aren't they here telling us what happened?"

"A detective checked in with your mother when we first got here. He'll report back as soon as he has any more information. They're investigating the crime scene now."

"What was my father doing in Chinatown?" She didn't like the way Martin avoided her gaze. "If you know, you have to tell me. My mother said something about a woman?" She lowered her voice, not wanting her mother to hear her, but Victoria and Joanne were engaged in a low conversation of their own. "Do you know who that would be?"

Martin shifted in his seat and tugged at his tie. She'd never seen him appear so uncomfortable. "What matters right now is your father's health." He took her hand in his.

His fingers were colder than Riley's had been. His reassuring squeeze chilled rather than comforted. Maybe because she knew he was keeping something from her, and she didn't like it. That was one of the problems with their relationship; she didn't think Martin respected her, or perhaps it was just that his loyalties always seemed to lie more with her parents or her grandfather than with her.

"I'm sorry, Paige," he said quietly, concern in his eyes. "I wish I could make this go away for you."

Now she was sorry for being so annoyed with him. He was a good man. And he'd come running to the hospital as soon as he'd heard the news. "I'm just on edge." She pulled her hand from his and stood up. "I can't sit here. I'm going to take a little walk, see if I can find someone who knows something. I'll be back in a few minutes. Watch out for my mother, all right?"

"Always," he said reassuringly. "And you, too, if you'll let me."

That was a question she'd save for another day.

Riley ran into the police detective getting off the elevator. A short, squat, muscular man with thick brown hair and cynical black eyes, Tony Paletti was a third-generation San Francisco Italian and a fifteen-year veteran with the SFPD. Riley knew Tony from some of the events on which they'd coordinated security.

"Hey," Riley said with a nod. "Are you working the Hathaway mugging?"

"You know something about it?" Tony stepped off to one side to avoid an orderly pushing a wheelchair down the hall.

"I was with Paige Hathaway when she found out about her father. Was he robbed?"

"Looks like it. Wallet, money, credit cards are missing. Hathaway was in the wrong place at the wrong time."

"Was anything else found at the scene?"

"Like what?"

Riley hesitated, debating the wisdom of saying anything, but then again secrecy would help the Hathaways more than his grandmother. "A statue that looked like a dragon?"

Tony's eyes narrowed. "No, but do you want to tell me why you're asking?"

"My grandmother found an antique statue in her attic. Hathaway's was appraising it."

"And you think he had it with him?"

"Possibly."

"Is this thing worth much?"

"Could be worth a lot, but we don't know yet."

Tony took out a small spiral notebook and jotted down some notes. "I'll speak to Mrs. Hathaway. See if she knows what her husband was doing in Chinatown, who he might have gone to see. I need to drum up some witnesses fast. I already got a call from the mayor. The Hathaway family is very important to the city. They want his assailant behind bars ten minutes ago, if you know what I mean."

Riley nodded, knowing the pressure the cops would be under to solve this case as soon as possible. By morning the press would be all over it, too.

Paige came around the corner, startling him with her sudden appearance. She looked just as surprised to see him standing with the police officer.

"Are you the officer investigating my father's attack?" she asked Tony.

"And you are?"

"Paige Hathaway. I'm his daughter."

"I'm sorry about your father, Ms. Hathaway."

"Thank you. Can you tell me any more about what happened?"

"Not yet, I'm afraid. We're still investigating the scene. Do you know what business your father had in Chinatown?"

"I have no idea."

"Did he have friends there? Business associates?"

"Probably both. My father specializes in purchasing Asian art. He has many contacts in the Chinese community."

"Sounds like we'll need a big net. I'll need you to sit

down with someone and give us a list of names. But right now I'd like to speak to your mother. Is she available?"

"She's in the waiting room."

Before Tony could move down the hall, the elevator doors opened and a uniformed officer stepped out. Tony walked over to greet him, and they began to converse in hushed tones.

"What do you think that's about?" Paige asked Riley.

"Probably your father's case."

"I hope they caught the bastard."

"If they didn't, they will," he reassured her.

"They better. It's cold in here, don't you think?" She shivered, clasping her arms more tightly about her waist.

Riley shouldn't have put his arms around her. He knew it as soon as her breasts brushed his chest. But it was too late then. Her cheek was pressed against his heart, her hair tickled his chin, and her arms crept around his body, holding on to him with a tight desperation that he suspected had a lot to do with fear. He wished he had as good an excuse for hugging her back.

"I'm sorry," Paige said, pulling away far too soon. "I don't know what came over me. I don't usually throw myself into people's arms like that."

"Miss Hathaway?" Tony walked back to join them. "Do you recognize this bracelet?" He extended his hand, a gold bangle in his palm.

She shook her head. "I've never seen it before. Where did you find it?"

"It was found near your father. It might not have anything to do with him, but there's an inscription. It says '*Jasmine, my love*'. Do you know anyone named Jasmine?"

"Jasmine," Paige echoed, looking confused. "I -- I don't think so."

Despite her denial, Riley had the feeling something in the name had registered with Paige.

"I'll ask your mother." Tony closed his fingers over the bracelet.

"Wait," Paige said. "Do you need to ask her now? She's upset."

"If this bracelet can help us find who assaulted your father..."

"You're right," Paige agreed. "Go ahead."

"From what I've seen, your mother is a very strong woman," Riley said quietly as they watched the detective stride away.

Paige looked at him with indecision in her eyes. "Yes, she is."

"You've heard the name Jasmine before, haven't you?"

She hesitated. "There's a painter named Jasmine Chen. We've bought some of her work for the store. But that doesn't mean that she and my father... He wouldn't do that. He's not a bad man. At least, I don't think he is." She pressed a hand to her temple, looking paler than she had before. "The truth is I don't know what kind of man he is, and I'm terrified that I won't have the chance to find out. What if he doesn't make it? God, I shouldn't have said that."

"Give yourself a break. You're human."

"No, I'm a Hathaway. The press will be all over this before morning. And if there's speculation about another woman..." she let out a sigh. "I should get back to my mother. She might need me." She paused, then let out an odd laugh that sounded incredibly sad. "Who am I kidding? She doesn't need me. I didn't even think she needed my father until a few minutes ago." Paige seemed to be talking to herself more than to him. She suddenly started. "Was I talking out loud?"

"I didn't hear a thing," he lied.

She stared at him for a long moment. "I can't quite figure you out."

"Likewise," he replied.

"Thanks for the ride."

Riley watched her walk away, the stiffness of her spine no doubt worthy of the very best Hathaway. She had her game face back on, and she would do anything to protect her family.

But right now he had his own family to worry about -- his grandmother's possibly priceless dragon. And the only clue he had was Jasmine Chen, a local painter. She shouldn't be that difficult to find.

Jasmine turned over in bed, her legs twisting in the hot sheets. She wanted to escape from the dream that raced through her head once again, but it had her in its grip, the jade green light burning from two bright eyes, the makeshift altar with the candles, the fireworks bursting outside. Then there was nothing but darkness, the swish of fabric against her face, the terror of no way out, the screaming, the terrible, terrible screaming of a woman, the harsh grip on her arm, the wrenching pain...

She woke up abruptly, sweat dripping down her face. The dream always began and ended the same way. But tonight was worse, because today the dream had become a reality.

The dragon from her nightmares existed. It wasn't a figment of her imagination, as her mother had assured her over the years. It was real. David had shown it to her. It matched the vision in her head, the one she had painted so many times, trying to understand what her dreams might mean. For there had to be a meaning, a reason why her mind kept taking her back to that place. What was she was supposed to learn? And why couldn't she learn it, understand it?

Untangling herself from the sheets, she walked over to the window and threw it open. The cold air washed over her, cooling the fever in her body, in her head, but she still felt frustrated. She was close to something. She could feel it in her heart, a heart that sang to the past more than to the present. It was a love she shared with David, a love of history, of China, of people and places that seemed both magical and yet very real, as if she had lived there once. But she hadn't lived there. Her parents had been born in China, but she had been born here in Chinatown, just a few blocks away in an apartment that she'd shared with her three brothers and one younger sister. How could she know of things that had happened a continent away and several lifetimes ago? Was it just her imagination, or did she have an old soul, as a fortune-teller had once told her?

Shivering, she stayed by the window, refusing to give in to the cold or to the reality of her life. She tried not to look down, not to see what was right before her, because so much of her present was not what she wanted it to be. Instead, she looked up at the moon and the stars, to her dreams, her desires. She was a fool, she knew that, too. Foolish to believe in miracles. Her life had been hard since the day she was born missing the index finger on her left hand, a sign of just how inadequate she was and would be. She had disappointed so many people in her life. So why was she here on this earth? What was she supposed to accomplish with her life?

The answers had something to do with the dragon.

She knew it with a certainty that she couldn't explain. David knew it, too. He was as much a dreamer as she was. And her persistent dreams had always intrigued him. Over the years, they had looked through centuries of stories about dragons to find some similarity to the one in her dreams. Only one tale had come close, but that tale involved two dragons connected together. She never dreamed about two, only one. Unless they were a perfect match, unless they blended together as one in her dreams. She remembered seeing a rough sketch of those dragons in a book of Chinese fairytales, and there had been a small similarity, but neither had really matched the dragon in her dreams. Another dead end, she had thought. But today... when her fingers had traced the joint opening where two dragons could become one, she had known the truth.

And if there were two dragons...

Where was the other one?

Chapter Six

Paige walked through the front doors of the hospital and blinked against the brightness of the early Thursday morning sun. She couldn't believe the night had finally ended. For a while she had thought it might go on forever.

Her father was in a coma, the doctors said. There was severe swelling in his brain. They didn't know the extent of the damage, if it was permanent or temporary. In fact, they didn't know much of anything. Only time would tell. So they waited and they waited. When the sun came up, Paige had ventured down to the lobby, grabbing a cup of coffee from the cafeteria, finally making her way out here, to the front of the hospital where a horseshoe driveway allowed for pickups and drop-offs.

She sat down on a cold bench and let out a long, frustrated, anxious breath -- the breath she'd been holding most of the night. But she couldn't relax, not yet. The immediate danger wasn't over. And she had to be ready for everything that would follow, the press, the police, Riley McAllister. She knew he'd be back. And she'd have to deal with the question of the missing dragon.

Maybe it was somewhere in the store. She would have her secretary search every floor. She'd ask Martin, too, and whomever else she could enlist to both help and keep the search confidential. The last thing she wanted was for the public to catch wind of not only her father's attack but also the fact that a piece of art that Hathaway's had not yet acquired had disappeared from their care.

"Paige, there you are." Martin came through the hospital doors, looking as crisp as he had appeared the night before. She couldn't imagine how he did it. "I'm glad you waited," he said. "I'll drive you home."

"I'm not going home yet."

"You've been here all night. You need some sleep."

"I can't sleep now, not until I know for sure my dad is all right."

"Paige, it could be hours."

"My mother should be back shortly," she said, taking a quick look at her watch. "I'll leave when she gets here."

"Do you want me to wait with you?"

She shook her head. "No, but thank you for the offer. You've gone above and beyond the call of duty."

"It's not duty. I care about you."

She looked away, not liking the gleam in his eyes.

"Paige, I know this isn't the time, but--"

"You're right, it's not the time. I have a lot on my mind."

He frowned. "I'm sorry. Is there anything I can do for you before I go?"

She thought about that for a moment. "There's something you can do when you get to the store. You can find out if that dragon statue is anywhere on the premises. I think my father had it with him, but I have to know for sure. I don't want to think there's a connection between the dragon and my father's attack, but it's possible."

"Does your mother know about this?"

"I mentioned it to her last night before Dad got hurt. I don't think it's at the top of her list right now. And I really don't want Grandfather to know, although I suspect he already does. He seems to have an uncanny ability to know every single thing that goes on at the store."

Martin smiled. "The sign of a good executive. Don't worry, Paige. I'll do everything I can to help." He leaned over and kissed her on the cheek. "Maybe someday you'll realize I'm a good guy to have around."

She was saved from answering by the appearance of her grandfather's car pulling up in front of the hospital. She stiffened at the sight. Wallace Hathaway was the most intimidating individual she had ever known. He demanded perfection, and he made no allowances for family. If anything, he expected more from those who shared his blood. She stood up as her grandfather got out of the backseat of his black BMW, which was driven by his longtime chauffeur.

Eighty-two years of living might have turned his hair a pepper gray and drawn thick lines across his forehead and around his dark eyes, but time had not lessened his stature. At six foot four, her grandfather still seemed like a giant.

"Grandfather," she murmured, walking over to him. "I didn't expect you back so soon."

"What are you doing out here? Why aren't you upstairs with your father?" he demanded.

"I was just--"

"How is David?" he interrupted.

"The same," she said.

Her grandfather's lips tightened with anger, or maybe it was fear. He was a difficult man to read. She wanted to tell him she was scared and worried and have him respond that it would be all right, that her dad would pull through. But to do that would mean admitting personal weakness, something her grandfather never wanted to see.

"I've hired a private nurse," Wallace said abruptly. "I want someone with him at all times."

Paige immediately felt guilty for having abandoned her post for even a few moments.

"I'll walk up with you, Mr. Hathaway," Martin said. "Paige needs a little air."

She sent Martin a silent thank you, knowing he'd made the offer to give her some space. She sat back down on the bench, retrieving her rapidly cooling cup of coffee.

Martin and her grandfather got along well, she thought, taking a sip of the tepid liquid. Another item to put in the pro column. And he'd just saved her a few minutes of awkward tension. But deep in her heart she knew there was still something missing in their relationship. Despite all of Martin's good qualities, she couldn't seem to feel more for him than fondness and appreciation. Her mother would say those emotions were enough to base a marriage on. But she wanted more. She wanted that reckless, breathless, falling-in-love kind of feeling. She wanted her stomach to do flip-flops when Martin was close by. She wanted to be acutely aware every time his hand touched her shoulder or the small of her back. She wanted to be swept off her feet. But Martin didn't make her feel any of those things.

He was a good date. Generous, concerned, able to pick fine wines, good restaurants, appropriate movies. He read extensively, traveled when he had the chance, worked out, kept fit, handled money well, had a good job. Damn. She was doing just what her mother had suggested, making a pro and con list in her head. Only the pros were all logical, and the cons were all emotional. Big surprise there. She'd spent most of her life torn between reason and desire. And she always chose reason. She always did the right thing in the long run. That was who she was; even when she wanted to stray, she couldn't. She should probably conserve her energy and just agree to marry Martin now, save herself all the stress and turmoil of a decision that would probably end up there anyway.

With a sigh, she leaned back, resting against the building. This wasn't the time to be thinking about marriage. Not with her father's life on the line. A rush of worry hit her once again. She didn't want to lose him. It couldn't end like this, without warning, without a chance to say good-bye.

She closed her eyes for a moment, seeking a peaceful image, but she was taken back to an even more painful place -- her sister's bedroom. She'd had more than one chance to say good-bye to her sister, but she hadn't been able to make herself go into the room, so she'd stood in the doorway as her parents sat by Elizabeth's bed. She could see them now, the sunlight streaming in through the window, lighting up Elizabeth's face as if she was already an angel, already gone to heaven. Her mother had asked Paige to come in, to say good-bye to her sister. But she hadn't been able to enter that room. Not with Elizabeth lying so still, her eyes closed, her small hands folded on her chest. It was the way she would look a few days later when they put her in the casket, like she was sleeping, only she wasn't.

God, how Paige wished she hadn't had to see that. But her mother had insisted that she face it, that she understand that death was a part of life. *You must be strong, Paige. You must not cry. You must go on with your life*. She hadn't been strong, and she hadn't understood. She'd been six years old and terrified that whatever was happening to her sister would happen to her, too. She hadn't been able to sleep on her back for years. In fact, she still hated that position, still refused to put her hands together on her chest, as if she were inviting the same result.

Her eyes flew open so she wouldn't see the images in her head. She knew that the reason she was sitting out here was so she wouldn't have to look at her father in the same position. She was twenty-eight years old now, but seeing her father lying so still in bed, looking so old, so fragile, made her feel as if she were six years old again. She wanted it all to go away. She wanted everything to be the way it was yesterday.

Rolling her head around on her shoulders, Paige felt the aches of the long, stressful night. The sudden ringing of her cell phone made her jump. She answered the call with a wary hello.

"Paige? This is Riley. We need to meet."

"What? How did you get this number?"

"It wasn't difficult. How's your father?"

"No change."

"It sounds like he's holding his own."

"For the moment, yes."

"We need to talk, Paige. I think you should meet me in Chinatown."

"Why?" she asked, shocked by the suggestion. She never went to Chinatown. Her mother insisted it was a tourist trap, a neighborhood where Hathaways didn't belong. Even on the few occasions when a girlfriend had dragged her there for dim sum, it had always been to visit a certain restaurant, not to go anywhere else, not to walk down the streets, or stop in the shops, or talk to the people.

"Paige? Are you still there?"

"I can't go to Chinatown. Why would you ask me to? The police are investigating the area. There's nothing I can do. There's nothing you can do, either."

"I've already done something."

"What?" Her heart beat in triple time. "What have you done?"

"I found Jasmine Chen. She lives two blocks from where your father was attacked. I want to talk to her. Don't you?"

Her mind whirled with the information. Did she want to talk to Jasmine? Did she want to face the woman who might be her father's lover? Oh, God. She couldn't do this, not on no sleep, not with her brain in a fog. "I can't leave right now," she said hastily.

"All right. I'll go on my own."

"No. This is family business. I want you to stay out of it."

"Until I get my grandmother's dragon back, your family's business is my business. I'm going to see Jasmine Chen with or without you. If your father went there yesterday, he might have had the dragon with him. She might be the last person who spoke to him. I'm sure the police won't be far behind me, but I figure she might rather talk to me than a uniform, especially if her relationship with your father--"

"Stop." She couldn't let Riley, then the police, then God knows who talk to Jasmine without her there. What if Jasmine said something to compromise her father, his reputation, his name? "I'll go with you. I don't want you to talk to her without me there."

"Do you need a ride?"

"I'll take a cab." She made a mental note of the address he gave her, then closed her phone and stood up. Her grandfather and Martin were with her dad, and her mother would be back soon. She might as well take care of this now. She hoped Jasmine Chen had nothing to do with her father, that all they'd had was a business relationship. Just because the woman lived in Chinatown near the scene of her father's assault didn't mean anything. Her bracelet could have fallen off at any time. It didn't have to be connected to her father. It didn't have to be from him. The rationalizations made her feel better. With any luck, this whole misunderstanding would be cleared up within the hour, and they'd never have to talk about Jasmine Chen again.

Riley walked down one of the many alleys that ran behind the main streets of Chinatown. David Hathaway had been attacked some thirty yards into the alley, and apparently no one had seen or heard anything, not an unusual occurrence in a neighborhood where it was better for your health not to be too observant. Even now, a young man sweeping the brick in front of his store hurried quickly inside and shut the door, obviously not wanting to engage in conversation.

Riley stopped at the spot where remnants of yellow tape lay on the ground and wondered again what the hell a rich man like David Hathaway had been doing down here. A glance around the alley showed nothing out of the ordinary. The bottom floors of the buildings housed various businesses, a trading company, a photography studio, an accounting office, certainly nothing that would appear to have anything to do with a dragon statue. There were, however, several unmarked doors opening off the alley that could have led anywhere, to anyone.

He looked up, noting the apartments on the second,

third, and fourth floors. There were clothes drying off fire escapes, open windows with tattered curtains blowing in and out in the breeze, and a halfhearted attempt at a window garden in the dark alley. Everything he saw spoke of people struggling to survive in a densely populated city. He imagined that the apartments above were cramped, the plumbing and electrical antiquated, too many people living in too small a space. Was it any surprise that David Hathaway had been robbed in a place like this? He should have had more sense than to come here alone at night.

Bringing his gaze back down to the ground, Riley checked to see if anything else had been missed by the police, but found nothing. A few feet away was a doorway set back from the street, an overhang offering shelter, perhaps a hiding spot as well. He walked over to the door and saw women and sewing machines through the metal grille that protected the shop from burglary. He rang the bell. A moment later, a short young Chinese woman approached the door. She looked through the upper glass portion of the door, then tentatively opened it, leaving the metal grille between them.

"Hello," he said, offering her a friendly smile. "I wonder if I could talk to you for a minute."

She said something to him in Cantonese and started to shut the door.

"Wait, I wanted to ask you about a man who was attacked here last night."

"No English," she said in a heavy accent. Another woman came up behind her and grabbed her by the arm, forcing her away from the door.

"Police?" the other woman asked him.

"No. I'm a friend of the man who was assaulted in the alley last night. Were you here when it happened?"

She shook her head, then shut the door firmly in his face. He had no idea if they were protecting someone else, or just themselves.

Checking his watch, he realized he had only a few minutes to meet Paige. He walked down the alley toward the main street, passing a temple on the corner. Gold dragons were wrapped around two columns in front of the doorway that boasted a sign with Chinese writing. Below, in English, those seeking blessings were invited to enter. He wondered if David Hathaway had stopped at this temple, seeking a blessing on the dragon. Apparently, dragons were quite a symbol in Chinatown. He saw them virtually everywhere, promising protection, long life, and good fortune. But he hadn't experienced any good fortune since his grandmother discovered the dragon, and David Hathaway certainly hadn't, either.

Leaving the alley, Riley traversed two short blocks, leading him away from the commercial area to a neighborhood of apartment buildings that shared common walls. He wondered again if he shouldn't have gone ahead and talked to Jasmine on his own. While he wanted to believe Paige knew nothing about the dragon's disappearance, another part of him, the part that reminded him that women could lie and cheat with smiles on their faces, told him to be wary and not to take anything at face value. Paige Hathaway had grown up in a different world with different rules.

David Hathaway had already broken one rule by taking the dragon from the store. Who knew what else he'd had in mind? Riley needed to do more research on the art world, find out what scams were running. He was concerned that someone might try to copy the dragon, return the counterfeit version to his grandmother, insisting it was a fake, and sell the real thing on the black market.

He would not allow that to happen to his grandmother.

A taxi pulled up alongside the curb, and Paige stepped out, still dressed in the navy blue leggings she'd worn the night before. She'd brushed her hair, put on some pink lipstick, but her eyes were tired, her face drawn. She was scared. He could see it in every tiny, tense line.

"You look like hell," he told her. "Why don't you go home and let me handle this? I can call you and tell you what I find out."

"You'll tell me what you want me to know," she said tersely. "Which one is her apartment building?"

"It's at the far corner."

"She probably doesn't have anything to do with my father," Paige said as they began to walk in that direction. "It's just a coincidence that her bracelet was found in the alley. It didn't have my father's name on it. Any man could have given it to her. Or it could have been there for days. Maybe she goes through that alley all the time."

The explanations tumbled out of her mouth one after the other. Paige was already deep in denial. That meant she had doubts about her father's fidelity, suspicions that had probably been hidden away with the family jewels all these years. "Relax," he said, halting in front of the building. "Let's take it one step at a time. No one is accusing your father of anything."

"You are. You've been accusing him of all kinds of things. And me, too."

"I'm simply opening my mind to the possibilities. The truth will come out in the end."

"And then you'll owe me an and my family an apology."

"We'll see." He tipped his head toward the back stairs. "Second floor, 2C."

She paused. "Let me do the talking."

"I don't think so."

"It's my father who's lying in a hospital bed in critical condition. I have the most at stake here. Don't forget that."

She had a point. He waved her forward. "After you."

Paige took a deep breath. Now that she had the control, she wasn't quite sure what to do with it. Despite her best efforts to take charge, she was trembling. She kept thinking about the fact that her father might have taken this same route the day before, climbed these stairs, raised his hand to knock on this door. But why?

"Aren't you going to knock?" Riley asked when her hesitation lengthened.

"Just give me a second."

"To do what? It's a door. Knock."

She flung him an irritated glare, then rapped her knuckles against the wood. For a split second she thought no one might be home. Then she heard footsteps, a rustling, the jangle of a chain. The door opened slightly, the chain still in place. An Asian woman peered out suspiciously, her eyes as black as her hair.

"Yes?"

"Are you Jasmine Chen?" Paige asked.

"I don't have any money to give."

"Wait," Paige said, but the door shut in her face. She looked at Riley.

He simply reached over and rapped again. "Ms. Chen," he said loudly. "We need to speak to you, please. We're not leaving until we do."

The door cracked open again. "What do you want?"

"Tell her, Paige. Tell her who you are," Riley

instructed.

She hesitated, knowing this might be her last chance to forget the whole thing.

"Paige?" the woman questioned, her gaze narrowing. "Paige Hathaway?"

Her stomach turned over. This woman knew her. Okay, don't panic, she told herself. Jasmine did business with the House of Hathaway. She'd probably seen her in the store. There was nothing mysterious about that. "Yes. I'm Paige Hathaway. I think you might know my father, David." She drew in a deep breath. "He was hurt last night. He was mugged in an alley not far from here."

The woman put a hand to her heart, her eyes widening in shock. "No, not David."

"We need to talk to you."

Jasmine unhooked the chain and opened the door to allow them to enter. The living room was small and sparsely furnished, with a simple black couch and matching chair, a coffee table with candles on it, a sewing machine on an old desk, piles of fabrics stacked on the floor, and a few photographs of a young woman on a side table. But while the room was simple, the walls were cluttered. Paintings filled every available space, conveying a frenzy of emotions that were not reflected in Jasmine's now unreadable expression as she stood in the center of the room waiting for them to speak.

Now that they were here -- now that the questions could be asked -- Paige couldn't bring herself to speak. How could she ask a woman, a stranger, if she was sleeping with her father? She'd told Riley she wanted to take charge of this meeting, but now she looked to him for help.

"Did David Hathaway come to see you yesterday?" Riley asked Jasmine.

Paige let out a small breath of relief at the fairly innocuous question. It was certainly an improvement on the question she'd been considering.

"Yes," Jasmine said.

"Why?" Riley asked.

"He came to speak about a painting."

Maybe that was all it was, a simple business meeting, Paige thought desperately. Then she saw Jasmine's gaze stray toward the wall, toward one of the paintings, and she saw something she didn't want to see, something that appeared very familiar.

"Oh, my God," she whispered, as she walked over to the wall to take a closer look. "Riley, look. It's your dragon."

Chapter Seven

Riley met Paige's gaze in shocked awareness. He turned to Jasmine. "How did you come to paint that dragon?"

"I have seen it many times in my dreams."

"In your dreams? What does that mean?" he asked.

"What I said."

"Why don't we get more specific, Ms. Chen," Riley continued. "Did you see a dragon yesterday that looked like the one in your painting? Did David Hathaway show you just such a dragon?"

Jasmine hesitated again, then nodded. "Yes. David came by yesterday with a dragon statue that looked like that one."

Why?" Riley asked sharply.

"He thought I might like to see it."

"Because you'd seen it before?"

"In my dreams, as I told you. I didn't know it actually existed until yesterday."

Riley paced back and forth in front of the painting, his gaze darting around the rest of the room as if he were memorizing all the details. Paige thought she should probably get into the conversation, but for the life of her she couldn't think of a thing to say. Why had her father brought the dragon to Jasmine? How had Jasmine known to paint something that looked so similar? And what the heck did she mean by saying she saw it in a dream?

"What time was Mr. Hathaway here?" Riley asked.

"I think it was around five o'clock."

"Is that when he left or when he arrived?"

"When he left."

"Did he leave with the dragon?" Riley asked.

"Yes."

Jasmine was nothing if not brief. "Ms. Chen," Paige said slowly, "When my father was found last night, he didn't have the dragon with him. Do you know where he was going when he left you yesterday?"

"I didn't ask."

"Do you think he was taking it to an appraiser, someone here in Chinatown that I might not be aware of?"

"I don't know. You must go now. I have an appointment." Jasmine walked across the room and opened the door.

Short of being rude, Paige didn't see any alternative but to leave the apartment. Riley followed her out to the landing.

"Your father," Jasmine said, her expression softening, "Will he be all right?"

"They don't know. He's unconscious."

There was a tiny flicker of what looked like pain in Jasmine's eyes. "I will burn some incense for him, ask for blessings."

"Thank you. I'm sure he would appreciate that."

"What hospital is he in?" Jasmine asked.

"St. Mary's."

"And your mother -- she is with him?"

Paige stared into Jasmine's dark eyes. "Yes, my mother is with him."

Jasmine nodded, then gently shut the door in her face, leaving Paige feeling sick to her stomach. There was something between this woman and her father; she knew it. Jasmine hadn't called him Mr. Hathaway as most of their customers did. She'd called him David. And there had been more than a little familiarity in her voice.

"You could have asked her," Riley said, reading her mind.

Yes, she could have asked, but Paige couldn't bear the thought of an answer that would destroy her family. "It's not the issue. It's not important right now." She looked into Riley's eyes and saw understanding, compassion, pity. She stiffened. She didn't want this man feeling sorry for her. She was a Hathaway. No one should feel sorry for a Hathaway. "It's all speculation, anyway. You heard Ms. Chen. She and my father met to discuss a painting. End of story."

"That's not the end, and you know it. He brought the dragon to show her."

"You think my father was attacked because of the dragon, don't you?"

"I believe the dragon is involved in some way. He had it with him when he left this apartment yesterday. Now it's gone."

"But hours passed between the time he was here and when he was found in the alley."

"Exactly. Where did he go in between? What did he do with the dragon? Did he leave it somewhere else? That's what we need to find out."

She hated his even, cool tone. "Yes, that's what we need to find out. Because this isn't just about your dragon.

My father could die, and I will not let whoever did this to him get away with it."

"Then we're both extremely motivated," he said, meeting her gaze.

"But you don't trust me."

"No, I don't."

She stopped at the bottom of the stairs. "My father almost died last night. How can you possibly think I'm involved in something underhanded?"

"Sometimes events get out of control. Things happen that aren't meant to happen. People considered friends, family, associates turn out to be enemies. And money, greed, desire can turn a man's head; or a woman's for that matter."

His eyes hardened down to cold, blue steel. She sensed he spoke from experience, that there was pain behind the harsh words, but she doubted he would admit that. A less vulnerable man she had yet to meet. But at the moment his vulnerability was the least of her worries. His stubborn pursuit of the truth might take her to a place she didn't want to go. Not that her father was guilty of anything. He must have had a good reason for taking the statue to Jasmine. He just needed to wake up so he could tell her that reason.

"I have to get back to the hospital," she said abruptly.

"Do you want a ride?"

She hesitated, part of her wanting to get as far away from Riley as possible, but it would certainly be more convenient to accept his offer. "Yes, thank you. Actually, if you could take me back to Fast Willy's, so I could get my car, I'd appreciate that. I'd like to go home and change my clothes before returning to the hospital."

"No problem. I'm parked in the Portsmouth Square garage just down the street."

She had to walk quickly to keep up with his long-legged strides. When they reached the square, she moved closer to him. The area was crowded with Chinese men, mostly older men, she realized as they headed toward the elevator leading to the parking garage under the square. Their voices were pitched high and loud, the unknown words of their language producing an odd kind of music. She felt suddenly and self-consciously blond, aware of the looks she and Riley were generating. This was not her world. She didn't belong here.

"Relax. At this time of day, we're fine," he said.

"I'm not worried."

"Sure you are."

"Well, it makes good sense to be cautious." She stepped into the elevator, the walls of which were covered with Chinese graffiti. It was probably a good thing she couldn't read the characters.

"Too bad your father didn't think the same way."

"My father gets wrapped up in what he's doing. He loses track of everything and everyone around him."

"Which would make him an easy target."

"Yes," she agreed, as they stepped off the elevator and entered the garage. It was dark and quiet down here, and her uneasiness increased. She was grateful to see Riley's black Jeep Cherokee parked in a nearby spot. The car was sporty, rugged, and unpretentious, very much like its owner. She got in, fastened her seat belt, and pushed down the automatic door lock.

Riley smiled at the action. "I won't let anything happen to you, Paige."

"Yeah, right. You and I are such good friends."

"You're very important to me right now."

"A means to an end. I figured that out awhile ago. Just get us out of here. I hate underground parking garages."

"Better?" he asked a moment later when they pulled out onto the street.

"Yes," she said, letting out a sigh. "It's been a long night."

"You should go home and get some sleep."

"I need to see my dad, to be there when he wakes up. I shouldn't have even come here, but I didn't want you to talk to Jasmine alone." Paige looked out the window, feeling calmer as Riley drove away from Chinatown, heading toward the Financial District. "It's amazing how quickly the neighborhood changes."

"And how little the neighbors mingle. You live only a few miles from here, yet you never come here."

"How do you know where I live?"

"I have my ways."

"I don't like my privacy being invaded."

"Well, I don't like the fact that my grandmother's dragon is missing. So we're even."

He had her there. "What about you? Where do you live? It seems only fair that I should know as much about you as you know about me."

"I have a condo south of Market," he told her.

"The new 'in' neighborhood according to *San Francisco Magazine*."

"It's convenient to my work. I don't care much about trends."

"What about your grandmother? Does she live with you?"

"God, no." He uttered a laugh. "She has a house in the Sunset. It's too big for her now that my grandfather is in a rest home, so she's thinking about moving. That's why we cleaned out her attic last week."

"I am sorry about all this," she said, feeling even

more guilty now that she knew his grandfather was in a rest home. When I promised you that the dragon would be safe in our care, I was sincere."

He sent her a thoughtful look. "I'd like to believe that."

"You can. I'm a very honest person. I don't lie about anything."

"Everyone lies about something."

She shot him a curious look. "You're really a glass half-empty kind of guy, aren't you?"

He smiled at that. "When it's half empty, it *is* half empty."

"Or half full, depending on your point of view, and yours seems to be extremely cynical."

"And yours is extremely optimistic. You remind me of my grandmother. She still believes in Santa Claus."

"I liked your grandmother. She's really nice. Nothing like you."

"She'd be the first to agree with you."

"You're close, aren't you?"

"We're all we have left since my grandfather got sick. I try to watch out for her as much as I can. I don't let anyone take advantage of her. Although I may have screwed up in this case."

"You didn't. We'll get the dragon back."

"You can't make that promise. You don't even know where it is."

"Then we'll compensate your grandmother in some other way," Paige said, knowing her mother would probably have a heart attack at the thought of paying for a dragon statue she couldn't sell. But then again, Hathaway's had lost the statue, and Paige doubted the insurance would cover the item since it had been taken out of the store.

Riley concentrated on the traffic, maneuvering across three lanes. His profile was strong and masculine, his hands firm on the wheel, his shoulders broad. He was a beautifully made man, attractive, virile. Good heavens, where had that word come from? A knot in her stomach squeezed tight as she was overwhelmed by an unfamiliar feeling of lust. She had the sudden urge to reach out and trace his jawline, maybe run her fingers through the thick strands of dark hair.

What was she thinking? Her father was fighting for his life. Her family business was going to be under intense scrutiny when the press got wind of the disappearance of the dragon. Her mother would be beside herself. That's what she needed to be thinking about, not how good-looking Riley McAllister was, or how much she wanted to touch him.

She rolled down the window, letting in some fresh, cooling air.

"I can turn on the air conditioner," Riley said.

"This is fine."

He turned the corner and slowed down as Fast Willy's came into view. He pulled over behind her car, leaving the engine running.

Paige put her hand on the door handle, then paused. "What are you going to do now?"

"Follow the trail."

"There isn't a trail. The only evidence the police have is that bracelet. I can't believe we didn't even ask Jasmine about the bracelet," she added, realizing the subject had never come up.

"The bracelet doesn't matter. It led us to her. That's all we needed to get out of it."

"But she didn't tell us anything. I don't see any trail, Riley."

"The trail of the dragon. It came from somewhere. It seems to have some value. Maybe if we know more about it, we can figure out who would want it badly enough to steal it. Surely someone in your family or someone at Hathaway's might have more information about such a piece and its history."

"That someone would be my father. But I think you're overlooking something."

"What?"

"Your family. Where did your grandmother get the dragon?"

"She doesn't know."

"Maybe someone in your family knows," she said, repeating his earlier statement and liking the fact that the Hathaways weren't the only ones under the microscope.

"There's no one else in my family to ask. My grandfather has Alzheimer's. He can't even remember his name."

"No other relatives?"

"Nope. Dead or gone pretty much accounts for all of them."

She thought about that blunt statement. "What about your parents?"

"Dead or gone," he repeated.

She didn't know what to say to that. Riley certainly didn't know how to make polite conversation. "I'm sorry," she said awkwardly.

"It's not your fault. But you're right. We can't overlook anything, in my family or in yours. I'll do some digging. Hell, I'll even pay my grandfather a visit. Maybe he'll have a lucid moment."

"Does that happen often?"

"Almost never."

"That must be difficult for your grandmother."

"She was crazy about him. Still is, even when he doesn't recognize her, which is most days. The hardest times are when he's struggling to remember something, when he has enough awareness to realize it's gone. That's when it gets to me -- when I see that look of panic in his eyes, and I can't do anything to stop it." He shook his head. "I hate feeling helpless."

She knew exactly what he meant. She'd felt that way when her sister died, and she'd felt that way all last night. "Thanks for the ride. I guess I'll see you later."

"You can count on that."

By seven o'clock that night, everyone in San Francisco knew that David Hathaway had been assaulted in Chinatown, that he was fighting for his life, and that a potentially valuable Chinese dragon might have been the motivation for the attack. Riley hit the mute button on the television, irritated with himself for mentioning the dragon to the police detective the night before. Obviously, Tony had not kept that fact to himself. With the press watching the Hathaways every second, it was no wonder the news had leaked out. At least his grandmother's name had not been mentioned. He didn't care if the Hathaway reputation took a hit, but he'd prefer not to have his grandmother in the spotlight.

His phone rang, and he leaned over to pick up the extension, seeing his grandmother's number. "Hello, Grandma."

"Riley, I just saw the news. I feel terrible about what happened to poor Mr. Hathaway. And that my dragon might be the cause of it all is so upsetting."

"We don't know that for sure."

"The reporter who talked to me seemed to think it was the reason."

His gut tightened. "What reporter?"

"Someone from the *Herald* called. He was very nice. He asked me all kinds of questions about the dragon. Of course I could only tell him what they told us, and I didn't even remember all of that."

"I wish you weren't mixed up in this," he grumbled. "Don't talk to anyone else, Grandma. Just let the answering machine pick up the phone. Maybe I should come over there."

"And do what? Babysit me? I'm too old for that, honey. Besides, Patty and Lila are coming over to play cards in a few minutes. I won't be alone."

"What about later tonight?"

"I'm a big girl. I'll lock the doors and windows, and I'll make sure I turn on that security system your grandpa put in a few years ago."

"All right, but be careful."

"Of course I'll be careful, but I don't understand why you sound so concerned."

"I'm concerned because someone may have been willing to kill David Hathaway for your dragon." He heard Nan's small gasp of breath and cursed himself for being so blunt. He should have chosen his words more carefully.

"Well," she said, "I didn't quite see it like that, but I don't think I have to worry. After all, I don't have the dragon anymore."

She had a point, but he still couldn't shake the feeling that he was missing something.

"I'm beginning to think I wasn't meant to have that dragon, Riley," she added.

"Why would you say that?"

"I've been racking my brain trying to figure out where it came from. It had to have been brought into the house by one of two people, your grandfather or your mother. Now, I usually knew what Ned was up to. He didn't have many secrets. But Mary was full of surprises. I wonder if she didn't pick up that dragon on one of her trips. Maybe..." Her voice drifted away. "But I don't want to think that."

"That she stole it." The thought had already crossed his mind.

"Your mother isn't a thief."

"My mother doesn't know right from wrong, up from down, red from blue. Her vision of the world was skewed most of the time, even when she wasn't on drugs. You know that."

"If she took the dragon from somewhere, she didn't think it was stealing."

"It doesn't matter," he said, trying not to show his exasperation with Nan's loyalty. After all, she'd extended that same loyalty to him.

"It might matter. Maybe your mother saw us on TV the other day. I've gotten a couple of strange hang-up calls recently."

"Why would she call and hang up?" Riley asked, trying to be logical and practical instead of emotional. "Why wouldn't she just say hello?"

"She might be working up her courage. We had words that last day before she left, and I told her that she couldn't come back unless she said she was sorry. I had no idea I was asking something that was just impossible for her to give."

Riley knew his grandmother still wanted to hear those words, still wanted to believe that her daughter would one day realize how much she'd hurt them all and apologize. Riley had hoped for the same thing for a long, long time. But not now, not after fifteen years.

"She must think about you, Riley. I'm only her mother, but you're her son, her child. I know she thinks about you. I know she wants to see you."

"You don't know anything of the kind," Riley said somewhat harshly. "I'm sorry, Grandma, but the truth is we don't even know if she's alive. And the odds of her calling and hanging up are really long. It's more likely a wrong number, or maybe even Grandpa dialing the phone and forgetting who he's calling. You should have caller ID on your phone; I don't know why you don't. I'll get that added tomorrow."

"Oh, Riley, more security measures? I don't want to feel like I'm living in a prison. You're probably right. It's probably your grandpa. He does have that phone by his bed."

Riley paused as the buzzer for his apartment rang. "Someone is at the door. Call me if you have any problems." He hung up the phone and walked over to the intercom. "Yes?"

"It's Paige. I need to speak to you right away."

He buzzed her in, having a pretty good idea of what she wanted to see him about.

She made it to the second floor in less than a minute and, judging by the flushed red of her cheeks, she'd taken the stairs. He waved her into his apartment.

"Before you--" he began.

"What the hell were you thinking, talking to the press about this?"

"I didn't."

"You must have. They have the whole story. My phone has been ringing off the hook all day. They want to know about the dragon. And our other customers want to know if their priceless artifacts are in danger of disappearing. My mother is livid. This is the last thing we needed, with my father fighting for his life." She finally took a breath.

Riley jumped in. "I didn't call the media, Paige. I mentioned the dragon to the police detective last night. I asked him if they'd found anything in the alley."

"The police told the press?" she asked with a disbelieving frown.

"I'm sure someone has a source in the department. And you said yourself that the Hathaways are always news, aren't they?"

"Yes." She let out a sigh. "I need to sit down."

Riley swept a pile of newspapers off a nearby armchair so she could take a seat. "How did you find me, by the way?"

"Your secretary was very helpful."

"I'll fire her in the morning."

Paige smiled weakly. "I guess I should apologize. I shouldn't have come here. I just had to yell at someone."

"How's your father?"

"No change. It's hard to see him lying so still. My mother is there now, along with a private nurse. My grandfather is planning to stop by tonight. He'll probably just order my father to wake up."

"Does he have that much power?"

"He thinks he does, but my dad tuned out my grandfather years ago. The two of them have never gotten along. I think that's why Dad started traveling so much. It was his escape."

"Do you need an escape, too?" he asked curiously.

"I already made my escape. I moved out of the family house a few years ago. I couldn't breathe there. My grandfather has portraits of all the Hathaway ancestors lining the hallway. Every time I'd walk down that hall, I'd feel like they were looking at me, wondering why I should be the only Hathaway left to carry on the family bloodline. I can't even carry on the name officially, since I'm a girl, which has caused endless turmoil. I think my mother would consider adopting my husband just to give him the Hathaway name."

Riley smiled. "That would be extreme. And I can't see many men willing to give up their name."

"The woman gives up hers. Why shouldn't the man do the same?"

"Because it's very..."

"Very what?"

"Wrong. Trust me, Paige, if the man you marry is willing to give up his name to take yours, you should run away as fast as possible." He sat down on the sofa across from her, resting his arms on his legs. "Speaking of which, you're engaged, aren't you?"

"Who told you that?"

"My assistant, Carey."

"Then you should fire her."

He grinned. "Are you saying it's not true?"

"You don't see a ring, do you?"

"No, but I thought I saw a jealous boyfriend last night at the hospital."

She shrugged, avoiding his direct gaze. "Martin was just being protective. He wasn't jealous of you. Why would he be? It's not like you and I are together. You don't even like me."

"Did I say that?"

"Didn't you?" she countered, her gaze seeking his.

"I don't think so."

"You said you didn't trust me."

"That's not the same thing."

She tilted her head, giving him a considering look. "It's not just me you don't trust, though, is it? What made you so cynical -- or should I say who?"

"I was just born this way."

"No one is born distrusting. That's not how it happens."

"Why don't you tell me about it over pizza?" He got to his feet and moved toward the phone. "What kind do you like?"

She looked at him in surprise. "I'm not staying for pizza."

"Why not? Aren't you hungry?"

"Well, yes, but--"

"You can help me with some research while we're waiting for the food," he added, tipping his head toward the laptop computer on the table. "I've found some interesting dragon tales, but nothing that looks like my grandmother's dragon. Maybe you know of some better sites."

"I suppose I could try," she said slowly.

"What do you want on your pizza?"

"Surprise me."

He raised an eyebrow. "Are you sure? I don't want to hear any complaints later on."

She gave him a serene smile. "Hathaways never complain."

Forty-five minutes later, Riley knew that Paige liked black olives, mushrooms, pepperoni, and onions but picked off the bell peppers when no one was looking. Only, he was always looking; she just hadn't caught him at it yet. She'd been too busy surfing through various art sites on the computer.

He liked the way she worked, the way her eyes focused on the screen, sometimes squinting over tiny print. He liked the way she frowned with impatience when the computer worked too slowly or a lead turned into a dead end. But it didn't make her quit. She just worked harder. And she was right; she didn't complain, not about the fact that the only drink he had to offer was beer, or that he had run out of napkins and paper towels and had only toilet paper to offer for dripping cheese and tomato sauce.

She'd probably also noticed the fact that his apartment was decorated in leftovers, as he liked to call the furniture he'd collected from his bachelor friends every time they moved in with a woman or got married. It seemed that along with commitment came interior design. Sooner or later, his friends' furniture showed up at his place while the women filled their joint living space with new stuff.

Well, not for him. He was happy with his big-screen TV, his oversized reclining armchair, his leather couch and his football memorabilia, including a signed jersey from the San Francisco 49ers. No woman was worth losing that for.

"Hello..."

Paige's voice brought his attention back to her. "What?"

"I've been talking to you for five minutes."

"Sorry. What did you find?" He moved around the table so he could see the monitor better. Unfortunately, the close contact with Paige distracted him once again. Her hair smelled good, like a field of wildflowers that he wanted to roll around in for a few hours.

Paige tapped the screen with her fingernail. "A

legend about a dragon that looks a lot like yours."

Riley forced himself to focus. The unsophisticated sketch could be his dragon, he supposed.

"The period referenced is the Zhou dynasty," Paige continued, "Which is the period my father thought your dragon might be from. What's interesting about this story is that it actually speaks of two dragons that connect together and open a special box."

"That doesn't sound like what we have at all."

"Maybe not. But..." Her voice trailed away.

"But what?" he asked impatiently.

"It's a fascinating story. Do you want to hear it?" She turned her face toward him, and he saw the eager light in her brown eyes. Whatever she'd found had caught her imagination.

"Go ahead."

"It's about a little girl, the daughter of an emperor. The emperor suffered severe, violent headaches, and the kingdom was in despair over how to ease his pain. It was said that he went on rages during these episodes. People were killed. Things were destroyed. One day the daughter was in the woods, and she found a long piece of bamboo that made music when she blew through it. She took the bamboo flute back to the palace, and that night, when her father was suffering from another headache, she played it for him. The music was magical. It instantly soothed his pain. He pronounced the flute to be a gift from the gods, and this child, this daughter, had succeeded in comforting him when no one else could--"

"What does this have to do with a dragon?" Riley interrupted, sensing Paige could go on like this for a while. She was obviously captivated by the tale.

"I'm getting to that. The emperor decided that the flute must be protected above all else. He had a box created to hold the flute. Then he had two special dragons fashioned out of bronze to guard the box. The dragons had to be connected together in a special way in order to open the box. If either dragon was damaged or lost, the box could not be opened. And the little girl, the first daughter of his second wife, was treated like a princess."

"Yeah, yeah. So?"

Paige gave him an irritated look. "So, these three pieces were very valuable. Others in the kingdom were jealous of the little girl's new status. You can imagine what happened next."

"Someone stole the flute."

"The whole thing, the dragons, the box, and the flute. What was worse, the emperor had his daughter killed, because he was so angry. He then had a ton of bamboo brought to the palace, but no one else could make any of the pieces sing like the original flute. There was no longer any healing magic. Nothing could be heard but the sound of weeping throughout the kingdom."

"Where's the happy ending?"

"There isn't one. The emperor swore a curse of revenge on all first daughters. He said that until the box and the flute were put back in their rightful place, all first daughters of whoever came in contact with any piece of the set, the box, the dragons, or the flute would suffer terrible misfortune."

"So what happened?"

"I don't know."

"What do you mean you don't know?" He reached over and pushed the scroll key only to find that they had come to the end of the passage. "That's it? That's the whole story?"

"There's a moral."

"Right. I got that. Stealing is a bad thing. What I want

to know is who took the box and the flute and the dragons, and what the hell happened to them?"

Paige smiled. "That sounds like a security expert talking. You have to solve the crime, otherwise the world is off balance. One plus one always equals two. Missing things must be found. Every beginning has to have an ending."

"That's the natural order of things. I still don't see what that story has to do with my grandmother's dragon."

"Maybe nothing, but it might be worth looking into. Did you happen to notice a connecting joint on the dragon, a piece that looked like it might fit into another piece?"

Riley shook his head. "I didn't look at it that closely. I'll bet your father did, though. What about that other guy who was working in the lab that day?"

"Raymond Li?" Her eyes widened. "My God. I just remembered. I never spoke to Mr. Li. He called in sick yesterday. I know that, because I was looking for my father, and I went down there thinking they'd be together, but Mr. Li's assistant told me that he was out."

Riley felt his heart begin to pump faster. He checked his watch. It was almost nine o'clock. "Do you have his home number?"

"I'm sure it's in the personnel file, but I don't have that."

"You can get it, can't you?"

"Tomorrow when the store opens."

"What about tonight?"

"I don't have access to those files on my computer."

"Don't worry about that. You get me into the store. I'll get you into those files."

Chapter Eight

"This feels wrong," Paige said as she let Riley into her dark office just before nine thirty. The store closed by six o'clock on weekdays, five o'clock on the weekends. The Hathaways had never felt compelled to offer longer hours. Her grandfather always said if the people wanted to buy their goods, they could damn well find a way to come during the day.

She flipped on the lights, but it still didn't ease the tension in her body. She'd been at the store after hours before, but never for the purpose of looking into files that weren't any of her business.

"You own the store, Paige," Riley reminded her. "You have the right to access any information having to do with it."

"My mother would not agree with you." Paige walked around her desk to turn on her computer. "She's the boss."

"More so than your father? Isn't it his family's business?"

"Yes, but my mother doesn't think of it that way. She's probably more of a Hathaway than my father is. Once she married my dad, she got rid of her own family.

I've never even met my maternal grandmother or my mother's sisters."

"Really?" he asked with a note of surprise in his voice. "So your mother has some skeletons in her closet. That's interesting."

"My mother grew up poor and angry about it. Now, she's rich and angry about other things, like the fact that my grandfather won't name her CEO. She's not a blood Hathaway, and therefore she can't have the title. My father can't have it, either, because he doesn't spend enough time at the store. But that's not an issue, because he doesn't want the title."

"Which leaves you."

"Exactly. If I prove myself worthy, someday all of this will be mine, but it certainly won't be anytime soon."

"Sounds like your grandfather still runs the show," Riley commented.

"He's a very strong-willed person, strong in body, in mind, and in opinions." She punched a button on her computer, then stepped aside so Riley could sit down. She perched on the edge of the desk, watching as he quickly riffled through the programs.

"Passwords?" he asked.

She gave him the ones she had and watched his fingers fly across the keyboard as if this were very familiar territory. She couldn't help wondering about his background. "Where did you learn to do this?" she asked, noting how quickly he got into the personnel files.

"Self-taught," he said, his attention still focused on the screen.

"You majored in computers in college?"

"I didn't go to college."

"Really? Why not?" Everyone she'd ever known had gone to college. Even Jerry had managed to make it through a state school.

"No money. What's the name of the guy we're looking for?"

"Raymond Li. They have scholarships, financial aid to help you get through school."

"Yeah, what would you know about that?"

"Enough to know that you were smart enough to go if you wanted to go."

"I went into the service instead. Here it is, Raymond Li." He jotted down the address on a piece of paper.

Riley had been in the service? Although given his commanding air, that wasn't all that surprising. "Which branch of the military?"

"Marines."

"You seem to be more comfortable giving orders than taking them."

"One reason I'm an ex-marine," he said with a brief smile.

She frowned as her gaze drifted to the screen and she realized that Riley wasn't looking at the personnel files anymore. "What are you doing?"

"Just checking a few things out."

"Our inventory?"

"Wouldn't someone have recorded the dragon as part of the inventory on the day we brought it in? Your father gave us a receipt for it. But I don't see it."

"It would have been temporary, most likely under possible acquisitions or something like that." She paused, knowing she should probably stop him, but reviewing their inventory list was hardly worth shouting about, and at the moment she was interested in learning more about him. "What was it like being a marine? Did you see any combat?"

"Some. Nothing I want to talk about," he added,

flinging her a pointed look before turning back to the computer.

"What's that expression the marines always say? Semper something."

"Semper Fi. Always faithful."

"And are you?"

"To my country -- absolutely."

She picked up a pen from her desk and played with it. "What about with a woman?"

"I've never been married."

"But you've been in relationships."

"What makes you so certain?"

"Because you're -- you're not bad to look at."

He smiled. "You think so?"

She felt a wave of heat cross her cheeks. "I was speaking from a purely observational point of view."

"Is that what they call it these days?" He suddenly swung the chair around and stood up. He put his hands on either side of the desk, trapping her in what could have been an embrace, only he wasn't touching her, just crowding her, making her very, very aware of every inch of his long, muscular, masculine body.

"What -- what are you doing?" she asked quickly, her heart speeding up at the look in his eyes.

"Getting a better look at you -- from a purely observational point of view."

She licked her lips, then wished she hadn't as his gaze settled on her mouth. "We should get back to..." What were they supposed to be doing, anyway? She couldn't seem to remember. He was too close. He was stealing her breath, making it hard to think, to concentrate. And then he moved closer still, his mouth covering hers in a kiss that he hadn't asked for, a kiss he simply took, a kiss she couldn't help giving back. He tasted good, his mouth warm, demanding, impatient as his tongue swept inside, deepening the kiss, making her want to melt right into him. His hands were hot and firm on her waist as he pulled her against the solid wall of his chest.

She stroked his back, loving the feel of the hard muscles beneath her fingers. Their legs tangled up as they each searched for a better position. It wasn't until her back touched the top of her desk that she realized how quickly things were moving along. Was that Riley's hand on her leg, on her hip, sliding up under her shirt?

Good God! Another minute and she'd be having sex on top of her desk.

Paige hastily sat up, pushing him away with a breathless "Stop."

Riley stared at her with dark, intensely blue eyes that were filled with desire for her. She almost wished she hadn't asked him to stop. But this wasn't right. She wasn't the kind of woman to have sex with a man she didn't know. And she didn't know Riley, not enough, anyway. The fact that he was the sexiest, most attractive man she'd met in a long, long time, and that he made her want to do reckless, impulsive things wasn't a good enough reason -- was it? Suddenly logic didn't seem important. Nor did common sense or rational thinking.

Riley had made her feel good, like a woman, like a sexy feminine creature. But she wasn't just a woman. She was a Hathaway. Hathaways didn't have sex on the office furniture.

Paige drew a deep breath and ran her hand over her hair, still acutely conscious that Riley hadn't taken his eyes off her. "Why did you do that?" she asked, stumbling over the question.

He thought for a moment, then said, "I wanted to."

"Well, you can't just do what you want like that --

without asking."

"Do men always ask before they kiss you?"

"As a matter of fact, yes, they do."

"And what do you usually answer?"

"That depends on the situation and the man and everything else." She waved her hand in the air, not liking the grin spreading across his face. "It's not funny."

"Yes, it is."

"Well, don't do it again. Don't kiss me without any warning."

"So you didn't like it? I must have imagined your fingernails burrowing into my back, the little gasp you made when my tongue--"

"Would you stop?" she interrupted, feeling awkward and embarrassed. "It's bad enough that we kissed. We don't have to talk about it."

He laughed again. "God, you're funny. You're not a virgin, are you?"

She bristled in defense. "What I am or am not is none of your business."

"Maybe I'm making it my business."

"Why would you want to?"

"Because I want you, Miss Hathaway. What do you think about that?"

She caught her breath at his blunt words. She wasn't a virgin, but her experience wasn't all that extensive. In fact, she could count her lovers on the fingers of one hand, and she suspected Riley would need more than a few hands to total his conquests. He was cocky and confident, a man who knew he was attractive to women. That arrogance should have turned her off, but for some reason she found it oddly appealing, almost irresistible, in fact.

"You're just trying to get to me," she said finally. "And we're done here."

Sliding off the edge of the desk, she pushed him aside to look at the computer. Her eyes widened as she took in the details of the screen. Riley had somehow hacked his way into the accounting program -- not just the company's financial records, but what looked to be her father's personal money program. "What is this?"

"Your father's electronic checkbook. Apparently, he does all his transactions online. He's very efficient that way. Probably because he's out of the country so much."

"You should not be looking at that. It's private."

He leaned over her shoulder and hit the scroll key, showing the check transactions for the past few years. "See anything interesting, Paige?"

"No. I don't want to see anything at all. This is none of our business." She moved to close the window on the computer, but Riley stopped her.

"Wait a second. There's something I noticed before you distracted me."

"I didn't distract you. I was merely asking a few questions."

"Whatever. Check this out -- payments to Jasmine Chen, once a month like clockwork."

She saw the look in his eyes and knew what he was thinking. It was what she was thinking, too. "That probably confirms they were having some sort of an affair," she said slowly, a sinking feeling in the pit of her stomach.

"An expensive sort. We're talking several thousand a month. The number varies a bit." He scrolled through a few more screens, taking them back to the previous year and the year before that. "There are also several payments to UC Berkeley. Is that where you went?"

"I went to Stanford."

"Did you take classes at Berkeley?"

"No." She frowned, wondering why her father would have made payments to the university. "Maybe it was some sort of Hathaway grant, although that wouldn't have come out of my father's checkbook."

She moved aside as Riley sat back down in the chair, his fingers flying once again. She should stop him. This was going beyond the investigation of the dragon. Riley was delving into her father's business, his personal life, a life she was beginning to realize she knew very little about. She'd never given much thought to the possibility that there were other people who meant something to him, people besides her mother or her grandfather or herself. Friends never seemed to be that important to him. In fact, most of the couples her parents spent time with seemed to be her mother's friends, not her father's.

"Who is Alyssa Chen?" Riley asked, interrupting her thoughts.

"I don't know. Why?"

"She's the one who was going to Berkeley. Your father referenced her name on several transactions."

Alyssa Chen? A relative to Jasmine? A daughter?

Paige suddenly felt a knot in her stomach, a knot that grew tighter and twisted painfully with each passing second. "Turn it off."

Riley shot her a quick look. "Turning it off won't make it go away."

"Yes, it will. I don't want to know."

"Then don't look. But my gut tells me Jasmine Chen has something to do with the dragon. And maybe this Alyssa does, too."

Paige walked away from him, staring out the window behind her desk, which overlooked Union Square. She wasn't seeing the stores or the park; she was seeing Jasmine Chen's face, her apartment, the painting of the dragon on the wall, the photographs of a young woman on the table. Alyssa?

Well, so what if her father gave Jasmine money?

It also didn't matter if Jasmine had a daughter, and her father had generously given that daughter money for college. He was a generous man. He gave to lots of charities. Jasmine probably couldn't afford to send her child to college; she was a painter, an artist, and her father would have wanted to support an artist. He was all about art, about making it possible for people to create freely, to express themselves without worrying about how to make a living.

"Hmm, this is interesting," Riley murmured behind her.

She didn't like the sound of that. She was almost afraid to ask. But she had to. Turning, she asked, "What are you looking at now?"

"Vital statistics."

"Whose?"

"Alyssa Chen. She's twenty-two years old. Mother: Jasmine Chen. Father: Unknown."

Paige's heart skipped a beat. "Why is that important? Lots of women have children without knowing who the father is."

He cast her a speculative look. "True. But how many receive money from a complete stranger for that daughter every month for the past four years at least?"

"Okay, maybe my father has been involved with Jasmine, but that has nothing to do with your dragon, so turn it off."

"She has a picture of my dragon on her wall. I don't think that's a coincidence. And your father took the dragon to her. Another connection."

"He just showed it to her. He didn't leave it there."

"So she said."

"Their relationship is not relevant to you. An affair is only important to me, to my family."

He didn't say anything right away, but his silence was damning. She didn't need his words to put the equation together.

"Paige--"

"Don't say it."

"Fine. I won't say it."

She stared at him for a long moment. "You think Alyssa Chen is my father's..."

"Daughter." Riley met her gaze head-on. "And you think so, too."

It was easy to get his room number. Jasmine's neighbor's daughter worked in pediatrics. So Jasmine bypassed the information desk and took the elevator to the fourth floor. Visiting hours were almost over and the hallways were quiet. Now that she was here, she wasn't sure she could go through with it. She had spent most of the day worrying about David. What if he died? She didn't want to face that possibility, but it was there all the same.

David Hathaway had been so many things to her. She had liked him, loved him, hated him, then loved him again. Every time she had tried to cut him out of her life, he had come back in some unexpected way. He had brought with him nothing but trouble, nothing but pain. He had shamed her, and in turn she had shamed her family. She had spent the past twenty-two years being shunned by the people who had once loved her. And all because of David. So why had she come here now?

Because she still cared. God help her.

She found herself in front of his room. The door was closed. Was he alone? What would she say if he was not? They would wonder who she was, why she was here. Or maybe they knew. She thought back to Paige's visit. There had been a question in Paige's eyes that had nothing to do with the dragon or her father's accident. Paige suspected something; she just hadn't had the courage to ask, and for that Jasmine was grateful.

She tapped quietly on the door. No one answered. She slowly opened it. The room was small but private. There was a man in the bed, lying perfectly still. There were machines surrounding him but no one else. Where were they -- this family that he adored, that he could never leave, that he had chosen over her? Why weren't they here by his bedside, praying for his recovery, holding his hand, talking to him, pleading for him to wake up?

Once in the room, she stopped by the bed, her heart breaking yet again as she looked at his face. There was a huge, ugly bruise just beneath the bandage around his head. Her eyes blurred with tears. It couldn't end like this. The charming, outgoing David Hathaway, who spoke so passionately about art and history and life, could not go so quietly out of this world.

She picked up his hand. It had been a long time since she had held his hand. His skin was cool, as if the blood couldn't quite reach his fingers, as if his heart was slowing, his body shutting down. But the machine was still bleeping. She could see jagged lines of what must be his heartbeat. His chest moved in and out. He wasn't gone yet.

"Don't leave me," she murmured. "Not like this, not without a good-bye."

"What on earth is going on?" A woman's sharp voice broke through the silence.

Jasmine turned, knowing whom she would find behind her.

Victoria Hathaway stood in the doorway, her face shocked, her eyes angry. She drew herself up, throwing back her shoulders, lifting her chin. She was so beautiful, with her blond hair, her blue eyes, her perfectly made-up face, not a wrinkle, not a shadow anywhere, nothing to show she was worried about her husband. Dressed in a white suit with sheer stockings and high heels, she looked as if she'd come from work, as if her life hadn't changed at all since her husband's assault.

Jasmine felt short and heavy, uncomfortable with her old, unstylish clothes and her heavy, thick black hair that hadn't seen a hairdresser in several years. Not for the first time she wondered how David could have left Victoria to come to her. But she hadn't always looked this way. There had been a time when men thought she was pretty, when she had laughed and enjoyed life. Meeting David had changed all that.

"Who are you?" Victoria demanded, walking farther into the room.

"Jasmine Chen," she replied.

Victoria's face paled. Did she recognize the name? Had David actually spoken of her? Jasmine's heart lightened just a bit.

"You have no right to be here." Victoria's harsh words sliced through Jasmine like a knife. "How did you get in here? Where is the nurse?"

Jasmine didn't reply right away, not sure what she wanted to say. Although she had feared it was not her place to be, now that she had come, she wanted to stay. She had lost so much because of this man. Didn't she deserve to at least stand by his bedside at this moment? Everyone would say no. She was not the wife. She was not family.

"How is he?" she asked, ignoring Victoria's request that she leave.

"That is none of your business. Please go."

"Why haven't you asked me who I am, how I know David?" Jasmine saw the truth in Victoria's eyes. "You know, don't you?"

"I know that you don't belong here in my husband's room."

"I love him, too." Jasmine was shocked by the words that had come from her mouth. She hadn't said them in twenty years, not to anyone, not even out loud to herself.

Victoria stuttered over a reply, as if she couldn't believe what Jasmine had said.

But it was done. It couldn't be taken back. Jasmine looked at David, wondering if he would be angry when he woke up. He had asked her for secrecy, and she had always given it to him. Until now. She had betrayed him to his own wife. Would he be able to forgive her? She told herself she should not care. But she did. And she was sorry. Would she have a chance to tell him how sorry she was?

"Get out of this room now," Victoria hissed. "You have no right to be here. I don't care who you love. For that matter, I don't care who he loves. He's my husband. I'm his wife. And that's the way it will stay."

"I didn't come here to cause you trouble. I simply wanted to see him." Jasmine cast David one last lingering look, wondering if this truly would be the last time she saw his face. She wished she could commit it to memory forever, so that she would never lose him. Not that she had ever really had him. She had been his lover, not his wife. That title belonged to the woman on the other side of the bed. "I'm sorry," she added belatedly.

"I don't want your apology."

"I shouldn't have told you, but I--"

"I already knew," Victoria said harshly. "Did you think I was stupid?"

A look of truth passed between them, and Jasmine realized that she had not betrayed David's secret at all. It had never been a secret, or perhaps only for a short time. His wife was not the fool; Jasmine was. In some strange way, the secrecy of their affair had made the love between them seem deeper, more important. Theirs had been a passion forbidden by society. In her heart she had always believed that only great passions dared to cross the bounds of propriety.

"Did you think you were the only one?" Victoria added, taking delight in sending another shaft through Jasmine's heart. "Ah, I see. You did believe that. What a pity."

Victoria was wrong. David had told her many times that he had only come to her and no one else. *Was he the liar? Or was it his wife?*

She turned away from the bed, then stopped, startled by the presence of another woman in the doorway -- Paige. Behind her was the man who had come to the apartment with her earlier. She wondered how long they had been standing there, how much they had heard.

"Mother?" Paige asked. "Is everything all right?"

"Everything is fine," Victoria said with ice in her voice. "Ms. Chen was just leaving. And she won't be back."

No, she wouldn't be back. This was not her place. This was not her role. She didn't come to David; he always came to her, and having met the cold-hearted woman who called herself his wife, Jasmine understood much more clearly just why he had come to her in the first place and why he couldn't seem to stop himself from coming back. A spiteful part of her wanted to tell Victoria exactly that. But when Paige moved to stand next to her mother, the spitefulness faded. Paige was David's daughter, and unlike her mother, she seemed terribly worried about her father. Even now she had her hand on his arm, as if she would protect him from the tension in the room. Paige didn't deserve to be caught in the middle.

"I am leaving," Jasmine said. "I wish your father well."

"Ms. Chen, wait," Paige said unexpectedly.

Jasmine felt a shiver run down her vine at the question in Paige's eyes, the nervousness in her stance as she looked from her mother to her father, to Jasmine.

"Don't get involved in this," Victoria warned her daughter. "It does not concern you."

"I think it might. I think she's Dad's--"

"I know what she is." Victoria cut her off abruptly.

"You do?"

"Yes, I've known about her for years."

"Have you also known about Alyssa?"

Jasmine's heart stopped. How did Paige know about Alyssa? That was one secret she was sure David had kept. Victoria, too, looked taken aback, her face as white as her suit.

"Stop, Paige, please just stop. Don't say whatever it is you're thinking," Victoria said.

"I can't. I have to know. Do Alyssa and I share the same father?"

Chapter Nine

Alyssa checked her watch as she got off the bus early Friday morning and headed toward her mother's apartment in Chinatown. She hated going into the neighborhood, with its crowded buildings, the smells of fish and livestock in the butcher shops, her mother's small apartment with its dark rooms, its heavy cloud of incense, the memories of so many nights when she had gone to sleep hearing her mother cry -- because of him. The *him* who remained a mystery even today. The man who had fathered her, who had left her and her mother, who had caused them to live in shame, who had made her half white, half Chinese, half of nothing.

Her friends told her that her unusual looks -- her brown eyes, long black hair, pert, pointed, very un-Asian nose -- made her more beautiful, more exotic, but she knew the truth. Different wasn't beautiful; it was just different. And her looks made her feel... wrong. There was no other way to describe it. Her own family didn't accept her, especially her grandparents, who treated her illegitimate birth like a mark of shame upon the family.

Every New Year, they prayed at the family altar that her mother's sins would be forgiven and that the rest of the family would not suffer for those sins. They also prayed that she would not travel the same road, that she would not dishonor the family as her mother had done.

She had no intention of dishonoring anyone. She just wanted to live her own life. She had a college degree now and a career in banking. Maybe it was just an entry-level job as a loan officer in a downtown bank, but she thought of it as a stepping stone to a future in high finance. She would not live hand-to-mouth as her mother had done. She would not have to sew late into the night to make enough money to eat, or sell precious pieces of her soul, as her mother had sold her paintings, to keep a roof over their heads. Someday she would have plenty of money and she would buy her mother a big house, and it wouldn't be anywhere near Chinatown.

The familiar smells were already turning her stomach. She usually made her mother meet her downtown in a café where they could eat with a fork, drink Diet Pepsi, and munch on potato chips, instead of sipping tea and using chopsticks to scoop up endless piles of rice. It wasn't that she didn't like Chinese food. She did. She'd grown up on it. But she had a love-hate relationship with everything Chinese.

Sometimes she wondered what kind of ethnic background her father had. Was he Italian? Irish? German? English? Was he a mix of something like she was? The only thing she knew for sure was that he wasn't Chinese.

Crossing the street, she quickened her pace. She didn't know why her mother had asked her to come so early, but the tension in her voice had persuaded her not to argue. Still, she didn't want to be late to work. She took her job seriously. She supposed she took everything seriously, but she didn't know how else to be. It had become clear early in her life that she had not brought joy and lightness into the world with her birth. She had to work hard to make that better. To be worthy of being born.

She took the steps to her mother's apartment two at a time, grateful for the tennis shoes she wore to work. They might look silly with her business dress, but they were comfortable. At work, she would put on her heels and add three inches to her five-foot-two inch frame. Then she would be ready to deal with the world. But that world would have to wait, at least for a few minutes. She had this world to deal with.

Her mother opened the door before she could use her key.

"What's wrong?" Alyssa asked quickly, sure now that something was up. It wasn't that her mother was crying or looking stressed, but rather that there was an unusual light in her eyes, an energy in her stance, maybe even a bit of anger in the tilt of her chin. Anger? That wasn't Jasmine Chen. Her paintings could be angry, but she was always quiet, complacent, accepting of her fate, her penance, her punishments. Sometimes Alyssa wanted to shake her mother, tell her to get mad, to tell her family to go to hell -- that she didn't deserve to be treated like some lesser human being just because she'd had a child outside of marriage.

"Come in." Jasmine took her hand and pulled her into the apartment. "We must talk."

"You're not sick, are you?"

Jasmine shook her head. "No. It's not that. I wasn't going to say anything, but somehow they know. I don't know how they know, but they do. They'll come to see you. I couldn't allow that to happen, not without talking to you first."

Alyssa couldn't make sense of what her mother was saying. "Okay, start over and slow down. Who knows what?"

"Your father."

"My father?" Alyssa asked in wonder. She'd asked her mother many times to tell her about her father, to describe him, identify him, but Jasmine had always refused.

"He is hurt. Hurt badly."

"You know where he is? I thought you didn't know where he was."

Her mother's expression was usually unreadable, but not today. Today the truth was written all over her face. Her mother knew where her father was. She had probably known for a long time. Every time Alyssa had asked, she had been told that he had disappeared and that her mother could not bear to speak of him.

Jasmine wrung her hands. "I didn't want to tell you. I still don't. But I am afraid they will."

"Who? Who will tell me?"

"Paige."

The name didn't ring a bell.

"She is his daughter, too," Jasmine added, drawing in a breath. "Paige Hathaway."

"Hathaway? As in the Hathaways? My father is a Hathaway?" Alyssa asked in shock.

"David Hathaway. He was attacked in Salmon Alley two days ago."

"That's only two blocks away."

"He came to see me."

"He came to see you after all these years?" Alyssa's mind was spinning. "Why? Why now?"

"He has come before. I am sorry, Alyssa. I only wanted to protect you. But his family knows of your existence now, and they may want to talk to you."

Alyssa couldn't believe what she was hearing. "They want to talk to me? Why?"

"Because it's possible that your father may not survive."

She didn't know how she was supposed to take that information. Was she supposed to feel sad about a man she didn't know? Angry -- because now it might be too late to know him? But why would she want to know him? Had he known about her? Had he ignored her all these years? She took a breath. "You said he came to see you. Why?"

"That's not important."

"Of course it's important. Does he know about me? Does he know I'm his daughter?"

"Yes," Jasmine said quietly, painfully. "He knows."

"For how long?" Her mother's dark eyes pleaded with her for understanding, but Alyssa wasn't sure she could give it. "How long?"

"Since you were born."

Her mother's words were shocking. "How can that be? How can he have known and not come to see me? He doesn't live that far away. My God! David Hathaway is an incredibly rich man. He lives in a mansion in Pacific Heights. I know, because there's a picture of the house on the wall of the bank I work in." Her anger grew with each word, each new realization. "And he let us live here, in this small apartment? You had to work two jobs when I was small. We barely had enough to eat."

"I wouldn't take his money in the beginning. But when you got older, when you needed things, I asked him to help. He paid for your college. He bought my paintings to help us out."

"To ease his guilt, you mean. He should have supported us, or at least me. I don't care what you told him."

"He did give me some money. That's the only way I could afford for us to live here alone. But I hated every penny that I took from him. If I couldn't have him, I didn't want his money, but pride wouldn't pay the rent, so I took a little when I had to."

Alyssa sat down on the couch, not sure she would have the energy to get back up again. She'd never felt so overwhelmed in her life. She had hated not knowing who her father was, but now that she did, she almost wished for that innocence again. It was bad enough to know that her father hadn't loved them enough to stay -- but even worse to know he was a rich, powerful man who lived only a few miles away but had never wanted to see her.

Jasmine sat down in the chair across from her. She tapped the teapot on the table with her finger. "Would you like some tea?"

Alyssa shook her head. How could they have tea? How could they pretend that nothing had changed between them?

For long minutes there was nothing but silence in the room. It wasn't unusual that they were quiet. Her mother had never been a talker, but now the air was filled with tension and distrust. Alyssa couldn't help it. She loved her mother, but she couldn't understand how she had kept such a secret all these years.

"You don't have to see him," Jasmine said haltingly.

"Of course I don't have to see him. I don't want to see him. He didn't care enough to see me." Alyssa paused, her mind catching up with everything that had been said. "You said he was attacked in the alley?"

"Yes. He was struck in the head. He has been unconscious since then." Jasmine's voice caught, and she lowered her gaze to the floor.

Alyssa felt as if she were seeing her mother for the first time. She had known that her mother had loved a man, and obviously slept with him since she'd been born as a result, but Jasmine hadn't dated anyone since then. She'd always been alone, content she said with her daughter and her painting. Now Alyssa couldn't help wondering what her mother felt for David Hathaway. Was it possible she still cared about him? It seemed unthinkable. He had left her to fend for herself alone, with a child. But Jasmine had never said one angry word against him. She'd never complained about her life, just accepted her fate.

It wasn't fair. David Hathaway had so much, and they had so little.

"You must not blame him," Jasmine said, breaking the silence.

She met her mother's gaze. "How can I not?"

"There are things you don't understand. I feel responsible for what happened to him."

"Why would you be responsible?"

"He came to show me something. If he hadn't come, he wouldn't be hurt."

"What did he show you?"

Jasmine hesitated. "The dragon, Alyssa. He found the dragon."

Alyssa's gaze flew to the wall, to the serpent-like creature her mother had painted so many times Alyssa could have drawn it herself simply from memory. "You said it didn't exist."

"I know now that it does. I held it in my hands."

Alyssa's body tightened. That dragon had been a part

of her life for as long as she could remember. On many nights her mother had awakened from sweat-drenched nightmares, mumbling about the dragon. Sometimes it saved her. Sometimes it threatened her. Sometimes she couldn't find it.

"So he..." She couldn't bring herself to call him her father yet. "He has the dragon?"

"I think it was stolen from him in the alley."

"Why? Who would steal it? Is it valuable?"

"It must be."

Before Alyssa could ask her to elaborate, a knock came at the door, surprising them both. "I'll get it," she said, rising to her feet. She didn't know whom she was expecting when she threw open the door, but it certainly wasn't two uniformed police officers.

"Jasmine Chen?" one of the officers asked.

"I am Jasmine Chen," her mother said from behind her.

"We'd like to talk to you about a robbery that occurred down the street and a man you may know -- David Hathaway."

Paige walked into her apartment and shut the door with a weary sigh. She'd spent the night at the hospital, catching a few hours sleep on a couch in the waiting room. She could have gone home. Her grandfather had hired private nurses to stay with her father twenty-four hours a day, but after Jasmine's surprise appearance in her father's room, Paige had felt compelled to remain close by. Even though neither Jasmine nor her mother had answered the question about Alyssa's parentage, Paige knew the answer. She'd seen it in Jasmine's eyes. And she'd seen it in her mother's eyes before they'd both left the room, leaving Paige alone with her father. She'd stared down at him for a long time, wishing he would wake up so she could ask him the questions burning her tongue, but he had slept, and he was still sleeping now. At least, that's what she liked to call it. Sleeping sounded so much better than coma.

Setting her purse on the table, she considered her options. She could nap, go to work, take a shower... she usually had a dozen things on her to-do list and today shouldn't have been any different, but it was. Since her father's attack, her priorities had shifted. She picked up her favorite family photograph from the table. Her father looked so young, vibrant and healthy. How she wished she could have that man back. Her mother looked good, too, happy as they posed in the front yard on the occasion of her grandfather's birthday. Her grandfather stood in the back, his tall, sturdy body like a solid tree, his arms around his son on one side and his daughter-in-law on the other. Paige and her sister, Elizabeth, sat on a bench in front of them, dressed in beautiful, fluffy white dresses.

Looking at her sister's sweet face, a face that had never grown old, never worn makeup, never kissed a boy, made her incredibly sad. Maybe it was the reminder that it was almost Elizabeth's birthday that brought tears to her eyes. Her father had to wake up soon. He hadn't ever missed Elizabeth's birthday. He had a present for her, a present only he could give.

Maybe it was a sick tradition, as her mother thought. But at the moment Paige clung to it, because continuing the ritual meant everything was going on the way it was supposed to go on. Paige set the photo down. The happy family portrait was really nothing more than an illusion. Her father had had an affair. He'd slept with another woman. Jasmine Chen was hardly the prettiest, sexiest woman Paige had seen. Maybe she had been in her day. Obviously their affair went back twenty-something years.

Alyssa was twenty-two years old, and Elizabeth had been dead almost twenty-three years. That meant that her father had had this affair almost immediately after Elizabeth's death. Paige's pulse quickened as she calculated the possibilities. Was that why it had happened? Had her father been so lost in grief, despair, and unhappiness that he'd reached out to another woman?

Or was she just trying to excuse his behavior the way she always did?

The doorbell rang, and she started, glancing down at her watch. It was ten o'clock in the morning. Who would be calling on her now? She went to the intercom and said, "Hello?"

"It's Riley. Can I come up?"

Riley? Her heart skipped a beat. Did she want him to come up? It seemed as if they were living in each other's pocket these days. And yet, at the same time, it felt as if it had been too long since she'd last seen him. The bell rang again, more insistently. Patience was not his strong suit. She buzzed him in.

She made a quick dash to the mirror. Her hair was falling out of its ponytail. There was not a speck of makeup left on her face, nothing to hide the shadows under her eyes. And her clothes were wrinkled. She was basically a mess, and she hated to face Riley looking like this. But he was already knocking at the door; she had no choice but to open it.

She wished she could say he looked as bad as she did, but it was just the opposite. His hair was damp from a recent shower, his skin scrubbed and glowing. He smelled good. He looked even better in a pair of black trousers and a long-sleeve, gray knit shirt.

"You look awful," he said. "Did you sleep in those clothes?"

"As a matter of fact, I did."

"Any change in your father's condition?"

"None. I don't know why it's taking so long for him to wake up. But he will wake up. I just have to be patient."

Riley walked into her apartment. "This is nice."

The apartment wasn't really her. While she'd expressed her independence by getting her own place, she'd followed true Hathaway form by allowing her mother to decorate it with antiques, paintings, and expensive furniture. A cleaning lady came once a week to keep everything sparkling clean, and since Paige never made a mess, the apartment was always spotless, but not particularly warm and inviting.

"I feel like I just stepped into the page of a magazine," Riley continued. "Where's the clutter? The shoes you kicked off when you got home, the newspaper you just read, the keys you tossed on the table when you came in?"

"My shoes are still on my feet. The newspaper is in the recycle bin, and the keys are in my purse where they belong."

He raised an eyebrow. "Obsessive-compulsive?"

"Just neat. Do you have a reason for being here?"

"I have some information for you. I called Raymond Li at home. His daughter told me he's on vacation, and she doesn't know when he'll be back." He paused. "Raymond Li wasn't scheduled for a vacation, was he?"

"I don't know. I don't keep track of the vacation time of every employee."

"She said it was a sudden trip, destination unknown."

"You make it sound mysterious."

"As far as we know, Mr. Li is the only other person at Hathaway's who had a chance to examine the dragon. He might also be the only other person who knows why your father went to Chinatown. I'd say that makes him a key player. The fact that he's now nowhere to be found is too big of a coincidence for me."

"Do you think that Raymond Li had something to do with the assault on my father? I can't believe that. He's worked at the store for twenty years. He's had plenty of opportunities to steal, if that's what you're implying."

"I'm not implying anything. Just saying his sudden vacation is suspicious. Let's say that he knew your father took the dragon out of the store. He might have even known where David was going. Or he could have followed him. I don't think someone just happened by that alley, found your father, and took advantage of his presence by robbing him. Someone followed him to Chinatown or knew where he was going and set the whole thing up. We know your father saw Jasmine a little before five o'clock and that the police found your father around nine o'clock. It certainly didn't take him four hours to walk those short blocks from Jasmine's apartment. And it doesn't appear that he was lying there for four hours, either. I'm figuring he went somewhere else and was coming back, maybe to tell Jasmine what he learned. Or else he had business in that area and was leaving that location."

Paige hated the way Riley was dissecting everything so clinically, so dispassionately. This was her father they were talking about. Just thinking about his attack made her feel sick.

"I've asked my assistant to see if she can locate Mr. Li," Riley added. "For now, I think we should concentrate on the Chen family."

She turned away from the sharp look in his eyes. She knew what was coming next, and she didn't want to hear it. Instead she walked back over to the table and picked up the family photograph. She handed it to him. "This is my family."

"Nice picture. Who's the other girl?"

"My sister, Elizabeth. She died when I was six, and she was seven. That picture was taken just a few months before she got sick."

"You had a sister who died?" He looked surprised. "I never heard about that."

"It's not a secret, but it happened a long time ago."

"How did she die?"

"She had leukemia. It was awful." A word that didn't begin to describe the horrible disease that had stolen Elizabeth's life. "Nothing was the same after she died." Paige stared at the photograph in his hand. "It happened almost twenty-three years ago. If that girl, Jasmine's daughter, is really my half sister, then she was born in the year after Elizabeth died. Maybe that's why the affair happened. Or maybe that's what I want to believe. Either way, I'm not sure I can accept this other girl as my sister. Elizabeth is my sister. It would be wrong to put anyone else in her place. It would be as if she hadn't existed."

"Alyssa Chen isn't going to make you forget or love your real sister any less."

"I'm not so sure." She debated telling him what she was feeling, but her emotions and words seemed to run amok when Riley was nearby. "Sometimes I forget what Elizabeth looked like, sounded like, smelled like," she confessed. "I see the pictures and I remember her, but I'm not sure I remember her from my memories or from the pictures. Does that make sense?"

"It makes a lot of sense. It's been a long time, Paige. Memories fade. And you were a little girl. How much do you remember from when you were six years old?"

"Probably not as much as I should." She took the picture from his hand and set it back on the table. "Every year on Elizabeth's birthday, my father and I go to the cemetery, and he gives her a birthday present. It's always a dragon. She loved dragons. My father started her collection, and he still contributes to it every year. In fact, we're going to display the collection in the new Hathaway exhibit at the Asian Art Museum."

"A dragon like the one my grandmother had?" Riley asked sharply.

"Any kind of dragon. The gifts have all been different. But, yes, he was interested in your grandmother's dragon for that reason, as well as a dozen others, I'm sure. Elizabeth's birthday is next Wednesday. He has to wake up before then."

"I hope he does, but everything you've told me, Paige, only makes me believe that your father knew something about that dragon that we don't. We have to find out more about it."

"You're right. Now I wish I'd majored in art history instead of business economics."

"You majored in business economics?" he asked with a raised eyebrow.

"After my mother. She said it was more important to be able to run the business than to appreciate the goods that we sell. Unfortunately, right now that's not helping us at all."

Riley's cell phone rang, interrupting their conversation. "I better take this," he said, checking the number. "Hello? Grandma?"

Paige watched Riley's demeanor change. His face

tightened. His eyes grew hard. He looked as if he wanted to hit something or someone.

"Stay at Millie's," he said. "Don't go back to the house. I'll be there as soon as I can."

"What happened?" Paige asked as he ended the call.

"My grandmother's house was broken into."

"Is she all right?"

"She's fine. She wasn't home when it happened. I have to go."

"I'm coming, too." Paige grabbed her purse as she followed him to the door. "What do you think they were looking for? Your grandmother doesn't have the dragon anymore."

"Maybe someone thinks she has the other one." He sent her a pointed look. "Didn't that story say there might be two?"

Chapter Ten

The drive across town seemed to take forever as the Friday morning traffic was heavy in the downtown area. Riley hit the brakes hard as yet another red light stopped him in his tracks.

"You couldn't have predicted this," Paige said quietly.

"I certainly should have. Dammit." He hit the steering wheel with his fist. "As soon as you told me that story about the two dragons, I should have connected the dots. And those hang-up calls--"

"What hang-up calls?"

"My grandmother said someone kept calling and hanging up. She thought it was my mother, which I immediately dismissed as ridiculous."

"Why would your mother be calling and hanging up? That seems odd."

He uttered a short, bitter laugh. "That's my mother, odd."

"What do you mean?"

"Never mind." He turned the corner sharply and

pulled up in front of his grandmother's house before she could press him further.

Riley jumped out of the car and ran up the driveway to where Millie and Nan were standing. Paige followed, feeling a strange tightness in her throat as she watched him hug his grandmother with a fierce tenderness.

"Good heavens, Riley. You're squeezing the breath out of me," Nan told him. She smiled and stroked his face with her fingers. "I'm fine. But the house is a mess. They went through everything, dumping out my drawers and undoing all the beds. I don't know what kind of fortune they thought I was hiding in there, but I don't think they got much for their trouble. I couldn't have had more than twenty dollars in cash lying around. And my jewelry isn't worth much."

"I'm going to check it out. You wait here. Paige will keep you company."

"Oh, dear. I didn't even see you, Miss Hathaway." Nan looked from Riley to Paige, then back to Riley. "Did I interrupt something when I called?"

"Nothing that can't wait. I'll be back in a few minutes. Just stay put. You, too," he told Paige.

As Riley sprinted across the yard, Paige found herself being perused by two pairs of very curious eyes. "It's nice to see you both again. I'm sorry the circumstances are so distressing."

"Let's go to my house and have some coffee," Millie suggested, leading them next door.

Paige followed them into the kitchen, where Millie filled several mugs with coffee and placed a chocolate cake on the table in case anyone was hungry. Then she excused herself to answer the phone, leaving Nan and Paige alone.

"I was so sorry to hear about your father," Nan said,

patting Paige's hand where it rested on the table. "How is he doing?"

"He's still unconscious." Paige paused. "I'm sorry your dragon has gone missing in the midst of all this. I feel terrible. The House of Hathaway has never lost an art object before."

"Someone wanted that dragon very badly. What I don't understand is why anyone would break into my house. I don't have it anymore."

Paige wasn't sure if she should tell Nan about the possibility that there might be two dragons. It was only a theory, and not much of one at that.

"I'm a little afraid it might be Mary behind this break-in," Nan said, surprising her with the comment.

"Who is Mary?" Paige asked.

Nan looked a little guilty at the question, as if she wished she hadn't brought it up. "She's my daughter, Riley's mother."

"Why would your daughter break into your house?"

"Well, she wouldn't." Nan shook her head. "I'm sure none of this has anything to do with her. She left Riley with us a long time ago, when he was a teenager. Even before that she was barely around. She wasn't much of a mother to him, that's for sure."

"That's too bad. Riley said something about hang-up calls?" she queried.

"Sometimes I think Mary is calling me and hanging up because she just doesn't have the nerve to speak." She sent Paige a thoughtful look. "I'm surprised Riley mentioned his mother to you. He must like you."

"Barely mentioned, and he doesn't like me at all. He thinks my family is trying to cheat you."

Nan brushed that away with a wave of her hand. "Riley always believes people are out to con him. He doesn't trust anyone. That's the legacy my daughter left him with, I'm afraid. I wish I could have stepped in sooner to take care of Riley, but she took him away from us early on, and there were years when we didn't know where they were."

Paige saw regret and sadness in Nan's eyes. It must hurt her deeply to speak ill of her daughter. Nan seemed like such a nice lady. Paige couldn't help wondering how her daughter had turned out so badly.

"She got involved with drugs at a young age," Nan said, answering Paige's unspoken question. "Barely fourteen when she started. Mary had the kind of personality that needed a lot of attention. She was never happy with what she had. I thought it was teenage years," Nan said reflectively. "I blame myself for not seeing that she needed real help. I did so many things wrong."

This time Paige reached across the table and covered Nan's hand with her own. "Sometimes people are just born with a personality that takes them into trouble."

Nan smiled. "You're a sweet girl, and very kind not to blame me. Riley doesn't blame me, either, and he should. He's the one who had to pay."

"Riley seems to have turned out okay."

"I know it looks that way, but I still worry about him. Sometimes I wonder if I did the right thing asking him to come home and run his grandfather's business."

"The security business belonged to your husband?"

"Yes, but when Ned started getting sick about four years ago, I asked Riley if he could come back and help us out. He was debating whether or not to re-up with the Marine Corps at the time. He was doing so well in the service. He was always cagey about what he was doing or where he was going though. I knew it was dangerous, and he was probably being reckless, because Riley has always believed he has nothing to lose." She shook her head, with regret in her eyes. "At any rate, he came home to help out and has been here ever since. Now he runs the business better than my husband did, and he's settling down, a little bit, anyway. I wouldn't mind seeing a woman in his life," she added hopefully. "He is a good man. A little pushy sometimes."

"That's an understatement," Paige said with a wry smile. "How on earth did he ever learn to take orders?"

"It took awhile. But the marines straightened him out. He got into some trouble when he was young. Ned, that's my husband, thought the service would put Riley on the right track, and he was right. Riley is very smart, caring, and he's loyal to a fault. A woman could do worse."

Paige smiled. "Well, that may be true, but just so you know -- I have a boyfriend." It felt strange to call Martin her boyfriend, but she needed something to dampen Nan's growing enthusiasm for a possibility that would never happen. As soon as they found Nan's dragon, Riley would be out of her life, and she would be out of his.

"Of course you do. I keep telling Riley that if he doesn't hurry up and get serious, all the good ones will be gone."

"I don't think he'll have any trouble finding someone."

Paige looked up as Riley entered the kitchen, a grim expression on his face. "The house is a mess. It will take some time to clean it up. I think you should stay here for a while, Grandma. And I definitely don't want you in the house tonight."

"Surely they've taken what they wanted," Nan replied.

"They may have been interrupted when you came home."

"What do I have that anyone would want so badly?"

"There may be another dragon. Paige and I have been doing some research, and we've found information about two dragons that connect together, and they both look like the one you had. Someone might think you have the other dragon, too."

"I'm sure I don't. We cleaned out the attic last week, Riley. You know that."

"But no one else does. Why didn't you turn on the security system when you left the house?"

"I only went to the store. I thought I'd be gone for just a few minutes. And it's broad daylight. I thought burglars usually came at night."

"You should turn it on every time you leave, no matter what."

"I'll do better, Riley, I promise."

"And you'll stay here with me today and tonight," Millie said, returning to the room.

"I don't want to impose on you and Howard," Nan protested.

"You could never do that. We'll go shopping. You've been wanting to walk down Union Street. And tonight we'll have dinner and then you'll keep me company while Howard plays on that computer of his. I'll be glad to have the company."

"Then it's settled," Riley said.

"I'll still need to get some clothes. I don't have anything with me."

"I'll go with you to the house. We'll get whatever you need."

"Riley, the police are still there, aren't they?" Nan asked.

"Yes, but--"

"Then I'll be fine. I'll go over and talk to them. I

won't stay there alone. Once they leave, I'll come back here. You and Paige can go on and do whatever you were doing."

He frowned. "I hate for you to see your house that way, Grandma."

"I've already seen it, honey. It was a shock, I'll admit, but it is what it is, and not looking at it won't make it go away."

"I'll come back later and clean it up for you."

"Don't worry about that. It's nothing that can't wait. Maybe after we go to Union Street, Millie and I will drive out and see your grandfather. I want to ask him if he's been calling the house." Nan paused. "Thank you, Paige, for keeping me company. I'll pray for your father."

"I'd appreciate that," Paige said, getting to her feet.

"You take care of yourself, and don't let Riley boss you around too much."

"Don't worry. I'm used to bossy people," Paige said with a smile. She followed Riley out to the street. It bothered her to see the police car in front of Nan's house. She was a nice lady. She didn't deserve to have trouble like this.

Riley opened the door for her, closed it, then walked around the car to slide in behind the wheel. "Thanks for staying with my grandmother."

"It was no problem. Her house was in bad shape?"

"Ripped apart. Even her china was broken."

"It seems so pointless."

A lot of life is exactly that -- pointless. Just crazy people doing crazy things."

She wondered if he was talking about someone in particular. "Is it possible your mother is involved in this?"

He sent her a sharp look. "What did my grandmother tell you?"

"A little about your past. Doesn't it bother you -- not knowing if your mother is even alive?"

His eyes turned a cold, dark blue. "None of it bothers me anymore. I turned that page a long time ago. And I'm not turning it back."

"But the emotions aren't gone -- the disappointment, the bitterness, the hate, maybe even the love -- they're still there, aren't they?"

"Save the psychobabble for your own shrink, princess. I don't need my head examined by a rich girl who has no idea of the way I've lived."

"And you have no idea of the way I've lived," she retorted.

"I have a pretty good idea. I've seen the family mansion. It must have been rough growing up with your own bedroom, your own housekeeper. Hell, you probably had one of those butlers, didn't you?"

"Stop baiting me, Riley. I'm not getting into a competition with you on who had it the hardest."

"Because you can't compete. You can't even get in the starting block. You grew up in a rose garden."

"I grew up in a cold, lonely house." She gazed out the window and drew in a breath. "My parents barely spoke, and my grandfather's anger and bitterness chilled every room."

"And he had so much to be bitter about, all that money weighing him down."

She turned her head to look at him, but he was staring at the traffic, his profile hard. He seemed almost unreachable. She told herself not to try, but the words wanted to come out. "My grandfather lost his wife and daughter in a car crash when my father was nine years old," she said quietly. "He never recovered from their deaths. He hired housekeepers and nannies to raise my father because he couldn't do it himself. He was too full of hate at the universe for what had happened to him. When my father got married and started a family of his own, my grandfather felt renewed hope that the house would once again be filled with laughter and happiness. When I was really small he used to smile more, he used to laugh. Then Elizabeth got sick and died, and that ended. The last bit of life went out of our house for everyone. The rooms were so quiet I could hear my own heart beating, my own breath going in and out of my chest. It was that still."

She stopped herself from going on, wishing she hadn't told him so much already. She was opening herself up to get hurt. And he could hurt her. She didn't know why his opinion mattered, but it did. Maybe it was because she was used to people liking her, trusting her, and Riley's attitude was difficult to understand. Maybe she really was a spoiled little rich girl who didn't know how good she had it. Riley wasn't going to feel sorry for her; he'd grown up with a mother who was a drug addict, a woman who'd abandoned him.

"Say something," she muttered, wanting to get it over with. "Tell me how not sorry you are for me."

"I'm not sorry for you, Paige," he said, but when he turned to look at her there was a softness in his eyes that took the sting out of his words. "But maybe I understand you a little better. I shouldn't have judged you. I'm just in a bad mood. I don't like it when people I care about are in danger." He pulled the car up in front of her apartment building and shut off the engine. "How about a truce? We need to work together."

"You just want to keep an eye on me."

"That, too. Look, Paige, it's not just you. I don't trust anyone."

"Except your grandmother."

He tipped his head. "Except her. She's special."

"One day you might manage to feel that way about another woman."

"I'm not looking for a wife. I don't know what my grandmother told you; I'm happy with my life."

"I'm happy, too, and I'm not looking to make any changes," she said pointedly.

"You may not be looking, but your life is changing. You now have a half sister."

She sighed. "I've been trying to forget about that."

"You have to deal with her, sooner or later."

"Let's make it later. I want to change my clothes and get back to the hospital."

"I'll wait for you and give you a ride."

"You don't have to do that. I can get myself there."

"We're keeping an eye on each other, remember?"

"What do you think I'm going to do, make some shady deal with an art buyer while I'm in the shower?"

He gave her a sexy smile. "If you think I need to follow you into the shower, just say so."

She saw the gleam in his eyes and gave a bemused shake of her head. "I can't figure you out. First you're nice, then you're sarcastic and cold, now you're flirting. Who is the real Riley?"

He grinned. "You like me, don't you?"

"I said you were complicated; I didn't say I liked you."

"Same thing."

"It's not at all the same thing." But as she got out of the car and slammed the door on his mocking smile, she was afraid he was right.

Alyssa couldn't concentrate on the loan application she was reviewing. Usually she loved her job as a loan officer for the First National Bank in San Francisco, but today her mind was back in her mother's apartment, hearing the words *your father is David Hathaway*. She still couldn't believe it.

For so many years she had wanted to know her father's name, but now that she did, she didn't know what to do with the information. How was she supposed to feel? Her emotions were all over the place. She was angry, hurt, jealous, but at the same time she was curious about the man who had fathered her. She'd seen David Hathaway in the newspaper. She'd known that the House of Hathaway had bought her mother's paintings. She'd been in the store -- that beautiful, rich store. Her father owned that store.

Her father. She'd been without one for so long.

But she didn't really have one now. David Hathaway, was lying in a hospital bed, fighting for his life. Even if he weren't, would he suddenly recognize her as his daughter? If his other daughter, Paige, hadn't found out, would he have kept the secret forever? Would her mother have done the same? She suspected the answer was yes, but it didn't matter. The secret was out. Now she had to deal with it. She could wait for them to come to her, or she could go to them.

She got up and walked over to the desk where her manager, Jenny Conroy, was ending a phone call. "I'm not feeling well," she said. "I need to go home."

"Oh, all right." Jenny appeared surprised. No wonder: In the year that she had worked at the bank, Alyssa had never missed a day of work or been late. She was too focused on her goal to get ahead to allow her private life to interfere. Until today.

"I've finished a couple of loan applications and put them through," she added. "I'll leave the information with Mark in case anyone calls while I'm out."

"You do look flushed," Jenny commented. "I hope you're not catching that flu."

"Me, too." Alyssa returned to her desk, grabbed her purse, and left the bank, relieved to be out in the fresh air. Maybe the crisp breeze blowing between the tall buildings would clear her mind. It wasn't just her father she was thinking about; her mother was also on her mind.

The police had shown them a bracelet found near the scene of David Hathaway's assault -- a bracelet with the name Jasmine on it. Alyssa had recognized it immediately. She'd seen the bracelet in her mother's jewelry box, but she'd never known it was from her father. Another secret.

Her mother claimed she cut through the alley every day and that she didn't know when she'd lost the bracelet. The police had continued to ask her questions about her whereabouts on Wednesday night, about when she'd last seen David Hathaway and why he'd come to visit her. Her mother had given out little information. She was a pro at saying nothing.

How strange that, after all these years, the dragon from her mother's dreams should appear as an actual piece of art that someone had crafted, someone had owned someone had stolen. Alyssa sensed her mother knew more than she was saying. But the dragon was not her concern. She had a father at last. Now she just had to figure out what to do with him.

Paige walked into her father's hospital room and

smiled at the private duty nurse who sat by his bedside. "Why don't you take a break? I'm going to be here for a while."

Paige moved closer to the bed as the nurse left the room. She reached out and touched her father's arm. He didn't move. His breathing didn't change. His eyelids didn't flicker. He'd never been a heavy sleeper, but today he was lost in some other world.

"Daddy," she whispered. "I'm here. It's Paige." What could she say to bring him back? "It's almost Elizabeth's birthday. We have to go to the cemetery. It's tradition. We can't miss it. You know that." She wouldn't remind him that he'd missed her own birthday a dozen times, not to mention other important events in her life. This wasn't the time for accusations.

His skin was so cool. She pulled the covers up over his body, tucking in the blanket next to his side. "I need you, Daddy. Mother needs you, too, even though she'd never admit it." She paused. "Your secrets are spilling out. Jasmine Chen came to see you last night. She said she loved you. I wonder how you feel about her. I wonder how you feel about her daughter, Alyssa. I wonder if you have any idea how wrong all this is."

"I wonder that, too," a woman said from behind her.

Paige whirled around. The woman in the doorway looked very familiar, a little like Jasmine, and a little like... her father. "Who are you?" she asked with a shaky voice, even though she already knew.

"I'm Alyssa Chen." The woman gave her a hard, angry look. "I think I might be your sister."

Chapter Eleven

Sister? No.

Elizabeth was her sister, her only sister. Not this petite Asian woman, who was beautiful, exotic, and furious. There was no mistaking the anger in her brown eyes when she looked at David. Paige instinctively moved closer to the bed, feeling as if she had to protect him.

"He doesn't look like me." Alyssa walked around the other side of the bed and stared down at David Hathaway. "Not really. Maybe a little in the nose."

And in the shape of her face, and the freckle at the side of her nose, the Hathaway freckle. Elizabeth had had one. Paige did not. It bothered her that Alyssa did.

"I can't believe he's my father." Alyssa looked over at Paige. "How long have you known about me?"

"Since last night. I found out my father paid your college tuition. When I saw your mother, she didn't deny it or corroborate it. She said nothing."

"My mother is very good at saying nothing."

Paige heard the bitterness in Alyssa's voice and saw something else in her face: fear. "When did you find out he was your father?" Paige asked.

"This morning. My mother always refused to talk about my father. But she was afraid you were going to tell me the truth, so she told me first." Alyssa stared down at the man in the bed. "He never came by to see me, never wrote to me, never gave me anything that I knew about, although I guess he gave my mother some money."

"Quite a bit of money, actually."

"It couldn't have been all that much. We didn't live well."

Paige felt guilty, as if that was her fault, as if she should apologize for being the daughter he had raised and supported. But it wasn't her fault. And, to be fair, it wasn't Alyssa's fault, either. The man between them was the only one to blame.

Alyssa didn't say anything for a moment, then murmured, "I should go."

Paige wanted her to go, wanted to be able to pretend that she'd never come at all, but as Alyssa turned toward the door, she knew she had to stop her. "Wait. We need to talk."

"About what?" Alyssa asked warily.

Paige wasn't sure. Where could they begin? There were so many questions to ask. "About everything. About your mother and my father. About us."

"Look, just because we found out we're half sisters doesn't mean we have to have a relationship. I doubt we have anything in common."

"We have *our father* in common."

"You had everything. I had nothing. I don't want to like you. I'm not even sure I want to know you," Alyssa said.

Her blunt words hurt, but in a way they mirrored exactly what Paige was thinking. Wouldn't getting to know Alyssa only cause trouble? Her mother certainly wouldn't like it. Her grandfather would be furious. And her father... Her gaze drifted over to her father. What would he want? Had he ever thought about introducing them? Of course not. That would have meant admitting he'd cheated, confessing to his infidelity. He couldn't do that. He couldn't jeopardize his marriage. And what did that mean? That he had never loved Jasmine, that she had never been worth giving up what he already had? It seemed the most likely answer. An affair was an affair. A marriage was forever, or was supposed to be, anyway.

"I'm not sure I want to know you, either," Paige said finally. "I'm also not sure we have a choice. Something is going on between your mother and our father -- even now. He went to see her only hours before he was attacked."

"The police already spoke to my mother. She told them what she knew."

"Did she tell you about the dragon?"

"I know my mother is obsessed with a dragon that looks like the one your father supposedly showed her. I don't know anything more than that."

"Maybe if we put our heads together, we can figure out why that dragon is so important to our parents. It seems strange that your mother could have painted it without seeing it before."

"My mother paints from her imagination. She's a very good artist and an extraordinary person. She didn't deserve... *him*," Alyssa added, casting another angry glance at her father.

"Neither one of us knows much about their relationship, but what I do know is that your mother was quite possibly the last person to see him alive. And that makes her very important."

"What are you saying? That you think she assaulted him?"

"No. But she's going to be a part of the investigation. My family is very important to the city. The mayor, the police chief -- they want the assailant caught. The press is covering the story every day. As soon as they find out about your mother, they'll be all over her. She'll be under the microscope. She'll be asked tougher questions than the ones I'm asking. The press will delve into her background, where she came from, how she met my father. They might even find out about you."

"Is that some sort of threat?"

"I'm just pointing out the reality of the situation. I need your help. My father got hurt in Chinatown. I bet people there would be willing to talk to you before they would talk to me. You may hate him, but I'm sure you love your mother. We both want to protect our family."

Alyssa considered her words. "I'll think about it."

Paige took out her business card and scribbled her home and cell phone numbers. "Please call me. Don't wait too long."

Alyssa took the card. She paused on her way out the door. "Are you going to tell the press about me?"

"Are you?" Paige countered.

"Why would I?" Alyssa asked with surprise.

"Money. Someone would pay you well for the story."

Alyssa nodded, her mouth set in a bitter line. "I'll keep that in mind."

"Dammit," Paige swore under her breath as Alyssa left the room. She hadn't handled that particularly well. The door opened, and she wondered if Alyssa had come back with more to say, but it was the nurse and Riley.

"I found this man listening at the door," the nurse said with a frown. "Do you want me to report that to your grandfather?"

"No, he's a friend of mine." Paige moved into the hall to speak to Riley while the nurse moved to the bed to check on her father. "What did you hear?"

"Some of your conversation with Alyssa," he admitted. "I don't think I would have given her the idea of selling her story to the tabloids."

"She would have thought of it eventually. She's very angry. She didn't know about my father until today."

"Then she has a right to be angry. Let's go."

"Go where?" she asked in surprise.

"To follow Alyssa, of course," he said, taking off down the hall.

Paige jogged after him, barely keeping up with his long strides. As they exited through the front doors of the hospital, they saw Alyssa heading toward the bus stop.

"I'll get the car," Riley told her. "You keep an eye on her. If she gets on a bus, make a note of the number."

"Okay. But why are we following her?"

Riley just gave her a quick smile. "So we can find out where she goes."

Paige didn't particularly care for his sarcastic answer, and she couldn't see what following Alyssa would accomplish, but at least they were taking action. Anything was better than sitting in that hospital room wondering if her father would ever wake up.

Alyssa got off the bus and walked up the steps toward the top level of Portsmouth Square, a popular gathering spot in Chinatown. Her discomfort grew with each step, especially when she passed the children's playground where old Chinese grandmothers watched the babies for their young mothers who worked during the day. Chinatown never really changed. While new immigrants moved in and out of the neighborhood, there were many who lived their whole lives here, like her grandparents, who had gotten married just after the Second World War ended.

They'd spent several years living in a small, cramped apartment with two other families they referred to as uncles, aunties, and cousins. In truth there was no blood between them, just a friendship borne of being strangers in a strange land. Eventually, her grandparents had managed to get their own apartment, where they'd raised five American-born Chinese children. But while those children, her mother Jasmine included, grew up American, her grandparents still held tight to their traditions and superstitions.

Her grandmother, An-Mei, was a strong-willed woman who had worked hard to help support the family, shelling shrimp, sewing in sweatshops, and making fortune cookies for tourists. She had done it all while her husband, Lee, cooked herbs in the kitchen and eventually opened an herb shop on a narrow street in Chinatown, which they still ran together.

Alyssa had heard the many stories of their struggles to survive in America, and she admired the strength and courage it must have taken for her grandparents to start over in a new country. But she didn't admire the way they treated her mother and herself as outcasts who had dishonored the family name. Her mother was the true culprit, but by virtue of her illegitimate birth, Alyssa was considered a mark of shame as well, at least by her grandmother, who had told her many times that she would have to work hard to overcome her birth, that she would have to prove to the gods that she was worthy. Worthy of what, Alyssa wasn't quite sure, but she hadn't dared to ask.

Questions were never welcome in her family, not with her mother, not with her grandparents, not with anyone. So why had she come back to the old neighborhood with even more questions? Who did she think would answer them?

Part of her wanted to turn and run back across town to the small apartment she shared with three of her college friends, who didn't worry about old secrets, who were only concerned about getting ahead, meeting nice guys to marry, living their lives the way they wanted to live them. But she still had to worry about her mother. It was for her mother's sake that she had come here. Perhaps her grandparents would speak to her more freely than they would to Jasmine.

A cluster of men sat on the stairs, playing cards. She hurried past them, past the chess tables where more old guys turned to stare at her. The top level of Portsmouth Square was a male bastion of gambling and other vices she didn't want to consider. She remembered once walking alone through the square late at night and having men come up to her asking if she wanted a date. She'd been so frightened by those groping hands, those leering voices that she'd avoided the square for years. Even now she felt uneasy.

But it was daytime and no one bothered her. She paused, seeing a familiar stooped figure bending over a bench where several men were playing Mahjong. It was her grandfather, Lee Chen. She hesitated, then approached the group, careful not to disturb anyone during the play. Her grandfather must have sensed her presence, for finally he turned and looked at her. He broke away from the group and walked over to join her. He was a short, square man; at one time, he had been a gymnast, but that had been a very long time ago. Now he was thin and frail and occasionally seemed confused by his very existence. Since he had turned seventy-nine years old on his last birthday, she supposed some confusion was understandable. She smiled as he put a hand to his head to pat down the few loose-flying strands of hair he had left. His face was square, plain, his eyes somewhat hidden by the old-fashioned black-rimmed eyeglasses he wore. But he had a smile on that face, a cautious smile, as if he wasn't sure he should give her one.

"Alyssa, what are you doing down here?" he asked.

"I'm on my way to the shop. I need some herbs."

"You are too thin. Must eat more. You come for New Year's. An-Mei fatten you up."

"You know Grandmother won't let us come for New Year's. It's a sacred holiday. We have too many sins, we taint the New Year with our presence." Alyssa heard the bitterness in her voice, but she couldn't do anything about it. While their presence was tolerated at other family parties, the traditional New Year's Eve dinner had always been held just out of reach.

"You come anyway. I invite you," Lee said firmly. "She do what I say. She's my wife."

"I can't come without my mother."

"Jasmine lay in the bed of her making. Not you. You come."

"I'll think about it." She paused. "Do you remember Ma telling you of her dreams about a dragon?"

He frowned. "She dream too much. She must stop."

"Ma thinks she saw a dragon just like the one in her dreams."

"She always see dragons. She imagine it."

"A man," she said, deliberately not calling David

Hathaway her father, "brought her a dragon statue the other day. She said it looked exactly like the one in her dreams. But that man was robbed, and the dragon was stolen." Alyssa watched her grandfather's face for a reaction but saw nothing in his eyes. He might be the friendliest of her relatives, but he had the same unreadable expression as the rest of the Chens. "Did you hear of a robbery in Salmon Alley on Wednesday night?" she added.

"I hear many things, some lies, some truths. Who knows which is which?" he said with a shrug.

"The man who was robbed was David Hathaway. I don't suppose you know who he is?"

"I must go. It is my turn to play. You be a good girl, Alyssa, go home, go to work. Make good life for yourself. Forget about dragons."

Her grandfather was gone before she could say another word. He knew who David Hathaway was; that much she was sure. Although that wasn't completely surprising. The Hathaways were a famous San Francisco family. Did her grandfather know that David Hathaway was also her father?

With a sigh, she walked out of the square. She was tempted to end her quest and go home, but Paige's reminder that her mother might be connected to their father's attack worried her. She couldn't let her mother get into any more trouble than she was already in. The Hathaways had a lot of money. They could make things happen. She hadn't needed Paige to tell her that. It was strange to think she had a sister now -- a half sister, but still a sibling. She'd been an only child forever.

Paige was beautiful -- blond, sophisticated, smart. She'd never had to struggle, never worried about her family name or lack thereof, never wondered where she came from, who her parents were. It wasn't fair, and Alyssa was jealous. Not really of the money, although it would have been nice to grow up rich. No, what she really hated was that Paige had grown up with two parents who loved her, two parents who could probably trace their family tree back to the Mayflower. Paige had never had to be half of anything.

Not that it was Paige's fault. She wasn't responsible for the situation any more than Alyssa was. In a way, Alyssa was surprised that Paige had been friendly. She wondered if she would have felt the same way if the situation was reversed. Well, she'd have to deal with Paige later. Right now she had to speak to her grandmother, and that would require all of her attention, strength, and courage.

Squaring her shoulders, she headed down the street and opened the door to the family herb shop. The smells of ginseng root and honeysuckle made her want to breathe deeply, to inhale the peace and calm that filled the shop. Despite her often anti-Chinese stance, she secretly loved the herb shop: the floor-to-ceiling mahogany cabinets filled with hundreds of long, narrow drawers where the various herbs were stored; the soft flute music that played in the background; the rows of books on Oriental medicine, self-healing, meditation; the candles that burned brightly along the counter no matter what the time of day.

Her cousin Ona, who at thirty-five was the oldest of the cousins and a favorite of their grandmother's, was helping a customer complete a purchase. She smiled at Alyssa and said she'd be just a moment.

"Is Grandmother here?" Alyssa asked deliberately using the word grandmother. While the other grandchildren affectionately called their grandmother Nai

Nai, Alyssa refused to do so. Her grandmother had made it clear that, because of her mixed blood, she wasn't a true member of the family.

"No." Ona bagged the customer's order and wished her a good day. "Can I help you with something? Maybe some ginkgo biloba or some licorice. You look anxious, tense. What have you been eating? Are you drinking too much coffee again? You know you have to keep a balance in your life."

"Yes, yes, I know." Unfortunately balance was the last thing she had right now. She was so weighted down it was hard to stand upright, but she didn't want to tell Ona the reason for her anxiety. As the oldest, Ona was also the nosiest, believing she had some inalienable right to butt into everyone's business.

"You're a big-time banker now," Ona continued. "You should take care of your health."

"I take ginseng every day."

"What about ginger? It disburses the cold, adjusts nutritive and protective qi."

"Fine, I'll take some ginger. But I think you're just trying to show a profit so our grandparents will leave the shop to you and not to cousin Lian."

Ona smiled. "You are a smart girl, little cousin."

"Don't let the family hear you say that or you'll be disowned for good."

"It's the twenty-first century. Our grandparents need to get over the facts of your birth," Ona said firmly.

"They never will. I don't expect it anymore. And I don't really care."

"Don't you?" Ona asked softly, compassion in her dark eyes. "It's not right the way you've been treated. I wish you would come to New Year's. I miss you every year."

"That's sweet of you to say, but I won't come without my mother, and she's not welcome." Alyssa took the bag of herbs off the counter. "By the way, I heard there was a robbery in Salmon Alley two nights ago. Do you know who did it?"

"I have no idea. Why do you ask?"

"Just curious. I read about it in the newspaper. You always seem to know what's going on in the neighborhood. I heard the victim was a Hathaway and that he might have had a priceless statue with him."

"I heard the same thing. Assaulting rich white men is very bad for business. If the tourists are afraid to come here, we'll all suffer."

That was Ona, a homeopathic herbalist but also an unemotional pragmatist. Of course, Ona didn't realize that the rich white man was Alyssa's father.

"Our grandparents were very upset about it," Ona added. "I heard them talking in the back room. They don't like it when crime gets too close. It makes them remember the old days when they had to pay for protection from the gangs running through the streets."

"They had to pay for protection?"

"Of course. It was a way of life for many years, but thankfully not now."

"Do you think a gang was responsible for the attack?"

"No one is boasting about it, but who can say? Ancient art pieces can be sold on the black market for a lot of money. I'm surprised Mr. Hathaway didn't have more security with him. Actually, I'm surprised he was here at all. I bet he was going to see Lonnie Yao. He's an expert on Chinese bronzes. He has a reputation for being able to spot a fake from three feet away."

"You'd think a rich man like Mr. Hathaway would have his own expert right in the store."

Ona shrugged. "Is something wrong? You seem awfully interested in this robbery."

"Nothing is wrong. So, where is our grandmother?" Alyssa asked, deciding she better change the subject before Ona became more curious. "Is she upstairs cleaning the apartment for the New Year's celebration?"

Ona groaned. "Every day she cleans -- up there, down here, in the garden. And every night she buys fresh oranges and tangerines and tells me to take them home so I can have more babies. She doesn't think my two are enough."

Alyssa laughed. Ona's two energetic boys were more than enough. "Maybe she wants you to have a girl."

"I don't think so. She says three boys would be lucky."

"I think I'll go upstairs and see her."

"She isn't upstairs. She went out, and she didn't say where. She was in a bad mood, so I let her go without asking why."

"Why was she in a bad mood?"

"She's seventy-eight years old. Does she need a reason? Besides, she's always in a bad mood around the New Years'. I guess counting up all her sins for the year depresses her." Ona rested her arms on the counter as she leaned forward. "So, how are you, Alyssa? Any new men in your life?"

"I'm too busy for men."

"Ben was asking about you the other day. He always asks about you when he comes into the shop."

"I'm sure he was just being polite."

"You know, he might get tired of waiting for you."

"He's not waiting for me, and I'm not interested."

"Because he's Chinese."

"Because we're too different."

"You should talk to him, Alyssa, give him a chance. He might surprise you."

"I doubt it. He wants a traditional Chinese wife, and I could never be that."

"Do you want me to tell Nai Nai you came by?"

"No, I'll catch up to her later. Thanks."

Alyssa stepped onto the sidewalk and paused, debating her options. Maybe she should talk to Ben. Not about her love life, but about the dragon and the robbery. Ben was a reporter for the Chinese Daily News. He covered everything that happened in Chinatown.

Still, she hesitated. She hadn't seen Ben in several years. They'd been friends throughout childhood and had started dating in high school, but when she'd moved away to college, she'd ended their romance the same way she'd cut the ties to the old neighborhood. There was no future for her in Chinatown. And that's where Ben wanted to be.

He probably didn't care about her anymore, she told herself. He just asked about her out of politeness and friendship. He probably had a girlfriend. There was no reason not to see him. She needed answers, and he was in the position to give them. They'd have a simple conversation, and that would be it. Thankful she had a plan, she walked briskly down the street.

"She's leaving," Paige said, watching Alyssa from Riley's car. "Are we going to follow her again? I don't really see how this is accomplishing anything. We've seen her talk to an old man and go into an herb shop. What have we learned? Nothing."

Riley ended the call he'd been making on his cell phone to his assistant. "The herb shop is owned by

Alyssa's grandparents, An-Mei and Lee Chen. They've owned it for the past thirty-five years."

"Your assistant got that information in the last five minutes?"

"It's all a matter of public record."

"I have a feeling everything is public where you're concerned."

Riley laughed. "True. I believe the old man she was talking to in the square was her grandfather, Lee Chen."

"So what now?"

"I think you're looking a little stressed, Paige."

"Thanks for pointing that out." She pulled down the sun visor and checked her face in the mirror. "I don't look that bad."

"You look perfect, but maybe the herbalist won't notice, especially if you tell him or her how tired you are all the time, and how you need a pick-me-up."

"And why can't you be the tired and pale person in need of an energizer?" she asked, realizing his intention.

"Me? I'm the picture of health."

Riley was the picture of a gorgeous male in the prime of life and didn't she know it. "Fine. But I draw the line at actually taking anything. You don't know what's in those Chinese herbs. They could be dangerous."

"Or they could save your life. Chinese medicine has accomplished some amazing things. In fact, many of our modern medicines are based on herbs that first appeared almost two million years ago."

Paige raised an eyebrow. "Who are you?"

He laughed. "Sorry. I have one of those minds for trivia. Things come into my brain, and they don't leave."

"And it doesn't get crowded in there?"

"The human brain is quite a large organ--"

"Please. I do not want to hear about the size of your

organs," she said with a mischievous smile. She hadn't seen Riley in this lighthearted mood before. Everything had been so intense, so fast-paced, so filled with drama that they hadn't had much time to laugh, and she was enjoying it -- probably more than she should be.

He smiled back at her. "It doesn't have to be just talk."

She shook her head. "Let's stay focused on the task at hand." She opened the car door and stepped out onto the sidewalk.

"Okay, all kidding aside," Riley said, as they paused in front of the door. "You distract the clerk. Do whatever you have to do while I look around. My assistant told me the grandparents live upstairs over the shop. If I can get up there or in the back office, I will."

"What are you looking for?"

"I'll know when I find it."

"This doesn't seem very efficient."

"And Hathaways are always efficient?"

"Always," she said with a nod. "If you don't find anything, you're buying me lunch."

"Or you're buying me lunch. I have a craving for a lobster and steak combo at the fanciest restaurant in town."

"What? Do you think I'm made of money?"

"You said it; I didn't." He opened the door to the herb shop. "After you."

Chapter Twelve

Paige had no idea that *do whatever you have to do* would mean participating in an acupuncture demonstration. But when Riley had asked for a restroom, and the clerk had sent him toward the back room, she'd known she had to do something to keep the clerk busy until he returned.

"Have you done this before?" she asked nervously, watching the woman, who had introduced herself as Ona, twirl a long needle between her fingers.

"Lots of times. Now, tell me where the pain is."

Paige had made up a headache on the spur of the moment, which was what had led to the acupuncture demonstration, but now the prophecy was actually coming true. Anxiety had brought a throbbing to her left temple. She pressed the point of pain with the tips of her fingers.

Ona nodded. "That is an easy spot to fix. You'll feel better within a few moments."

"You're not going to stick that thing in my head, are you?"

"No. There are pressure points throughout the body that can relieve pain."

Paige lost track of what Ona was saying as her mother's voice entered her head. Are you out of your mind, Paige? That needle could be unsanitary. You could be sticking yourself with a fatal disease. You don't let some woman in an herb shop in Chinatown stick a needle into you.

"Um, maybe I don't want to do this," Paige said anxiously.

"The needle is sterile. You saw me take it out of the package. And I've worn latex gloves the entire time, yes?"

"Yes, but--"

"It's perfectly safe. I promise you. Now give me your hand."

Damn that Riley. Where the hell was he? Paige extended her hand, watching as Ona slowly inserted the needle into the back of her hand, the fleshy part between the thumb and first finger. There was a little pinch, but no real pain. Ona turned the needle back and forth, concentrating on her task. Paige was so tense she felt as if every muscle in her body was on red alert, ready to flee at any second.

"Relax," Ona said softly.

"I don't think--"

"Close your eyes. Let your mind drift. Find a picture that pleases you."

She closed her eyes and Riley's image came to her mind, unbidden and unwanted. His image did please her, but it did not make her feel relaxed. On the contrary, she felt her heart speed up and her palms dampen with sweat. Not that she was sweating because of him. Her nerves had more to do with the needle in her hand. Didn't they?

She saw his laughing face in her mind, his sexy smile, the lazy grin, and she wanted to smile back at him, run away into the sunset, find a deserted sandy beach and a big soft blanket, and fall into Riley's arms.

"Paige?"

His voice was so clear. She could hear him calling out to her, see him raising his hand to beckon her forward.

"Paige?"

She started, realizing his voice was much too clear to be part of her dream. Her eyes flew open, and she looked into his astonished face.

"What are you doing?" he asked.

"I -- uh, I had a headache."

"And how is it now?" Ona asked, as she removed the needle from Paige's hand.

"Oh, my goodness, it's gone." She wrinkled her brow, surprised that the tension had eased. Had the acupuncture done the trick, or was it due to the fact that Ona had removed the needle from her hand? Or maybe it was because Riley had returned, and she no longer had to cover for him. Whatever the reason, she felt a lot better.

"I told you," Ona said. "Now what else can I do for you?"

Paige looked at the array of herbs she'd already agreed to buy. "I think we have everything."

"You bought out the store, honey." Riley put his arm around her. "I hope you have something to take away those headaches every night," he said suggestively. "Or maybe a little aphrodisiac that won't make you feel so tired around bedtime."

Paige elbowed him in the gut, but Ona laughed. "Oh, we can take care of that, no problem. In fact, I have something for you, too," she said to Riley.

"That's good," Paige said, "because you know your stamina isn't what it used to be, sweetie."

Riley's jaw dropped. "My stamina is just fine."

Paige exchanged a commiserating look with Ona but

said out loud, "Of course it is."

"Don't worry, we'll fix you right up," Ona said, reaching for some other herbs.

"I don't need fixing. Thanks, anyway," Riley said quickly.

"Now, dear, you know we agreed we'd keep an open mind," Paige reminded him. "Just give us whatever you think, we need," she said to Ona. "Honey, why don't you give her your credit card, so we can pay up?"

"You'll be paying up later," Riley said in hushed annoyance as he handed Ona his credit card.

Paige simply smiled. Hey, she'd had a needle stuck into her hand. The least he could do was pay for the herbs. She wondered if he'd found anything on his search through the back room.

"Thank you. Come again." Ona handed Riley his purchase, then said to Paige, "If your headache comes back, you can always massage and put pressure on the point in your hand where we did the acupuncture. Sometimes that works, too."

Paige nodded and followed Riley out onto the sidewalk. "Well?" she asked impatiently.

"In the car," he muttered.

She got into the car and shut the door. "Did you find anything? Or did I just get myself stuck for no good reason?"

He reached into his pocket and pulled out a piece of paper. It was a newspaper article written in Chinese characters. She had no idea what the article said, but she recognized the picture of the dragon that accompanied the piece. "That's our dragon," she breathed.

"The photograph could have been taken from the antiques show," Riley said. "I know there were photographers there as well as the television cameras. Or it might have come from somewhere else."

"How do we find out?"

"I think we should pay a visit to the *Chinese Daily News*." He pointed to the byline. "Benjamin Fong should be able to tell us where this photograph came from and what else he knows about this dragon." He started the car engine. "By the way, you owe me lunch."

Alyssa could see Ben through the plate-glass window that separated the small lobby of the *Chinese Daily News* from the ten or so cubicles that made up the newsroom. Ben had a computer at his elbow but was writing on a yellow pad of paper, his fingers painstakingly precise, his attention focused on the task at hand. It reminded her of when they'd both taken calligraphy lessons from his uncle Guy. Ben had loved calligraphy, putting ink to paper, detailing the Chinese characters with absolute perfection.

She had been too impatient to take such time. But not Ben; he loved tradition and history. He was a twenty-four-year-old dinosaur in the twenty-first century. Which was why she was here. If anyone could tell her where to start her search for an ancient dragon, it was probably him.

"Can I help you?" the receptionist asked as she entered the lobby from a back room.

"I'd like to speak to Benjamin Fong."

"May I tell him your name?"

"Alyssa Chen."

Alyssa watched Ben through the glass as the receptionist made the call. He looked up as soon as he heard her name, his gaze meeting hers. He was surprised she had come. Why wouldn't he be? She'd cut the ties to their friendship a long time ago. "

“You can go on back," the receptionist said.

Ben waved to her, but now that she had the okay, she was hesitant to take it. What on earth would she say to him? She saw him get to his feet and realized she hadn't moved an inch. The last thing she wanted was to have this conversation in front of the receptionist, who was already giving her a curious look. Forcing herself to put one foot in front of the other, she walked down the hall, meeting Ben halfway.

"Hi," she said, offering him a tight smile. She'd never been a warm, affectionate person, and she didn't think she could start now.

"Alyssa. It's good to see you." Ben's eyes were truly welcoming, and she relaxed a bit.

"How have you been?”

"Great. Busy. What are you doing here?"

"I need some help, and I thought you might be the right person to ask. It's not personal," she said hurriedly, then wished she hadn't added the disclaimer as his smile dimmed.

"Business, of course. Come on back." He walked toward his cubicle and waved her toward a chair by the desk. "Have a seat."

"Thanks." She sat down, holding her purse on her lap.

"What's up?”

"My mother saw a statue that she thinks might be really old, maybe valuable, and I thought you might be able to tell me about it. You always seemed to know so much about Chinese art"

He shrugged somewhat modestly. "I know a little. What does the statue look like?"

"It's a dragon with a serpent-like body, about ten to twelve inches tall. The eyes are jade. There's a gold strip around the neck. It probably sounds like a million other statues."

Ben's eyes darted to the newspaper on his desk. He reached for it and handed it to her. "Does it look like this?"

"Oh, my God! That's it exactly." The dragon in the photograph resembled the painting on her mother's wall, which her mother said was a perfect match to the statue David Hathaway had brought to show her. "Why do you have this picture in the paper?"

"That statue was discovered on the television show *Antiques on the Road*. It's believed to date back to the Zhou dynasty. You can read the article, unless you've forgotten how to read Chinese characters."

She frowned at his reminder that she had not always embraced her culture. "Does it say anything more than what you just told me?"

"Not much."

"Do you know more about the history of the dragon?"

"There are several theories. Unfortunately, no one has gotten a good look at it. The owner took it to the House of Hathaway to have it appraised. Since David Hathaway was assaulted a few days ago, no one has been able to get any information on the statue."

Alyssa nodded, her body tensing at the mention of her father's name. She had no intention of sharing that information with Ben. As long as she and her mother didn't speak of it, no one else would know. She doubted anyone in the Hathaway family would rush to tell the press about a long-lost illegitimate daughter. Unless, of course, as Paige had suggested, the disappearance of the dragon drew a connecting line between David and Jasmine. That's what she had to prevent from happening.

"Does anyone have any idea who might be responsible for assaulting Mr. Hathaway?" she asked.

"Not the usual suspects, from what I've heard."

"What does that mean?"

"That someone with experience and knowledge of ancient art was behind the theft. That it was more than likely David Hathaway was mugged because he had the statue with him and not just because he was in the wrong place at the wrong time."

"You said there are several theories about the dragon," she continued.

"There are, but I have a meeting in a few minutes. Perhaps we could do dinner."

She didn't like the wicked sparkle in his eyes and knew getting involved with him again was probably a bad idea, but she needed his help. "Where do you want to go?"

"I'll cook for you."

"You'll cook for me?" she echoed in astonishment.

"Yes, and trust me you won't starve. I'm a very good cook." He jotted down an address.

She saw the street names and realized he hadn't gone far. "Chinatown, Ben?"

"Is that a problem?"

"No, of course not."

"Good." He got up and walked her out to the lobby area. "Is seven o'clock good for you?"

Before she could answer, the outer office door opened. To Alyssa's surprise, Paige and Riley walked into the lobby. They stopped abruptly when they saw her.

"Alyssa?" Paige questioned, her gaze narrowing suspiciously. "What are you doing here?"

"I could ask you the same thing," she retorted.

"We'd like to speak to Benjamin Fong," Paige said, giving Ben a questioning look.

"That would be me," Ben replied. "You're Paige Hathaway, aren't you?"

"Yes, and this is Riley McAllister. We'd like to speak to you about the article you wrote regarding the dragon belonging to Mr. McAllister."

"It seems that many people are interested in that story. Do you all know each other?" Ben asked, his gaze moving back to Alyssa.

"We've met," Alyssa said shortly. "They spoke to my mother earlier. You know she has sold several of her paintings to the House of Hathaway."

"What do you want to know?" Ben asked.

"Paige and I have read about a legend involving two dragons, a box, and a flute," Riley said. "Have you heard of such a thing?"

Alyssa started. This was the first she'd heard that there might be two dragons. Or a box. Or a flute for that matter. She glanced over at Ben and saw a spark of excitement flash in his black eyes.

"I know the story," Ben replied. "It is believed that an emperor had the box and dragons made out of bronze to protect a flute that his daughter, the first daughter of his second wife, found in the woods. When the daughter played the flute for her father, his violent headaches would ease. He was so happy that he treated the daughter like a princess and her mother like a queen. The first wife, however, did not like the change in status. She had a son who was meant to be emperor, but now there was talk of this girl becoming an empress. In a fit of rage, she stole the dragons and the box. With the flute gone, the father's headaches returned. In a violent frenzy, he had his daughter killed for losing the flute and swore a curse on all first daughters of anyone who should touch the dragons or the box or the precious flute."

"That's very similar to the story we read," Paige said. "Do you know if the pieces ever resurfaced since the origin of the legend and the curse?"

"I believe there have been several sightings of the pieces, whether as a unit or individually I'm not sure. However, the age of the bronze alone would make it of great value today. Of course, if all three pieces of the unit were together, it would be even more valuable. Where did your grandmother get her dragon, Mr. McAllister?"

"She has no idea, unfortunately. She found it in the attic."

"Too bad. It would be easier to trace." Ben paused. "If there was a curse on the dragon, it might have affected your grandmother."

"I don't believe in curses," Riley said sharply.

"You might want to rethink that," Ben said. "To not understand the power of the past is to be a fool."

"Is that a Chinese saying?" Riley asked.

"No, it's good advice." Ben checked his watch. "I'm afraid I have a meeting."

"Thank you for your time," Paige said. "If you think of anything else, please call me." She took out a business card and handed it to Ben.

Alyssa lingered behind as Paige and Riley left.

"I guess I don't need dinner after all," she said. "Interesting story. You could have shared that with me when I asked."

He smiled. "I needed a bargaining chip so you'd come to dinner. We haven't seen each other in a long time. I'd like a chance to get reacquainted." He paused. "If you give me a few hours, I'm sure I can find out something else about the dragon."

"That sounds like bribery."

"Whatever it takes."

She hesitated, then said, "All right. I'll come to dinner."

"Good. I'm sure we'll have plenty to talk about -- including how you know Paige Hathaway and why you're both interested in a dragon statue from thousands of years ago."

"I can't believe Alyssa came here, too," Paige said to Riley as they waited in the hall for Alyssa to emerge from the newspaper office. "She obviously knows Benjamin Fong."

"Yes, she does," Riley mused. "There are a lot of players getting in this game."

"It's not a game."

"I think it might be," he said.

"You think everyone is conspiring against you. That's called paranoia."

"That's called being smart," he said, tapping his temple with his finger.

"Too smart to believe in legends or curses, right?"

"My grandmother had that dragon in her attic for God knows how long. Nothing happened to anybody."

"Are you sure?" She saw his eyes darken and had second thoughts about bringing it up, but it was too late. "The curse is about first daughters. Wasn't your mother a first daughter?"

"Don't be ridiculous. I'm not going to blame a statue for my mother's problems. She created most of them herself. It's just a story, Paige. It doesn't mean anything. It isn't real."

She'd been working around antiques too long not to believe in the power of the past, but she didn't know enough about Riley's mother to pursue an argument.

The door opened and Alyssa stepped out.

"I figured you'd be waiting," she said with a sigh. "How is your -- our... I don't even know what to call him."

"He's the same," Paige said quickly, not eager to get into labels either. "Is Mr. Fong a friend of yours?"

"Since childhood."

"You came to ask him about the dragon, didn't you?"

"He didn't tell me anything he didn't tell you."

"But he might," Paige said. "We need to work together."

"I'll think about it, but right now I have other things to do."

"Alyssa..." Paige didn't know what she wanted to say, but she felt as if she had to say something. "I'd like to know more about you. I think we should talk or something."

Alyssa sent her a wary look. "Why? Just because we share a few genes doesn't mean we have to know each other."

"It doesn't mean we can't, either. Wouldn't it be easier if we tried to get along?"

"Easier for who -- you? You've always had it easy. I'm used to it being hard, really hard." And with that she walked away.

"That went well," Paige said. "Alyssa has a chip on her shoulder that's almost as big as yours."

"You can't just expect her to open up her heart to you. She's protected it for too long."

"I think she has the Great Wall of China built around it. I can understand her distrust of my father, but why doesn't she want to know me? What have I done to her?"

"You haven't done a thing. But you had everything she didn't, especially a father. It would be natural for her to resent you."

"That wasn't my fault. And I do feel bad about the fact that my father ignored her. He shouldn't have done that, and when he's better, I'm going to tell him so." Riley didn't look as if he believed her, so she added, "I won't sweep this into the closet like a dirty little secret."

"I doubt your mother will let you make anything public. It is a dirty little secret, Paige. And if it gets out, your high-society friends will have a field day gossiping about it."

He was right. Victoria would fight any kind of public disclosure. But this wasn't about the public acknowledging Alyssa; it was about her father doing the right thing.

"Come on, Paige, it's time for a break," Riley said. "You owe me lunch."

"Fine, I'll buy you lunch. Just remember when you're ordering that I don't come into my trust fund until I'm thirty."

"How old are you now?"

"Twenty-eight."

"Looks like we're going to have a very long lunch."

Chapter Thirteen

"I told you I wasn't cursed," Riley said as he pulled into a parking spot directly in front of a restaurant called the Mad Hatter on Union Street. Because it was a popular shopping street just a few blocks from the marina, Riley had indeed scored a coup.

"I didn't say you were cursed. I said your mother might have been," Paige reminded him. "The curse has nothing to do with sons."

"That's because men don't believe in curses."

"Need I remind you that it was a male emperor who put down the curse?"

He smiled at her. "You can remind me over lunch. I'm starving. Let's go."

Paige followed him into a small sidewalk café. A hostess wearing a top hat with sequins and feathers asked them if they'd prefer to sit inside or out. Out of habit, Paige chose an inside table, but almost immediately regretted her choice when they were seated at a cozy table in a dark corner of the room. It was difficult to keep their relationship in perspective when they were alone.

"This is nice, private," Riley said with a wink. "I like it."

"I should have figured you'd feel comfortable in dark corners." She paused. "I feel a little guilty that I'm having lunch instead of going back to the hospital to see my dad."

"Your father is not alone, and we're working hard to figure out who hurt him. That's worth something."

She sighed. "Fine, you've convinced me. You're very persuasive and good at coming up with excuses. I'll be sure to call you when I want to get out of a root canal or something."

"I can't be of any help to you there. I love going to the dentist."

"No one loves the dentist."

He smiled. "The chairs are cool. When I was a kid I felt like I was in a spaceship."

"What about the drill and the shots of Novocain?"

He shrugged. "A little pain is good for the soul. It builds character."

"Who told you that -- the dentist?"

"As a matter of fact, yes," he said with a laugh. "My first crush was on a female hygienist. I was thirteen. I loved the way she smelled, the way her hair drifted against my face, her breasts -- they were so perfect--"

"I get the picture," Paige said, holding up a hand. "You're a fan of big breasts."

"I'm a fan of any female breasts."

"Of course." She picked up her menu, deliberately placing it in front of her not overly endowed chest.

"Hiding?" Riley asked.

"Just trying to order."

He pushed the menu down so that it lay flat on the table. "I think you have beautiful breasts, Paige."

She cleared her throat, hating the way her breasts responded to his words, her nipples drawing into tight, hard peaks that she prayed weren't evident through her silk blouse. "This isn't exactly lunch conversation."

"We can talk about them over dinner if you prefer."

"We're not talking about them at all, unless you want to talk about a few of your own private parts."

"Whatever you want."

What she wanted was to slap that lazy, knowing grin right off his face. Actually, she didn't want to slap it off; she wanted to kiss it off. "There must be something terribly wrong with me," she muttered.

"Why? Because you're turned on? It's a natural response. It happens all the time."

"I'm so happy to know that you turn on all of your lunch companions. But thanks for reminding me, because you just turned me off."

"No, I didn't."

"Oh, shut up," she said in exasperation. "Can we just order some food and talk about something else?"

"Sure. Have you ever been here before?"

"No. Is the food good? Or are the hats supposed to distract you from what you're eating?"

"The food is excellent, especially the hot roast beef sandwich."

"That sounds perfect. I'll have that."

He raised an eyebrow. "It's a good size and it comes with fries -- do you know how many calories are in that?"

"I don't want to know. But since I've missed most of my meals the last few days, I think I have room for a few extra calories. Do you watch your weight?"

"Do I look like I should?"

He looked like a man in perfect condition, muscled, toned, trim, but she didn't want to make his ego any bigger. "How old are you?" she asked instead.

"Thirty-one. Does that make a difference?"

"Of course it does. Once you pass thirty, it's all downhill."

"I thought that was forty."

"That's what all thirty-one-year-olds think," she said with a smile.

"Well, you don't have to worry since you haven't hit the magic number yet."

"That's right. I can even order dessert."

"You're paying," he reminded her.

She looked down at the menu in front of her. "It could have been a lot worse. Where's the steak and lobster combination? Did you decide to go easy on me?"

"Since you don't have your trust fund yet, I had no choice."

The waiter came over to take their order and for a few minutes they were busy answering questions about drinks and food and whether or not they'd like to purchase one of the hats on display. When the waiter left, a silence fell between them, a tense silence, Paige thought, the teasing laughter of a few minutes ago no longer in evidence. She glanced over at Riley and caught him staring. A little shiver ran down her spine. "What are you looking at?"

"You."

"I know that, but you look like you have something on your mind."

"I do. You," he added with a slow smile that took her breath away.

"I'm sure you have a lot more interesting things to think about."

"I can't remember one." He paused, his gaze still intent on her face. "Are you really going to marry that stiff shirt who was at the hospital the other night?"

"Martin? I told you I'm not engaged to him."

"Does he know that?"

"He should," she replied. But she had a feeling she'd let things drag on too long where Martin was concerned. "It's a tricky situation. Our families are friends. Martin works at the store. He's a vice president now. Somewhere along the way someone got the idea that we would make a good match. So we started going out, but--"

"But you don't want him," Riley finished.

"He's a good man. I could do worse."

"You could do better."

"You don't even know him. And why should I care what you think?"

"No reason," Riley agreed. "It's none of my business. A week ago I probably would have thought you were a good match, too."

"Not now?"

He didn't answer right away, just continued to study her with a thoughtful expression on his face. Then he said, "You're not exactly what I thought. You're more complicated. The person most people see isn't the person you really are, is it? Somewhere in there lies the problem with Martin."

How could he know her so well after a few days when people she had known her whole life didn't have a clue?

"I think on the outside you're cool and collected but inside you're teeming with frustration and maybe a little anger," he continued.

"That's enough," she said, shaken by his assessment.

"Am I wrong?" he challenged.

"You're oversimplifying things. And even if you're not, you're no different. You play the tough guy, but that's not who you are."

"That *is* who I am."

"And more. Caring and loyal... Your grandmother said you gave up your career in the marines to come back and take care of the family business when your grandfather got sick."

He shrugged. "It wasn't a big deal. I was ready to come home."

"And your family was important."

"My grandparents are important to me, just those two people. I wouldn't use the general term *family*. Are you done with the analysis, Princess, or is there more?"

"You always call me princess when we get too friendly. I wonder why."

"It's a reminder that we don't travel in the same circles."

"Today we do."

"Tomorrow we won't."

He was probably right, and she should be happy about that. He'd been a thorn in her side since the day they'd met. But he'd also been other things, including the first man in a long time she felt she could really talk to, say the things she wanted to say, not the things she was supposed to say.

"Riley?" a feminine voice called out with a delighted squeal.

Paige looked up to see a gorgeous, statuesque redhead heading straight toward them. Riley jumped to his feet just in time to be swept into a tight hug against a pair of very large breasts. He must be in heaven, Paige thought, sitting back in her seat.

"Riley, you devil, I've missed you," the woman said with a sparkling laugh. Then she planted a long, smacking kiss on his lips that he didn't make any move to avoid.

As their kiss went on, Paige cleared her throat. Riley still didn't look over at her. "Riley," she said more loudly as the two broke apart. "Who's your friend?"

He finally turned toward her. "This is Brenda Sampson -- Paige Hathaway."

"Paige Hathaway?" Brenda raised an eyebrow as she cast Riley a speculative look. "Moving up in the world, are you?"

"Right now I'm having lunch."

"Did you order the hot roast beef sandwich?"

"It's the best," he said.

"I put it on the menu just for you. I'll go have a word with the chef, make sure you get extra meat and fries. It was nice to meet you, Miss Hathaway. I hope you enjoy your lunch. And, Riley, you better call me soon. It's been too long."

"I will," he promised. He returned to his seat as Brenda moved on to greet another table of customers.

"You have lipstick all over your face," Paige told him.

Riley picked up his napkin and wiped off his mouth.

"It's on your cheek. You didn't get it," she said.

"Maybe you could help."

"Fine." She dipped her napkin into her water glass and leaned across the table to wipe the lipstick off his face. Unfortunately, the move put her into closer contact with his body. Her leg brushed his under the table. Her shoulder collided with his arm, and she became acutely aware of how near his mouth was to hers. It wouldn't take much to lean in just a little bit farther...

She heard a catch in his breath, and her eyes met his in shocking awareness.

"Do it, Paige," he said huskily. "You know you want to."

"I -- I don't know what you're talking about," she lied. She rubbed at his face with brisk ruthlessness, then sat back in her seat. "It's gone now."

"So is half my skin." He put a hand to his cheek. "What the hell is wrong with you?"

"Nothing is wrong with me."

A gleam entered his eyes. "You're jealous."

"I am not. I've never been jealous in my life."

"You didn't like Brenda."

"She's a pushy redhead, and the two of you made a scene."

He sent her a knowing grin that irritated her more. "You didn't like that she kissed me."

"I couldn't have cared less. You know, I'm not hungry. I think I'll catch a cab and go to the hospital."

"Running away, Paige? I thought Hathaways had more guts than that."

He knew just which buttons to push. She tapped her fingers on the table, considering her options. Why was she acting so crazy? Was she jealous? Was that possible? She certainly wouldn't admit that to him, nor was she going to admit that she had actually wanted to kiss him a moment ago. She needed to calm down, pull herself together, and--as he'd reminded her--act like a Hathaway.

"Fine, I'll stay."

"Good." He paused as the waiter set down his beer and her diet Coke. He raised his glass. "To your father's speedy recovery and to finding the dragon."

She hesitated, but how could she resist that toast? She clinked her glass against his. "Thanks for putting my father first. I know you believe he created this situation."

"I think he had a lot to do with it, yes."

"Guilty until proven innocent."

"Most people are guilty."

"I'm not. And we're on the same side, Riley."

"Maybe for the moment." He leaned forward, resting his arms on the table as he gave her his full attention. "We don't know yet how this will play out. We don't know what your father's intentions were. But we do know that you are a loyal Hathaway. And at some point you may have to choose between doing what's right and supporting your family."

"That won't happen. My family is as trustworthy and honest as I am."

"I hope that's the case, Paige, I really do. Because if it comes down to your family or mine, who do you think I'm going to pick?"

Paige was reminded of Riley's words an hour later when she approached the front doors of the hospital. Off to the side of the main entrance were at least two television crews lying in wait. Unfortunately, they spotted her just a second after she spotted them. There was no time to escape.

"Miss Hathaway, how is your father?" a young woman asked as she stuck a microphone in Paige's face, nearly knocking out her teeth.

Paige jumped back, only to trip over a man coming up on the other side of her.

"Is it true that your father was robbed of a valuable piece of art that didn't belong to Hathaway's?" he asked.

"What is Hathaway's doing to recover the piece?"

"Do the police have any leads on your father's assailant?"

"Do you think this was a personal attack? Does your father have any known enemies?"

Paige blinked at the rifle-shot questions. She could barely keep up with them all, and each time she turned her head, there seemed to be another reporter in her face as well as more microphones and cameras. She certainly hoped this wasn't a live shot, because she had the distinct feeling she was coming across as an idiot.

Think, Paige told herself. You're a Hathaway. You can do this.

"My father," she began, drawing immediate silence with the mere sound of her voice. The sense of power gave her confidence. "My father is in stable condition, and we expect a full and complete recovery."

"What was your father doing in Chinatown?"

"The police are continuing their investigation," she replied. This wasn't so bad. A lifetime of watching her parents handle reporters had prepared her for this moment. She hadn't realized just how well prepared she was until now. "Thank you for your concern. As soon as we know more, we'll be sure to inform you."

"Is it true that your father went to see a woman in Chinatown?"

The question pierced Paige's confidence like a pin to a balloon. Jasmine? They knew about Jasmine? Oh, God. What about Alyssa? Did they know about her, too? She had to say something to head them off.

"No further comment," Martin Bennett said, appearing at her side. "The Hathaways will be holding a press conference later today."

Paige felt Martin's strong grip on her arm as he pulled her through the crowd of reporters and into the hospital lobby. They didn't stop walking until they were on the elevator, and even then he put a finger to his lips, motioning for her to be silent until they were alone. They got off at the fourth floor, and she yanked her arm out of his grip.

"Why on earth did you do that?" she demanded.

"Do what? I saved you from saying the wrong thing. You know you're not supposed to talk to reporters. What were you thinking?"

"That I could handle the situation," she snapped. "Which I was."

"No, you weren't. They were leading you for a fall, and you were going right along. You should have done what I did, told them there will be a press conference forthcoming and any further questions should be directed to me as the spokesperson for Hathaway's in this time of crisis. That's the way we do things. You know that."

She stared at him in amazement. He was talking to her like a child. "I'm a Hathaway, Martin. I know how to handle myself and the press. And if I want to speak on behalf of the store or my family, I will. I don't care if you're the designated spokesperson or not."

"Your mother won't feel the same way."

"My mother isn't here."

"No, she's with your father, talking to him instead of the media, which is where you should be."

"And where I was going." She saw the anger in his eyes but didn't understand it. "What are you mad about, anyway? I'm the one who has the right to be annoyed. You came in and swooped me away like an eagle snatching an unsuspecting bird."

"You are an unsuspecting bird," he said as he ran his hand through his hair in obvious frustration. "Where do you think those questions were going, Paige? Someone has obviously been following the police investigation. They know by now that the police went to see Jasmine Chen. Curiosity as to how a simple Chinese woman could be connected to David Hathaway was sure to follow."

"And we should have an answer ready. *'No comment'* will only fuel the curiosity."

"The answer is coming from your mother. We've already planned a press conference for early this evening. That's why the media are outside right now."

"No one told me that."

"I tried calling you earlier, but your message machine was on at home, and you didn't pick up your cell phone. Where have you been?"

She felt a slight surge of guilt at the memory of her delicious lunch. "I've been doing some research of my own about the dragon."

"With Riley McAllister? What are you doing with him, Paige? He's not on our side. He's using you."

"And I'm using him. We both want to get the dragon back. We both want to know who is responsible for the attack on my father and who might have the dragon now. Riley is a security expert. He has connections. He can get information I can't."

"Like what?"

"Like he's the one who figured out Jasmine's daughter, Alyssa, is my sister," she said.

Martin's jaw tensed. He cast a quick look around them to make sure they were alone. "What the hell are you talking about?"

"My father's illegitimate daughter."

"Damn," Martin frowned, then shook his head. "Now McAllister has ammunition to blackmail you."

She was shocked by the suggestion. Riley wouldn't do that. He was an honorable man. Wasn't he? A niggle of doubt crept into her mind. Was she being naive? He'd laughingly told her she shouldn't have suggested to Alyssa the possibility of selling her story to the tabloids, but couldn't Riley do exactly that? If they couldn't find his grandmother's statue, maybe Riley would have to find another way of getting his grandmother the money he thought she deserved.

"I need to see my father," she said abruptly, hating the way Martin had derailed her.

"Look, Paige, I'm sorry if you think I came down too hard on you. I just want to protect you from more pain. And I don't think hanging around with this McAllister guy is a good idea."

"You don't need to protect me. I can take care of myself. Understood?"

"As long as you understand that there's a good possibility your father was up to something by taking that dragon into Chinatown in the first place."

"Up to what? We know he took it to show Jasmine. Big deal."

"She might not be the only one he showed it to. Maybe he took it to someone who could make him a fake."

His suggestion left her speechless. "My father doesn't deal in fakes. How can you say that, Martin?"

"Because he didn't have a good reason to take it out of the store. It went against company policy, our insurance guidelines, our security measures, everything."

She couldn't refute that. She didn't know why her father had taken the dragon from the store, but Martin's doubts gave her even more motivation to find out. "When he wakes up, he'll tell us why he went to Chinatown. And his reason won't have anything to do with the commissioning of a fake statue. He cares too much about art to even consider such a thing. You'll see I'm right. When my father wakes up, he'll tell us what really happened. And then there won't be any more doubts or questions."

"I'm looking forward to that moment," Martin replied. "Until then, don't talk to any more reporters, Paige. You'll only add fuel to the fire."

The fire eating away at her family's reputation. She had to find some way to put it out.

Chapter Fourteen

After discussing her husband's case with the private duty nurse, Victoria dismissed the woman so she could be alone with her husband. As she stood now by his bed, she couldn't remember the last time she'd watched David sleep. He looked old, she thought, panic filling her chest. And he was two years younger than she was. This shouldn't be happening now. They weren't the right age to be facing this crisis. They had so much left to do.

But she wasn't dying, she reminded herself quickly. She was okay. And David would be all right, too. She had to believe that. He was the foundation of her life. Maybe not him exactly, but who he was. She hadn't married just him; she'd married his family, his heritage. She knew more about his ancestors than he did. She was the one who made sure the distant relatives got Christmas cards and birthday presents. She was the true Hathaway, and she wouldn't lose that.

She certainly wouldn't lose it to divorce. She still couldn't believe the nerve of that woman coming here to her husband's bedside. Well, it wouldn't happen again.

The nurses had strict instructions not to let Jasmine Chen anywhere near David.

How could he have picked a woman so unattractive, so unappealing, so unstylish, so lower-class? He had a wife who was beautiful, smart, sophisticated. Why had he needed someone else?

Angry tears blurred her vision, and she drew in a sharp breath, hating the fact that she still cared about him at all. Look at how he had treated her, cheating on her with another woman, and God knows how many others. And now the daughter had surfaced. She had known of Alyssa's existence, of course. Her private investigator had researched every aspect of Jasmine Chen's life, including the birth of her daughter, Alyssa, nine months after she'd slept with David. If Jasmine had gone after David then, Victoria would have stopped it. But it appeared that the woman actually cared about David, maybe even loved him -- too much to go after his money. What a fool Jasmine Chen was.

But she was a fool, too. She should have made sure that the connection between Alyssa Chen and David could never be made. She'd slipped up. Now Paige knew about the whole sordid mess. It was embarrassing and awkward, and Victoria dreaded the conversation she knew was coming. Paige would want to talk about the affair, the last thing Victoria cared to discuss with her daughter. Her marriage was personal and private and none of Paige's business.

"Damn you, David," she said aloud. "The least you could do is have the guts to wake up and face this mess you've created."

"Do you really think yelling at him is the best approach?" Paige asked as she entered the room.

"I've run out of other ideas," Victoria retorted, glad to

see Paige was alone. She suspected that Riley McAllister was behind her daughter's newfound knowledge, and she resented his intrusion into their lives. "What's wrong?" she asked, noting a flush on her daughter's cheeks.

"I ran into some reporters downstairs."

"You didn't tell them anything, did you?"

"Not really. Martin cut them off at the knees." Victoria nodded approvingly. "He's a very smart businessman. Where is he?"

"He said he'd be by later. How is Dad?"

"I don't know. The same, I guess."

They both glanced down at David, who seemed to be barely breathing. "He sleeps so deeply," Paige murmured. "You're worried, aren't you?"

"I'd feel better if he was awake." Victoria felt Paige's gaze on her face, but she didn't want to look into her daughter's eyes and see the questions there. "Now isn't the time," she muttered.

"I wasn't going to ask."

"Thank you for that."

"But you knew, didn't you?"

"I thought you weren't going to ask."

"I'm sorry. It's just so confusing. I believed our family was so solid, so secure."

"Our family is fine. A few bumps in the road along the way, but nothing more than that." Victoria looked at her daughter's worried face. "We are Hathaways, Paige. And we're survivors. Don't ever forget that."

"I hope Dad hasn't forgotten. What would we do without him?"

"Hopefully, we won't have to find out."

"You still love him a little, don't you?"

"Good heavens, why would you ask that?" "That's not an answer, Mother. Do you still love him?"

"We've been married for thirty-one years. Love isn't that easy to define at my age."

"I don't think it should be that difficult, either."

Some latent motherly instinct made her want to reassure Paige. "Your father and I are not going to split up. We'll never get a divorce, if that's what you're worried about."

"Because you love him, or because you want to be a Hathaway?"

"I am a Hathaway. I'm more a Hathaway than he is. I've worked hard to be one. I won't give it up. I don't care how many women and daughters come out of the woodwork."

"I guess I have my answer."

"No, you don't have your answer." Victoria took a deep breath. "I love him, and I hate him. I can't help it. I'm sure he feels much the same way. We've shared some of the best days of our lives and some of the worst. We understand each other, and yet we don't. We make each other laugh, and we make each other cry."

"I guess that's better than feeling nothing."

"Sometimes I'd rather feel nothing." Victoria stared down at the familiar lines of her husband's face and realized that what she felt was fear. She didn't want to lose David. She didn't want him to die.

"Damn you, David, wake up. Wake up and answer your daughter's questions." She smiled at Paige, and for the first time in a long while there was a connection between them. "I shouldn't be the only one on the hot seat. He has a lot more to answer for than I do."

"That's for sure." Paige put her hand on her father's arm. "Come on, Daddy. Open your eyes. We need you."

"Oh, my God," Victoria whispered as David's eyelids began to flicker. "I think he's trying to wake up." She leaned over in excitement. "David? Can you hear me?"

His eyelids moved. Another blink and she was staring into his brown eyes.

"Jasmine," he said, and then his eyes shut again.

"You bastard," Victoria hissed. "You lying, cheating bastard."

"He didn't know what he was saying," Paige said quickly, trying to defuse the situation.

"The hell he didn't."

"Mother, please." Paige pressed her lips against her father's cool cheek. "Daddy, try to wake up again."

"Bright," he murmured in a raspy voice.

"I'll turn off the light," Paige said, hurrying over to the light switch.

"Vicky? Is that you?" he asked, squinting as he tried to focus.

"Who did you think it was?"

"Mother," Paige warned. "He's coming out of a coma. Try to remember that."

Victoria drew in a long breath and slowly let it out as she gazed into his dazed eyes. "How do you feel, David? Do you have any pain?"

"Head hurts. Where am I?"

"You're in the hospital." She leaned over and pushed the button for the nurse while Paige took her father's hand.

"It's going to be okay, Dad. Just relax and don't try to do too much too soon."

A few moments later the nurse entered and proceeded to check David's vital signs.

"Welcome back, Mr. Hathaway," she said.

"What happened?" David murmured, continuing to blink in confusion.

"You were attacked," Victoria answered. "Don't you

remember?"

David slowly shook his head, then winced at the pain the movement generated.

The doctor entered a moment later and conducted a brief examination. "You're doing well, Mr. Hathaway. I'd like to run some tests, but it looks like you're on the road to recovery. It's about time, too."

"What -- what day is it?" David turned to Paige with desperation in his eyes. "Elizabeth's birthday. When is her birthday? I didn't miss it, did I?"

Page shook her head, tears filling her eyes. "Today is Friday. Her birthday is next Wednesday. You have plenty of time."

"Thank God."

"I'll be back," Victoria said, following the doctor out of the room and leaving Paige alone with her father.

"You had us worried, Daddy."

"What happened to me?"

"You were mugged in Chinatown."

"What? Why was I in Chinatown? God, I'm tired."

"Dad, before you go back to sleep, I have to ask you. Do you know what happened to the dragon?" He looked at her in confusion. "What dragon?"

"The dragon that belongs to Mrs. Delaney, the one you took out of the store when you went to Chinatown."

"Did I go to Chinatown to meet Mr. Yee for dim sum?"

"Mr. Yee? No, that was last month. I'm talking about this week."

His eyes drifted shut, and Paige realized he had fallen asleep. Why didn't he remember? Was there something wrong with his memory? She walked quickly from the room, finding her mother and the doctor in the hall. "He doesn't remember the dragon or going to Chinatown or anything that happened recently," she blurted out. "Something is wrong with his mind."

"Short-term memory loss is common in cases of trauma like this. It usually comes back," the doctor reassured her. "He just needs time. I'll check him in the morning, but I think you can both relax. He'll probably sleep for a while. His body is still recovering. But the worst is over."

"So you think his memory will return?" Paige asked.

"I'm fairly certain it will. Maybe not the actual event of the assault, but probably most of what occurred before that time."

"Thank you, Dr. Crawley," Victoria said.

"No problem. Now, both of you go home and get some rest. That's an order." He smiled and tipped his head as he walked away.

"Well, it looks like your father will make it," Victoria said with relief.

"Yes, it appears that way."

"What's wrong now, Paige?"

"I wish he could have told me what happened to him."

"He will. He needs time. You heard the doctor. Why don't you go home? The nurse will stay with your father through the night. If he wakes, she'll make sure he has whatever he needs."

"I'm wondering if we shouldn't have more than a nurse."

"What are you talking about?"

"I'm talking about a security guard. What if whoever tried to hurt Dad finds out he's awake? He might be afraid that Dad can identify him. He might come back."

Victoria's gaze narrowed suspiciously. "What else aren't you telling me?"

Paige hesitated. "There may not be any connection, but Mrs. Delaney's house was broken into this morning."

"Mrs. Delaney, the owner of the dragon?"

"Yes, and I've been doing some research. It's possible that her dragon is part of a set. It's Riley's theory that--"

"Riley McAllister? The grandson?"

"Yes, he's a security expert, and he thinks that someone might have broken into his grandmother's house to see if she had another dragon."

Victoria let out a long, weary sigh. "Fine. I'll call our security company and have them send someone over here right away. Will that ease your mind?"

"Yes, thank you." Paige paused, watching her mother's gaze drift back to her dad's hospital room. "Are you going to stay?"

"For a while."

"What Dad said when he first woke up--"

"I didn't hear a thing."

"I didn't, either," she lied.

"Go home, Paige, and for God's sake, run a comb through your hair. It looks like a bird made a nest in it. And put on some lipstick. There could be press snapping your picture on your way out of the hospital. You have to think about these things, you know. Appearance and image are very important, especially when we're under such close scrutiny. Speaking of which, I think you should distance yourself from Mr. McAllister. We need to keep our business private."

"Our family business went public when Dad lost Riley's grandmother's dragon. Riley is determined to find out what happened, and I can't blame him. I feel bad for his grandmother. One minute she's sitting on a possible fortune, and the next minute it's gone."

"There's no room for sentiment in business, Paige,"

her mother replied. "Mr. McAllister is a customer, not a friend. Try to remember that."

She would try, but her mother had no idea how difficult that would be, because Paige wasn't thinking of Riley as a potential friend but as a lover.

"So you decided to actually come to work," Carey said, dumping a pile of pink message slips on Riley's desk late Friday afternoon. "Where have you been all day?"

"I've been trying to track down my grandmother's dragon," he replied. "I knew I could count on you to keep things going."

"You can -- for most things," she said somewhat ominously.

Riley sat back in his chair. "What does that mean?"

"The three musketeers want another assignment."

"Bud, Charlie, and Gilbert?" he asked, referring to the three older men who'd been with the company since his grandfather had started it forty years ago. They were now in their early to mid-seventies and insisted on continuing to work. His grandfather had made him promise when he first came back to help out that he would not terminate their contracts for any reason except gross negligence, certainly not for age or any other discriminatory reason. "Actually, I have a job for them," he said. "I want them to take turns monitoring my grandmother's house. I'm not expecting any trouble, but another pair of eyes wouldn't hurt."

"I'll let them know. They'll be thrilled."

Riley smiled. "Maybe we should look into getting them into some computer classes. If they're going to work for me, I need to find something worthwhile for them to do."

"And you're too soft to fire them."

"Hey, they're cheap, loyal labor. I'm looking out for my own interests."

"Yeah, yeah, tell it to someone who doesn't know you."

"What else is going on?"

"Tom picked up a new Internet client. Richie called in and said the film company shooting in Marin needs security guards for three more days. That's about it. Oh, and Josh called and said he got an A on his chemistry test, so can he please come back to work?"

Riley smiled at that. "Good for him."

"Good for you for making him care about his grades. You're pretty smart when it comes to teenagers and old guys. Women -- now that's another story. And speaking of women, or woman in particular, are you going to be tagging along with Paige Hathaway all night, too? Just so I know where to reach you in case of emergency."

He ignored her amused smile. "You can always reach me on my cell phone. You don't have to know where I am."

"That's no fun. Seriously, Riley. Is this thing with Paige Hathaway business or funny business?"

"It's none of *your* business," he said pointedly.

"Just be careful," Carey warned. "Don't fall in love. Girls like Paige can break your heart."

"That's never going to happen."

Carey walked out of his office with a disbelieving laugh. But she was wrong. He had no intention of falling in love. Long-term commitments were not for him, and not even a beautiful, brown-eyed blonde was going to change that. Besides, he had more important things on his mind right now. He had a dragon to find.

When Jasmine opened her door, she was shocked to see her mother, An-Mei, on the doorstep. She couldn't remember the last time her mother had come to visit. They lived only a few blocks from each other, but the distance between them was as big as a continent.

"Ma," she stuttered. "Is everything all right?"

"No, all wrong," An-Mei said shortly, brushing past her into the apartment.

Jasmine closed the door and waited for An-Mei to state the purpose of her visit. A flicker of nervousness ran down her spine as she watched her mother critically peruse the contents of her apartment. Her mother would find some fault with the way the furniture was arranged or the color of the painted walls. There would be something to criticize. She waited quietly, patiently, feeling as if she deserved whatever criticism was coming. Because she was bad; she'd always been bad. Her mother had told her so over and over again.

Sometimes she wondered if anyone else saw the temper in the tiny, barely five-foot-tall woman in front of her with the long black braid down her back and the baggy clothes that covered her from head to toe. Jasmine couldn't remember the last time she'd seen her mother's bare legs or arms. Modesty was a virtue, An-Mei believed, along with many other virtues that Jasmine had never been able to live up to, even before the biggest sin of them all.

She'd always been a disappointment. When she'd been born missing a finger, her mother had screamed in fury, according to her auntie Lin. Ever since then, Jasmine had been treated as an outcast. Her mother had once told her that the missing finger was the mark of shame she would grow into. And Jasmine hadn't disappointed her.

By sleeping with a married man, she'd committed a terrible sin, and having an illegitimate baby made it even worse. Her mother probably wouldn't have spoken to her again if it hadn't been for her father's influence. His heart attack a few years earlier also had softened her mother's stance, perhaps made her realize that too many years had passed with this anger between them.

Jasmine wouldn't have taken the scraps of affection if it hadn't been for Alyssa. She'd buried her pride and forged a tenuous relationship with her parents so that Alyssa would become part of the family. But that hadn't really happened despite her efforts. The sins of the mother were forever visited on the daughter.

An-Mei walked over to the painting of the dragon that hung on the wall. She stared at it with piercing black eyes, then turned those same eyes on Jasmine. "You take down. Hide away. Never speak of dragon again." Her heavily accented voice was sharp, pointed, definite. Despite the fact she'd lived in San Francisco for fifty-some years, An-Mei still spoke as if she'd only recently gotten off the boat. Her heart had never really left China.

"I saw it," Jasmine said somewhat defiantly. "I saw the dragon. It's real."

"You are a liar. You make up stories."

"I'm not lying. I saw the dragon." She watched her mother closely, seeing something in her eyes that looked like fear.

"You see nothing. You are a bad girl."

"I'm not a girl. I'm a middle-aged woman with a grown child of my own. When are you going to realize that?"

"You send Alyssa to see your father. She make him worry about dragon. She tell him you in trouble. Mixed up in Hathaway robbery."

"I'm not in trouble. But David Hathaway did show me a dragon statue that was taken from him later that evening. Someone else must have wanted it very badly." Jasmine paused, seeing the pulse beating rapidly in her mother's neck. An-Mei knew something about the dragon. But what? "I read a story about my dragon. I think there are two, and together they open a box," she continued.

An-Mei didn't blink, her gaze unwavering.

"I wonder if whoever took Mr. Hathaway's dragon has the other one."

"If you know of such a set, you know there is a curse. Your dreams come from the curse reaching out to touch you. You must not let it touch you. And you must not touch the dragon."

"I held it in my hands," Jasmine said with a shiver of uneasiness as she remembered the coolness of the bronze beneath her fingers.

"Where is Alyssa?"

"Alyssa? I don't know."

"You must find her. You must make sure she is safe."

"Why wouldn't she be safe?"

"The curse is on first daughters."

The words stabbed deep into her heart. So it was true, the story she and David had found. And something else was suddenly clear. "I'm a first daughter."

"Yes," An-Mei said, meeting her gaze. "And your dreams have cursed you, too."

"My dreams?" Jasmine echoed. "Or the dragon?"

"No more!" An-Mei shouted, her eyes blazing.

Jasmine took a step back, feeling suddenly afraid. But why did she fear her own mother? This small woman had cut her many times with unkind words, but she had never actually struck her. At least, she didn't think that had happened. Sometimes her childhood seemed like a vague, dull memory that never came into focus.

"The gods are watching," An-Mei said, her voice quieter now but still sharp.

Jasmine crossed her arms over her chest, fighting the impulse to look around and see if someone was watching. "Why can't you just tell me the truth? Did I see the dragon somewhere?"

An-Mei stared at her for a long moment. "Yes. You see the dragon at the museum in Taiwan when we went there on a trip. I tell you don't touch, but you do. Bells go off. Guards come running. Lee almost go to jail. You touched it, and you were cursed."

Jasmine stared at her mother in confusion. The story sounded convincing, but it was so innocent, so bland. Why hadn't they told her before where she'd seen the dragon? Why pretend it didn't exist, that it was only in her dreams? Was her mother lying?

It seemed an impossible thought. An-Mei had punished each of her children for every small lie she had caught them in. She believed that lies told eventually came back and stabbed you in the heart. In fact, she thought heart attacks were caused by too many lies. When her husband had had his attack, An-Mei had prayed for forgiveness every minute of every hour until his heart was beating strongly again. Which made Jasmine wonder something else. What were the lies her father had told?

"Please," An-Mei said. "No more, Jasmine. No more talk of dragons. Stop now, before it is too late."

Jasmine had the terrible feeling it was already too late for her. But maybe not for Alyssa. She had to find her daughter. She had to make sure Alyssa stayed away from the dragon before she, too, was forever cursed.

Chapter Fifteen

"Alyssa, come in," Ben said, as he opened the door to his apartment. "You're right on time. Can I take your coat?"

Alyssa was tempted to hang on to her coat so she wouldn't get too comfortable, wouldn't let down her guard, but it was warm in the apartment, so she took off her suede jacket and handed it to Ben. Underneath she wore a red knit sweater and a pair of black pants.

"Nice sweater," he said approvingly. "At least you haven't shunned red."

"Why would I? The Chinese don't have a monopoly on the color."

He smiled at her. "It's still considered lucky, you know."

"I look good in red. Don't read anything more into it than that."

"You do look good." He hung up her coat in the closet. "Joey is out for the evening, so make yourself comfortable."

"You still live with your brothers?"

"Henry lives in Seattle, but Joey lives here. He has a night class. So it's just you and me."

"Great," she murmured warily. A few minutes with Ben had reminded her of why she had avoided him all these years. He was too attractive, too likeable. And he had a way of seeing into her head that made her feel uncomfortable. Besides that, he reminded her of the past and a lifestyle she'd rather forget. Even now, looking around his apartment, she saw all the signs of a traditional Chinese family getting ready for the upcoming New Year's celebrations. There were fresh flowers everywhere as well as a platter of oranges and tangerines and a candy tray that she was sure was filled with eight varieties of dried sweet fruit.

"My mother," Ben said quickly, following her gaze. "She brings flowers and fruit every day. I tell her we have more than enough, but she won't stop. She wants to make sure we have good fortune in the New Year. Would you like a drink?"

"Absolutely," she said with a fervor that made him laugh.

"I take it that means alcoholic."

"If you have anything like that -- wine, beer?"

"I'll get you some wine."

"Thanks." While he was getting her a drink, she looked around his apartment. The furniture was mostly old and comfortable. Nothing really matched, and it was clear that it was a male-dominated room, no traces of female sentiment anywhere in sight. Three tall bookcases overflowed with books, and she moved closer to take a look at the titles. "Have you read all of these?" she asked, taking the glass of wine from Ben's hand when he returned to the room.

"Most of them."

She pulled one out of the stack. "The History of Porcelain. That looks fascinating."

"It is, if you like porcelain." He tipped his head toward the couch. "Sit down. Tell me what you've been doing with your life since you moved away from Chinatown."

"Getting a college degree, a job, an apartment. I live in Noe Valley with three girls I went to school with," she said, taking a seat.

"Sounds good. I heard you graduated from Berkeley with a four-point GPA."

"Who told you that?"

"Someone in the neighborhood."

"I can't imagine how they'd know." She didn't keep in touch with any of the kids she'd grown up with, just a few of her cousins, and that was because they insisted on keeping up with her.

"How's your mother? I haven't seen her in a while." He sat down in a chair facing her.

"She's all right, I guess." Alyssa set her glass of wine on the coffee table between them. She had the sudden urge to tell Ben everything that had happened, which was unusual. She always kept her thoughts private. It was easy to keep quiet with her other friends, none of whom were Asian, because they wouldn't understand the way her family operated. But Ben wouldn't need long explanations. He'd seen firsthand how she and her mother had been treated by the rest of the Chen family.

"Alyssa?" His gentle voice called her back to the present.

"Sorry. I was just thinking."

"Want to talk about it?"

She looked into his kind eyes and knew she could trust him. "My mother might be in some trouble. David

Hathaway brought that dragon statue to my mother's apartment the day he was assaulted. The police came to visit her. They asked all kinds of questions about where she was, and why he was there, and where he was going when he left. But she couldn't tell them anything, because she didn't know."

"Why would David Hathaway visit your mother?" Ben asked curiously.

"He purchased several of her paintings in the past."

"Right. I forgot about that. Is that how you know Paige?"

She hesitated, tempted to share it all, but in the end her guard came back up. "Yes."

"Now, tell me again why he took the dragon to your mother. Surely that didn't have anything to do with her painting?"

Damn, he was too smart. She should have remembered how quick his mind was. She cleared her throat, stalling. "Actually, my mother painted a dragon that looks exactly like the one he found. That's why he wanted to show it to her. And that's why I'm interested in finding out more about it. You said you'd research it for me. Did you find out anything?"

"Are you going to run out the door as soon as I give you my answer? I've worked very hard on dinner."

"Of course I won't run out the door. That would be rude."

"I did make Chinese food. Still sure you'll stay?"

"Yes," she said, seeing the challenge in his eyes. "I know you think I'm wrong to feel the way I do, but I wasn't raised to be proud of who I am. I was raised to be ashamed of my mixed blood."

"You can't run away from who you are, Alyssa."

"My God, Ben, you think I don't know that? I've

spent half my life wishing I could wake up in a different body and be someone else."

"You shouldn't feel that way. I hate that your family made you think you were unworthy. It was wrong."

"Well, I don't think they'll agree with you. But it doesn't matter anymore. I have a good life away from here. And I'm never coming back."

"I know," he said softly, meeting her gaze. "I figured out a long time ago that you probably hated Chinatown more than me, but it was easier to get rid of us both."

His words reminded her of how much there was between them. "Maybe this wasn't a good idea," she said.

"I want you to stay for dinner."

"I don't want to discuss the past, Ben. There's no point. We broke up a long time ago."

"You broke up with me."

"You would have done it eventually, if I hadn't. We want different things out of life."

"We used to want each other," he reminded her. "I don't think that desire is gone. I felt it the moment you walked into my office this afternoon."

She swallowed hard at the look in his eyes. "Ben, I only came here to discuss the dragon. If that's not going to happen, I should leave."

"It will happen. I made you a promise, and I'll keep it. As for the rest, we'll see how it goes. Now stay here, drink your wine, and let me show you what a good cook I am. I've got some appetizers you will love."

And if she stayed too long, she'd fall in love with more than his appetizers. He was right. The desire was still there, maybe even stronger than before. When had he become so good-looking, so grown-up, so manly? Why was she feeling such a strong attraction to him? They should have felt comfortable around each other, like two old shoes, not tense and nervous and on edge. She picked up her glass of wine and took a long sip, willing herself to relax. This was just Ben. This was just dinner. Nothing was going to happen.

"So, what have you been doing with your life?" Alyssa asked a while later as they finished the incredible dinner Ben had prepared. She was feeling calmer now that she had a full stomach. She rested her arms on the dining room table and smiled at him. "Are you happy writing only for the Chinese audience? Is that enough for you?"

"Probably not," he said, surprising her.

"Really?"

"You're not the only one with ambition, Alyssa. I'd like to work for one of the bigger metropolitan newspapers, or maybe an arts magazine "

"That might mean moving away from Chinatown."

"It's not a ball and chain around my leg. I could leave -- if I had a good reason." He paused. "I like your hair. I'm glad you left it long."

"It's too thin and too straight."

"It's perfect. You're perfect."

"I'm not," she said with a shake of her head.

"I wish you could see yourself the way I see you."

Alyssa got to her feet, suddenly restless under his intense gaze. She walked over to a desk that held a computer and more books. "What's all this?"

"Research on your dragon." He came up behind her. "I found out that the set I told you about was discovered in an archaeological dig in southern China in the early 1900s. The pieces were sent to China's National Palace Museum, but at some point they were lost."

"From a museum? That sounds odd."

"There was a lot of turmoil and war in China. Many artifacts were lost."

"My mother only saw one dragon. She didn't see a box or another dragon."

"It's not surprising that the pieces have been separated. It would probably be more shocking if they were still together."

"True." She picked up a pile of newspaper clippings. "What are these?"

"I'm doing a story on the Chinese New Year celebrations in San Francisco, a composite look at the traditions. My cousin Fae is going to be Miss Chinatown this year."

"That's great. She must be excited."

"She is, because she's the third generation." He flipped through the photos on the desk. "Here's the one of her mother getting crowned, and here's the one of her grandmother."

Alyssa looked at the photos. The Miss Chinatown Pageant was a very big deal. When she was a young girl, she'd even had thoughts of trying out for it herself. Until she was reminded that only a pure Chinese girl could win.

"See anyone familiar in this picture?" Ben asked her, pointing to the one of Fae's grandmother. It had been taken at the party after the pageant, and there were a number of people in the picture, but none really jumped out at her. Although...

"Is that my grandfather?" she asked in astonishment, recognizing the familiar profile.

"Yes, and he's talking to Wallace Hathaway. David Hathaway's father."

And her grandfather.

A shiver ran down her spine at the connection.

"Hathaway was probably the Master of Ceremonies for the pageant," Ben continued. "They usually had someone from the city council or chamber of commerce announce the winner."

"I had no idea they'd ever met," she murmured. These two men, who had shaken hands some fifty years ago, were her grandfathers.

"It's a small world," Ben commented.

"Yes," she agreed. And it was getting smaller by the moment.

Riley set his grandfather's armchair back into its upright position and adjusted the cushions. He looked around at the living room his grandmother had always kept so neat and wondered if it would ever look that way again. Whoever had ransacked her house had been hastily and ruthlessly brutal in their search. Obviously time had been a factor. There was also a sense of purpose. This hadn't been a random burglary. It didn't appear that anything had been taken.

He moved over to the end table, staring down at the piles and piles of photographs that had been dumped out of the box his grandmother kept them in. It had been a family joke for years that Nan was not a photo-album kind of person. She'd been talking about organizing the photos of her life for as long as he'd been alive, but here they were, a mass of black and white and color photographs from a lifetime of living.

He sighed. He wished he could just hire a cleaning service to come in and tackle this mess, but his grandmother had already told him that she didn't want any more strangers in the house. She'd do it herself tomorrow, and that would be fine, but he couldn't let her face this.

His cell phone rang, and he answered. "Yes?"

"There's a beautiful blonde casing the house,"

Gilbert, one of his security guards, told him. "She's been standing on the sidewalk for almost five minutes. You want me to talk to her?"

"No, I think I know who it is," he said, feeling an unexpected jolt at the information.

"She's walking up to the door now."

"I've got it, thanks."

Riley slipped his phone back in his pocket and went to open the front door. Paige was in the process of reaching for the doorbell. "Looking for me?" he asked, surprised and pleased to see her. He'd spent most of the day with her, but he'd missed her the past few hours. Damn, not a feeling he wanted to examine too closely.

"How did you know I was out here?" Paige asked.

"I have a sixth sense."

Her gaze narrowed speculatively. "You have an undercover guy sitting in a car at the corner."

He grinned at her. "Very good, Miss Hathaway. He said you were stalling. Why?"

"I was having second and third thoughts. Can I come in?"

Riley held the door open for her. "It's a mess, I warn you."

Paige walked into the room, her eyes widening as she took in the destruction. "My goodness. When most people say their house is a mess, it's usually spotlessly clean. But this really is a mess."

"They did quite a job. Take a look." He led her around the downstairs, showing her the living room, dining room, and kitchen, where they had to step over pots and pans to get to the back stairs. The upstairs was just as bad. The bedding had been tossed off all the beds, the drawers upended, items pulled off the shelves.

"Oh, Riley." Paige shook her head at the sight of his

grandmother's bedroom. "Whoever did this was very serious."

"I know. You live in a secure building but you should be careful, Paige. Until your father can tell us what happened, we need to be cautious."

Paige's face lightened at his words. "That's what I came to tell you. My father is awake."

"That's great. How is he?"

"He's okay, I think. But he doesn't remember what happened this week at all. He only spoke for a few minutes, and he seems to have lost a few weeks. I asked him about the dragon, but he didn't know what I was talking about. The doctor said it's not unusual for there to be short-term memory loss."

"Probably not, but it's damned inconvenient," Riley grumbled. He couldn't help wondering if David really couldn't remember or if this was just another trick, but in light of Paige's happiness at her father being awake, he decided to keep that thought to himself.

"Everything seems so much better now," she said. "I know we don't have the dragon back yet, but I feel as if we're getting closer. As soon as my dad can tell us why he went to Chinatown, we'll have an idea of who is behind all this."

Her smile took his breath away. He liked the optimism in her voice. She reminded him of his grandmother in that way, always wanting to see the best, the potential, the possibilities. Meanwhile his brain was spinning with the complications. "Your father may not be safe," he began.

"My mother is hiring a security guard."

"That's good. We don't want anyone to take another shot at your father."

"My mother will make sure that doesn't happen. She

knows how to protect what's hers." She paused. "Anyway, why don't I help you clean up? That's what you came here to do, right?"

"Surely Hathaways don't clean."

Her brown eyes sparkled. "Not usually, no. But I think I can stumble my way through the process. Besides, I've seen your apartment, and I don't think you're exactly an expert."

"You don't have anything better to do with your Friday night? No hot date with Marty?"

"Martin."

"Whatever. How come you're not out with him?"

"He didn't ask."

"Are you one of those girls who must be called by Wednesday for a Friday date?"

"Monday or Tuesday at the latest. What about you? Are you one of those guys who calls at four o'clock on Friday and says, " 'Hey, babe, want to hang out tonight?' "

"What's wrong with that?"

"No finesse. No style." She walked into Nan's room and picked up one of the drawers from the floor. She set it on the bed and began folding his grandmother's shirts and shorts.

Riley watched her from the doorway. Once again her behavior was surprising him. She should have been out celebrating her father's awakening with her fancy friends in a fancy restaurant. Instead she'd come here -- to him. That thought was more than a little disturbing. What was she doing here? What did she want?

"Are you going to help?" She cast him a curious look. "Or are you going to stand there and stare at me?"

"I haven't decided yet."

Paige finished with one drawer and returned it to the dresser. "You probably don't want to go through your grandmother's underwear, do you? I can understand that women's lingerie would make you a little uncomfortable."

"My grandmother's underwear definitely makes me uncomfortable," he said with a smile. "Women's lingerie is another story entirely."

"I'll bet. Red teddies and black garter belts, right?"

"I keep an open mind. And I don't discriminate."

She rolled her eyes. "I'm sure you don't. Do you have a woman in your life right now?"

"Yeah, an irritating, nosy blonde who asks a lot of questions."

Paige finished with another drawer. "Help me get the bed together," she said, ignoring his comment. "Maybe we should wash the sheets. I bet your grandmother would feel better if everything was cleaned."

"She is a big believer in clean sheets. I had to strip my bed every Saturday morning like clockwork. For the first fourteen years of my life, I was lucky to sleep on any kind of sheets. Sleeping bags and old blankets were more the norm." He was sorry he'd mentioned it when he saw the pity come into her eyes. "It was like camping. It was fun," he added, not wanting her to feel bad for him

"It was wrong. Every child deserves at least the basics -- food, shelter, clothes, security."

"That requires money. I don't expect you to understand."

Paige tossed the bedding in a pile on the floor, leaving the mattress bare. "You always bring up money. You always point out how different we are. It's as if you want to make sure I know there's a line between us that we can't cross."

She was right. He was drawing a line between them, because right now, alone in a bedroom with a bed only a few feet away, it would be easy to forget there was anything to keep them apart. Her flowery scent was tantalizing, her brown eyes beckoning with the fire of challenge in them. And her body. Hell, he'd have to be a saint not to notice the curve of her breasts through her silk blouse or the shapely ass encased in a pair of black pants. She was quite a package, and he was dying to unwrap her.

"Well? Nothing to say?" she asked.

"You seem to be talking enough for both of us."

"Show me your room, Riley."

"I haven't lived here in a long time."

"Show me where you slept when you did live here."

It was another dare; he could see it in her eyes. She wanted to get to know him better, to get inside his head. And he wanted to get inside her body. Two distinctly opposing goals. Although they didn't have to be, if he gave her what she wanted ..

He turned and walked down the hall to his old bedroom. It had been his mother's room when she was a girl, but there was no sign now that any female had ever lived here. Now the room housed a full-sized bed with a blue bedspread, a simple oak dresser and matching desk where he'd once done his homework. There were a few items from childhood in the room, the model airplanes he'd made when he'd dreamed of being a pilot and flying away from it all, the posters of football players that had never quite come down. Now he was almost embarrassed to see them.

"Did you make these?" Paige asked, pointing to one of the airplanes.

"Yeah." He picked up the globe and the stand that his grandfather had given him. It had been knocked over during the burglary.

"You like to fly."

"I do. I like looking down on the world. How about

you?"

"I love flying, especially takeoff, when you're speeding down the runway and the plane is shaking and suddenly you're up and away. It's a wonderful feeling."

He frowned, hating the way she'd echoed his own feelings. He didn't want to have anything in common with her. "I'm sure it's a better experience in first class than in coach."

She groaned. "Oh, my God, Riley, would you knock it off? You may have grown up poor, but you're not poor anymore."

"How do you know?"

"Because I know. There's nothing wrong with this house, either. It's nice, comfortable, a lot warmer than the one I grew up in."

She sat down on the bed, which was disheveled but intact. Apparently, their uninvited guest had done only a cursory run through this room. Probably because there wasn't much in it. Riley swallowed hard as Paige did a little bounce on the bed. His bed. His teenage bed. The bed he'd dreamed of sharing with a beautiful, sexy blonde like Paige.

"This is much softer than mine was," she told him. "My mother believes a firm mattress keeps the posture straight and the body supported. It's also extremely uncomfortable. I used to pile extra blankets on the mattress and sleep on top of them. Now, of course, I have a nice soft mattress, like this." She laid back on the bed, her legs dangling off the end. "Look, you have the universe on your ceiling. That is so cool."

He glanced up at the ceiling, which his grandfather had painted like a nighttime sky, a dark blue with twinkling gold stars. "My grandpa got tired of me climbing up on the roof. When my mom would leave, I'd go up there to watch for her. Then I started stargazing."

"What's that one?" She pointed to the ceiling.

"Orion. Get up, Paige."

"What's the problem?" She sat up halfway, resting on her elbows.

"I want you out of my bed." He could have bit his tongue at the way that came out, but he was fighting an overwhelming feeling of lust at the moment, and it was that or jump on top of her and show her just how much the bed could bounce.

"Sorry," Paige said hastily as she scrambled off with a hurt look on her face.

He caught her by the arm. "That's not what I meant."

"You were pretty clear."

He gazed into her face and knew he couldn't look away, couldn't walk away, couldn't make her go away.

"Riley," she whispered, "let me go."

"I can't." He leaned over and covered her mouth with his. She tasted sweet, sinful, sexy, sophisticated. It was a heady combination and completely irresistible, especially when she moved into his body, when her breasts came into contact with his chest, when her hands crept around his waist. She should have been resisting, pushing him away, not kissing him back like she didn't want to stop. And when he slipped his tongue into her mouth, she absolutely should not have met him halfway. Nor should she have made that lusty little gasp of desire that he wanted to hear again and again.

"Riley, I need to breathe," she murmured against his mouth.

He played his lips across her face, her neck, the curve of her shoulder. He moved behind her and used his hands to memorize her body, from her slim waist to her soft breasts. He rolled his palm over one breast, feeling the nipple tighten beneath his fingers. It was too much of an invitation to resist. He slipped his hand inside the V neck of her blouse, into her lacy bra so he could touch her bare skin, feel the heat rising between them. He used his other hand to bring her bottom flush against his groin, where he was hard as a rock.

There was that little gasp of desire again. It made him crazy.

His name rolled off her lips like a plea for more. And he intended to give her more, much more. He turned her to face him again, backed her up against the bed until the backs of her knees hit the mattress, and they both went down. He landed on top of her, exactly where he wanted to be, and found her mouth again. He wrestled with the buttons on her blouse, one, two, three. Finally, he had them undone, and as he pulled open her shirt, he broke away from her mouth to gaze down at her. Her beautiful breasts were rising up and down, her nipples peaking through the sheer lacy cups. God, he was in heaven.

He leaned over and pushed her bra aside, putting his mouth to her breast, rolling his tongue around her nipple until she groaned. But she didn't push him away; she put her hand around the back of his neck and pressed him closer.

"Don't stop," she whispered. "Don't stop."

"I won't," he promised. But the words had barely left his mouth when the sound of a door slamming penetrated his foggy brain.

A voice came from down below. "Riley? Riley, are you here?"

Paige shoved him off, panic in her eyes. "Is that your grandmother?"

"Riley?" Nan called out again.

"Oh, my God. She can't see us like this," Paige said.

Riley sat back in a daze, watching as Paige fumbled with the buttons of her shirt. She looked incredible, with her blond hair tangled from his fingers, her lips red from his kisses, her breasts moist from his tongue. He knew he needed to move, get up, go to the door, tell his grandmother he'd be right down, but all he could do was look at Paige and wish to hell they could go back to doing what they had been doing.

"Riley, help me," Paige begged as they heard footsteps on the stairs.

He finally got his brain to function. "I'll head her off." He got off the bed and took a deep breath, willing the rest of his body to cooperate. His grandmother might be in her seventies, but her eyesight was still perfect.

"I'll be right there, Grandma," he yelled. He gave Paige a rueful smile. "She always did have bad timing. I'll get rid of her."

"How are you going to do that?"

"I don't know."

"Don't tell her I'm here."

"I wasn't planning on it." He walked out of his bedroom and took care to close the door behind him. He found Nan in her room, staring at the mess.

"It's worse than I remembered." She walked over to the dresser and set up the photo of herself and Ned at their fortieth anniversary party. "That's better."

Riley's heart began to slow down as he realized his grandmother's distraction was definitely to his benefit. "What are you doing here? I thought you were staying at Millie's."

"I needed my robe. I forgot to get it earlier. I saw your car so I figured it would be all right to come in. Plus, I saw Gilbert sitting in his car at the corner, so I know I'm safe. You hired those old boys to watch over me, didn't you?"

"Yes," he admitted, still feeling a bit uncomfortable when she turned her gaze on him.

She stared at him for a long minute, and he wondered what she was seeing. Did he have lipstick on his face? Was his hair as messy as Paige's? He distinctly remembered feeling her fingers run through his hair.

"What's wrong?" she asked him.

"Nothing."

"You look -- funny."

"It must be all the dust I've been stirring up."

"Must be."

"There's your robe." He grabbed it off the chair in front of her dressing table. "This is your favorite one, isn't it?"

"Yes, it keeps me warm." She gave him another long look. "I guess I'll go back to Millie's, unless you want me to stay and help."

"No. You take the night off. There will be plenty to do tomorrow."

"Are you going to sleep here tonight, honey?"

Sleep was the last thing he had on his mind. "I don't know yet. I'll see how late it gets."

"If you are, you should change the sheets on your bed. I have extras in the hall closet. Why don't I help you do that before I go?"

"No," he said abruptly. "I mean, I already did it. So you can just go back to Millie's."

"You already did it? I must have taught you something after all." She smiled at that. "Well, don't work too hard."

He followed her down the stairs, praying she wouldn't suddenly stop and decide she needed to get something else. But they made it to the front door without a hitch.

"I'll watch you walk next door," he said.

"You always take good care of me, Riley."

"That's my job."

She stood on her tiptoes and gave him a kiss on the cheek. "Good night, honey." She walked down the steps, then paused. "By the way, tell Paige I said hello." Her knowing grin made him feel fourteen years old again. "I hope you didn't make her hide in the closet like you did Jenny Markson."

"Paige is definitely not in the closet," he replied. Her laughter lasted all the way next door. When be shut the door, Paige was right behind him.

"I am totally embarrassed," Paige said. "She knew I was here the whole time."

"I never could get away with anything." He took a step toward her. "Now, where were we?"

She put a hand on the middle of his chest, holding him at arm's length. "Who is Jenny Markson?"

"She's not competition, if that's what you're worried about. I think she has a couple of kids by now, and at least one husband."

"Was she your girlfriend?"

"For about two weeks in the tenth grade."

"Did you make out in your bedroom?"

"We tried, but my grandmother came home early."

"So I wasn't the first." Paige crossed her arms in front of her chest, a sexy little pout on her face.

He grinned. "You were definitely not the first."

"Did you have sex with her?"

"Unfortunately, that bedroom has never been lucky for me in the sex department. I'm hoping tonight we can change my luck."

She dodged his oncoming embrace. "Are you kidding

me? Your grandmother knows I'm here. I can't possibly have sex with you in that bedroom tonight."

"The idea wasn't bothering you a few minutes ago."

"I went a little crazy," she admitted.

"I like you a little crazy." This time when he put his hands on her waist, she didn't move away. "Want to know what else I like?"

"I don't think so," she said breathlessly. "I should go home."

"I could come with you. Your bedroom would certainly be more private."

She hesitated, and he saw the answer in her eyes even before she said it. She'd had time to think -- too much time, apparently.

"You have a lot to do here," she said.

"It's not going anywhere."

"Riley--"

"The moment is over. I get it."

"It's not that I don't want to." She looked at him with her heart in her eyes, and he felt a rush of emotion as well as panic. What was he thinking? What was casual for him would probably not be casual for Paige. She wasn't a one-night-stand or a three-day-fling kind of girl. She was marriage and children and happily ever after, and he'd given up on that a long time ago.

"Fine. Whatever," he said.

"It's just more difficult to make the choice than to simply let it happen, you know? I guess that makes me a coward."

"Or smart."

"I don't feel smart. I feel... frustrated."

"That makes two of us. You should go."

"I want to help you with the cleaning."

"Why?"

"Because I do, and because, dammit, I don't want to go home yet. Is that the deal, if I don't sleep with you, I have to leave?"

He smiled at her obvious annoyance. "That's usually how it works."

"That's not the way it works with me. But to be on the safe side, we'll clean down here." She entered the living room. "Has this room been lucky for you?"

"Nope."

"Good."

He laughed. "Not so good for me."

She knelt down next to the pile of photographs on the floor. "This is quite a mess. Your grandmother sure has a lot of pictures."

"My grandmother has been talking about putting those in photo albums since I was a kid. She just never gets around to it."

"Is this you?" She held up a baby picture.

He squatted down beside her, his chest tightening. "No, that's my mother."

"Oh, I'm sorry. I should have guessed." She picked up more pictures of his mother at various stages of her life. Riley didn't want to look. He tried not to remember his mother at all. He certainly didn't want a visual reminder. But as Paige went through them, he found himself looking over her shoulder. His stomach clenched at the one in her hand. His mother was holding him in her lap at what was probably his third Christmas. She was trying to hand him a doll, but he was pushing it away.

"Now, I know this is you." Paige looked at him with tenderness in her eyes. "I recognize the scowl."

"I wanted a fire truck. Not that stupid rag doll."

"Oh, this is you, too." She pulled out a photo his grandmother had taken at his junior high school graduation. "There's that scowl again. Do you ever smile for the camera?"

"I didn't see any point in recording those moments in my life." He paused, remembering that day. He'd only been at his grandmother's house since that Christmas. He'd transferred into yet another school to finish up the eighth grade. His mother was supposed to be at the graduation, but she'd gone off on a weekend retreat that had lasted six months. That's when his grandparents had told him he would be living with them from now on.

"Aren't there any of those naked baby pictures in here? I'd like to see your bare ass on a blanket," Paige said, lightening his mood.

"I'd be happy to show it to you. It's much more impressive now than it was then."

Her brown eyes sparkled at him. "So you say." She picked up another photograph. "This must be your grandparents at their wedding."

"You're really going back in time now As I said, my grandmother never organized any of these. She always said she was too busy living life to look at it."

"That sounds nice." Paige let out a sigh. "There are six photo albums of my life to date, every minor or major event captured on film for generations to see."

"Who was the photographer? Your mother or your father?"

"They usually hired photographers."

"Of course. My mistake."

"They were at my kindergarten graduation and all the other school graduations to follow, birthday parties, Christmas, holiday events, and of course the off-the-shoulder drape portrait for my debutante ball."

"Poor little rich girl. My heart is bleeding."

She tossed the pictures at him. "Then you can clean

these up."

"Fine with me." He swept them into a pile, then stopped. The photograph in front of him was an old black-and-white taken in San Francisco. It was the sign in the background that made him pause. "Look at this."

Paige peered over his shoulder. "That's my store," she said in wonder. "That must have been taken years ago. Look at the car."

"I was looking at the men in front of the store." Riley pointed to a man wearing a security uniform. "That's my grandfather. Do you happen to know who he's shaking hands with?"

"Oh, my God. I certainly do. That's my grandfather, Wallace Hathaway."

Their eyes met as they both came to the same conclusion.

"My grandfather must have worked for Hathaway's," Riley said.

"It sure looks that way. And he obviously knew my grandfather. It's quite a coincidence, isn't it?"

"I've never believed in coincidences." Riley felt sick to his stomach. He glanced over at Paige. "Have you spoken to your grandfather about the dragon?"

She shook her head. "No."

"I think it's time you did."

Chapter Sixteen

The store clerks chatting behind a counter stopped the instant they saw him. Good, but not good enough, Wallace thought. They shouldn't have been wasting time in the first place. Their business was to serve the public, not to entertain each other. He stopped in front of the counter, eyeing the name tag on the younger woman, Megan.

"May I help you, Mr. Hathaway?" she asked nervously, sending a pleading look to her cohort, a man who quickly busied himself with the countertop display.

"What time do you begin work?" he asked. "Ten o'clock."

"What time is it now?"

"Ten thirty."

"Exactly. I assume your duties do not include pointless conversation with other store clerks?"

"No, sir. But there aren't any customers right now."

"Whether there are customers present or not does not mean you should shirk your duties. Am I clear?"

"Yes. It won't happen again."

"See that it doesn't." He strode briskly away. Now that his presence had been noted in the store, everyone got busy. He walked down the aisles, surveying the displays, making mental notes that he would later dictate to his secretary. He made the same inspection on each subsequent floor, stopping at times to speak to the department managers. Some had been at the store for decades, but he didn't allow any friendliness to creep into his voice. There was a line between them. He liked it that way. He trusted no one, not even those who reported to him on a daily basis. They served a purpose, but that was the extent of the relationship.

As he headed toward the executive offices, he couldn't help but worry about what would happen to Hathaway's when he was gone. Paige needed to step up to the plate. Maybe she didn't have it in her. He hated the thought of his store going into anyone else's hands, including Victoria's, but he had to admit that so far his granddaughter was a dismal failure as an only heir.

"Is my grandfather coming in today?" Paige asked, when her grandfather's secretary answered the phone. Although it was Saturday, she expected him to make an appearance. Saturday seemed to be his favorite day for checking up on employees, especially her mother. Victoria acted as if she didn't care and made a point of not coming to work on the weekends, but Paige suspected her mother made sure there was nothing out of order for Wallace to find.

"I expect him any minute," replied Georgia Markham, her grandfather's longtime secretary who always worked on Saturday. "Would you like an appointment?"

"Yes. I mean no. Well, maybe."

"Which is it, dear?"

"I'll check back with you in a few minutes. I'm not sure about my schedule yet." Paige hung up the phone, feeling like a big fat chicken. The man was her grandfather, for heaven's sake. There was no reason to be intimidated by him. Unfortunately, logic did little to dispel the nervous butterflies in her stomach.

Well, it could wait a few more minutes. While she was stalling, she decided to tie up some of the final arrangements for the grand opening party of the Hathaway exhibit at the Asian Art Museum, now only two short weeks away. She updated the response list, reviewed the catering, floral, and photography arrangements, and took another look at the budget. Everything was as it should be. In fact, her assistant had done most of the work, reminding Paige that she wasn't all that vital to the success of the company.

Paige looked up as a knock sounded at the door. "Come in," she called.

Martin walked into the office, dressed in his usual Armani business suit. "Hello, Paige. It's good to see you back at work and things returning to normal. I just came from the hospital. Your father looks well."

"Yes, he does. I stopped in early this morning and caught him having his first real meal in a while. Of course, he complained about the eggs and the toast and the fact that there was no bacon. But he seemed in good spirits."

She got to her feet as Martin walked around the desk to offer her a hug and a kiss on the cheek. His touch did absolutely nothing to raise her blood pressure, and she couldn't help thinking about the night before when she'd had a meltdown in Riley's arms. At least one truth had come out of this past week. She didn't feel enough passion for Martin to even consider marrying him. It wouldn't be fair to either one of them.

"How are you doing?" he asked.

"I'm fine. Catching up."

"I'm happy to see you concentrating on work instead of pursuing that dragon."

"It needs to be pursued. We still don't know what happened to it. My father's short-term memory is apparently absent at the moment"

"That's what I hear."

She didn't like the doubt in his voice. "You don't believe him?" She paused, tilting her head to one side. "You don't really like my father, do you?"

"Don't be ridiculous. I have a great deal of respect for him."

The words were right, but the lack of emotion in his voice told Paige that Martin wasn't being completely honest with her. "You already suggested to me that my father might have been looking into commissioning a fake. There's no point in backtracking now."

"That was a mistake on my part. I realize your father would never do such a thing. As for the dragon, our security people are investigating it, Paige. You don't need to do it personally. In fact, your mother and I both agree that it would be better if you stayed out of it. Your father has already been hurt. We certainly don't want you in the line of fire. Your mother tells me that the Delaney woman's house was broken into as well. Another sign that you should leave this to the experts. This is not the job for you."

She couldn't stand his patronizing tone, never mind the fact that he glossed over the words with a smile. "I don't think it's up to you, Martin, to decide what job is right for me."

"I didn't mean to offend."

"But you did."

"Paige, you're misreading me."

"I don't think I am. I realize you have an important job here at the store, that Mother considers you her right-hand man. But I'm the Hathaway heir, not you."

He looked shocked by her words, and she had to admit she had surprised herself by speaking so bluntly. Maybe Riley had rubbed off on her.

"I didn't mean to overstep--" he said.

"You did overstep. It is obvious that as far as you're concerned, I'm pretty much good for planning parties and nothing else, but you're wrong. And so are my mother and my father and my grandfather and whoever else thinks that way. I intend to do more for this store than party planning."

"That's great," he said soothingly. "My point and concern were only for your safety. I wasn't criticizing your judgment."

"I appreciate that. Thank you."

He looked at her for a long moment. She refused to glance away, knowing that they had to get something else straight between them.

"You're not interested, are you?" he asked.

"I like you as a friend and a coworker."

He offered her a wry smile. "Not exactly what I was hoping to hear."

"I'm sorry, Martin. I realize I may have given you the wrong idea in the past, but I don't want to lead you on any further."

"We could be good together. We have so much in common. I feel as if you and I are a perfect match."

"Maybe on paper, but a marriage is real life. Quite frankly, I don't think you have any idea who I really am. I suspect I haven't seen the real you, either."

"I am what you see."

"I doubt that," she said with a softening smile. "You're going to make someone a great husband."

"But not you."

"Not me."

He tilted his head to one side, studying her thoughtfully. "You've been different this past week. Your father's brush with death sparked something in you."

"That was part of it," she conceded, not wanting to mention that the real spark had come from Riley. She liked Martin far too much to throw another man in his face.

"You've come alive." He nodded approvingly. "It looks good on you. And I don't think all you're capable of is party planning. I simply followed your lead, Paige. If you've been unhappy or feeling restricted, you should have said something. After all," he added with a smile, "you are the Hathaway heir, as you just reminded me."

"I guess that sounded a little high-handed, didn't it?"

"Actually, you sounded a lot like your mother."

"God forbid."

Martin laughed, and she realized in that moment that he wasn't at all disappointed that their relationship wasn't going to be more than friendship.

"You aren't upset about this, are you?" she asked.

"Don't get me wrong, Paige. I like you. However, I must admit I was feeling a little heat from our respective mothers. I've been so focused on my career the past few years that I hadn't given much thought to marriage and, well, you are pretty near perfect."

"Not even close."

"Let me know if you want to branch out into some other areas of the company," Martin said, as he opened her office door. "I'd be happy to explore the possibilities with you."

"Thanks. That's very generous of you."

Martin paused, his expression turning serious. "I do think you ought to stay out of this dragon business. Your father was almost killed. I don't want you to get hurt."

"I'll be careful, but I have to see it through. I have to know what happened, not just to Dad, but to the dragon. Mrs. Delaney put her trust in me, and I failed her. I want to make it right."

"To her or to her grandson?"

"To both. My family's reputation is on the line."

"And you are the Hathaway heir. Don't forget to remind your mother of that."

She made a face at him. "I don't think she'll take it as well as you did."

"I don't think she will, either."

"I have to talk to someone else first," she said. "My grandfather."

"Are you sure you want to climb that mountain?"

"I've been putting it off for far too long."

"Your grandfather knows everything that happens around here. He's uncanny that way."

"I suspect he has a few spies helping him out. Maybe even you," she added thoughtfully. "Hmm. I'm right, aren't I?"

"I'm a loyal employee, Paige. That's all I am."

As Martin left, Paige couldn't help wondering if that's really all he was. Her grandfather did seem to know everything that occurred in each nook and cranny of the store, and she knew he had to have help. Why not Martin? He'd risen through the ranks faster than anyone.

Not that it mattered. Whether he had a spy or not, her grandfather was the boss. He had a right know to what was going on in his own business. But she knew it was past time for her to find out exactly what he knew about the dragon. Picking up the phone, she dialed his secretary's extension.

"Hello, Georgia, it's Paige again. I would like to make an appointment to see my grandfather, as soon as possible."

"I'm sorry," Georgia replied, "but your grandfather has already left the store. Can I give him a message for you?"

"No, I'll catch up to him later," she said, hanging up the phone. Maybe it would be better to talk to him at home, anyway. There were too many eyes and ears at the store, and this was one piece of business she'd prefer to keep private.

Ned Delaney lived on the second floor of the Woodlake Assisted Living Center, a three-story building set in a quiet grove of trees on the western edge of San Francisco. Riley and his grandmother had chosen the center after looking at all the available options and had found this one to offer the most in terms of quality surroundings, care, and compassion. But it was still a depressing place, and Riley had to force a smile as he opened the door.

His grandfather sat in a chair by the bed, staring at the television set. There was a basketball game on, but whether he was actually watching it was debatable. Dressed in casual clothes, Ned looked normal, as if nothing was wrong with him. He'd always been a big man, taller than Riley's own six feet by another two inches. But his girth had diminished in the past few years, and now he was dangerously thin, Riley thought. Not like the man who used to chow down three hamburgers or a twenty-ounce steak at one sitting.

In fact, the man in the chair was nothing like the man who had taken him to task, made him clean up his act. His grandfather had once dragged him out of a pool hall where he'd gone to hustle money when he was fifteen. That Ned had been larger than life, an Irishman who talked loudly, gestured with every word, and knew how to tell great stories. Where had that man gone?

His body was still there, debilitated by various illnesses that came with old age, but still relatively stable. It was his mind that was off balance.

Maybe Riley would get lucky. There were times when his grandfather was coherent, when he remembered somebody or something. This could be one of those times. Damn, he was starting to sound like an optimist, a role better left to his grandmother or to Paige.

Ned's head turned as Riley entered the room, a good sign that he was alert.

"Hello, Grandpa." Riley deliberately used the title to help his grandfather remember.

"Who are you?" Ned asked, a somewhat belligerent note in his voice.

"I'm Riley, your grandson."

Ned narrowed his eyes suspiciously. "You're that guy who owes me twenty bucks. Did you come to pay up, or do you have another sob story?"

"I've come to pay up." Riley took his wallet out, removed a twenty-dollar bill, and handed it to Ned.

"What's this for?" Ned asked, already confused.

Riley shook his head and took the bill back. "You

okay? You got everything you need?"

"I'm cold. It's damn cold in here. Can't get no heat. They don't turn it on for me. They're cheap."

"How about a blanket?" Riley took a blanket off the edge of the bed and put it over his grandfather's legs. "I remember when you tucked me in that first night I came back to your house. You made sure the covers were real tight."

His grandfather looked at him with bemusement, his dark eyes suddenly clearing as if a cloud had passed. "Riley?"

"It's me." He squatted down next to the chair. "How's your grandmother? I haven't seen her in a long time. Is she still mad at me?"

"She's not mad at you. How could she be? You always make her laugh."

Ned grinned at that. "She was the prettiest thing I ever did see. I remember when I met her the first tune at a dance at the YMCA. She had beautiful legs. I loved those legs."

"Do you remember Wallace Hathaway?" Riley asked, knowing he had to take the shot while he had an opening.

"Is that you, Wally?" Ned's eyes changed once again as he tilted his head and studied Riley's face. "You hate when I call you Wally, don't you? Well, I don't care. I saved your sorry butt more than once, and what did you do? You turned on me, that's what you did."

"I didn't mean to," Riley said, trying to keep the conversation going.

"It wasn't right what you did, Wally. I thought we were brothers."

"I'm sorry about what happened."

"That was a hell of a crash. I can still hear the engines screaming as we went down, the treetops splitting off as we hit 'em. Hell of a ride. We were lucky he found us."

Was he still talking about Wallace Hathaway? Riley couldn't make sense of the rambling sentences.

"Do you remember working at Hathaway's store as a security guard?"

"Damn fire ruined everything. Nan doesn't know. Can't tell her. Want to tell her but can't tell her. She'd get mad." Ned grabbed Riley's sleeve. "You don't tell her, Wally."

"I won't," Riley promised as his grandfather grew more and more agitated.

"Where's Betty?"

"Betty? I don't know a Betty."

"Who are you?" Ned asked, lost again. His gaze drifted back to the television set, and he lapsed into silence.

Riley stared at him for a long moment, feeling incredibly depressed by the sight of his grandfather, once so vital, so strong, so important to him, fading away, adrift in a mind that raced from one subject to the next. At least his grandfather didn't know that he didn't know. That was a cold comfort, but it was all Riley had to hang on to..

"Riley? I didn't know you were coming here." Nan entered the room with a vase of fresh flowers in her hands. "You should have told me. We could have driven over together."

"I didn't know until this morning."

She leaned over and kissed Ned on the cheek. "Hi, honey. I love you."

Ned pulled away from her, his gaze focused on the television. Riley saw the hurt in her eyes and wished he could take the pain away. "He asked about you. Talked about your beautiful legs."

"He did? Really?"

"Yes. He was sort of clear for a couple of minutes."

"Did you come here to ask him about the hang-up calls, about whether he was trying to call the house?" Nan asked.

"I didn't get a chance. I think the hang-up calls were someone casing the house, to see if you were home or not. The next thing we need to do is get you an unlisted number."

"If you do that, I'll start to feel invisible. It's bad enough getting old. I don't want to disappear, too."

"That could never happen."

"Did your grandpa say anything else?" Nan asked.

"I asked him about Wallace Hathaway, Paige's grandfather. When I was going through your photos, I saw a picture of Grandpa in a security uniform posing in front of Hathaway's store with Wallace Hathaway."

"I don't remember a picture like that. But I hardly ever look at those old photos."

"Grandpa must have worked at the store."

"Well, yes, he did, when we were first married. Didn't I tell you that?"

"No, you didn't."

"It was a long time ago. And he worked at so many stores in those early days; I could hardly keep track. I was too busy having a baby and making a home."

"Did you ever meet Wallace Hathaway?"

"Good heavens, no. I would have remembered that, Riley. He's quite famous in San Francisco. But your grandfather was a security guard. He didn't spend time with the Hathaways."

"Grandpa mentioned someone named Wally. Did you ever hear him talk about a Wally?"

She pondered that. "I know your grandfather flew with someone named Wally in the war. I don't think it was

Wallace Hathaway, though. He talked about Wally like he was a friend. If Wallace Hathaway was Wally, I think he would have mentioned that to me at some point."

"You're right. Wally is probably somebody completely different. I doubt a Hathaway would ever let himself be called Wally."

She smiled. "How was your evening with Paige'?"

"Too short."

"I'm sorry I interrupted."

"It was probably for the best." He glanced over at his grandfather, whose eyes had drifted shut. "Looks like he's going to sleep for a while."

She nodded. "I'll just leave the flowers and hope they cheer him up."

"I'll walk you to your car."

"Good-bye, Ned," she said quietly and kissed him on the cheek once again.

Riley drew in a sharp breath of air, feeling as if he'd been punched in the stomach. The look in her eyes when she gazed at her husband just about undid him. The only real love he'd ever seen in his life had been between these two people. Even now, it was still there, at least on his grandmother's part.

"He squeezed my hand," she said, her eyes bright, drawing Riley's gaze down to their hands clasped together. "I think he knows it's me."

"I'm sure he does."

"I feel better. I can go now." She squeezed Ned's hand again. "I'll be back soon."

Riley was glad she didn't say anything as they left the room. He didn't know why he felt so choked up. He'd come here before. He'd seen how bad it was. He knew it wasn't going to get better. So why was it still getting to him?

Paige, he thought with annoyance. It was her fault. He'd been living a nice emotion-free existence up until a few days ago. She'd knocked down some of his walls, and he needed to get them back up fast. He didn't want to feel like this, like there was a pain in his heart. He didn't even want to admit he had a heart or that it could break again.

"I'm going back to clean the house," Nan said when they reached her car, parked just a few spots down from his own. "You made a good start on putting things right. I can finish the rest."

"I'll come stay with you tonight."

"No. I'm a big girl, and I have my watchdogs out in front. In fact, I told Bud he could stay on my sofa tonight instead of the car. He'll be more comfortable there, and I'll have someone right in the house."

"Someone who is seventy-four years old. I'm not sure what good he'll do inside. At least out front, he can call 911 if he sees anything."

"I trust Bud. And I'll put on the alarm so you don't have to worry. I'm sure you have better things to do than babysit your grandmother. It's Saturday. Maybe you should make a date -- maybe with Paige."

"You have to call Paige by Monday or Tuesday at the latest for a weekend date."

"Somehow I think she might make an exception for you. You've got a devilish charm when you choose to use it."

"Don't go thinking there's some possibility of a longterm relationship with Paige. That won't happen."

"Why not?"

He shrugged. "Because we aren't right for each other and we are definitely not in the same financial bracket."

"So what? Money isn't everything, not if you love each other. But that isn't the real problem, is it? You don't think you know how to love. And you're afraid to trust anyone who says she loves you."

He shifted his feet, uncomfortable with the conversation. "Paige hasn't said she loves me, because she doesn't, and I sure as hell don't love her. I barely know her."

"You knew her well enough to make out with her last night. Or are you going to tell me you were just talking?"

"It's a different world, Grandma."

She laughed at that. "It's the same world, Riley, and I'm not so old I don't remember what desire feels like."

"You know, I have to go." He was not going to discuss desire with his grandmother.

"To see Paige? Give her my love, or better yet -- give her yours."

Paige let herself into the mansion in Pacific Heights that had housed four generations of Hathaways. She was met almost immediately by the latest housekeeper, Alma Johnson.

"Let me take your coat, Miss Hathaway," Alma said. "Did you come to see your mother? Because she's at the hospital."

Paige handed over her coat. "Actually, I came to see my grandfather. Is he in?"

"Yes, he is."

"I'll go on up, then. Thanks." Paige made her way to the third floor with heavy feet and a reluctant heart. She told herself that her grandfather wasn't a bad guy; he was just impatient, opinionated, ruthless. Okay, maybe he was a little bit of a bad guy. He certainly didn't suffer fools, and he could definitely hold a grudge. He'd told the story a hundred times of a childhood friend who'd asked out the girl he was interested in. Wallace had never forgiven him. Their ten years of friendship had ended with that one lapse in judgment.

Which was why Paige hesitated in the hall outside his study. Talking to her grandfather about the Delaneys and the dragon or even her role at Hathaway's could be a definite lapse in judgment on her part. She wished Riley were here, but she knew she had to do this by herself. This was her family, after all.

She glanced at the portrait of her grandmother that hung on the wall near the door to her grandfather's study. It had been painted on the eve of her wedding to Wallace. Dolores Cunningham Hathaway had a beautiful smile and a serene expression on her face, as if she knew exactly what she wanted out of life. Paige wondered if her grandmother had been able to soften the sharp edges of her husband, if she had stood up to Wallace, or if he had controlled her the way he did everyone else. Unfortunately, she would never know. Her grandmother had died long before her birth, and Wallace had been single ever since. She supposed there must have been other women in his life at some point, but if there had been, he'd kept them away from the family.

Was that because he'd been so in love with her grandmother he couldn't bear to be with anyone else? Was that the kind of love he'd known? It seemed difficult to believe. He was such a hard, cold man. Maybe he'd been different then. Maybe he'd changed. The death of a wife and child would be enough to change any man.

How odd that both her father and her grandfather had lost their daughters -- their first daughters.

An eerie shiver drew goose bumps along her arms. They weren't part of this curse. They didn't have the dragon, which had only just surfaced in Ned Delaney's attic. If anyone had felt the curse, it would have been Ned. But Ned Delaney and her grandfather had known each other. They'd posed for a photograph together. Was that all it had taken? Had just touching Ned Delaney's hand, the hand that had held the dragon, been enough to launch a curse? Or was all this foolishness?

Shaking her head, she pushed the disturbing thoughts to the back of her mind. She needed to concentrate on the present, not the past. Although, she might have to bring up that past in order to get to the present. Damn, she was going in a circle.

She raised her hand and rapped on her grandfather's door. A moment later, she heard his gruff, "Come in."

He stood in front of the fireplace, poised to hit a golf ball into a can of some sort. He raised a hand when she began to speak, and she waited patiently while he sank the putt.

"There," he said with satisfaction, reaching down to take out the ball. He finally looked at Paige. "What's wrong?"

Okay, so it wasn't the warmest greeting. She didn't need warmth; she needed answers. "Nothing is wrong. I just wanted to talk to you about something."

"Did something happen at yesterday's press conference?"

"I don't know. I haven't heard anything. But that's not what--"

"You weren't there?" he interrupted with annoyance. "Why weren't you there?"

"Mother wanted to handle it, the way she always does."

"Goddammit, Paige, you're the Hathaway, not your mother. When are you going to start acting like one?"

She was taken aback by the question. "I, uh, Mother is the CFO of the company. She outranks me."

"You let her outrank you."

"Excuse me?"

He sat down on the arm of the couch, golf club still in hand. "I haven't stepped down as CEO because you're not ready to step up. Maybe you never will be. Maybe you've got more of your father in you than I thought."

"I don't understand. I can't just take over. I don't even have a title."

"You don't need a title. You're a Hathaway."

"All I've been doing is planning parties."

"And that's all you will do until you stand up for yourself."

She stared at him in bemusement. "I didn't know you wanted me to."

"You're all I've got," he said in a tone that didn't sound exactly loving or appreciative. In fact, it was almost an insult. "If your father had had a son, that would have kept our line alive, but no, he had to have girls," Wallace continued. "He couldn't even do that for me."

His words cut her to the quick. "I'm sorry we were such a disappointment."

"You don't have to be. You've been well educated, well trained. You know what to do, so do it. Prove you're worthy of being a Hathaway."

She didn't know what to say, how to react to the challenge he'd thrown down before her.

"Well, cat got your tongue? Speak up, girl."

"I came here to ask you about something else." She needed more time to think about what he'd just told her. "There's a dragon statue that my father wanted to acquire. We got it in the store on Tuesday afternoon, but it disappeared along with Dad on Wednesday."

"Do you think I'm a fool, Paige? I'm eighty-two years old, for goddamn sake, but I can figure out what's going on in my own company. Your father was an idiot for taking it out of the store. Insurance won't cover the loss." His angry brown eyes held not a hint of concern for the son he'd almost lost.

"That's true, but we can't change what happened. Right now I'm more interested in trying to find the statue."

"How the hell will you do that? Whoever took it probably sold it the same day."

"Sold it to who? Do you have any ideas?"

"Could be thousands of people. Ask your father. He's the Chinese art expert."

"He doesn't remember what happened or why he even went to Chinatown." She watched her grandfather's face carefully, wondering if he knew about Jasmine and Alyssa, but he didn't give a thing away. "It's possible that this statue," she continued, "might have been part of a set consisting of two dragons and a box. There's a legend, a curse, the whole bit. I've been reading up on the subject."

"There are always legends, always curses. What else have you got?" He stood up and placed the golf ball back on the carpet in preparation for making another putt.

"Ned Delaney. Do you know who he is?"

"I don't think so," he said.

"He was a security guard at Hathaway's. I saw a photograph of the two of you together."

"I've taken a million photos with a million different employees."

"He was also the owner of the dragon in question. His wife, Nan Delaney, is the one who brought it to us. It seems an odd coincidence that he would have worked for us a long time ago."

"A lot of people have worked for us over the years."

"Not people who have priceless artifacts discovered in the attics of their modest homes. This is not a man who collected antiques or Chinese art. He had nothing except this statue, and no one seems to know where it came from." She paused, debating whether or not to ask a question that had been bothering her for some time now, a question she didn't really want to put into words because it made her feel disloyal to Riley. But that was wrong. Her loyalty was to her family. She had to remember that. "Are you sure that Hathaway's never owned a statue like this a long time ago?" she finally asked.

"You think this Delaney stole the statue from us?"

"It did occur to me, yes."

He focused on his putt, sending the ball into the can. "Interesting theory."

"Unfortunately, the computer records at the store only go back ten years and the files another ten. Judging by the photo I saw, Mr. Delaney must have worked for Hathaway's in the fifties or sixties. And I don't think we still have those records anywhere, do we?"

"No. That's that, then," Wallace replied. "Anything else?"

"You're sure you don't remember the dragon statue?"

"I've bought and sold thousands of statues in my lifetime, Paige. Not many stand out in my mind."

"I guess not." She turned toward the door, but his voice stopped her.

"What happened to this Delaney guy? Is he dead?"

"No, he has Alzheimer's. He's in an assisted living place. Riley says he doesn't remember much."

"Too bad." Wallace picked up the golf ball and set it up again. She watched him measure the distance to the hole. Then he stroked the ball. It missed by a good two inches. Wallace Hathaway was nowhere near as steady as he usually was. Paige wondered why.

Chapter Seventeen

An hour later, Paige was still thinking about her conversation with her grandfather as she leaned over the pool table, trying to concentrate on the shot in front of her. It was nice to focus on something simple for a change. All she had to do was hit the ball into the corner pocket. She slid the cue between her fingers and took the shot. It was perfect. She stood back, admiring her handiwork.

"Not bad," Jerry said as he stepped into the back room of Fast Willy's in search of empty glasses. "But don't you think it's kind of pathetic that you're here all by yourself on a Saturday afternoon shooting pool?"

"It's not nice of you to point that out."

"How's your father?"

"He's much better, almost ready to go home. I'm incredibly relieved."

"Are you?" Jerry picked up two empty beer bottles and set them on the tray. "Then why are you shooting pool today? You usually only do that when you've got some problem on your mind that you can't figure out how to solve."

"I do not have one problem, I have many problems," she replied.

He gave her a thoughtful smile. "Any involving that guy who followed you here earlier this week?"

"That is none of your business."

"Come on, Paige. Give a little. This is your old pal Jerry you're talking to."

She let out a sigh. "I think I'm falling for him."

"Does he feel the same way?"

"Who can tell? I know he wants me, but the rest, all the emotional stuff, I don't think it's going to happen." She sighed. "But my love life or lack thereof isn't really the problem. It's my family, it's my job, it's what I want to do with the rest of my life."

"That's going to take a lot of games of pool to figure out."

"Tell me about it." She set her cue back in the rack. "What's up with you?"

"Actually, I'm thinking about moving on. I have a job offer, if you can believe it."

"Seriously?"

"Yes. I know that surprises you but I don't want to tend bar forever."

"What kind of job is it?"

"Computer programming. It's in Seattle. And I've always wanted to live in the Pacific Northwest."

She frowned. "Since when?"

"For a while," he said with a shrug.

"It rains all the time in Seattle."

"I like the rain."

She snapped her fingers. "That's not it. There's a girl there."

His freckled face flushed at her statement. "Maybe,"

he conceded.

"No maybe about it. Is it serious?"

"There's some of the emotional stuff, as you called it, involved."

She threw her arms around him and gave him a big hug. "I'm so happy for you."

"All right, don't get mushy."

She felt mushy. She felt like crying. She was happy for Jerry, but it seemed like everyone was moving on except her. Why was she stuck in one place?

"I need a drink," she said as she let him go.

"I'll get you one."

"Don't bother; I've got it covered," Riley said. He walked into the back room with a beer in one hand, a diet Coke in the other.

Her jaw dropped at the sight of him. "Did you follow me again?"

"Actually, I came on a hunch. Couldn't find you at home, at the hospital, or at work. Process of elimination."

"You went to all those places?" she asked, amazed at his persistence.

"I called around."

"Oh." So he hadn't tried that hard; but he had tried a little. And here he was, looking even better than he had the day before. And she wanted... she wanted a thousand things that all had to do with kissing and touching him and getting really, really close. She was still kicking herself for not making love to him when she'd had the chance. Maybe she should have thrown caution to the wind instead of playing it safe the way she always did.

"I don't think you two need me anymore," Jerry said with a laugh, since Paige seemed unable to do anything but stare at Riley. "And, Paige, I don't think you're going to need to play as much pool as you think."

"What did he mean by that?" Riley asked when they were alone.

"Nothing. What's up?"

"How's your father?" Riley asked.

"Getting better. He's coming home tomorrow. He still has no memory of what happened, though." She paused. "You don't think he's faking, do you?"

"You know him better than I do," he said, his expression carefully neutral.

Did she know her father? She used to think so. Now she wasn't nearly as sure. "I suppose if he was trying to cover up going to Jasmine's apartment, he might claim a memory loss. I'm not sure. I'll ask him about it when he gets stronger. I don't want to put too much pressure on him too soon."

"That's understandable. Why don't we sit down?" he suggested as a group of men came back to play pool. He chose a table by the window. "I think we need to talk."

"Yes," she said, joining him at the table. "I spoke to my grandfather today. I asked him if he'd met your grandfather."

"And his reply?"

"He said the name sounded familiar. Then he pointed out to me that he's eighty-two years old, and he's met a lot of people in his life. He also said that he's sold thousands of statues in his time and none stand out as the one we're looking for."

"That sounds about as productive as my conversation with my grandfather." Riley took a sip of his beer. "Although, he did ramble on about someone named Wally. I wondered if Wally was short for Wallace, but my grandmother said she didn't think so."

"I don't either," she said with a shake of her head. "I can't imagine my grandfather allowing anyone to call him

Wally."

"My grandmother did mention that Ned worked at Hathaway's when they were first married, which would explain the photograph."

"Yes. And it might also explain where your grandfather got the statue," she said.

His gaze narrowed. "What are you talking about? You think that statue was owned by your family?"

"It's a possibility, isn't it? I mean, think about it. Where would your grandfather have gotten such a piece?"

"Just what are you accusing my grandfather of doing? Stealing from Hathaway's?" he demanded, protective fire in his eyes now.

"I didn't say that."

"Yes, you did. I knew you'd go down that road, Paige. It just came a little sooner than I thought."

"What came sooner?"

"The choice between your family and mine."

"I'm not making a choice; I'm just pointing out some things."

He jumped to his feet, obviously angry.

"Riley, wait. Don't go."

He paused at the door, his blue eyes as cold as steel when he looked at her. "Why not?"

"Because we're not done."

"I think we are. You've already decided--"

"I haven't decided anything." She got to her feet and walked over to him. "I just said what came to my mind. I'm sorry. I thought we were past the point of having to pick and choose our words. I thought we were friends."

"How could we ever be friends?" he asked, as if that would be totally impossible.

"We can be friends if we're honest with each other."

"My grandfather wouldn't have stolen a statue from

your store. He wasn't that kind of man. He was honest to a fault. He set the standards of behavior for me. He taught me what was right and what was wrong."

In other words, Riley couldn't bear to believe his grandfather wasn't perfect. She understood that. Too many people had hurt this man with their actions; he couldn't afford another disappointment.

"Okay," she said evenly. "Then there must be another reason why your grandfather had the statue. Don't make me the enemy, Riley, because I'm not. I'm your partner. Now, what do you say to starting this conversation over?"

He hesitated, then let out a long sigh. "Fine."

"You can finish your beer. I'll drink my diet Coke. And we'll both take a deep breath."

Riley sat back down at the table and picked up his beer. "I'm sorry if I jumped on you, but my grandfather was a good man, Paige. He ran into a lot of prejudice when he was young. He used to tell me that when he was a teenager, the Irish in San Francisco were considered second-class citizens, thieves and robbers. It made him very determined to live the kind of life he could be proud of. I won't let his reputation be smeared at this late date."

"I understand. And I was just talking off the top of my head. From here on out, let's try not to point any fingers unless we have hard proof. Deal?"

"Deal." Riley ran his finger around the edge of his glass beer mug.

"What was your grandfather like before he got sick?" she asked curiously.

"Typical Irishman. He liked his drink, his food, his wife, his stories. He wasn't wild, though. He had all these rules for himself."

"Like what?"

"Like no more than two drinks before dinner. No

dancing with anyone other than his wife. No stories that made fun of women. No laughing in church." He smiled to himself as if he were lost in a fond memory. "That was a tough one, though. Father O'Brien used to fall asleep during the readings and snored so loud he could have woken the dead. My grandfather and I could barely get through those moments without a laugh." Riley took another drink. "For the most part his rules worked for him. He said they kept him out of trouble."

"He sounds like a good man."

"He is -- or he was. He's not the same now. I must admit I've wondered where he got that statue, but if anyone stole it from somewhere, it was my mother, not my grandfather."

"Or maybe it wasn't stolen at all," she said soothingly. "We really don't know. It is odd though, isn't it -- this connection between us, between our grandfathers."

"So, did your grandfather have anything else of importance to say?"

"Not about the statue. We did talk about my position at Hathaway's. He shocked the hell out of me by telling me that I can take control at any time. I just have to stand up and do it. I'm not quite sure how that's supposed to happen since I have no title, no real power."

"Do you want to take control of the store?"

"I think so," she said slowly. "I've been raised to believe it's my destiny. Everything I've done has been to that end. I've never worked anywhere else. Every summer since I was fifteen, I've been at the store, filling out sales slips, working the floor, tracking inventory. But now all I do is plan events or host tea parties for clients whose art objects we wish to acquire."

"So do what your grandfather said, take charge."

"And what do you think my mother will do, roll over and get out of the way?"

"You need to be as smart and ruthless as she is."

She sent him a doubtful look. "I'm not sure I have it in me."

"And that's the problem," he said with a knowing nod. "You have to believe in yourself before anyone else will."

"I'm trying."

"I have an idea," he said after a moment. "Are you free for a few hours?"

"Why? What do you have in mind?"

"Just answer the question."

"I guess. My father is resting. My mother has hired a private detective to look for the dragon. Alyssa has not returned my calls. And I'm not accomplishing anything here, so sure, I'm free."

"Good. I know just the thing for you. Come with me." He stood up, holding out his hand. She hesitated as anticipation raised the hairs on the back of her neck.

"Where are we going?"

"To my apartment."

His eyes dared her to say no, but she couldn't. There were a lot of things she wanted to do at his apartment, and they all involved saying yes.

"Bike riding?" Paige asked in surprise as they stood in the center of his small garage a few minutes later. "You want me to ride this bike somewhere?" She looked down at the mountain bike he'd pushed over to her.

Riley laughed at her look of dismay. "It's a good bike. There are fifteen speeds."

"I don't ride bikes that actually move."

"Then you've been missing out. This is a great city we live in. You should be out in it."

"I was just out in it -- in your warm, comfortable car. Besides, it's cloudy. It might even rain."

"And your point is? Come on, live a little. You might like it."

He walked his own bike out of the garage, pleased when she slowly followed. He handed her his extra helmet. His bike riding passion had grown so much over the years that he was always replacing his equipment with newer and better, which meant he had extras to share.

"Are we planning on crashing?" she asked.

"No, but Hathaways aren't the only ones who are prepared for every possibility. You need to wear the helmet."

"There's so much traffic in the city. Why don't we drive to a park and start there? Golden Gate Park is really nice."

"It's too flat." He adjusted his helmet and watched as she reluctantly put hers on.

"This isn't really my color," she said, referring to the bright orange helmet now covering her blond hair.

"But the cars will be able to see you." He was actually surprised she was such a good sport. Most debutantes probably would have bailed on him by now. He handed her a clip for her pant leg. "Put this on. It will keep your pants out of the chain area."

"You are prepared for everything." She clipped her pant legs and straddled the bike. "You couldn't have had a girl's bike, could you?"

"I think you can handle it."

"Okay, I'm ready, but I haven't ridden an actual bike since I was a kid, and I only did that about three times."

"You'll be fine. Just follow me, and yell if you have a

problem." He got on his bike and began to pedal slowly down the street.

"Riley," she yelled.

He stopped immediately, turning his head in anticipation of seeing her sprawled on the ground, but she was still standing where he had left her. "What?" he asked with annoyance.

"Just testing to see if you'd really stop."

"Get on the bike, Paige."

"Okay, okay." She perched gingerly on the seat and began to pedal so slowly the bike was in serious danger of falling over.

"Faster," he encouraged. "It will be easier."

"So you say," she grumbled, increasing her speed until she passed by him.

He headed after her, pleased to see her gaining confidence as they moved down the block. The beginning of their ride was flat. He took her along the Embarcadero, past the magnificent Bay Bridge that connected San Francisco to Oakland, the ferry buildings where the cruise ships docked, and the downtown Financial District that edged North Beach and Fisherman's Wharf, closer to the hills he wanted to tackle today.

He motioned for her to follow as he cut across the Embarcadero toward a residential area. The hills of San Francisco called to him like a beacon in the night. But Paige's voice yanked him back. He stopped his bike and looked over his shoulder at her. "What's the problem now?"

"We're not riding up that hill, are we?" she asked in disbelief.

"Sure we are."

She shook her head. "It's too steep. I'll never make it."

It wasn't nearly as steep as the next one, but he wasn't about to tell her that. "I thought you wanted to find out what you were made of."

"By riding a bicycle up a hill?"

"It's a test of your strength, courage, stamina, stubbornness. You can do it."

"I don't think so."

He saw the uncertainty in her pretty brown eyes and knew that she needed to do this for herself. "You're stronger than you think, Paige."

"This isn't going to prove anything."

"Try it and see."

"I don't like to fail."

He smiled. "So don't fail." He sent her an encouraging look. "It's not a test if it's too easy."

"Who said I wanted to take a test?"

"Fine. I'm going up this hill with or without you. Your choice."

"That's not very gentlemanly."

He laughed. "I thought you'd figured out by now that I am not a gentleman."

"You're not a very good date, either. I can think of a lot of other things that would be more fun than this."

"You haven't even tried it yet. And this isn't a date." He turned his head toward the hill in front of them. He drew in a deep breath and counted to ten. Then he got on his bike and pedaled hard, wanting to get as much speed as possible for the ascent. He heard Paige muttering to herself and saw from the corner of his eye that she was on the bike and riding after him.

So far so good. He just hoped she really could make it up the hill. Maybe she was too pampered, too spoiled, too weak for such a challenge, and maybe he was a fool, wanting to believe she was someone she wasn't.

Paige knew she'd passed the insanity mark when her legs began to burn and her chest tightened with each breath. She was only halfway up the hill; there was no way she would make it. She wasn't in shape for this. She should have trained, prepared, worked up to it. But wasn't that what she'd spent the last thirteen years doing at Hathaway's: training, preparing, but never actually doing? At least here she was being aggressive, taking a chance.

But it hurt.

And damn Riley. He was already at the top, off his bike, watching her, waiting for her. He shouted words of encouragement.

If he believed in her, maybe she needed to believe in herself. So she told herself to focus, keep pedaling, and don't even think about quitting.

"Come on, Paige. A few more feet," Riley yelled.

The last part was very steep. She really didn't think she could do it. Her eyes were glazing over from sweat or terror or exhaustion, she didn't know which. The road was wavy, the bike was wobbling, her hands were beginning to cramp from her grip on the handlebars.

"You're almost there, Paige. Bring it home!"

Her heart pounded against her chest as she forced her feet down again and again and again, until she hit the top and the ground flattened.

"Keep riding, Paige, take a circle around the intersection," Riley said.

She wanted to get off the bike the way he'd done, but she needed to bring her heart rate down to a safer level. She knew that much from her cardio classes at the gym. So she took a wide circle around the quiet intersection, finally returning to his side, her breath still ragged but her heart slowing to a more reasonable beat.

His smile was her reward. It was big and broad and totally amazed. She couldn't help smiling back. And when he tossed his bike on the ground and held out his arms to her, she slid off her bike and ran to him.

She threw her arms around his neck. "I did it," she said with more joy than she could ever remember feeling.

He hugged her tight and hard, as if he didn't want to let her go. They were both hot and sweaty, their helmets clanking as Riley swooped in to kiss her mouth. He tasted so good, better than the last time -- better than any time. He tasted like success, freedom, wonder, and all the emotions that seemed so often out of reach for her. But he'd made her feel them.

He pulled back and undid her helmet, taking it off of her head. "You're awesome."

"I'm a mess." She put a hand to her hair, which was loose and tangled, then laughed. "But I don't care."

"Neither do I." He took off his own helmet and tossed them both to the ground. "Now, let's do this right."

She met him more than halfway, as eager for the kiss as he was. She wrapped her arms around his waist, pressed her breasts against his chest, and let her tongue sweep the inside of his mouth with a demanding need she hadn't thought herself capable of. Today was a day for firsts.

A honking horn broke them apart as a car maneuvered around them and headed up the next hill.

Paige knew she should have felt embarrassed, ashamed by her behavior on a public street no less, but there was laughter bubbling up from deep down inside. And she couldn't stop it from bursting out, especially when Riley was already laughing.

"Stop," she said, getting a side ache. She turned away

from him. "If I look at you, I'm going to keep laughing."

"It's good for you."

She turned back around. "You're good for me." His laughter stopped. His expression changed like a cloud over the sun. "Paige--"

"Don't say anything." She held up her hand. "This is a great moment. Let's just leave it at that."

"I knew you could make it up that hill."

"You had more faith in me than I did. You've done this before, haven't you?"

"A few times."

"Like every day?"

"Three or four times a week," he admitted. "But not just this hill. There are always higher hills to climb, especially in this city."

She wondered what the hills really stood for. She doubted he would tell her even if she asked. Instead, she looked down the hill from where they had come. "I did pretty good."

"You did. Ready for the next one?"

"No way."

"You said that before."

"Maybe next time."

He studied her thoughtfully, then nodded. "Maybe next time. Ready for the best part?"

"Going down?"

"Absolutely. You earned it. Now enjoy it."

She put her helmet back on and picked up her bike. She had a momentary fear of the steepness of the downhill ride, but she pushed it away. Today was not a day for holding back but for going forward.

She sailed down the hill, the wind in her face bringing tears to her eyes -- at least that's what she wanted to blame the emotion on. She knew she was lying to herself. It wasn't the wind making her cry; it was the feeling that she'd finally broken through. And the odd thing was she hadn't even realized she was holding back until now.

"How was that?" Riley asked her as he joined her at the bottom.

"It was good, but it wasn't the best part," she admitted. "The best part were those last few feet at the top of the hill."

His eyes burned bright at her reply, and they exchanged a long look of complete and total understanding.

"Was it that way for you, too?" she asked.

"It usually is," he admitted. "But today the best part was when I was kissing you, and you were kissing me back."

She smiled at him. "I hate to break this to you, Riley, but you could have had that kiss an hour ago when we were standing in your garage."

He laughed. "Now you tell me."

"I'll race you back to your apartment."

"Feeling cocky, are you?"

"Absolutely. And I like it!" She hopped on the bike and began riding back the way they had come. It didn't matter if she beat Riley or not. She'd already won the biggest battle of the day, the one going on inside herself.

Chapter Eighteen

Alyssa jogged up the stairs to her mother's apartment Saturday afternoon and knocked on the door. As she waited, she found herself foolishly smiling, which was pretty much what she'd been doing since she'd left Ben's apartment the night before. She'd had a good time with him, better than she'd expected. In fact, he'd reminded her of what she'd liked in him before, his intelligence, his dry sense of humor, his ability to see into her head, to make her take life less seriously.

If only he weren't Chinese, or, at the very least, if only he didn't live in Chinatown and wasn't so closely tied to this neighborhood, maybe then she could consider him as someone she could date. But... she glanced over her shoulder, realizing how close he lived to this building, only three short blocks away. It wasn't nearly far enough.

Her mother finally opened the door and beckoned for her to come in. "Are you all right?" Jasmine asked, her gaze traveling up and down Alyssa's body, as if she were checking for bruises or broken bones.

"I'm fine. Why wouldn't I be?"

"I've been calling you since yesterday. Why didn't you call me back?"

"I didn't get a chance," Alyssa said, knowing that she'd had plenty of chances, but she'd been battling herself over how much she wanted to get involved with the missing dragon, her mother, and her newly discovered father. "What's wrong?" she asked, seeing the deep worry lines stretching across her mother's forehead. "Why are you so upset?"

"You shouldn't have spoken to your grandfather about the dragon."

"Oh. Well, I ran into him in the square. I was going to talk to Grandmother, but I couldn't find her. She wasn't at the shop."

"She came to see me."

"She came here?" Alyssa echoed in amazement. "What did she say? What did she want?"

Instead of answering her, Jasmine walked over to the nearby easel and stared at the still-wet painting. She was stalling, Alyssa thought, wondering why. She also noticed that her mother had once again painted the dragon, and this one was more distinct, the details sharp and clear where before they had always been hazy.

"You can't stop painting it, can you?" she asked.

"I try, but whatever object I start to paint always turns into this."

"What did Grandmother want?"

"She told me that I had seen the dragon at a museum in Taiwan, that I had tried to touch it, and the alarms went off, frightening me. That's why I have such bad dreams about it."

Alyssa considered the explanation. It was so simple, so easy. "Why didn't she tell you that before? When I asked Grandfather, he said you had never seen a dragon like the one you dream about."

Her mother looked as confused as she felt. "I don't know, Alyssa."

"They're not telling us the truth, are they?"

"We should not speak ill of our elders. It is wrong, disrespectful. We must honor them."

Alyssa had heard those words a thousand times, but she had always had a difficult time equating her grandparents' behavior with honor.

"My mother reminded me that the story of the dragons includes a curse on all first daughters," Jasmine continued. "Because I touched the dragon the other day, I may have brought the curse down upon you, Alyssa. I am worried about you."

Her mother's words rocked her back on her heels. She'd never thought about the curse in terms of herself. Did she even believe in curses? Wasn't that just more superstitious foolishness?

"I'm not worried," she said, trying to ignore the unease sweeping through her body.

"You should not taunt fate."

"Ben already told me about the curse, but we don't even know if the dragon you saw is part of that story, that set."

"You went to see Ben?" her mother asked in astonishment. "Why? Why would you do that? You don't care about the dragon or Ben."

"I care about you. I care about the fact that the dragon is missing, and you might have been the last person to see it before Mr. Hathaway was attacked just a few blocks from here." She couldn't quite bring herself to call him her father. It still didn't seem real.

"I didn't hurt David."

"Of course not. But he's a rich man, and his family has connections. If they need someone to blame, who better than you?"

"You don't have to worry about me."

"I'm afraid that's not possible. I love you. You're my mother."

Tears came to Jasmine's eyes. "I brought you into a world of shame."

"You brought me into a world of opportunity. And I thank God that you did. I can be whoever I want to be."

"I know it hasn't been easy for you."

"You were the one who had it the worst," Alyssa said generously, even though she still couldn't quite forgive her mother for withholding the name of her father for so many years.

"What about David?"

"What about him? He obviously didn't want to know me. If he did, he would have asked you about me. He would have wanted to see me."

"It is much more complicated than that," Jasmine replied with a helpless wave of her hand. "He did ask at times. I refused. I had my reasons. I didn't want you to be confused any more than you already were."

"That I don't understand, but it was your choice."

"Yes, perhaps it was wrong. I don't know anymore, but he is awake now."

"He is?" she asked, her body tightening.

"It was on the news last night."

"Well, that's good, I guess. He can clear you if the police come back." Alyssa paused, not sure she was ready to ask the question in her head, but it came out before she could stop it. "How did you two meet? How did a humble Chinese girl from Chinatown meet a rich, handsome man like David Hathaway?"

"It is a long story."

Alyssa sat down on the couch. "Tell me."

Jasmine stood in the center of the room, looking decidedly uncomfortable, but finally she began to speak. "I met him at a party at his home. I was working as a waitress for a caterer, and the Hathaways had ordered a special Chinese feast in honor of David's birthday." She paused. "He was very sad that night. His daughter had died only a few weeks earlier."

"His daughter?" Alyssa asked in shock. "I thought Paige was an only child."

"No, there was an older girl. Her name was Elizabeth. David left the feast as soon as possible. I was on the terrace collecting glasses. He started talking to me. I think for some reason I was the only one in the house that night that he could talk to. He said they were all pretending -- his wife, his father, his friends. They were acting as if life was normal, but he didn't think it would ever be normal again." She took a breath, collecting her memories. "I don't know how it happened. One minute we were talking, and the next minute we were kissing. It was wrong. He was married. But there was something between us, a connection. I felt as if we belonged together, as if this was meant to be for some reason."

Her mother made it sound romantic and lovely, but the consequences of that night had been anything but. Her own existence was a testament to that fact.

"I fell in love with him at first sight," Jasmine continued. "I've loved him ever since."

"But he never really loved you, did he?" she asked sharply.

"I suppose not," her mother admitted, her voice edged with pain.

"And he never loved me, either." Alyssa made it a

statement, not a question.

"He couldn't. He thought loving you would be a betrayal of his love for his daughter Elizabeth. He had come to me out of grief. When I became pregnant; when I had a daughter, he didn't know how to react. For him to care about you seemed wrong."

"Were you together after I was born?"

Jasmine cleared her throat somewhat awkwardly. "A few times in the early years, usually around Elizabeth's birthday. I thought that's why he had come this past week to see me. Her birthday is on Wednesday. I was surprised when the reason for his visit was the dragon."

Alyssa nodded, her mind reeling with the information she had just received. "So you and my father met by chance at a party. It seems like such a coincidence."

"What do you mean?"

"When I was at Ben's apartment, I saw a photo of my two grandfathers. Wallace Hathaway was shaking Grandfather's hand at a New Year's celebration a long time ago. Don't you think it's odd that they knew each other?"

"It's not odd at all. When my father first came to San Francisco, he worked at the House of Hathaway."

"He did?" Alyssa asked in amazement, wondering when she would stop being surprised.

"Yes, but it was only for a short time. It was a long time ago, before he and your grandmother started the herb shop. I used to wish when I was a little girl that he worked at Hathaway's still, so he could take me inside. At Christmas when we'd walk by the store, I thought it was so beautiful, all the lights, the glass, the fancy people. My mother would never let me go inside. She said it was not the place for a poor girl from Chinatown."

Alyssa heard the wistfulness in her mother's voice

and wondered if that was when the love was born. Had her mother coveted something Hathaway from the time she was a little girl? Was that why she had an affair with a married man twenty-something years later? "Do my grandparents know that David Hathaway is my father?" she asked.

"No, they don't," Jasmine said immediately.

"Are you sure about that?"

"Yes, absolutely. I told no one."

"Did my father tell anyone?"

"No, he kept it a secret. He couldn't bear for his family to know what he had done."

She could certainly believe that. "Well, they know now."

"We can't cause them any trouble, Alyssa. I have always promised David that I would not hurt his family."

"I'm his family, too," she reminded her mother. "In fact, I just realized something. I'm a Hathaway. And I should own a piece of that fancy store that a poor girl from Chinatown didn't belong in."

"Alyssa, no. You can't upset things."

She was tempted, very tempted. She could make big trouble for David Hathaway and his family. She could sue him for paternal support, for a stake in Hathaway's and the rest of the family investments. She could win enough money to support her mother in the fashion she deserved for the rest of her life. Even if she didn't win a lawsuit, she could sell their story to the tabloids for a fortune, as Paige had suggested. The Hathaway's deserved everything they got.

Well, maybe not all the Hathaways, maybe not Paige. She seemed nice, friendly. Of course, Paige had also reminded Alyssa that her mother could be in a heap of trouble if the stolen dragon was linked back to her. Maybe

Paige had only been looking out for her own interests. Maybe that was the Hathaway gene she had truly inherited, the one that was telling her now to look out for herself and her mother and not to worry about anyone else.

"I love him. I love you," Jasmine said, interrupting her plan of attack. "Alyssa, listen to me -- I don't want you to fight with David or his family. I couldn't bear it. I committed the sin. If you must punish him, you must punish me."

"You've already been punished enough," Alyssa said.

"And so have you. I want you to have your life, Alyssa, the life you want, wherever you want to live it. I don't want it to be a life based on pain and anger. You have told me many times that you know what you want, and you know how to get it. So get it. Don't do it by hurting the Hathaways. I already did that, more than you can ever understand."

Paige didn't understand how Riley could change gears so quickly. Since they'd returned to his apartment from their ride an hour earlier, he'd parked himself in front of the computer, pounding the keyboard in search of more information on the dragon. He seemed to have forgotten all about her, about their kiss, about the fact that if they'd wanted to continue that kiss in the privacy of his apartment, they could have done just that. Obviously, he'd had second thoughts. But why?

She felt annoyed, restless, wanting answers to questions she didn't have the courage to ask, so she did what he was doing, turned her attention to the mystery surrounding them.

"Have you found anything?" she asked.

Riley didn't answer her. She wasn't even sure he'd heard the question. That was the thing with him. He gave one hundred percent to every task, whether it be attacking a monster hill on a mountain bike or researching an ancient artifact. She liked that about him. She liked a lot of things about him. More important, she liked the way she was when she was with him.

Sitting down on his couch, she stretched out her legs, feeling a delicious ache of weariness. Defeating that hill had given her a sense of confidence and self-worth that she hadn't felt in a long time. She remembered the feeling from when she was at college and she'd spent two years on the crew team. Rowing had also made her feel as if she was using her body, her muscles, her mind, accomplishing something. She'd been drifting the past few years, going from one mundane task to the next. She'd lost her focus, her purpose. She'd just been waiting, counting minutes, passing time until the magic moment when she would assume her intended role at Hathaway's.

She realized now that taking over Hathaway's would not happen by chance, that she would have to make it happen. She couldn't keep moaning about unimportant duties; she needed to find her own work, her own role at the store. Maybe it wouldn't be as CEO or CFO, since those jobs were already taken, but surely there was something she could do to leave her mark on the company. She just had to find it and then do it -- tomorrow or the next day. She didn't have to find herself a job right this second. In fact, she could think of lots of other things she could be doing right now, including finishing that kiss she'd started with Riley in the middle of an intersection in San Francisco.

She was tempted to get him out of his chair and into

the messed-up bed she could see through the half-open door to his bedroom. Sheets and blankets were tossed in abandon, making her want to jump into the middle of them and roll around with Riley. A shot of heat swept through her body at the thought. She couldn't do what she was thinking, could she?

She had to get a grip. Sex with Riley would only complicate things. They'd never work out as a couple. *Would they?*

Even if they could get past the differences in the way they'd grown up, what about the way they lived now? She might rail against Hathaway standards, but there was no denying the fact that she liked some of the culture she'd grown up with -- the ballet, the symphony, the art museums. And she wanted commitment, a husband, children, the happily-ever-after she'd read about in so many books.

Did Riley want any of that? He loved his grandparents, but he couldn't seem to let himself get close to anyone else. She knew his mother had hurt him deeply. Too deeply for him to be able to trust, to love another woman?

"Paige. Yoo-hoo, Paige."

She started, realizing the object of her thoughts was now staring at her. "What?"

"I've been talking to you for three minutes."

"That's funny. I asked you a question awhile ago, and you didn't even answer."

"I found something," he said, ignoring her comment.

"About the dragon?"

"About my grandfather."

She looked at the screen. "Where are you?"

"Social Security. My grandfather worked at Hathaway's from 1946 to 1952, when the store burned to the ground."

"That makes sense, because the store was closed down while it was rebuilt. I'm sure a lot of employees were let go."

"I'm sure they were." He closed one screen and went to the next. He brought up an old newspaper article. "Did you know that the fire occurred during the Chinese New Year's Parade?"

Another bell went off in her head. "I remember hearing that. They thought it might have been started by some errant fireworks."

"Actually, the article claims there were traces of gasoline in the basement and suspicion of arson."

"Really? I never heard that, but it happened a long time before I was born."

"Do you know who was the first man on the scene?"

"Your grandfather?" she ventured.

"Guess again."

"My grandfather?"

"You've got one more choice."

She frowned. "I don't see what it is."

"Lee Chen."

"Lee Chen?" she echoed, seeing the excited light in Riley's eyes.

"Alyssa's grandfather," he said. "We're connected, Paige, all three of us. It says in the article that Lee Chen, an employee at the store, was the first one on the scene. He tried to put the fire out but it was too hot, and he suffered burns on his hands before he was pulled out of the store."

"What a strange coincidence," she said, still trying to make sense of all the connections.

"Is it a coincidence? What do you bet that Lee Chen was never rehired after the fire?"

"Why wouldn't he have been -- if he tried to save the store?"

"Did he try to save it? Or did he start the fire? The first one on the scene could have also been the person who started it."

"That's quite a leap. You got angry at me for making that same jump to your grandfather. We should be careful who we accuse."

"Agreed. But at least we're narrowing down the suspects."

"The suspects to what, Riley? Are we trying to figure out who set fire to the store fifty years ago? Or are we trying to figure out what happened to a dragon that disappeared last week?"

"That depends on whether that dragon ties the two events together."

"Which would take us back to the idea that the dragon might have been owned by the store at one point. You didn't like that scenario, remember?"

He tipped his head. "I still don't think my grandfather stole it. But I'm willing to keep an open mind on where it's been in the last hundred years."

"That's big of you."

"I also think that the fact that these three men knew each other at one point is somehow very important. They all worked at Hathaway's in some capacity."

"I agree," Paige said. "Maybe Alyssa or Jasmine could tell us about Lee."

Paige's cell phone rang as she finished speaking, and Paige had the eerie sensation that someone had been reading her mind. Her suspicion was confirmed when Alyssa's voice came over the phone.

"Alyssa," she said. "Riley and I were just talking about you. We found an odd connection between not just you and me, but Riley, too. Your grandfather's name is Lee Chen, right?" It suddenly occurred to her that Lee Chen was a fairly common name.

"Yes," Alyssa said. "Why do you ask?"

"We discovered that he worked at Hathaway's a long time ago."

"I just learned that as well."

"Riley's grandfather worked there, too. And, of course, my grandfather. They must have all known one another. I don't know what it means. It could be a small world, a really big coincidence, or a great lead. That doesn't narrow it down much, does it?"

"No, but perhaps we can narrow it down further," Alyssa said. "I spoke to Benjamin Fong again. He says his uncle has some information for us about the dragon. I'm meeting them in a half hour -- that's why I'm calling."

She was thrilled that Alyssa had thought to let her know. "I'd love to come with you. Riley would, too."

Alyssa hesitated. "I've been thinking about everything. I don't completely trust you, Paige. You might be trying to frame my mother for some sort of theft."

Paige's heart sank. Another distrusting soul. She seemed to be surrounded by them. She looked at Riley and caught him watching her with a thoughtful expression on his face. He didn't completely trust her, either. She would just have to prove herself to both of them. "I don't want to hurt your mother in any way," she said firmly, returning her attention to the phone call. "What's between my father and your mother is separate from all this. I want to know who attacked my father, and you want to protect your mother. We're on the same side. And we want to make sure no one else gets hurt. The only way we can do that is to find out what happened to the dragon, if we can."

"All right. Meet me at 3712 Stockton Street, Jimmy Lee's martial arts studio."

Paige ended the call and explained the situation to Riley. "We can go if we want," she told him.

"Of course we're going."

"You're loving this, aren't you?" She could see the sparkle in his eyes, hear the energy in his voice.

"I've always liked a puzzle, and this one is finally starting to come together." He stretched his arms up over his head, then got to his feet. "So, thirty minutes, huh?"

"Yes." She stiffened as Riley took a predatory step in her direction. "What are you doing?"

"I'm walking over to you."

"I can see that, but why are you -- Oh," she gasped as his mouth pressed against hers in a crushing, passionate kiss. "You're never going to ask me first, are you?" she muttered when he let her catch her breath.

"Are you complaining?"

"Yes, I'm complaining. I've been here for almost an hour, and this is the first move you've made."

He laughed. "You never say what I think you're going to say." He swooped in and stole another kiss.

"We only have thirty minutes," she reminded him.

"There are a lot of things we can do in that amount of time, princess," he said, a husky note in his voice.

"Like what?" she asked breathlessly.

"Use your imagination."

David felt himself sliding into sleep. The familiar dream welcomed him home.

He was walking through the long dark alley, hearing footsteps coming closer. There were eyes following him, watching him, or maybe it was the dragon's eyes. They glowed in the night, two jade points of light from thousands of years ago. Jasmine's dragon. He had to get back to her. She was the only one who understood. Why couldn't he get to her? Why didn't the alley end? Was it always this long, this narrow? He heard voices hushed, then growing louder, one especially cold and shrill -- Victoria? She stepped in front of him, and something flashed in her hand. A knife? A gun?

"I know what you did, David. You betrayed me. You ruined our name. You hurt your daughter. You must pay."

The gun was pointed straight at his heart. It exploded. He jerked, feeling the shock, the pain, the knowledge that he had really screwed up this time.

"Mr. Hathaway. Mr. Hathaway?"

He blinked as a bright light blinded him. Was this it? The light that would lead him straight to heaven? No, he probably wasn't headed there. Not after the way he'd lived.

"Mr. Hathaway. Wake up. You're dreaming." The hand on his shoulder was firm.

He opened his eyes, looking into the concerned face of the nurse who'd been hired by Victoria to babysit him

"Are you all right?" she asked him. "You screamed bloody murder a minute ago."

"I'm fine." He put a hand on his chest, feeling as if Victoria really had shot him. But there was no bullet hole, no blood, no pain. It was just a nightmare. She didn't know. She couldn't know. He'd never said a word, and Jasmine certainly wouldn't have told her.

Jasmine. She'd been on his mind since he'd woken up. She must have heard the news of his attack. She was probably worried.

"Can I get you anything, Mr. Hathaway?" the nurse

asked.

"Yes," he said huskily. "Could you get me a soda from the cafeteria downstairs?"

"There's water right here."

"I'm tired of water. I want a Coke." And he wanted her to leave him alone for a few minutes so he could call Jasmine. Maybe Jasmine could tell him why he'd gone to Chinatown. He didn't know why he couldn't remember anything since Christmas, which according to Paige was a month earlier. Why had his brain cut off the last few weeks? What was his mind hiding?

"All right. I'll get it for you. Shall I have the security guard stand inside the door?"

"No, you shall not," he said grumpily. "I'm fine. Go. And take your time."

She did as he asked, and he was blessedly alone. Thank goodness. He wasn't used to having anyone around twenty-four hours a day, and even though it hadn't been that long, he was already tired of the constant attendance of nurses. He wanted to go home, to his own room, where he could sort things out.

Reaching for the phone, he dialed Jasmine's number, hoping she was home. She always told him not to call or come by, but he needed to talk to her.

The phone rang three times, then her voice came over the line. "Hello?"

"It's me," he said, relieved that she was there.

"David?" she asked in wonder. "Are you all right?"

"They told me I was assaulted in an alley near your apartment, that I was in a coma for a few days."

"You don't remember?"

"I wish I could." Silence followed his words. "Why did I come to see you?"

"You showed me the dragon."

"The dragon I bought for Elizabeth's birthday?"

"No, David, it was the dragon from my dreams. Someone brought it to your store to have it appraised. You showed it to me. I held it in my hands." Her voice wavered. "I believe now that it was part of that set, the one we read about, the one with the curse on first daughters. And I touched it. I released the curse on my own daughter, on our child."

His brain was still too foggy to follow her reasoning. He knew about the dragon, of course. It was important to Jasmine. "Are you sure the dragon was the same one?"

"Exactly the same. You saw it, too, David. I am so afraid of what will happen next. First, you are almost killed. Now I worry about Alyssa, and what the curse will do to her. You must remember, David. You must remember where you went when you left me. You didn't go back to the store. If you had found the dragon, where would you have gone?"

"I don't know," he said slowly. "I wish I did." He strained to remember, but the effect only brought a throbbing pain to his head.

"There is something else. I told Alyssa that you're her father."

"Why? Why would you do that?" he asked, shocked to the core. They had kept the secret for so many years. It was difficult to believe it was out.

"Your daughter found out about Alyssa."

"Paige? That's not possible."

"It's the truth. I don't know how she did, but she did. I couldn't let Alyssa be blindsided. I had to tell her first."

Paige knew about Alyssa and Jasmine? His heart sank to the bottom of his toes. She must hate him. She hadn't said anything yet, probably because he'd been so badly hurt. But when things were back to normal, she would remember that he'd betrayed her and her mother. And she wouldn't understand. He couldn't bear it if Paige turned on him. She was the only daughter he had. Except Alyssa, of course, but he didn't know her. She didn't know him. It was a choice he'd made a long time ago. There was no turning back now. Unless .. .

"Does Alyssa want to see me?"

"She isn't sure. But you know she will not make trouble for you, and neither will I."

No, the trouble would come from Victoria. No doubt about that.

"I have to go," he said, hearing the nurse outside his room. "I'll call you when I get home." He hung up the phone, almost wishing he could return to the unconscious state he had just left. His daughter and most likely his wife knew about his mistress and his illegitimate child. Maybe he would have been better off dead. The thought sent a shiver down his spine.

Someone had wanted him dead.

Who? Did he know? Was that why he couldn't remember? Maybe he didn't want to remember. Maybe he didn't want to know who had attacked him.

Or worse, maybe the person who had attacked him was someone he knew. He wasn't the only one with secrets.

Chapter Nineteen

"You're awfully quiet," Paige said as Riley drove them across town.

"Just thinking about everything."

"It makes my mind spin. There seem to be so many secrets."

"Yeah," he said. But he wasn't thinking about secrets; he was thinking about Paige, about the kisses they'd shared before she'd reminded him that they had to leave, that they didn't have time to take those kisses into the bedroom, which was the only place at that moment he wanted to go.

He needed to stop kissing her, stop torturing himself with possibilities that could never be. Paige was a long-term girl; he was a short-term guy. He could have women in his life without making a commitment. In fact, he'd probably get more sex if he stayed single; at least that's what most of his married friends told him.

If Paige wanted a fling, he was her man, but anything longer, forget about it. He didn't carry the commitment gene. He knew that without a doubt. Neither his mother nor his father had been able to handle a relationship or a family. Although... his grandparents had had a good marriage.

Sure, they'd fought over the years. He'd heard them yelling at each other and driving each other crazy about not filling up the car with' gas or forgetting to buy toilet paper. But they'd also hugged and kissed and laughed together. They'd been best friends as well as lovers. They'd had a special connection, something rare, something most people didn't have. What was the likelihood of him finding such a connection? A million to one.

And the truth was -- he didn't have the stomach for those odds. He didn't want to put his heart on the line, make himself vulnerable. He'd lived his childhood like that. The pain was still with him years later. He'd loved his mother and she'd abandoned him. She'd lied so many times, broken so many promises. He sighed, wondering why the memories were coming back now. It was because of Paige. She was breaching the emotional wall he'd built. He would have to be careful, or she'd sneak in when he least expected it. And he couldn't let that happen.

It would all be over soon. They might not find the dragon, but he was confident they would get closer to the truth. The pieces were falling into place. He just had to concentrate on the task at hand and forget about the woman sitting next to him. If only she didn't smell so good. Did she wash her hair with perfume? The scent of sweet wildflowers seemed to fill the car. He pushed the automatic button for the window to let the breeze in, anything to break the intimacy growing between them.

Paige shot him a curious look. "Are you all right?"

"Fine," he said gruffly.

"You're not acting fine. You seem tense. You're

angry because we didn't get to finish what we started."

"We were finished," he said shortly.

"Really? I wasn't."

"Well, you don't get everything you want, Paige. I know that's probably a foreign concept for you, but it's the truth. Some things, some people you just can't have, and it doesn't matter what your last name is."

She sent him a curious look. "Jeez, what brought that on?"

He shrugged. "It's just the way it is."

"Are you under the impression that I think I can get anything or anyone I want? Because believe me, that's not the case. In fact, very few people in my life ever do what I want them to do. I've often thought I have absolutely no impact on anyone's choices."

"That's not true."

"Oh, it's true. For example, my mother let me get a cat when I was a little girl. She thought it would keep me company after my sister died. It was a small black-and-white kitten and I adored it, but it refused to sleep on my bed. When I tried to pick it up, it hissed at me."

"You should have gotten a dog."

"The point is I couldn't even make my own cat do what I wanted it to do." She shook a finger at him. "And don't you dare call me poor little rich girl again. You'd feel bad if your pet didn't like you."

"I never had a pet, not one that belonged just to me. There were some animals at one of the communes we lived in. It was actually more of a farm with pigs, chickens, dogs, cats."

"You lived in a commune? Like a cult kind of place?"

"More like a transient, don't-feel-like-being-a-responsible-citizen kind of place."

"What a crazy life that must have been."

"It was. Moving into my grandparents' house was culture shock. They ate dinner every night at six o'clock, not six-fifteen or six-thirty, but six. My grandfather always had the same cocktail before dinner, a Manhattan. And my grandmother used to watch game shows on a small television set in the kitchen as she cleaned up after us. They had so many rules I thought I'd gone to prison."

She smiled at him. "You liked it."

"I liked the structure, the predictability," he admitted. "It was sometimes stifling, and I complained a lot, but deep down it felt good to know what was going to happen from day to day."

"And that's what you liked about being a marine, too?"

"Yes. Plus I got to combine that structure with danger and excitement."

"Do you miss it?"

"Sometimes." He thought about her question far more seriously than she'd probably intended, but then again, he'd been considering the subject a lot lately. "But this is where I'm meant to be."

"Do you like the security business? Or are you doing it out of a sense of responsibility to your grandparents?"

"I like it. There are certainly opportunities for improved security these days."

"So it's going to be a long-term commitment?"

"Did I say that?"

She smiled. "You don't like that word -- commitment."

"Most things don't last. Not jobs, not relationships."

"You're very cynical. And yet you have grandparents who adore each other. They grew together not apart."

"They're the rare exception."

"Maybe," she admitted, her smile dimming. "My

parents certainly aren't a shining example of anything."

"Let's go find your sister," he said, as he pulled the car into a parking space.

"Words I never thought I'd hear again," she muttered. "I'm not sure I want you to call Alyssa my sister. We haven't figured out what we are to each other yet."

"You're sisters by blood."

"But we don't know each other. She doesn't trust me. I'm not sure I trust her."

He smiled. "Sounds like every family I've ever known, Paige. At any rate, she called, and we're here, so let's go meet her. The trust issues can wait."

"The class started a little late," a young Asian woman told Alyssa. "Ben said to tell you to wait for him." She waved her hand toward the gym. "There are chairs along the wall if you want to sit down."

Alyssa walked into the studio and paused just inside the door. Ben and another man faced off in the middle of the room. They were both bare to the waist, dressed in black pants and barefoot. She watched in fascination, every move, every attack, every defense. There was strength, skill, stubbornness, determination, agility, and courage in the way they fought.

Ben had taken martial arts classes for years, but she'd never actually seen him fight, and she hadn't realized he'd become so masterful at the art. She tended to think of him as an intellectual man, not a strong physical being, but it was quite clear now that that impression did not do him justice. She felt her heart speed up at the sight of him.

Today, at this minute, he wasn't a modern-day reporter. He was an ancient warrior, a man of power, a force to be reckoned with, a man who was making her feel really hot and very female. She waved her hand in front of her face and sat down in a nearby chair. The match continued for another five minutes. Ben finally took his opponent down with a spinning kick.

She let out the breath she had been holding as Ben extended his hand to his opponent. He helped him to his feet, then they bowed to each other. The instructor said a few words to both of them, then Ben turned toward her, a soldier returning from battle to the woman left waiting for him. She had to fight back the ridiculous impulse to run into his arms and hold him tight, to make sure he hadn't been hurt.

This wasn't a fantasy. This was reality. Ben was her childhood friend, her pal, not some godlike warrior out of a movie. So why did she feel so anxious and tense around him?

"Hi," he said, his voice deep and husky.

Had he always sounded this sexy? She cleared her throat. "Hi. You said you had some information?"

"Actually, I said we should talk to my uncle."

"Right." She could barely remember what he'd said. "Do you want to put on a shirt or something?"

A small smile played across his lips, and she damned herself for being so obvious.

"Sure, I'll put on a shirt." He walked over to a chair and grabbed a T-shirt, pulling it over his head in one swift gesture. "Better?"

"I don't really care. I thought you might be cold. It's not good to get sweaty and then walk around in the cold air. You'll stiffen up."

"Thanks for the concern."

"There's something else. I called Paige Hathaway and asked her to meet us here. I hope that's all right?"

"That depends on why you called her." His eyes sharpened with curiosity. "I know she's interested in the dragon, but there's more to it than that, isn't there?"

"Yes." She took a step back, drawing him into a private corner so they wouldn't be overheard. "My mother actually had a more personal relationship with David Hathaway than I led you to believe." She drew in a deep breath, not sure she could actually say the words. It would be the first time she'd said them out loud to anyone except her mother. But Ben was her friend. She could trust him. "David Hathaway is my father."

His eyes widened. "You're kidding."

She shook her head. "No, I'm not."

"That's quite a piece of news." His expression changed. "Oh, wait a second, he's hurt, isn't he?"

"He's getting better. He's conscious now."

"Have you spoken to him?"

"Not yet. Which is fine, because I'm not even sure what I want to say to him."

"So Paige Hathaway is your half sister," he said slowly. "And the two of you are interested in the dragon because... Okay, I've lost the thread."

"Because David Hathaway showed the dragon to my mother the day he was assaulted. She might have been the last person to see it."

"You want to protect your mother."

"And Paige wants to protect her company from a lawsuit since they hadn't purchased the statue when Mr. Hathaway took it from the store."

"Do you think you should be calling him Mr. Hathaway when he's your father?"

"I don't know what to call him," she said with frustration. "The whole thing is strange. I've wanted to know who my father was for so long. I had this dream that I fit in better with him and his family than I did with my own. I used to think about running away to find him."

"Alyssa--"

"Now I know who my father is," she said, cutting him off, "and it doesn't make any more sense. I'm not a Hathaway. I can't fit in with them."

"You don't know that. You don't know who they really are."

"What would we have in common?"

"You won't find out if you don't try. And I suspect you want to try, or else Paige wouldn't be joining us."

"I just don't want her making trouble for my mother." She wouldn't let herself look at any other motives right now. "I think it's better if I know what she's up to than let her do this on her own."

"Whatever your reason, it's a start." He looked up as the front door opened. "There they are now." He waved them over.

"I hope we haven't kept you waiting," Paige said as she and Riley joined them.

"Not at all," Ben replied. "I need just a moment, and then I'll take you upstairs."

"Upstairs?" Riley queried.

"My uncle knows a great deal about Chinese artifacts. I asked him to speak with us about the dragon you're seeking. I'll be right back."

"Thanks for calling," Paige said to Alyssa. She could see that Alyssa had stiffened upon their approach, and she wanted to put her at ease. "We really appreciate your help."

"Whoa, what is this?" Riley murmured in amazement.

Paige turned to see two men sizing each other up in the middle of the studio. In their hands were long, curved, single-edged blades.

"They are using broadswords," Alyssa said.

"I didn't think weapons were involved in the martial arts," Paige replied.

"The swords were used in ancient times, as the hand weapons of military foot soldiers."

"I would have liked one of those," Riley said with macho enthusiasm.

Paige rolled her eyes. "You are such a guy," she muttered. They all sat down together in the corner as the sparring proceeded.

Alyssa leaned in closer to explain what was going on. "The use of the broadsword requires speed and strength and excellent footwork. One wrong move could mean death."

"It looks dangerous," Paige commented.

"It is, but these two are highly skilled. And they will use every resource they have. Wisdom and courage, sharp eyes, fast hands, and the ability to confuse the opponent."

Paige saw exactly what she meant as the two men spun and kicked, thrust and parried, moving like dancers in an odd, brutal, killing ballet. Yet there was something beautiful about the fight, something intriguing. Ever since that dragon had appeared, her days had taken such a strange turn, leading her into a world she'd never seen before. She wouldn't have believed she'd enjoy watching a fight like this, but these men were so warrior like, so elemental in what they were doing. They were pushing themselves to the limit, a mental, physical, emotional, and spiritual battle. They were living the way she should be living.

A few moments later the sparring ended. The two men bowed to each other and moved off the floor amid sporadic clapping from the spectators sitting around the room.

"That was very cool," Riley said with enthusiasm. "I think I might have to take a class."

"Have you studied martial arts?" Alyssa asked.

"A little tai chi, some kickboxing, karate, nothing for any length of time. I think I'll grab a flyer from the front desk."

Paige shook her head, a rueful smile on her lips as she saw him heading fast and furiously into something new and exciting. What kind of woman could ever keep a man like this happy and feeling challenged? It would take a unique person. Someone who lived life to the fullest, who wasn't afraid of new experiences, who loved a good fight. Was that her? Or was she just kidding herself?

"Is there something between you two?" Alyssa asked, her question mirroring Paige's own thoughts.

"Well, uh, Riley's grandmother is the owner of the dragon."

"That's not what I asked. He's very attractive."

"Yes, he is."

"And you like him?"

"Yes, I do," Paige admitted. "Although I'm not sure I want to."

For the first time Alyssa smiled, and they exchanged a female look of commiseration.

"What about you and Ben?" Paige asked.

"He's been a friend to me my whole life, but we've seen little of each other since high school. I'm not sure it's wise to get involved again, but here I am."

"That damn dragon is causing all kinds of trouble."

Alyssa nodded her head in agreement. "I'm not sure we'll be able to find it. But I want to make certain no one thinks my mother had anything to do with its disappearance."

"I don't think that." And Paige realized it was true. Jasmine might be her father's lover, but she didn't seem like someone who would steal an ancient artifact. She was an artist herself. Still, she couldn't help wondering... "I don't quite understand why my father took the dragon to your mother. Why was it so important that she see it?"

"She has dreams."

"She told me that. But it's not clear to me what the dreams mean."

"Or to me. She has always had them. They're nightmares really. They leave her shaking and trembling, as if she is terrified of something. We have both wondered if there was some experience in her early life that was tied to seeing such a dragon. She told me today that her mother now says she saw the dragon on a trip to Taiwan when she was a small girl. That it was in a museum, and she tried to touch it, setting off many alarms."

"Really? That's interesting."

"I don't think it's true. Which makes me wonder why my grandmother would make up such a story."

"If it isn't true, where did your mother see the dragon?"

"I don't know. Maybe it truly is in her dreams. She's very spiritual. Not at all like me."

"Or me. My father -- our father -- he's a dreamer, too. Maybe that's what they had in common," Paige added. "I used to be so jealous of his fascination with China. I loved hearing his stories when he came home from his trips, but in a way I hated them, too, because he was so much happier when he was there than when he was home, when he was with me."

"He loved all things Chinese, and yet he couldn't love me," Alyssa said, bitter irony in her voice. "But then, I'm only half Chinese. He made me that way."

Paige didn't know what to say. The hurt in Alyssa's eyes was so deep, so dark, she wondered if it could ever be mended. "I'm sorry," she said with heartfelt sincerity. Even though her father hadn't always been there, at least he'd been around some of the time.

"It doesn't have anything to do with you."

"I know that. What you should know is that I wasn't the favorite daughter, either. I had a sister. Elizabeth died when she was seven and I was six. She was his favorite. He loved her more than anyone or anything. He still goes to her grave every year on her birthday to give her a present. It's on Wednesday, by the way -- her birthday. I think he might have woken up just so he could make that trip. God, I sound like a jealous sister, don't I?"

"I don't know. I was an only child."

"Not any more." Paige didn't know when she had decided she wanted Alyssa to be part of her life. An hour ago, she'd been waffling, but it suddenly seemed clear that she had a chance to make this relationship whatever they both wanted it to be. "We've got the power now," she said. "My father didn't tell me about you. Your mother didn't tell you about him. But now it's just about us, what we want to be to each other. That's a good thing."

Alyssa seemed a bit taken aback by her words. "I suppose," she said slowly. "I understand our father is awake now. Has he told you anything more about his visit to Chinatown?"

"No. He can't remember the last week. Hopefully it will come back. Until then, we'll work together to protect our parents." Paige looked up as Riley returned with a flyer in his hand. "Find any classes?"

"A few, not that I have time."

"I have a feeling you'll make time."

"You could take the class with me."

She laughed. "You'd trust me with a long blade in my hand?"

"Only if mine is bigger."

"Spoken like a true man."

Before Riley could reply, Ben rejoined them. "I'm ready now. Please forgive the delay. If you'll follow me, we'll go see my uncle."

Paige smiled at Riley as he sent a look of longing at the sparring about to take place, this time with long, pointed spears. "Come on," she said, grabbing his arm. "You can play later. We have work to do."

Chapter Twenty

"My uncle, Guy Fong, still teaches calligraphy classes every Saturday night," Ben said as they approached the upstairs apartment. "He may be finishing up with his students. If so, we will have to wait patiently and quietly. He does not tolerate interruptions."

Paige nodded as Ben opened the door. As he had said, there were three adolescents sitting at the dining room table, carefully painting Chinese characters with long, ornate brushes.

They moved in closer so they could watch what the children were doing. Paige was surprised by the preciseness of their script, the attention to detail, the concentration of three kids who surely would have wanted to do something else on a Saturday night. Ben's uncle stood at one end of the table, a short man with a square face and thick black hair. His eyes were a piercing black, his expression stern and uncompromising as he watched his young charges. If she'd had to guess at his age, she would have said mid-forties, but she couldn't be sure. Perhaps it was the otherworldliness of what was happening in the room that made him seem older.

Time obviously passed slowly in this apartment

where an ancient art was being taught to children who were being raised in an age of video games and fast food, fast everything. It seemed extraordinary that they would be painting characters instead of pounding a keyboard or moving a mouse. But apparently Mr. Fong was a man who believed in traditions. Paige respected that. It was nice to see something being preserved and passed on from one generation to the next. There was too little of that in the world.

She was also beginning to see where her father's passion for China and everything Chinese had come from. He loved old things, traditions that never changed, rituals and ceremonies. He'd been born in the wrong century and the wrong place. Maybe it was people like her father and Mr. Fong who were meant to show others the value of such time-honored customs.

A few moments later, the children set down their brushes and the tension in the room eased as Mr. Fong nodded approvingly at each paper passed to him. He said some words in Cantonese that Paige didn't understand. The children's faces broke into smiles that were matched now by the one on their teacher's face. He reached into the cabinet and pulled out three bright oranges and handed one to each.

"For prosperity and good luck," Alyssa said, answering Paige's unspoken question. "A long and fruitful life."

"Uncle," Ben said as the children left the apartment. "These are the friends I spoke to you about. You remember Alyssa Chen."

"Alyssa." Guy bowed to her. "How is your family? Your grandparents are well?"

"Yes, thank you."

Ben continued the introductions and Mr. Fong

greeted each of them with a welcome and a bow. After refusing his offer of refreshments, they sat down together in the living room.

"As I told you on the phone," Ben said, "my friends are seeking information about three pieces of art, two dragons that join together to open a box that we believe once held a flute."

"Yes." Mr. Fong picked up a folder from the table. "I made a copy of the article I found."

At Ben's nod, he handed it to Paige. She opened the folder, sensing that she was about to see something very important. Her instincts were right on the money. The photograph in front of her showed two dragons, one facing to the right, one to the left, interlocking together in front of a long, rectangular box. "This is it," she murmured. Riley and Alyssa crowded in next to her as she read the caption under the photograph. "*An ancient Chinese bronze excavated from a burial site in 1903, now on display at the National Palace Museum.*" She looked at Mr. Fong. "Where did you get this?"

"From a very old book I have on Chinese art. Is this the piece you are seeking?"

She glanced at Riley. He was staring at the picture with an intense frown. "What do you think?"

"I think that's my grandmother's dragon on the left, with the head going to the right, don't you?"

"I don't really remember."

"It looks a lot like the dragon in my mother's painting," Alyssa commented.

"If it was in the museum, what happened to it?" Paige asked.

"The National Palace Museum was taken apart piece by piece during World War Two," Mr. Fong replied. "Almost thirty thousand crates filled with artifacts were sent all over China for protection against the invading enemies. After the war it took sixteen years to put the museum back together. Some items were lost during that time, the dragon set among them."

"Do you know what happened next?" Riley asked. "Is there any record of these pieces reappearing at auctions or in private collections?"

"Some believe the box and the dragons came to the United States along with other pieces of art that were sold discreetly and privately."

"But there are no records, no proof that these pieces, this set, still exists?" Paige asked.

"Not until Mr. McAllister's grandmother found a dragon in her attic," Mr. Fong replied. "Ben told me what happened. I wonder how it got there -- in your grandmother's attic."

"I wonder the same thing," Riley said, his expression grim. "Do you mind if I keep this photo?"

"Please do."

"Thank you for your time," Paige said as they all stood up and walked toward the door. "Just out of curiosity, Mr. Fong -- if someone were looking for that dragon or its match here in San Francisco's Chinatown, where do you think they would go?"

"They would follow the pattern. The dragons and box connect. I suspect the owners do as well. If Mr. McAllister's grandfather had one dragon, then who do you think would have the other?"

Wallace Hathaway or Lee Chen. Those were the connections, Paige realized. But both of those men denied having knowledge of the dragons. Someone was lying.

Victoria raised her hand to knock on the door of David's bedroom late Sunday afternoon, knowing she'd put off this visit as long as she could. She'd managed to avoid her husband since she'd brought him home in a limousine just before lunchtime. She'd rationalized that she was letting him rest, but in truth she was avoiding him. His near brush with death had scared her more than she wanted to admit. Although she and David had grown apart in recent years, she didn't want him to die. In fact, faced with that possibility, she'd been shocked at how much she wanted him to live. She'd prayed for another chance, but now that she had it, she didn't know what to do with it.

They could no longer pretend that Jasmine and Alyssa did not exist. Jasmine might be willing to stay hidden, and Paige might be willing to let Jasmine stay that way, but not Alyssa. Paige wouldn't take kindly to sweeping Alyssa under the carpet. Victoria would have to deal with Alyssa herself, make it clear to her that she wasn't going to be a part of anything Hathaway. Victoria couldn't bear the thought of her husband's lover's daughter getting anything that she, Victoria, had worked so hard to achieve for herself and her own child.

One of the maids walked down the hallway. Unwilling to be caught waffling in front of her husband's door, she knocked and entered without waiting for a reply. David was still dressed in the casual clothes he'd worn home from the hospital. He was lying on the middle of his bed surrounded by art and antique books.

"What are you doing? You're supposed to be resting."

He looked at her with bemusement in his eyes, as if he wasn't quite sure why she was there. "I'm reading."

She picked up one of the books and saw a photo of a dragon. She sighed. "Dragons and more dragons. Is this the same one?"

"No."

"I thought you didn't remember the dragon statue."

"I asked Martin to send over a copy of the videotape from the antique show so that I could see the statue that sent me to Chinatown."

She wasn't quite sure she believed him -- he'd lied about so many other things -- but his words had a ring of truth to them. "Maybe you just went to Chinatown to see that woman. It wouldn't have been the first time. We both know that."

David took off the reading glasses that had slipped to the bridge of his nose and put them on the bed. "Must we deal with this now?"

"Paige knows about your illegitimate child. That damn security expert she made friends with has dug into our personal life."

"But you already knew about Alyssa, didn't you?" he said, through shrewd, tired eyes.

"I know everything, David." She could have sat down on the chaise lounge next to the bed, but she preferred to stand, to be taller, bigger, more in control than he was.

"Why didn't you say anything?"

"It wasn't important as long as she stayed away."

"What do you want to do now?"

"Pay her off, of course."

"Of course," he echoed wearily. "It doesn't matter that she's my daughter."

"You haven't acted like her father, have you? I didn't think so," she added when she saw him flinch. She knew this man too well, maybe better than he knew himself. She knew what made him strong and what made him weak. She knew his fears and the limits to his courage, and once upon a time he'd known something about her.

But he'd forgotten or she'd changed -- maybe it was a little of both.

"Alyssa is a young woman. She can't hurt us," David said.

"I won't be made a target of gossip."

"Don't worry, Vicky, you can play the martyred wife and become even more popular."

She ignored his cutting comment. "The least you could have done was use birth control. Where was your mind anyway? Forget it, I don't want to know. What I do want to know is if there are any other children about to come out of the woodwork."

"No," he said shortly.

"Thank God for that." She walked over to the window, gazing down at their beautifully manicured backyard lawn, next to the swimming pool and the gazebo. The sight of her surroundings immediately calmed her.

"You're so cold, Victoria. So sure of yourself, so self-righteous. I almost died this week, but all you can think about is your image, your reputation."

"You almost died this week because you went to see her," she said fiercely, turning to face him. "How do you think I felt knowing you were almost killed two blocks from her apartment? What do you think the press has been asking me all week? '*Where was your husband going? What was he doing in Chinatown?*' I'm lucky I managed to cover up your connection with that woman. Thankfully our good friend the police chief made sure that piece of information was put to rest by suggesting that the police visit to Jasmine's apartment had no connection to your attack."

"You mean your good friend, don't you? I'm not the only one with friendships in unlikely places, but while you can take the girl out of the slum, you can never quite take the slum out of the girl."

"How dare you!"

"How dare you?" he echoed. "You haven't said a kind, warm word to me since we buried Elizabeth, since you decided to blame me for her dying. It was my fault she got cancer. It was my fault the doctors couldn't save her. It was all my fault."

"Yes, it was," she hissed. "It was your fault. It was your fault I had to hear the diagnosis by myself because you were out of town. It was your fault that Elizabeth didn't go to see that specialist in Europe because you let her pleas that she just wanted to stay home sway your judgment. Maybe he could have saved her."

"And maybe he would have caused her more pain. She was dying, Victoria. You knew it, and I knew it, and neither one of us could stop it, not even you, the superwoman, and certainly not me, because I've never been good enough to do anything in your eyes. Except marry you. I got that right, didn't I? It wasn't me you wanted. It was my name, my house, my business, my parents. But was it ever me? Tell me the truth for once in your life."

Staring into his demanding eyes, she wondered -- had it ever been him? She'd set her sights on him and made sure she got an introduction. She'd learned everything she could about him, his likes, dislikes, ambitions, fears, and she'd made herself into the perfect wife-to-be. She wouldn't apologize for it. She'd been a good wife. She'd given him children, managed his house, taken over his company, made his life simple and easy. "You've had it good, David. You have nothing to complain about. You had what you needed."

"I didn't have love."

She shook her head, remembering those same words coming out of her poor, drunken mother's mouth. "What is love, anyway? It doesn't pay the bills. It doesn't get you through life. It doesn't make trouble go away. You have to fight for things. You have to take care of yourself." She walked back to the side of his bed. "Haven't you figured that out yet?"

"I figured out I couldn't depend on you, except for the basics of our life together. What about friendship? Companionship? Caring? Kindness?"

"Is that what *she* gives you?"

"She did at one time."

His gaze was clear and direct. She found herself feeling uncomfortable, but she wasn't the one who was wrong; he was. So why was she feeling as if she had to explain or justify her own actions? "Don't turn this around on me."

"Was I doing that?"

"I never walked out on you. I never cheated on you."

"You never wanted anyone more than you wanted the store. That's why you didn't cheat. It wasn't out of faithfulness to me; it was out of your desperate need to keep your position. That's what you love. That's the only thing you love."

"That's not true," she said, her voice shakier than she wanted it. "I love Paige. And I loved Elizabeth. And at one time I even loved you, dammit. Is that what you want to hear? Well, there it is. When we first got married, I thought I was the luckiest girl in the world, because you didn't just have everything I wanted; you *were* everything I wanted -- funny and passionate and charming. But when things got tough, I couldn't count on you. And you're right, I want more for my life than someone who drops in and out of it every few weeks, whose heart is on another continent. If I'm cold, it's because it got damn chilly in our bed."

"You locked your door against me. The day Elizabeth died, you turned away. Every night that week you went into your room alone, and every morning when you came out, there was another piece of you that you'd hidden away from me. It was the same with my father. When my mother and sister died in that car crash, he turned away. He couldn't love me, because I had survived. Just like you couldn't love me, because Elizabeth was gone and I was still there."

His words shocked her to the core with a truth she couldn't refute. She put a hand to her heart, feeling weak. A moment later she was sitting on the edge of his bed, looking into the eyes of a man she had never really seen. "You never said that before."

"I was hoping you'd figure it out for yourself. You were so damn smart about everything else."

"I -- I never wished you dead in her place."

"It doesn't matter anymore, does it, Vicky? We're done. We've been done for a long time. What are we trying to hang on to, anyway? What do we have left? Why don't you just give me a divorce and call it quits? You can have the store. You can have whatever you want."

"And what will you have?" she asked. "Will you have her?"

"I hurt Jasmine more than I ever hurt you," David said with brutal honesty. "I used her for comfort and friendship and kindness. When she got pregnant, I gave her money to get an abortion, money she threw back in my face. When she had Alyssa, I offered to send support, but she turned me down. For years I didn't give Jasmine or our daughter one penny of my money. Finally, Jasmine broke down. She needed help. Her family had turned against her because she'd had a baby out of marriage and out of her own race. So I sent her a few dollars when she asked, never one cent more than she requested, and I never saw Alyssa, never even spied on her in the playground. Jasmine didn't want me to confuse Alyssa, and I couldn't betray..." He rubbed a rough hand across his eyes, eyes that were suspiciously wet.

Victoria was still reeling from his suggestion that they get a divorce; she could barely keep up with what he was saying, the words pouring from his heart. The dam had burst and twenty years' worth of feelings were rushing out in a wild torrent of emotion. She was feeling it, too, more than she wanted. All those old feelings of young love were coming back. She'd told herself for so many years that she hated David, but she'd never really told herself why. Now she wasn't sure she could remember why. She just knew how badly he had hurt her, and she supposed she had hurt him, too. She'd known that he didn't get along with his father, but she hadn't realized that it stemmed from the accident in which David had survived and his sister and mother had perished. Why hadn't she put those facts together?

Everything made so much more sense -- even to some extent the affair that he had had. Deep down in the honest part of herself, she knew she had turned away from him. She'd been overcome with sadness, depression and pain; she just hadn't wanted to feel anything else.

"I don't expect you to forgive me," David said wearily. "I'm too old to start over, to change, to make things better. I'm too damn old."

Now here was one good reason why she had grown to dislike him so. "You're such a quitter, David. Why don't you ever fight for the things you want? Why didn't you fight for your father's attention, for my attention?

Why didn't you fight Jasmine so you could see your own daughter? Why do you always give up, take the easy way out?"

"Because I never win, even when I try."

"I don't think you try. You blame yourself the way you expect others to blame you. I think you're the one who feels bad for surviving all the tragedies."

"You've been in therapy too long, Vicky."

"I *have* been in therapy too long," she agreed. "I realize now I wasn't the one who needed it. It was you, always you." She got up from the bed. "Here's the bottom line, David. If you want a divorce, you're going to have to fight like hell to get it. Maybe it's time you found out what you're made of. Maybe it's time you gave me a chance to see if you're worthy of my affection."

He uttered a short, bitter-edged laugh. "Goddamn, Vicky. Do you know how crazy you are? You're saying the only way you'll love me again is if I can beat you, if I can make you divorce me."

"I need an equal, not a doormat. It's your call. Frankly, I don't think you have it in you to do anything more than run back to China and lick your wounds in private. I fully expect things to go on exactly the way they've gone for the last twenty years at least."

"We'll see about that."

"Yes, we will."

Chapter Twenty-One

"I cannot believe you want to sneak into my parents' house and search the cupboards and closets for a dragon statue," Paige said. "This is your worst idea yet."

"You didn't have a better one," Riley replied as he settled himself more comfortably in the driver's seat of his car. "Mr. Fong told us to look for the connections, and we both agree that your grandfather is one of those links."

That was true, she silently conceded. She'd been thinking about their grandfathers' connections ever since she'd left Mr. Fong's apartment, but she hadn't had time to do anything about it, having spent most of the day helping her mother get her father settled back home. "Did you talk to your grandmother again?" she asked.

"No. Not yet," Riley said.

She stared down the dark shadowy street. Riley had parked several mansions down from the one she'd grown up in, and she couldn't shake the uneasy feeling that they were heading into trouble. But they weren't really breaking in anywhere. They were just going to take a look through the family home while her mother and grandfather were out. She checked her watch. It was nearly six. "They should be heading out any minute now."

"If they're as punctual as you say they are."

"They are, trust me. I inherited the on-time gene. But don't forget my father will still be in the house, not to mention his private nurse and a couple of servants. We won't be alone."

"Too bad." He smiled. "So what was it like to grow up with servants. What did they do for you?"

"They kept the house, cooked, that kind of stuff."

"So if you dropped a candy wrapper on the ground, someone was there to rush over and pick it up for you?"

"I wasn't allowed to eat candy. It's bad for you."

"Some bad things are really good," he said with a wicked smile.

And suddenly the quiet in the car grew more intimate. She'd been trying to keep her attraction to Riley at bay, to remind herself that Riley didn't want the things she wanted, like commitment, marriage, family. Maybe she didn't want all that tomorrow or the next day, but eventually she would. What was the point in wasting time in a relationship that wouldn't lead in that direction? She wasn't twenty-one anymore. She was almost thirty.

So why couldn't she listen to her head instead of her heart? When he'd stopped by her apartment an hour earlier, she'd jumped at the chance to join him on this latest escapade, not even asking him what he had in mind until they were in the car. She was crazy. *Crazy in love*.

She'd just have to get over it. Treat it like a bad cold or a case of the flu. She could recover. She'd just have to work at it.

Of course, working at it probably didn't include spending more time with him. Well, she'd start working on it tomorrow. Her weary sigh drew his attention.

"Something wrong?" he asked.

"Just thinking."

"You do that too much." He shifted, putting his right hand along the back of her seat.

"What are you doing?"

"Passing the time."

She scooted to the edge of her seat. "We can't do that here."

"I think we can."

"This car is way too small," she protested, just before his hand crept around the back of her neck and pulled her toward him.

"It's perfect. You're perfect," he muttered.

He sealed the words with a lingering, tender, playful kiss that wasn't really meant to start anything. Just the same she felt her body responding with passion and intensity that went far beyond his intention. He seemed able to light her up without even trying.

Riley must have read her mood, because the kisses suddenly changed, deepened, intensified. Or maybe he was just feeling what she was feeling.

When they broke apart, there were no smiles, no teasing jokes, nothing to ease the tension between them.

"Dammit, Paige."

"What?"

"I shouldn't have done that."

"And you're blaming me."

"Yes, because you're irresistible. Every time I kiss you it's better than the last time. I keep telling myself that can't possibly be true, but it is."

His look of bemusement made her like him even more. "I feel the same way," she confessed. "I keep thinking it will burn itself out."

"We might have to make that happen."

"You mean, get each other out of our systems?"

"It's an idea."

She couldn't help smiling as she shook her head. "Another bad one. You're full of them tonight."

Before he could reply, their attention was drawn to the street where her grandfather's car pulled out of the drive. They could see two people in the back, the driver in the front.

"Looks like it's show time," Riley murmured. "Ready?"

"Yes." Because right now she had a feeling her grandfather's rooms were far less dangerous than this car.

Alyssa spotted her grandfather through the blinds of the Plum Rose Café. He was seated at the second booth, the newspaper in front of him. it was probably the racing form, she thought. When he wasn't playing mah jong or pai gow he went to the track at Golden Gate Fields and watched the horse races from around the country. She knew this was her best opportunity to speak to him alone. Tomorrow was New Year's Eve and the entire family would gather together for a huge feast of Chinese specialties that her grandmother and a half dozen cousins were working on even now. Of course she hadn't been invited to help prepare the food. Just another slight to make her remember that she didn't quite belong.

She shook the thought from her head. She had more important things to worry about right now than fitting into the family. Since Mr. Fong had suggested the possibility that the connection between the dragons and the box might mimic a connection between the various owners of those three pieces, she couldn't stop thinking about the connection between the three grandfathers. If Riley's grandfather had a dragon, then it made sense that one of the other two men might also have one. But probably not her grandfather. He'd simply worked in the stockroom at Hathaway's. He hadn't been in a position of power.

Still... there was something about the dragon that bothered her grandparents, and she had to find out what that something was.

"Alyssa?"

She turned her head to see Ben crossing the street. "What are you doing here?" she asked in surprise, feeling her heart skip a beat at the sight of him.

He smiled at her. "Trying to catch up to you. I saw you as I was leaving my friend's apartment." He pointed to a building down the street. "I couldn't believe you were actually making another trip to Chinatown."

"I want to talk to my grandfather. He's in the café."

"I can see that. He's eating alone. Hiding out from the family?"

"Avoiding the New Year's Eve preparations, I'm sure."

"You're going to ask him about the dragon?"

"I thought I might ask him about Wallace Hathaway instead, see if I can find another way into the conversation."

"Want some company?"

"I don't think so. Although he did always like you."

"What's not to like?" Ben asked teasingly. "Wait, forget I asked. You probably have a list somewhere."

"I left it at home."

Ben glanced toward the window of the café. "He's having pie. Looks like dinner is almost over. If you're planning to go, you better do it now."

"All right. Would you wait for me out here? Unless

you have other plans or something. You probably do have other plans. I don't know what I'm thinking. Forget I asked."

"You are one crazy woman," Ben told her. "You argue both sides before anyone has a chance to say anything."

"I know. I should have been a lawyer. But I wanted to make money now, not in three years. I couldn't wait any longer to be independent. And I want to get this issue with the dragon resolved so I can go back to my own life." Her words erased the smile from his face, the light from his eyes.

"I'm sure you must be eager to get away from here," he said. "I actually have something to do. I'll see you around."

"Ben, wait."

"What?"

"I didn't mean it the way it sounded. I'm grateful for all the help you've given me, and especially for your friendship, which I don't deserve."

He walked back to her with deliberate, purposeful steps that made her want to step back, but she couldn't move. Because this was Ben, and she suddenly wanted very much to hear what he had to say.

"You deserve everything you want, Alyssa. And I hope you get it all."

"I wish you wouldn't be so nice."

"That's my problem. I'm the nice guy, the one who doesn't get the girl."

"It's not you, it's me," she whispered. "Until I figure out who I am, I don't feel as if I have anything to offer."

"I already know who you are. I've known for a long time. When you figure it out, give me a call." He put his hand under her chin, tipping up her face so he could look into her eyes. "Just don't wait too long."

Before she could reply, he brushed her lips with his, a brief, teasing kiss that made her want more. He was halfway down the street before she got her breath back. Turning toward the café, she forced herself to move, up the steps, through the door, and into the seat across from her grandfather.

"Alyssa," he said with surprise.

"I saw you through the window," she said. "Did you play the races today?" She tipped her head toward the racing form that was marked up with numbers and circles.

"I won a few dollars. I don't bet much, you know that. Your grandmother counts every penny. Do you want something to eat?"

"No, thanks. I actually wanted to talk to you about something."

He grimaced. "Not the dragon, please."

"About your work at Hathaway's."

His gaze dropped to his empty plate. "I worked in the stockroom. Nothing more."

"Did you get to know Wallace Hathaway?"

"He was a big man. I was a small man."

She waited for him to elaborate, but he didn't say more. Instead, he picked up his empty coffee cup and waved the waitress over. He remained quiet while his cup was refilled. Even after the waitress left, he still didn't speak.

"Can you tell me anything more about him?" Alyssa prodded. "Or about the fire? I know you stopped working there after the fire."

"I can still see those flames in my mind, jumping up the walls like angry snapping snakes." He shook his head as if to dislodge the memory. "It was the end of everything."

"The end of what?" she asked.

His gaze sharpened. "The end of my job."

She had a feeling that wasn't what he'd been thinking at all.

"Why do you ask these questions -- because of the dragon that your mother can't forget?"

"Partly. But also because I want to know more about the Hathaway family."

His lips formed a tight line. "Do not speak of it, Alyssa."

And just like that she knew that he knew -- about David and her mother and herself. She had been brought up not to ask questions, especially of her grandparents, and she had always respected that policy... until now. There was a need to know burning inside of her.

"Just tell me one thing -- did my mother's affair with David Hathaway have anything to do with your relationship, whatever it was, with Wallace Hathaway?" she asked. "I know why my mother wanted David, but I don't know why he wanted her. And I can't help thinking, that maybe getting my mother was some sort of revenge or payback or a way of getting in someone's face, maybe even yours."

Her grandfather's face tightened. "You talk crazy. He pulled out his wallet and tossed some money on the table.

"I'm sorry if I upset you," she said as he got to his feet.

"You go home, work hard, forget about this. It was over a long time ago."

That was the problem. It wasn't over, not by a long shot.

"What do you think are the odds that we're actually going to find something in here?" Paige asked as she and Riley entered her grandfather's study. She turned on the small lamp over his desk. "I've been here before. In fact, I was here yesterday. And I didn't see a dragon or anything else suspicious."

"He wouldn't have it sitting out on his desk," Riley replied, glancing around the room. "This is nice. A man's room." He nodded approvingly at the dark wood, the heavy furniture. "Is this where your grandfather spends his time?"

"Yes. He considers these rooms his private sanctuary. Which is why we shouldn't be doing this. We have no right to be in here."

"Paige, get a grip. We're not stealing anything. We're just looking. You know your grandfather is hiding something. Asking him straight out didn't get you anywhere."

"That's true," she conceded.

"Don't forget, this missing dragon almost sent your father to the morgue."

Riley had a way of cutting to the chase that was really effective. "All right. You've convinced me. But be careful. I don't want him to know anyone was here." She glanced around the neat room. "Where do we start?"

"You check out the desk. I'll look through the filing cabinet."

Paige did as he asked, and for a few moments there was nothing but quiet rustling in the room. The desk revealed common business items, stationery, paper clips, pens. Everything was organized, nothing out of place. She closed the desk and waited for Riley to finish with the filing cabinet.

"Nothing," he said. "Where would your grandfather

hide something incriminating?"

"I don't think he has anything incriminating." She couldn't stop the automatic defense. It was second nature to protect the family name.

"Let's go into his bedroom," he said, ignoring that comment. He walked through an adjoining door. She hastily followed. If there was anything to find, she wanted to be with him when he found it. She stood in the middle of the room as Riley went through the drawers of the bureau with a quiet efficiency that scared her. He looked very at home in this role of burglar. It reminded her of how different they were, where they'd come from, the lives that they'd led up until this point.

Maybe Riley was right. Maybe they were too different to belong together. Her head told her he might have a point. Her heart told her the differences didn't matter. And weren't those differences in the past? They were together in this. She might be hesitating, but if she were really honest with herself, she'd have to admit that he hadn't dragged her into it. She wanted to find the answers as much as he did. She was just letting him be the one to do it.

Wasn't that cowardly? As if not helping in the search made her actual participation seem less. But it wasn't less. They were a team, a partnership. And she'd come into this room with her eyes open. She couldn't pretend Riley was making her do it. He wasn't.

She turned and deliberately opened the door to her grandfather's walk-in closet. It was lined with suits on one side, shirts and pants on another, everything from formal to casual wear, dozens of shoes on racks, ties, hats, sweaters. It was the closet of a very rich man. She looked to the shelves that ran around the top of the closet. Her gaze caught on a square plastic container in which there appeared to be several books. She looked around for a step stool but couldn't find one.

"Anything in here?" Riley asked, moving into the closet.

"I don't know yet. But that plastic container looks interesting."

Riley reached up and pulled it off the shelf, setting it on the ground between them. She squatted down, putting her hand on the lid, but she stopped when Riley covered her hand with his. She met his eyes. "What?"

"You don't have to do this. At least, you don't have to do this with me here."

"Why wouldn't I?"

"If I find anything to incriminate your grandfather, I'll use it," he said with his usual brutal honesty.

She drew in a tight, worried breath. Maybe she should be doing this alone. But she didn't want to do it alone. She wanted to do it with him. Gazing into his passionate blue eyes, she knew she could no more send him out of the room than she could send herself. They'd already crossed that line, and there was no turning back.

"We're in this together," she murmured. "And if I find anything incriminating against your grandfather, I'll use it, too."

"Then we know where we stand."

"Not really. But let's at least open this box and find out if it's anything at all."

She pulled off the lid and realized the box was indeed something. There were three photo albums inside and a manila envelope. She grabbed one album. Riley took another. Her album showed her grandfather's childhood, black-and-white photographs of her grandfather and his parents. She flipped through it, wishing she had more time to really think about where her grandfather had come from, what kind of life he had lived as a young man.

"What did you get?" she asked Riley.

"Your grandparents' wedding pictures. Your grandmother was a beautiful woman. Looks a little like you in the eyes."

"Yes," she murmured, gazing at the page he had turned. "I wish I could have met her. Anything else?"

"Doesn't look like it."

Paige reached for the third album, wondering where this book would take them. The first page of photographs sent goose bumps down her arm. "Hathaway's," she muttered. "Look, this is the store way back when."

"In the 1920s?" Riley guessed, coming around so he could sit next to her on the floor.

"It looks that way. My great-great-grandfather started the store in the late 1800s. The Hathaways were part of the gold rush, only we weren't digging for gold; we were outfitting the miners and selling dry goods."

"When did the focus turn to antiques and art?"

"After World War Two when my grandfather took over," she said, wondering if there was any significance to that. "I remember him saying that his own father never had much vision, but after he'd seen the world, he realized that bringing the rest of the world to San Francisco would be a gold mine."

"It certainly was," Riley agreed.

Paige flipped through several more pages, noting the mix of photographs and yellowed newspaper clippings. There were a few pages devoted solely to the 1906 earthquake that had flattened the city and the fires that followed. Hathaway's had moved to Union Square with the rebuilding of the square after the quake. The clippings from the next few decades showed the Hathaways gaining importance as city leaders.

"This is amazing," she murmured, seeing her family history unfold before her. "I wonder why this has been hidden away. I would have loved to see it."

"Your family was really something. It looks like they built half the city."

She turned another page and stopped, the headline turning her blood cold: W*allace Hathaway Missing In Action.* "Oh, my God. What's this?" She skimmed through the article, knowing Riley was keeping pace along with her. "My grandfather's plane was shot down over mainland China," she exclaimed.

Riley met her gaze with an excited gleam in his eyes. "We just hit pay dirt. Turn the page."

She was almost afraid to do that. Her grandfather had never mentioned being shot down over China during the war. In fact, she only vaguely knew that he'd been in the war, but that was it. No one had ever spoken about that time in his life.

Riley grew impatient and turned the page for her. "Damn," he said. "Would you look at that."

It was a newspaper photograph of two men dressed in ragged uniforms, their arms around each other: *Hometown Heroes Found Alive*

"Our grandfathers," Paige said in amazement, recognizing both men.

"Two of San Francisco's finest, shot down over China almost three months ago, were found alive," Riley read. " 'They credit their survival to a young Chinese man named Lee Chen, who gave them food and shelter and kept them hidden from the enemy.' "

"Lee Chen?" Paige could hardly believe it. "The same Lee Chen who is Alyssa's grandfather?"

"The third connection," Riley said, meeting her gaze. "This is amazing, Paige. It's all coming together. Our grandfathers flew together in the war. Wallace must have been the Wally my grandfather talked about."

"And Alyssa's grandfather was the one who saved their lives in China."

"When they returned from the war, they all went to work at Hathaway's with a new focus, Asian art. Imagine that," Riley continued.

"The three of them worked together until a fire destroyed the store," she continued. "They went their separate ways, nothing connecting them to each other until now."

"Until a dragon statue in my grandfather's possession came to light."

"The dragon set that was lost in China during the war."

They both came to the same conclusion at the same time.

"You think they brought it back from China?" she asked.

"It sure looks that way to me."

"But that would mean they stole it. Not just my grandfather, Riley, but yours, too. Is that what you're saying?"

He ran a frustrated hand through his hair. "Someone stole it. I'm just not sure who."

"You can't still be trying to pin this all on my grandfather?"

"He did end up with the most money."

"He had the most money to start with."

"Okay. Let's back up a little."

"Good idea, because I don't think it would be that easy to smuggle national art treasures out of a foreign country. In fact, I wonder how Lee Chen got out of China so quickly."

"Probably courtesy of your grandfather, Paige. He came from a powerful family. He had political connections, didn't he?"

"I'm sure my great-grandfather did."

"There you go. Your grandfather was grateful for the rescue, and in return he got Lee Chen to the States."

"I suppose it could have happened that way. But that still doesn't explain the dragon."

"It was wartime. I have a feeling a lot of things were smuggled out of China."

"You can't just steal ancient artifacts and sell them without anyone noticing," she argued.

"The black market has been around forever. Who says you can't do exactly that?"

"I don't know, but we still don't have real proof of any of this. It's all speculation. The only person we know who had a dragon was your grandfather. I'm not accusing him of anything," she said hastily as the storm clouds gathered in his eyes. "Like you said, he could have gotten it anywhere. He could have come across it at a flea market. The possibilities are endless."

"The possibilities are not that endless, Paige, not when we now know that the three of them were in China together during the war, the same time these art pieces were being shipped around the country." He paused. "Let's go over it again. When they came back to the States, Wallace returned to work in the family business. My grandfather was hired as a security guard, and Lee Chen went to work in some capacity in the storeroom."

"Then there was a fire," Paige continued.

"Discovered by Lee Chen."

"After the fire, neither your grandfather nor Lee Chen returned to the store."

"There was speculation that the fire was arson, but no

conclusions. The Hathaways didn't press for an investigation."

"How do you know that?" she asked.

"Simple. If they had pressed for an investigation, it would have happened. They had too much clout to be ignored. Which leads me to believe that Wallace, for whatever reason, didn't want to pursue the arsonist. Hell, maybe it was him."

"He wouldn't have burned down his own store."

"Maybe for the insurance money? Things couldn't have been that good after the war."

"They weren't that bad, either," she replied. "It's just as likely that Lee Chen or your grandfather was responsible. And if you're going to accuse my grandfather, then you can take some heat yourself. Because everything you're implying, including getting national treasures out of China, involves all three of them."

Riley thought about that for a moment, and she could see he wasn't too pleased by the idea. Which was tough. Because she didn't want to believe her grandfather would have done any of the things they were talking about, either.

"Is there anything else in the album?" Riley asked. She checked the next page, but it was empty.

"Nothing," she said, closing the book.

"What's in the envelope?" he asked.

She pulled a stack of letters from the manila envelope. "They're all addressed to my grandfather." She opened the first one and began to read aloud.

"Dear Wallace, I miss you so much already. I hate this war. I hate that we can't be together. And most of all I hate that we didn't get married before you left. I think about you every day. You have my heart, Wallace. Keep it safe until you return. Love always, Dolores."

Paige felt a wave of emotion as she folded the paper and returned it to the envelope. "A love letter from my grandmother. Who would have thought anyone could love that cranky old man?"

"He probably wasn't always so cranky."

She opened the next one and read softly, "Dear Wallace, I'm so afraid. We haven't heard from you in a long time. You've been declared missing in action. I was with your parents when they were told. Your mother fainted. Your father said it wasn't true, that you couldn't be gone. I don't believe you're gone, either. In my heart I know that you're alive and that you're coming home to me. We're going to have a future together, children, grandchildren. We'll grow old together. I miss you so much, Wallace. I'd do anything to get you back, and I know you'd do anything to get back to me. You're so strong, determined, stubborn. You'll get through this. We both will..." Paige's voice trailed away as she glanced at Riley. "She must have been so scared."

"She didn't give up on him."

"No, she didn't. And he came back to her just like she said he would."

"He did whatever he had to do to get back."

"Maybe," she said, wondering what bargains her grandfather had made to get himself out of China. "Anyway, I'm sure these letters are more of the same. I don't feel right reading them. They're so personal." She placed the envelope and the photo albums into the box and stood up. Riley put the box back in its place on the top shelf. "I think we're done in here."

"Yeah." Riley took one last look around the bedroom before they turned out the light and walked into the hall. "There's one more place I want to see before we go."

"We can't do the downstairs," she said quickly. "The housekeeper is here, maybe one of the maids. And my father is resting in his bedroom."

"I'm not interested in the downstairs or your father's bedroom. It's time for payback."

"What does that mean?"

"I showed you mine. Now you show me yours."

"Just what exactly are we talking about me showing you?"

"Your bedroom. I want to see where the princess slept for most of her life."

Chapter Twenty-Two

Against Paige's better judgment, she snuck Riley down the stairs and into her old bedroom, which was thankfully at the far end of the hall on the second floor, separated from both of her parents' bedrooms by several guestrooms and two bathrooms. She'd moved down the hall just after her thirteenth birthday in a moment of pure teenage rebellion. Her mother had pouted for a week, but it was one of the few times in her life that her father had actually stuck by her and stood up for her decision, saying she needed more space and privacy.

"This isn't nearly as nice as I thought it would be," Riley said with some disappointment. "Where's the canopy bed and the pink rug?"

"I hate pink," she retorted.

"You must hate every color."

She saw her room through his eyes, cream-colored walls, cream-colored carpet, cream-colored bedspread on the double bed with just a hint of a flower pattern. At least her bed frame, desk, and dresser were a dark wood.

"Where are the teenage rock star posters, the sports

trophies, the antique porcelain doll collection?" he asked.

"How did you know I have one of those?"

"Lucky guess." He sat down on the bed, stretching out against her fluffy pillows, and he had the nerve to actually put his feet, shoes included, on the comforter. "You really were raised to be a princess, weren't you?"

"Do you mind getting your feet off the bed?"

"Afraid of a little dirt?"

"Not afraid of it. I just don't feel like cleaning it."

"Don't you have housekeepers for that?"

She crossed her arms and studied him thoughtfully. "This is another test, isn't it? I'm starting to recognize them. I constantly seem to be auditioning for you, but I'm not quite sure what part I'm trying out for."

His eyes darkened. "What part would you like?"

"How about the part where I get to be myself and you stop judging me by all the stereotypical rich girls you've met in your life?"

"I haven't met any rich girls before you."

"Now, that I find hard to believe."

"Why?" he challenged. "Do you think they lived in my neighborhood? That they were in the marines with me? Or maybe you think they work for my security company?"

"If you aren't comparing me to anyone in particular, then why do you have so many critical judgments about me?" He didn't answer, but she could see she'd struck a nerve by the way his jaw tightened. "I know why. It's because you're still trying to convince yourself that this attraction we're both feeling will take you someplace you don't want to go."

"At least you admit you're attracted to me."

"You know I am. And I think we could be good together."

"What makes you think that?"

Sensing he genuinely wanted to know, she decided to tell him, even though she felt as if she'd run into another test. "You need someone like me in your life to make you see the other side of things, to make you believe in the good stuff again."

"And what about you? Do you want someone to drag you down, to mire you in the bad stuff the way I would?"

"Maybe I need someone to hold my feet to the fire, the way you do." She moved closer to the bed and sat down next to him, putting her hand on his very solid chest. "I need someone to challenge me, and you do that."

"Paige," he warned, "don't start something you can't finish."

"Who said I can't finish it?"

"We're in your bedroom at your parents' house. There is no way it's going to happen here."

She almost laughed at the desperation in his voice. "You don't think so, huh? I seem to have a thing for childhood bedrooms where you're concerned."

"I don't think you want your mother to see my bare ass on your bed."

"That would shake her up," she said with a little laugh. "But I actually like the sound of that." She dropped her hand to the snap on his jeans and heard the sharp intake of his breath. She didn't have to look down to know that his body was not fighting her nearly as hard as his mind was. Since she was a curious woman by nature, she let herself look anyway and was more than a little pleased by what she saw. When she glanced back at Riley, she couldn't hide the smug satisfaction she was feeling.

"I'm a man," he told her. "It doesn't take much."

"That's what you'd like me to believe, but I know it's me making you crazy."

"Feeling awfully sure of yourself all of a sudden."

"At one time, in my youth, I was an inexperienced virgin sleeping in this bed, but that was a long time ago, Riley. I want you to understand something important, all joking aside."

"Okay, tell me."

"I'm not a princess. I'm a woman, a complicated woman with good sides and bad sides. This room is part of who I am. I won't try to defend my family or my background or the privileges I grew up with, and I don't expect you to defend yours. What's important is not where we come from or how we were raised, but who we are today, what we want out of life."

"It's hard to forget where you come from."

"Maybe I can help you forget." She put her hands on his shoulders and leaned forward, whispering in his ear. "I want to make love to you."

"God, Paige, you can't just say it like that."

"I can say it any way I want."

"If you want to go back to my apartment--"

"I don't. And I don't want to go back to my apartment. I want to make love to you here."

"Why here?"

She gazed into his dark blue eyes and knew she had to tell him why. "Because this is where I first dreamed about you."

"Not me. I'm not some prince. You must have me mistaken for some other guy."

"I know who you are, Riley. And I have a pretty good idea of who you're not. I don't mean I dreamed of you exactly. I just dreamed of feeling this way, a little bit wild, reckless, like I'm about to jump off a cliff and I'm not sure where I'm going to land."

"Maybe you should back away from the edge."

"You're the one who makes me want to go higher and see what's on the other side." She touched his lips with hers, tentative at first, then with more confidence when he didn't reject her. "I'm going to make you forget who you are and where you are. The only thing in your head and your heart will be me," she whispered against his mouth, feeling his warm hands run up her back as she pressed her breasts against his chest and ran her tongue along the line of his lips.

Riley groaned deep in his throat. "You're killing me, Paige. I'm going to stop saying no if you're not careful."

"Good, because I don't intend to be careful." She covered his mouth with hers, diving into the kiss with her heart and her soul, giving him everything she'd dreamed of giving a man. No holding back. No second thoughts. It was all about this one moment, this one incredible kiss.

She threaded her hands through his hair, drawing him as close as she could, and when his arm slid around her body and hauled her up tight against his chest, she knew there was no turning back. She let reality go, stroking his tongue and feeling the rest of her body respond with a sense of desperation she'd never experienced before. She wanted him more than she wanted to breathe. She'd never felt so needy, so starving.

A moment later, the breath was completely knocked out of her when Riley moved suddenly, tossing her on her back, his hard body pushing her into the soft pillows.

"You didn't think I was going to let you call all the shots, did you?" he asked.

A shiver of anticipation ran down her spine at the intense male look in his eyes. He cupped her head with his hands, imprisoning her face for his very thorough kiss. Then his mouth left hers to dance along the side of her cheek, down the column of her neck across her collarbone as if he were following a path straight to her heart. But it wasn't just her heart calling him. Her breasts were tight and fun, eager for the touch of his fingers, his mouth. Her legs were moving restlessly between his, her body yearning to complete the connection between them.

"Damn." Riley pulled back with a breathless curse. "What's wrong?"

"I don't have anything. Protection. Safe sex. You know." He ran a frustrated hand through his hair.

"Oh. Don't you have anything in your wallet?"

"I don't have my wallet."

"You don't have your wallet? But you drove us here. Did you drive us here without your driver's license?"

He stared at her in amazement. "Is that really the most important thing on your mind right now?"

"Sorry."

"What about your purse? Don't you keep anything handy in your purse?"

"I own a dozen purses, Riley. And today I used the sneak-into-my-mother's-house purse, which does not come with condoms."

"Then that's that."

No, this couldn't be happening, not now when she wanted sex more than she'd ever wanted it in her life. Think, she told herself. "Wait. Oh, my God. I think I can save us."

"I sure as hell hope so."

"You'll have to let me up."

He sat back and she slid off the bed, walking over to her bookcase. She ran her fingers along the spines of novels she'd read during her high school years. There it was, The Odyssey, a thousand pages that her mother would never dream of reading. She flipped through the pages until two foil-wrapped condoms dropped out. She picked them up and held them out triumphantly to Riley. "They're still here."

"From what decade, Paige?"

She pursed her lips. "They're not that old. I didn't buy them until after I graduated from college. I was trying to be a grown-up."

"So you bought condoms and hid them in a book," he said with a laugh.

"I didn't want the housekeeper to find them and report them to my mother, because then I'd get the lecture on strange men and strange diseases."

"You are crazy."

"You want me anyway." She walked toward him, dropping the condoms on the comforter.

"I do," he agreed, taking her hand and pulling her back down on the bed.

"Good."

He pushed her back against the pillows. "Now, where were we? I know." His hand went to the buttons on her shirt, his fingers playing with those buttons for long minutes, while he leisurely kissed her as if they had all the time in the world. She wanted him to pick up the pace. She wanted that hand on her breast, and it seemed to be taking forever for him to undo the buttons.

"You're torturing me," she muttered.

His grin told her just how much he was enjoying the process. "I know."

"Riley."

"Paige," he echoed.

"Touch me."

"Oh, I intend to. I intend to do a lot of touching." His hand slid inside her shirt, his fingers slipping under the lace edge of her bra, circling one nipple and then the other as they tightened and peaked under his caress.

His mouth touched hers again as he explored her breast with his hand and his leg insinuated itself between hers. She moved her hand up under his shirt, caressing the taut muscles of his back. He was a strong, powerful man, and she loved the solid feel of his body, the way they moved together so perfectly. She had always believed that when it was really right, she would know it. And she knew it now. Knew it with all her heart.

Riley sat back, pulling his shirt over his head. She followed his lead, removing each item of clothing with a deliberate seriousness, her gaze never leaving his, answering all the questions in his eyes. She'd never stripped herself so bare before, lights blazing overhead, bodies completely exposed. That's the way she had wanted it. And she faced him bravely, offering herself to him in a way that she'd never offered any other man.

"I don't think I deserve this," he muttered. "Yes, you do. Let me show you why."

They met each other halfway, the slow teasing of the past few minutes replaced by breathless passion as they kissed, touched, stroked, caressed, made love to each other with their mouths, their bodies, their hearts, and their minds. Her dreams had never been this good.

Paige woke up disoriented. The bed didn't feel quite right, and there was something weighing her down. Blinking, she realized there was a strong male arm, flung heavily over her stomach. As she stirred, Riley's hold on her grew tighter, as if he didn't want to let her go, even in sleep. The events of the past few hours came flooding back into her mind. Making love to Riley had been better than she had imagined. He was a generous lover, inventive, adventurous, demanding, making her stretch, reach, be more than she thought she could be. And she'd tried to give him back what she suspected he needed, genuine caring, unconditional love.

Love. The word took her breath away. They hadn't used the word, but she didn't have to say it to know she felt it. She'd been falling in love with him since that first awkward tea party at the store. And she'd tumbled further and further each day. When would it end? When would she stop falling? When would it feel like every other relationship?

The cynical man in her bed would probably predict that possibility happening today or tomorrow or the next day. But she knew deep down it wasn't going to happen. She hadn't gone into this with blinders on. She knew what kind of man Riley was. He was terrified of commitment. He could risk his life on a battlefield but not his heart on a woman. But she also knew that he could love with loyalty and devotion; she'd seen that with his grandparents.

She wouldn't try to change him; she would just wait him out. Eventually he would realize what she already knew, that feelings like this didn't come around more than once in a lifetime. For the first time in her life that she'd made love to a man without all the trappings of romance, dinner, dancing, music, candlelight, flowers, candy. They hadn't needed any of those things, only each other. She put her hand on his arm and smiled to herself. Even if she didn't have tomorrow, she would not regret tonight.

A wave of light flashed through the window and she heard the sound of a car pulling into the garage. "Oh, my God, my mother is home," she said, shooting up in alarm.

"Paige?" Riley muttered in a sleepy voice.

"They're home. My mother and grandfather are home."

"Huh?"

"Jeez, you don't wake up very fast, do you?" She put her hands on his face. "Focus. My mother and grandfather are home. We have to get out of here without anyone seeing us."

His gaze sharpened. "Got it. You don't want Mom to see me."

"See us," she corrected. "Especially not naked here in my old bedroom."

"Right."

Paige scrambled out of bed, tossing clothes at Riley as she tried to find her own. "What time is it?"

Riley looked at his watch. "Ten forty-five."

"I can't believe we slept so long."

"Well, you wore me out." He smiled. "You're not going to turn into a pumpkin, are you?"

"Ha-ha." She walked over to the door and turned off the light, not wanting her mother to see the light when she came down the hall. "She must still be downstairs. What do you think we should do?"

"We could have sex again until she goes to sleep."

She rolled her eyes. "We already used up my stash."

"Are you sure you didn't hide anything in another book, maybe *The Little Princess* or how about *The Scarlet Letter*?"

"You're quite the funny man tonight, aren't you?"

He offered her an unrepentant grin. "I like you flustered."

"You just like me."

"Maybe a little."

"More than a little." She saw him stiffen and added, "Don't worry, this isn't the *tell me you love me and want to be with me forever* moment."

"It's not?" he asked, unable to hide the note of relief

in his voice.

She laughed. "You scare so easily." She stopped abruptly at the sound of footsteps on the stairs. They slowed down by her door, and Paige had the sudden thought that maybe her door was usually left open, not closed. Holding her breath, she hoped her mother wouldn't take this moment to notice the anomaly, although her mother was certainly one to notice just such things. The footsteps moved on, and she let out her breath.

She wondered if her mother would check on her father or go straight to bed. Thinking about her father made her feel a little guilty that she hadn't bothered to check on him herself. Not hearing anything more, she opened her door a crack and peeked out. The hallway was empty. "I think it's safe," she whispered. "But be quiet. My mother has excellent hearing."

She took Riley's hand as they crept down the stairs. They managed to make it down the stairs without any doors opening behind them or voices calling out. They were almost to the front door when she realized someone was in the living room. She grabbed Riley and pulled him across the hall into the dining room. There was no way they could open and close the front door without whoever was in the living room hearing them.

"Is that my mother?" she whispered.

Riley peered around the corner then looked back at her. "It's your grandfather. He's opening a safe."

"There's no safe in the living room."

Riley took another look. "Behind the portrait by the window."

"That's not possible." She pushed him aside to take a look herself, and what she saw was shocking. She'd thought she'd known where all the family safes were.

There was one in the study, one in her mother's bedroom, another in the linen closet, although why there was one there she'd never been able to explain. But no one had told her about the one in the living room. She was so annoyed by the oversight that she stepped into the hall.

"What are you doing, Paige?" Riley asked. "Do you want him to see you?"

"I think I do," she said decisively.

"You're going to take a step you may not be able to take back," he warned her.

"It seems to be the night for that. Are you coming with me?"

"After you, princess."

She drew in a deep breath, walked across the hall, and entered the living room just as her grandfather turned away from the safe with a very familiar object in his hands.

Her body stiffened in amazement. "Oh, my God! That's the other dragon."

Chapter Twenty-Three

Her grandfather drew himself up to his full height, his eyes blazing with anger. Paige couldn't help but take a step back. Actually, she was tempted to run out of the room, but Riley's solid body blocked her exit.

"What the hell are you doing here, Paige?" her grandfather demanded.

She couldn't speak. The dragon in his hands was the last thing she had expected to see. "I -- I came to...." She couldn't think. Her grandfather had the other dragon. How? When? Why? The questions raced around her mind, but she couldn't get any of them out.

"Who are you?" her grandfather asked, his gaze now fixed on Riley.

"Riley McAllister. Ned Delaney's grandson."

Wallace was not surprised. That small fact registered with Paige before anything else. He knew who Riley was. In fact, it was obvious now he knew a lot more than he was telling.

"Where did you get that dragon?" she asked, finally putting a voice to her thoughts. "You told me you'd never seen a dragon like the one that was stolen last week, but this is an exact duplicate. You lied to me. Why?"

"It's none of your business. This is my property. I don't owe you any explanations."

"But you owe me." The voice came from the doorway. David Hathaway entered the room wearing a silk robe over his pajamas. He looked tired and pale, but his eyes were filled with excitement. "Where did you get that dragon?"

"You should be in bed. You look like death," Wallace replied, ignoring the question.

"I got up to get some water. I heard voices." David stared at the dragon in Wallace's hands. "I remember now. I saw the dragon on the television show, and you--" His gaze swung to Riley. "You and your grandmother brought it in to the store."

"That's right," Riley said tersely. "And you took it without telling anyone. The next thing we knew, the dragon was gone and you were in the hospital."

"I took it to show Jasmine. Then I went to show it to someone, a man who can spot a fake bronze from a mile away. I had to be sure my excitement wasn't misleading me."

"Why didn't that man tell the police he had seen you that day? You were on the news every other hour," Paige said.

David hesitated. "He's very private."

"He works the black market," Riley interjected.

"Let him talk," Paige said. "What happened next, Dad?"

"I remember thinking that I needed to get home. I cut through the alley. And then--" He stopped. "There were footsteps behind me. Someone was running. I was struck by a terrible force. I felt myself falling." He shook his head. "That's all I remember."

"You hit your head on the pavement," Paige said.

David drew in a breath, then let it out as he nodded.

"Why did you think you needed to get home and not back to the store where my grandmother and I were waiting?" Riley asked.

David glanced at Riley, then back at his father. "I wanted to speak to you," he said to Wallace. "A long time ago I saw a box that you had, and I thought it could be the one that goes with the dragons. I didn't realize you also had the other dragon--"

"What? He has the box?" Riley interrupted.

David didn't answer. Neither did her grandfather. The two men were staring at each other, a look passing between them that spoke of unfinished business. Paige couldn't help wondering just what her father knew and what else her grandfather was hiding.

"The box you saw was from the Ming dynasty," Wallace replied. "It has no connection to the dragon."

"I find that difficult to believe. It looked exactly the same."

"I don't care what you believe."

"Where did you get the dragon, then?" David asked.

"From a private collector. I thought I might one day find the other dragon and the box. Until then, I would keep the dragon safe." Wallace turned abruptly, putting the dragon back into the safe before anyone could move. He slammed the door shut and flicked the combination lock. Paige was startled by the movement. Her father, too, seemed taken aback. But Riley... She could feel the angry energy emanating from his body. She glanced over at him and saw a determination in his eyes that told her he wasn't about to let her grandfather end the conversation so quickly.

"I'd like to see that dragon," Riley said.

"I would, too," David added.

Wallace shrugged. "It's no one's business but mine."

"My grandfather had one just like it," Riley said. "And he worked for you. You were friends."

"We were friends until Ned betrayed me," Wallace replied. "I gave him a job. I treated him like a brother. And he paid me back by stealing the dragon and setting fire to the store to cover up his crime."

"That's a damn lie," Riley said.

"It's the goddamn truth," Wallace said, his eyes blazing. "And you gave me the proof when you and your grandmother showed up on television with the dragon he'd been hiding in his attic all these years."

"I don't believe you. My grandfather is an honest man."

"Then how did he get the dragon?"

"I don't know. But then, we don't know how you got yours either, do we?"

"I told you, a private collector--"

"You also told us only a minute ago that you only had one," Riley reminded him. "Now you're saying you had two, and my grandfather stole one."

For the first time, Wallace looked confused. "Yes, well, I had both originally."

"But not the box?" David asked, rejoining the conversation. "Are you sure the box I saw didn't go with the dragons? If you had both dragons, where was the box?"

"That box wasn't part of the set."

"Open the safe," David said. "I want to see the dragon again."

"No."

"Dad almost died because of that dragon," Paige

interjected. "Don't you think he has a right to see the matching one?"

There was a strange glitter in Wallace's eyes as he looked at David. "I'm sorry you were hurt. That shouldn't have happened."

"Why are you sorry? You didn't have anything to do with it." David's eyes narrowed, the expression on his face changing several times. "Did you have something to do with the robbery?" he asked in shock.

"I'm eighty-two years old. You think I go around knocking people off in alleys?"

"Maybe not just anyone," David said slowly, his mouth set in a grim line. "But I'm not just anyone, am I?"

Paige had a sick feeling in the pit of her stomach. "Dad, you can't believe--"

"Can't I?" David interrupted, his gaze still fixed on his father.

The two men exchanged a long look that Paige couldn't begin to decipher.

"Your grandfather certainly could have hired someone to do whatever he needed to have done," Riley said to Paige.

"No!" Paige turned on him in fury. "Don't accuse my grandfather of hurting his own son. Are you crazy? He wouldn't do that."

"Wouldn't he?" Riley looked her straight in the eye. "Look at the facts, Paige."

"There aren't any facts, just speculation. We need to calm down, talk this through."

"Playing the peacemaker again, princess?"

"Someone has to."

"You just want to give your grandfather and your father time to cover up. A Hathaway to the bitter end."

She was stung by the cold fury in his voice and felt

her own temper rise. "Maybe you should go."

"So you can hide the dragon?"

"I'm not hiding anything. But you're not helping."

"She's right. Get out," Wallace said shortly. "Or I'll have you thrown out."

"And who's going to do that?" Riley challenged. "Are you going to call the police, Wally? Because I think I'd like them to come. I'd like you to tell them why you have a dragon in your safe that looks exactly like the one that was stolen from me."

"We know there are two," Paige said desperately. "They're identical. This could be the other one."

"Take off the rose-colored glasses, Paige. This isn't the other one. This is the same one."

"Please, just go." She had to think. She needed time to sort things out, to make sense of it all.

He looked as if she'd just stabbed him in the heart. "You really are choosing them, aren't you?" he asked.

"It's not a choice. It's too much too fast. I can't keep up with it all."

"Sure you can; you just don't want to. But this isn't over. I'll find out the truth, and when I do, someone will pay."

"That someone will be your grandfather," Wallace said.

"We'll see about that." Riley strode from the room without another glance in Paige's direction. His exit was punctuated by the slamming of the front door.

For a moment there was only silence in the room. Paige was afraid to look at her father or her grandfather, afraid of what she would see in their eyes. She had a terrible feeling that Riley might just be right about everything.

"I want to see the dragon again," David said. "Open

the safe, Father."

"It's late. I'm going to bed."

She looked up as David moved in front of Wallace, blocking his way. There they stood face-to-face, shoulder-to-shoulder, father and son. Paige had always believed her grandfather was the stronger of the two, but right now her father was holding his own.

"The dragon in the safe is the same dragon I held in my hands," David said slowly. "Mr. McAllister was right. That's what you don't want me to see, isn't it? You didn't have two dragons. You had none. Until you stole the one from me in the alley."

"No," Paige breathed, but neither one of them was paying any attention to her.

"Did you mean to kill me, too?" David asked in a voice that sounded almost dispassionate. "Was that part of the plan?"

Wallace didn't say anything for a moment, then said, "I didn't want you to get hurt. They were supposed to take the dragon and bring it back to me. No one was supposed to get hurt."

Paige sank down on a nearby chair as her legs gave out from under her. Her grandfather had had his own son robbed? And she'd just stood up for her family? Taken their side over Riley's? She'd made a terrible, terrible mistake.

"Why didn't you tell me you wanted the dragon?" David asked. "Why steal it?"

"I didn't want to pay for it. It was mine. Ned stole it from me. I wanted it back. It was simpler just to take it"

"Simpler?" Paige echoed in disbelief, drawing their attention back to her. "Dad was almost killed. You call that simple?"

Wallace's face tightened at her criticism. "I told you

that was an accident."

"And you expect him to forgive you for it? I don't understand you at all."

"You don't have to understand. I was settling an old debt. And your father will be fine." He paused. "No one will ever know. It's done now. Tomorrow this dragon, too, will disappear."

"It's not done," Paige countered. "Riley won't let it go. He's probably on his way to tell the police right now. He'll get a search warrant. They'll come to get the dragon."

"It won't be here, and surely you don't think Mr. McAllister is any match for a Hathaway?" Wallace's cool, ruthless smile made Paige shiver. "The police chief is a friend of ours. He will not be obtaining any search warrants. Your Mr. McAllister will run into one brick wall after another until he gives up."

"He doesn't give up easily."

"He'll have no other choice, not if he wants to run his business in this city."

"You're really flexing your muscles, aren't you?"

"I'm showing you what it means to be a Hathaway. Maybe it's time you decided whether or not you're up to the challenge."

And with that Wallace left the room, leaving chaos and confusion in his wake.

David sat down on the couch, resting his head in his hands, looking exhausted, overwhelmed, and defeated. "He always wins, Paige. He always wins."

She went to him, kneeling down in front of him, putting her hands on his knees, forcing her father to look at her. "Not this time," she said. "We can't let him win this time. This isn't about honor. It's about cheating. That's not what Hathaways are about."

"Isn't it? I cheated on your mother."

"That's not the same thing."

"Your mother cuts corners at the store every chance she gets."

"That's just good business sense."

"And your grandfather -- well, where do you think he got the dragon in the first place, Paige? You're the only one who still has some goodness left. You should get out of this family while you have the chance."

"I don't think I can." Paige sat down on the couch next to him, her mind reeling with information. They'd never spoken this frankly in their lives. It was difficult to take it all in.

"I've made so many mistakes," David said.

Which reminded her... "You have. You should have told me about Jasmine and Alyssa, especially Alyssa. She's my sister. I should have known about her," Paige said. "Why didn't you support her? See her, even if it was only in secret?"

"Her mother wanted it that way. And your mother would have wanted it that way, too. I'm a very weak man, Paige. I couldn't stand up to either one of them. The last thing I ever wanted was for you to know the truth about me. But now you do. And I'm sorry."

A part of her wanted to put her arms around him and give him a hug, tell him that it didn't matter, that he would always be her father. But that was the old Paige. Sometime in the past week -- or maybe in the past few minutes -- she'd grown up. "I don't think sorry is enough. Maybe for me, but not for Alyssa. You owe her, Dad. You owe her support, love, and acceptance. She's your daughter. She deserves that as much as I do or Elizabeth did."

"I was missing Elizabeth," he said quietly. "That's

how it started. Jasmine was there. She was kind. She listened. It's not an excuse, just a reason. We met at a party. She was a waitress working for the caterer. She was beautiful then, warm, kind. She reminded me that there was still some life in me. But I destroyed her life just as she gave me mine back."

"Did you know that Jasmine's father, Lee Chen, was the man who rescued Grandfather during the war?"

"What?" David looked surprised. "How can that be?"

"The three of them knew each other, Ned Delaney, Lee Chen, and Grandfather. I think they found at least one of the dragons and maybe even the box in China and brought them back here to San Francisco. After that, I'm not sure what happened. But it's strange that you and Jasmine should end up together. And that she should dream of dragons. It all seems so unexplainable."

"The mysteries of the universe. Perhaps I've spent too much time in the Far East, but I believe that there are patterns and connections everywhere. Destiny plays a bigger role than we imagine. Maybe those dragons want to come back together. That's why they're pulling all of us toward each other."

It was an eerie, mystical explanation for what was happening, but there seemed to be some truth in it. The dragons were bringing them together, this third generation. Maybe they were the ones who were meant to put the pieces of the set back together, too. "Do you still think Grandfather has the box?"

"Yes," David said without hesitation. "I'm sure of it."

"Then that leaves one dragon missing. If Ned had a dragon and Grandfather had the box, then it stands to reason that Lee Chen had the other dragon. I think it's time you and Jasmine had a talk. And Alyssa, too," she added. "We'll need everyone to get to the bottom of this."

Riley didn't sleep all night, considering the options available to him. After leaving the Hathaway house, he'd gone to the police station but hadn't gotten beyond leaving messages for the officers investigating the robbery. He'd gone home, tried to sleep, but gave up as the sun rose.

Getting out of bed, he went on a grueling bike ride around the city, watching San Francisco come to life. It was the day before the Chinese New Year he realized as he passed by traffic control officers putting up signs and roadblocks for the parade that would begin at five o'clock in the afternoon. Tonight all of Chinatown would celebrate the dawning of a new year.

He wished he could feel a sense of hope and wonder, that he could look forward to a new year filled with good fortune, but he couldn't feel any of those things. He'd left them behind in the Hathaway mansion. He still couldn't believe Paige had stood up for her grandfather. The old bastard was a liar. That was obvious to anyone. But no, not Paige. She still couldn't see past her last name. Well, why should he have expected it to be any different? He knew who she was. He'd known all along. He'd just forgotten for a while.

Lost in her arms, in her kiss, in her body, he'd forgotten pretty much everything. Even now his body was hardening at the thought of her, which was damn uncomfortable considering he was riding a mountain bike. But the pain in his body was nothing compared to the pain in his heart. He'd let her in. And she'd hurt him. When was he ever going to learn to stop believing in fairy tales and happily ever afters? They didn't happen to guys like him. They never had, and they never would.

He pedaled harder, keeping his head down, his heart

racing, his mind occupied so he wouldn't have to think. Somehow he ended up at his grandmother's house. He got off the bike and walked up to the front door. It was almost eight now, and he suspected his grandmother was already up and making coffee for whichever one of the three musketeers had spent the night on her couch. He could probably call them off now. He suspected Wallace Hathaway had been behind the burglary. He'd probably been looking for the other dragon, the one still missing.

Bud opened the door for him. "Riley. Saw you coming. Anything wrong?"

"No," he lied. "How's my grandmother?"

"I'm fine, honey," Nan said as she came down the hall from the kitchen. "And while I've enjoyed having the company of Bud, Charlie, and Gilbert, I think their wives would be happy if you ended this assignment."

"I was just thinking the same thing. You can go on home, Bud. Thanks for your work."

"Are you sure it's safe now? I don't want to leave Nan in any danger."

"I think she'll be all right, and I'll keep an eye on her."

"I'll be fine," Nan said with a firm tone.

Bud grabbed his jacket and headed out the door without any more encouragement. Riley followed his grandmother into the kitchen. "Is that bacon I smell?"

"Yes, it is. Take a seat. Do you want eggs, too?"

Riley sat down at the kitchen table as his grandmother put a plate of bacon in front of him. "This is plenty."

"You look like you sweated off enough calories this morning to eat whatever you want. Don't tell me you rode that bike of yours all the way over here?"

"Okay, I won't tell you."

Nan sat down across from him. "'What's wrong?"

"Everything," he said heavily.

"It's Paige, isn't it? I knew you liked her."

"Yeah, well, it doesn't much matter."

"Why not?"

"It's a long story, but let's just say that Paige will protect her family's reputation no matter who else gets hurt in the process."

Nan's eyes sharpened. "Who else is going to get hurt?"

"Maybe Grandpa."

"Oh, honey, I don't think your Grandpa could get hurt right now."

"Wallace Hathaway claims that Grandpa stole that dragon from him and tried to burn down the store fifty years ago. It's crazy, I know. Grandpa would not do any of that. And I know they don't have any proof, or they would have done something before now. But I don't want your name being dragged through the mud."

Nan's expression grew troubled. "Oh, dear. That doesn't sound good."

"You don't sound as shocked as I thought you would be." An uneasy feeling ran through him.

"I don't know anything about what you just said, honey, but I know Ned had a bit of a temper when he was younger. And he could be a show-off, a braggart. He liked to impress people. I thought it was rather charming. I kind of liked his bad boy image to tell you the truth."

Riley's eyes widened. " 'His bad boy image'?"

"He drank quite a bit when I first met him. He was always hanging out at the Irish pubs, telling stories. He was a little wild back then. All the girls loved him, but he didn't always treat them right. Until he met me, of course. Then he changed. Not all the way, though -- there was always a toughness about him " She paused. "Life wasn't that easy for Ned. He grew up poor, got drafted when he was eighteen, went to war, almost got killed from what I understand. Then when he came back, he had to find work in a city that didn't think much of Irishmen. He always struggled. But he always found a way to survive."

"Do you think he could have stolen something from Hathaway's?"

"No," she said quickly. "He wasn't a thief."

"I didn't think so," Riley said, much relieved.

"But there could have been a misunderstanding," she continued.

And just like that his relief fled. "What kind of misunderstanding?"

"I couldn't say. But now that we're talking about all this, I do remember that Ned was very upset after the fire at Hathaway's. I thought it was because he would be out of a job for a few months. Maybe there was more to it. I don't know. We didn't talk about his work much. I do know this. Your grandfather wasn't perfect. He made mistakes. He was human. I know you love and respect him, Riley, but don't put him up on a pedestal or under a microscope. Not many of us could withstand such scrutiny."

"It might not be my choice."

"Paige won't hurt you. She likes you too much. I saw it in her eyes." She smiled at him. "And I am never wrong."

"You might be this time."

"We'll see. I have faith in that girl. She'll come through. She'll do the right thing."

He had a feeling that Paige's idea of the "right thing" would be vastly different from his own.

Chapter Twenty-Four

"We need to do this," Alyssa told her mother as Jasmine prepared breakfast for them in her apartment.

"We are not invited to the New Year's Eve celebration."

"It's a family party, and we're family. I say we go."

"Why?"

"Because this is the most important holiday of the year. It's a time when families are supposed to be together, and I feel a strange and intense need to be with my family this year."

"You do?" Jasmine asked with surprise.

"Yes. I want you to come with me. I don't care what Grandmother has to say about it, or anyone else for that matter. Just this once, Ma. Please say you'll come with me."

"You're up to something," Jasmine said. "What is it? What are you planning?"

"Nothing," Alyssa lied. Actually, her plan was only half formed at the moment. She knew one thing for certain, though. She needed to stop running away from who she was and face up to it. Ben was right about that. Tonight would change that. Tonight would be a step forward for all of them. "Will you come?" she asked again. "I won't take no for an answer."

"I will bring dishonor to the occasion."

"No, you will bring pride and strength and love." Alyssa got to her feet and kissed her mother on the cheek. "It's about time the rest of the family sees what I have always known."

"You have such faith in me. I don't deserve it."

"Yes, you do. And you deserve a lot more. This past week has made me realize so many things."

"You are not still angry with me about your father?"

"Well, I wouldn't go that far," she said with a gentle smile. "Which brings me to my next request. I want you to ask him to come over here before we go to Grandmother's tonight. I want to meet him face-to-face."

"Oh, Alyssa, I don't know if that is wise. And he may not be strong enough. He just got out of the hospital."

"Ask him and see."

"I don't call him. I never call him."

"If you don't, I will. And I'll leave a message with his wife, if I have to."

Jasmine frowned. "I think I like it better when you stay away from Chinatown, when you want nothing to do with family."

"You're never happy. I'll see you after work. We have a new year to welcome in."

"Are you sure you won't change your mind?"

"I'm sure. Call my father. Tell him it's about time he saw his daughter."

⁂

Paige had plenty of time to change her mind on her way to Riley's apartment. In fact, she drove around the block twice before pulling into a parking spot and shutting off the engine. It was after nine on a Monday morning. He might not be home. But she'd already checked the office, and his secretary had said he hadn't come in yet. He could be on a bike ride. She'd have to check the highest hills in San Francisco next. But maybe she'd get lucky and find him at home.

As she walked down the street toward his building, she realized his garage door was open. Bypassing the front door, she slipped into the garage and saw that both bikes were there. Since she doubted he'd leave his garage open if he wasn't there, she went through the door leading up the stairs into his laundry room.

"Riley?" she called. There was no answer. Venturing farther into his apartment, she heard water running. He was in the shower.

Damn. She wanted to get this over with, wanted to apologize to him, beg his forgiveness, claim a moment of temporary insanity, and hope he was willing to meet her halfway. She had hurt him, and she regretted everything she had said. She knew the truth about her family now. And she knew that the man in the shower was the most honorable man she had ever met. The father she had adored was weak. The grandfather she had admired was a ruthless liar. But Riley -- a man who came from nothing, who had struggled to survive a neglected childhood, who had served his country, who had come back to support his grandmother -- was a strong, courageous man, an incredible human being. He was the man she really loved. And she hoped to God she hadn't lost him forever.

She walked into the bedroom and saw the open bathroom door, wisps of steam coming from the shower like tantalizing fingers beckoning her forward. She couldn't do that, could she? A knot of desire grabbed hold of her as she thought about stripping off all of her clothes and joining him. He'd be shocked. She'd be shocked. It was not Hathaway behavior at all. But then, Hathaway behavior wasn't what it used to be.

She unzipped her high-heeled boots and slipped them off. Her jeans and shirt followed. Standing in his bedroom in nothing but a bra and panties, she had more second thoughts. He'd been so angry with her last night. He was probably still furious. Maybe he wouldn't want her. Or maybe he would. Maybe they could connect in a physical way even if they couldn't connect on any other level. It was worth a shot. She was desperate.

She unhooked her bra and slid off her panties. She heard the shower being turned off. The shower door opened.

Damn, she was too late. She wanted to grab something to cover herself, but she'd made the dramatic point of tossing her clothes across the room.

Riley walked into the bedroom with a towel in his hand and nothing else on his body. He stopped in surprise when he saw her. "Paige'?"

"You weren't supposed to get out of the shower yet."

"I was done."

"I guess I'm too late then."

"That depends on what you want. I'm all out of hot water."

She took a deep breath. "I wasn't really looking for hot water. I was looking for you." “Why?"

"You're not going to make this easy, are you?”

"No way."

"I'm sorry, Riley. I was wrong. My family is basically pretty sick. I shouldn't have defended them. I shouldn't have asked you to leave. I was afraid." She drew in a deep breath. "I hope that maybe you can forgive me."

"Why? Because Paige Hathaway always gets what she wants?"

"No, because Paige Hathaway has finally found a man worth loving, and she really doesn't want to lose him because she was stupid."

His mouth tightened, and she could see a battle going on in his eyes. She didn't know if he was fighting himself or her. "You should have left well enough alone," he said harshly. "I told you before this wasn't going anywhere."

"I can't accept that," she said simply. "I love you, Riley. You don't have to say it back. You don't even have to feel it. I'm feeling enough for both of us right now. Just give me a chance to show you what kind of person I really am." She crossed her arms in front of her breasts. "Did you happen to notice that I'm naked?"

"I noticed."

"What do you think about that?"

"I think you're pulling out all the stops."

"That's right. Whatever it takes, I'm willing to do it."

"Anything I want, huh?"

She swallowed back a knot of nervousness. "Anything. I'm just hoping that anything includes making love to you."

"Oh, it definitely includes that."

"Good." She saw a teasing light blossom in his eyes and felt the ugly tension between them dissolve. "Now, let's see how willing you are." She walked over and grabbed the towel he was holding in front of himself. "Not bad. I know you're a guy, and it doesn't take much."

"Just you," he said on a husky note.

She tossed the towel on the floor with her clothes, liking the way it fell on top of her bra and panties. That's where she wanted Riley to be -- on top of her, inside of her, all around her. Their eyes locked in a moment of complete and utter intimacy.

His arms came around her body. His mouth claimed hers in a hard, passionate kiss. His hands cupped her bottom, puffing her into the heat she was craving. She was on fire, one burning need fueling every action. She wanted to get closer, but instead of letting her pull him into her very willing body, Riley took a step back, his breath ragged.

"We gotta slow down."

"No." She reached for him again, but he sidestepped.

"Patience, princess." He reached into the drawer by his bed and pulled out a foil-wrapped square packet. "Why don't you open this for me?"

She'd never done that before. What an odd realization that was. She smiled at Riley, then ripped open the foil packet with her teeth. She laughed at the astonished expression on his face, then moved forward until her body was only inches from his. She cupped him, hearing a deep groan of appreciation as she slid the condom on. "Is there anything else I can do for you?" she whispered.

"Hell, yes." He backed her up against the wall, gripped her bottom with his hands, and raised her until she could slide right down on top of him, taking him deep inside.

He filled her completely -- and not just her body but her heart and her soul. She closed her eyes as they began to move in absolutely perfect unison.

Paige was sleeping on him, her head on his chest, her arm flung across his waist, her leg over his, as if she wasn't planning to let him go any time soon. And that certainly wasn't a problem, since he didn't want to let her go, either. He couldn't believe she'd come into his apartment, stripped down, and offered herself to him. He'd spent most of the previous night trying to convince himself she was all wrong, and here they were -- back where they'd been yesterday. Because she was a beautiful, generous person, he realized. Because he cared about her more than he had ever thought possible.

"I can hear you thinking," Paige whispered. "Your heart started beating a little faster. What are you thinking about?"

"You," he muttered.

She raised her head and looked into his eyes. "Really?"

"You had a hell of a lot of nerve coming here like you did. How did you get in, anyway?"

"For a security expert, you don't keep your apartment very secure. I came in through the garage. It was wide open."

"Damn. That's right. The phone was ringing when I got back from my bike ride, and I must have forgotten to close the door. I bet half my stuff is gone by now."

"Do you want to go look?"

"Are you kidding? I'm in bed with a beautiful blonde. What's a bike or two?"

She laughed, her eyes sparkling with pleasure. God, she was pretty. Every time he saw her he thought she looked more appealing than the last time. Maybe it was because he wasn't just seeing her physical beauty now. He was seeing her, all the complicated feelings and emotions and actions that made her Paige.

Paige Hathaway, a little voice inside reminded him. A woman who'd only the night before chosen her family over him. Sure she'd apologized, but how could he be sure it wouldn't happen again?

"Now you're stiff, and I don't mean stiff in a good way," Paige said, frowning. "What's wrong?"

"Nothing."

"Liar. You're thinking about last night again. I was hoping we'd gotten past that."

"We will," he said, stroking her silky hair with his hand, "but we still have some things to resolve."

"I know -- the dragon for one. My father and I talked last night. We agree that the dragon in the safe is the one you brought in. We think my grandfather has the box, which means there's one dragon missing, and there's only one other person I can think of who might have it."

"Lee Chen," Riley said. "I think so, too."

"My father said something else that was interesting. He thinks the dragons are calling us together. They want to be reunited. They're making it happen."

"They're doing a damn good job of it," he said with a grin.

"Yes, they are. Now it's up to us, Riley, the third generation, to put those pieces back together and return them to China where they belong. What do you think about making another trip to Chinatown tonight?"

"It's a good idea."

"I'm going to call Alyssa. We'll go to her grandparents' house together."

"It's the Chinese New Year's Eve," he reminded her. "The anniversary of the fire."

"And the perfect time to figure out just what happened that night."

"What are we going to do until then?" He was getting hard again, already wanting her, already feeling as if it had been too long since he'd last made love to her although it had only been an hour or so.

"I can think of a few things," she said with a smile.

"So can I."

"Good. But this time you can open your own damn condom." She gave him a wicked smile. "I have a few other things I'd like to do with my mouth."

He groaned and knew he wasn't just lost; he was hopelessly lost.

"He's late. He's not coming," Alyssa told her mother as she paced restlessly back and forth across the living room. "It's almost five o'clock."

Jasmine sat on the couch, her hands folded calmly in her lap. "Sit down, Alyssa. You're wearing a hole in the carpet."

"This is a mistake. I shouldn't have asked you to call him. He doesn't want to see me. He doesn't want to know me."

"He will come. You will see."

"Fine. He'll come. I'll see. And then we'll go to my grandparents' house and ask them where the dragon is."

Jasmine's lips tightened. "I don't think it's a good idea. It's New Year's Eve. It is a special occasion. We cannot do it tonight."

"We have to do it tonight. I already spoke to Paige and Riley. We're going. And I hope you'll come, too."

"I will think about it."

A knock came at the door just as her mother finished speaking. Alyssa sent her a desperate look. "Maybe you should open it."

"You are my brave daughter," Jasmine said with a rare smile. "The one who always tells me I must not be so afraid. Now it is your turn."

Alyssa took a deep breath, squared her shoulders and answered the door.

"Alyssa." David Hathaway stood in the doorway, a handsome man with dark hair and dark eyes, eyes that looked like hers. Those eyes were pleading now, pleading for understanding. "I'm -- I'm your father," he said.

God. She felt like crying. Why did she feel like crying? He hadn't wanted her. He hadn't taken any time to see her before, and only now because he'd had a near-death experience. That had to be the only reason he'd agreed to come.

"Can I come in?" he asked tentatively.

She nodded, her throat still too tight for words. She took a step back as he entered the apartment, dimly aware of him greeting her mother.

"Alyssa, shut the door," Jasmine instructed.

She hesitated. This might be her last chance to run. But she forced herself to shut the door, to look at the man who had fathered her. He was tall, almost six feet. He still had a bandage on his forehead, but it was obvious he was almost back to normal.

"You look like your mother," he said. "As beautiful as she is."

"I'm afraid I look more like you," she said, speaking for the first time. "Ma has always said I have your nose."

"And the Hathaway freckle," he said idly. "Paige is the only one who doesn't have it." He paused. "You met Paige, I heard."

"Yes. She's nicer than I expected:"

"She chastised me for abandoning you."

"Is that why you've come now?"

"No. She only said what I have known for a long time. I want to apologize. I can't make up for what happened. But I want you to know that I do care about you, Alyssa."

"Why should I believe you?"

"I guess there's no reason," he said wearily.

"Why didn't you want to see me before?"

He sent Jasmine a desperate look, as if hoping she'd throw him a lifeline. Her mother remained stonily silent, letting him answer the question for himself.

"Ma already gave me the reasons she could think of," Alyssa told him. "I'd like to hear yours."

"It was never you I didn't want to see, it was myself. Looking at you would have been like looking at a mirror that showed all my flaws, all the bad things I've done in my life -- cheating on my wife and hurting your mother. And it was also because of Elizabeth, my oldest daughter. She was my heart. I loved her so much. I wanted to die when she died. It was the end of everything good. For those few years in my life that I had Elizabeth, I was happy." He took a deep breath. "I had lost a mother and a sister when I was a child. For the next twenty years I was searching for something good. Elizabeth gave me back the joyous feeling. And then that was gone, too." He took a breath and continued. "When your mother and I got together, I knew it was wrong, but I did it, anyway. When she became pregnant with you, I felt as if my sin was being held up for the world to see. Everyone would think I was trying to replace Elizabeth with you. It felt like betrayal. I couldn't bear it."

It hurt to hear how much he had loved her half sister. And she couldn't help noticing that Paige's name hadn't been mentioned throughout any of it. Hadn't Paige told her that their father had always loved Elizabeth the most? She wondered how Paige had felt growing up in a house with a favorite daughter, and how she'd felt afterward when she was the only one left, but not the child he really wanted.

"I can't change the past," he added. "I hope you'll give me a chance in the future to get to know you."

"Do you really want to? Or is this gesture just because you've been found out?"

"I want to," he said with surprise in his voice.

"Does your wife feel the same way?"

"No. In fact, she wants me to offer you a financial settlement to stay out of our lives."

Another stinging rejection. Alyssa didn't know why she hadn't expected it. The Hathaways weren't going to want her in their family any more than her own family did. "No, thank you," she said. "I don't need anything from you. In fact, I'm going to start repaying the money I owe you for my college education. It might take awhile, but I can do it," she said proudly.

"I don't want your money, Alyssa. And I'm not offering you a payoff. I'm done with hiding. I almost lost my life cutting through a dark alley." He smiled at Jasmine. "And I hope someday you'll forgive me, too, for not supporting you when you needed it the most."

"I always knew what I was getting," Jasmine said. "You never lied to me, David. Maybe to everyone else, but not to me."

Alyssa followed the look that passed between them and saw something that resembled love. Maybe she hadn't been the product of a sordid affair. Maybe her parents really did have feelings for each other. The thought made her feel better. "Why did you bring the dragon to show my mother?" she asked, the question still bothering her.

"I knew how much the dragon meant to her." He smiled again at Jasmine. "When I saw it, I wanted to give it to you, to free you from the dreams that kept you awake night after night. I probably should have left it with you. It would have been safer here. Or perhaps not. It might have brought you even more trouble."

"It is cursed, David. I believe that now even more."

"Yes." He paused. "I do need to ask you both a favor."

Alyssa's newfound serenity quickly fled. "What do you want?"

"Paige told me you are all going to your grandparents' house tonight. I want to go with you."

"Oh, David," Jasmine said. "They would not like it."

"Who cares if they like it or not?" Alyssa asked. "We know they've been lying to you about the dragon. We have to confront them, and you must come with us."

"I am afraid," Jasmine replied. "I don't have a good feeling about this."

David took Jasmine's hand in his "I will be there for you. It's about time I gave you back some of the strength you once gave me."

Chapter Twenty-Five

The colors were amazing, lighting up the twilight sky with mystery and excitement, Paige thought as she and Riley stopped to look at the parade that was currently blocking their way into Chinatown. There were children in costumes, some playing instruments, some dancing, others just walking and waving amid the colorful floats weaving their way down the street.

"This is incredible. I've never seen this before," she said loudly as Riley bent down to hear her.

"Me, either, except on the news."

He wrapped his arm around her waist and pulled her close, reminding her of just how close they'd spent most of the day. They'd made love several times, each time more passionate and demanding than the last, as if they both were testing the limits of their feelings. Her body felt sore and achy, but wonderfully satisfied, she thought with a smile. Whatever happened tonight, she would never regret this day.

"Look at that," Riley said, pointing to several enormous lions that were now dancing through the streets.

Each lion was operated by two men. The head was carried by one dancer who would rear up, then crouch down, while the other man carried the body, carefully copying his moves. The lion danced to the accompaniment of gongs and drums. As they watched, more characters, including monkeys and clowns, entertained the crowd with acrobatics.

"Amazing," Paige said. "I never knew until this past week how really isolated I've been. I live in a city of intensely different cultures, and I've hardly experienced any of them."

"Hard to do that from a mansion on the hill."

"I'll be spending more time on the street from now on. I like all the excitement, the music, the laughter, the life. Don't laugh at me," she said, seeing amusement on his face. "I can't help how I was raised. It's what I do with the rest of my life that counts, isn't it?"

"Absolutely," he said. "And I can't wait to see what you do with it."

"Neither can I."

"We better go."

"Wait, there it is, the dragon." But she wasn't talking about the dragon statue, she was talking about the enormous paper dragon coming down the street toward them. A man paraded in front of the dragon, carrying a lantern. The dragon's head was held up by a pole carried by another man. The tail of the dragon followed, as far back as she could see, with thirty, forty, maybe fifty people carrying the tail as it danced down the street.

Once the dragon had passed by them, Riley took her hand and pulled her down the street, looking for an opportunity to cross to the other side. Most of the crowd was following the dragon, so the streets were thinning out quickly. A few minutes later they were passing in front of the herb shop, which was currently closed. There was a door next to the shop leading into the building itself.

"I wonder where Alyssa is," she said, checking her watch.

"Right there," Riley replied.

She turned to see Alyssa coming down the street, flanked on both sides by her parents, Jasmine and David. Paige supposed she might have felt angry or upset to see her father with another woman, another daughter, but in truth she felt pleased that he'd done the right thing. When he'd told her his intention to accompany Alyssa to the Chens' tonight, she hadn't been sure he'd go through with it. Maybe there was hope for him yet.

"I'm glad you all came," she said, reassuring them with a warm smile. "There is strength in numbers."

Riley opened the door to the building. "Shall we go in?"

Paige stood back, allowing Alyssa and Jasmine to go first. It was their family, after all.

At the top of the stairs, Alyssa knocked on the door. "They might not be home," she said. "They're probably still at the parade. But everyone will come back here for dinner."

"Do you have a key?" Riley asked.

"I do," Jasmine said, holding up a long, silver key. "I haven't used it twenty-two years."

"Then it's time," Alyssa said.

They all waited as Jasmine inserted the key into the lock and turned the handle.

The Chens' apartment was small, crowded with mismatched furniture and knickknacks. The delicious smell of many Chinese dishes wafted from the kitchen. The dining room table was set for a feast. Paige had a terrible feeling they were about to ruin what was supposed to be the happiest day of the year.

A loud sound from the next room set them all back on their heels.

"Someone is here," Jasmine whispered in a panic. "We must go."

But it was too late to leave. A tiny Asian woman came through the door in a rush. Her eyes widened at the sight of them. "What are you doing here?" she demanded. "You go. You all go. Too early for dinner." She tried to shoo them away, but no one was moving.

"We want to talk to you," Alyssa said. "Before the others come back."

"No, you come back later."

The front door opened behind them to reveal a short, elderly man. Lee Chen, Paige realized, the man who had rescued her and Riley's grandfathers so long ago. He appeared taken aback by their presence, and as his gaze went from one to the other, he seemed to grow more alarmed.

"Jasmine, explain," he said. "Who are these people?"

Jasmine couldn't seem to get her mouth open. Paige almost felt sorry for her. She looked completely overwhelmed. Her father went to Jasmine's side and took her hand in his. Paige was stunned at how oddly dispassionate she felt. Her father was holding the hand of another woman, a woman not her mother. And while she would never have put Jasmine and her father together before, they seemed almost right for each other.

Jasmine needed him. And that was something his own wife had never felt -- need. Jasmine looked up to him as if he were important, and her mother had always looked down. It suddenly became so clear to Paige what had drawn these two rather eccentric people together. Alyssa was watching them, too. Alyssa, her sister, watching her own parents together for the first time. A rush of emotion threatened to overwhelm her. Paige sought out the hand of the man standing next to her, and his strength filled her with resolve.

"I'm Paige Hathaway," she said, taking charge. "This is my father, David. And my friend, Riley McAllister, who is the grandson of a man you might remember, Ned Delaney."

Lee Chen's face paled at her words. "Why did you come here? Why did you bring him?" he said to Jasmine in anger. "You dishonor us, dishonor the family. You should go."

"You're a fine one to talk of dishonor," a man said from the doorway.

Paige was shocked to see her grandfather, Wallace Hathaway, walk into the room like a king visiting the local peasants. He was dressed in an expensive suit, and he looked every inch the successful businessman, a direct contrast to the old, baggy clothes worn by Lee Chen. The room went still at his appearance. She had the distinct impression that this was the first time in many years that these two old men had laid eyes on each other. But they were looking now, staring at each other with an intensity that spoke of a troubled past.

"What are you doing here, Grandfather?" she asked.

"I came to get my dragon back. Where is it?"

"I don't have your dragon. You steal it and keep it for yourself," Lee Chen said.

"You and Ned conspired against me. If he had one, you must have the other," Wallace replied.

"I do not," Lee said firmly, waving his hand in the air. "Get out of my house. You are not welcome here."

"Don't tell me where I'm not welcome. I'm the one who got you to this country, and how did you repay me?

By stealing and burning down my store--"

"I thought you said my grandfather did that," Riley interrupted. "So you really don't know who did it, do you? Maybe you did it yourself. Maybe you wanted to cover something up, take the insurance money, start over."

"The person who burned down my store is the person who took the dragons out of the basement that night. That would be Ned or Lee," Wallace said. "I've known that all along."

"Why did you wait until now to come looking?" Riley asked, echoing the question in Paige's mind.

"Because I thought that the dragons had been destroyed in the fire. The store was a twenty-feet high pile of junk after that blaze. The cleanup wasn't as efficient as it would be today. I lost everything. When I saw your grandfather's dragon, I realized it had escaped the fire, and I suspected the other one had, too."

"And you knew my grandfather didn't have the other dragon because you had his house searched," Riley said. "You probably had my grandmother watched, too, didn't you? I knew someone was tailing us that very first day we went to the store."

Paige's eyes widened as Riley put together another piece of the puzzle that hadn't yet occurred to her. Wallace didn't confirm or deny the accusation, but Paige could see the truth in her grandfather's eyes. When he hadn't been able to get the dragon away from Riley and his grandmother, he'd had someone follow David until there was an opportunity to snatch the dragon back.

"Why did you wait until now to come here?" Riley asked.

"I don't have to explain anything to you. Where is the other dragon?" Wallace said turning his attention back to Lee. "I want it."

"I don't have it," Lee Chen stubbornly repeated. "I never had it. And I didn't set the fire."

"You were just the first one on the scene, is that it?"

"Yes. I was there. I tried to put the fire out. I tried to save the store. I never saw the dragons. I don't know where they are."

"You must know where one is," Jasmine said quietly. "It's here, somewhere in this apartment, isn't it?" Lee's face turned pale at his daughter's words. He started to shake his head, but Jasmine interrupted. "I saw it one night. A night like this."

Jasmine had barely finished speaking when a loud crack rocked the room. Fireworks! The parade must be over, for there was an explosion of noise, flashes of light coming through the windows. Jasmine jumped, putting a hand to her mouth. "It was just like this," she said. "I remember now."

"You remember nothing," An-Mei said fiercely. Suddenly the battle was between the two women and not the two men.

"I was frightened. I ran into your bedroom?" Jasmine's gaze darted to the door behind her mother, and she gasped.

Paige followed her gaze and saw the reason for the sudden horror on her face. Smoke was coming from under the door behind Mrs. Chen.

"Fire!" Alyssa cried.

An-Mei threw open the door to her bedroom, and they saw the curtains going up in flames. She ran into the room with a scream. Riley followed behind her, trying to pull her away from the fire. Paige rushed toward them both, while David, Jasmine, and Alyssa ran to the kitchen to get water to throw onto the fire.

"Get her out of here," Riley said. "Call 911." He tried

to push An-Mei out of the room, but she was surprisingly strong for a small woman of her age. Paige tried to take her arm as well but she shrugged it off. Jasmine came into the room and begged her mother to leave it alone, to get out. An-Mei wouldn't move. She looked at Jasmine with a gleam of madness in her eyes. "The curse. It has finally come true. We all die here tonight."

"We're not dying," Riley said as he ripped the curtains off the rod and stomped on them until there was nothing left but smoke.

An-Mei looked at Wallace with hatred in her eyes. "It is your fault. You make it all happen. You promise much gold and prosperity. But you curse us all."

"I made us a fortune. I brought your husband to this country. He was nothing without me. Then he betrayed me."

Wallace's eyes suddenly lit up, and as Paige followed his gaze, she saw the dragon on a table that was set up like an altar, the statue surrounded by dripping candles, one of which had fallen on its side, lighting the bedroom curtains that were now water-soaked and blackened. The dragon stared at them mockingly, as if wondering why it had taken them so long to come. Its jade eyes flashed through the lingering smoke, throwing colors across the ancient bronze.

"Oh, my God," Paige said.

"You had it all along," Jasmine said in a daze. "I saw it here before. You were praying at the altar. I came up to you and asked you about it. You threw me in the closet. You locked the door. It was dark. I could hear the fireworks. I was terrified." She looked at her mother. "And when you pulled me out, you almost broke my arm. You spanked me many times and told me I was bad, I must forget. I must never tell." Jasmine turned to her father, who stood in the doorway of the bedroom. "Did you know what she did to me? Did you?"

Lee Chen didn't answer right away. He stared at his wife, who was holding her arms around her waist and rocking back and forth. "An-Mei," he said softly. "It's all right."

"It's not all right," Jasmine said. "Don't you understand that?"

Lee wasn't looking at his daughter. He was looking at his wife.

"The dragons were not meant to belong to any of us," An-Mei said. "They should have been returned years ago."

Wallace turned to Lee. "After all we had been through together, you betrayed me. You stole this dragon. But you couldn't do anything without the other dragon and the box. So you kept this one hidden away all these years. Did you know Ned had the other dragon?"

"I wasn't sure," Lee said, coughing as he finished speaking.

"We should get out of this smoke," Paige said.

"She's right," Riley echoed.

No one moved. No one wanted to leave the dragon on the altar. But no one seemed to have the nerve to touch it.

Riley took a step forward. Paige called him back. "Don't," she said. "Don't touch it. It might really be cursed."

He hesitated, then moved ahead in typical Riley fashion. He picked up the dragon statue and walked out of the room. There was a scramble to follow him, people bumping into one another as they made their way into the living room. Paige was the last one out, closing the bedroom door behind her.

"Time for some straight talk." Riley set the dragon on

the coffee table. "Where did the dragons come from?"

"Tell him, Wallace," An-Mei ordered. "Tell him you steal dragons from China."

"I didn't do it alone," Wallace retorted.

"Then, how did you do it?" David asked his father.

"It was Lee," Wallace said. "He found the crate in the woods. It must have fallen off a truck. It was just waiting there, a treasure to be discovered. I knew right away we should keep it. We might need to trade it for freedom. It was wartime. The enemy was getting closer every day. Lee agreed with me. So did your grandfather," he added, looking at Riley. "We were good friends then, brothers. We smuggled the crate out of China and brought it back here to San Francisco. Inside, there were many artifacts from the museum."

"More than just the dragons and the box?" Paige asked.

"Yes," Wallace said shortly. "We knew we were sitting on a potential gold mine. We made a pact to sell the objects one at a time, discreetly of course, so no one would know. Ned and Lee worked at the store with me. We shared the profits from those sales equally. Until she" -- he tipped his head at An-Mei--"started worrying about the damn curse. She got Lee and even Ned all worked up about it. Stupid woman." He turned to Lee. "But you -- I couldn't understand why you would steal the dragons and burn down the store. We were friends."

For the first time, Paige saw a chink in her grandfather's armor, a sign that he wasn't as emotionless and cold as he pretended to be. He'd been betrayed by his friends. No wonder he'd never trusted anyone again.

Lee didn't seem able to speak. His eyes were watering. His shoulders shaking.

Paige wanted to tell her grandfather to stop, but she

couldn't interrupt. This was between the two of them, and it was time they settled it.

Lee put a hand to his heart. Jasmine ran to his side. "Papa," she said with concern.

He waved her off. "I'm okay." He drew in a breath, then said, "When I set the fire, I thought I could take everything, but only one dragon was there. The other two pieces were missing. I set the fire to cover the theft. It was my fault."

"No!" An-Mei cried. "Not you. *Me*."

The tiny Chinese woman walked to the middle of the room and slowly but defiantly pushed back her sleeves. Paige saw the crisscross of scars that ran from her wrists to her elbows, and suddenly the truth was clear.

"I start fire," An-Mei said. "I want to send dragons and box back to China. Break curse forever. I have no choice." She shook her head. "But only one dragon there. The fire jumped. Too late to stop." She looked at her husband. "I hide it away. You don't see. You don't know."

"I knew," Lee said heavily, meeting her gaze. "I saw it a long time ago, but I didn't want to speak of it."

"And I saw it, too," Jasmine reminded her once again.

"I tell you to forget. You never forget. You cursed."

"I think it was the moment I realized how much you hated me," Jasmine said. "That's why I couldn't forget. I knew I was a disappointment, but I didn't know why -- a disappointment long before David came along."

"You first daughter, Jasmine. You born with no finger. The curse struck you because of him," she said, shooting another dark, stabbing look at Wallace. "He say they too valuable to send back."

"They were too valuable, and it was too late to turn back," Wallace replied. "We would have had to reveal where we got the dragons in the first place. And we couldn't do that. The scandal wouldn't have just done us in; it would have hurt the entire country. The United States and China were not exactly friends." He looked at the statue on the coffee table. "And neither were we -- after the fire."

"I can't imagine that my grandfather ever went along with this theft, this plan," Riley said.

Paige heard the pain in Riley's voice; it matched the pain in her own heart. It was hard to believe that the men they loved and respected had made a very bad decision a long time ago.

"He went along with it," Wallace said. "You don't have to understand. It was a different time. We'd seen our friends die in front of us. We'd faced our own mortality, and when we got back to the States, times were hard. Those art pieces gave us a leg up. Lee and Ned were able to start their own businesses with the money they made, and I put Hathaway's back into the black. No one got hurt."

"How can you say that?" Paige asked. "It looks to me like a lot of people got hurt, our families most of all."

"I don't understand," Jasmine interrupted, looking at her mother. "If the dragon was cursed, why did you keep it all this time?"

"I couldn't do anything else with it," An-Mei said. "The pieces were separated. I thought they were destroyed in the fire. So every New Year I pray to the Dragon God for forgiveness and a chance to make it right. When the other dragon came to light I thought -- but then it was gone again."

"How did my grandfather get the other dragon?" Riley asked.

"I think Ned must have taken it to show some friends at the bar, to impress them," Lee replied. "He was always doing that. I didn't realize he hadn't returned it to the store before the fire."

"But then the store burned down, and my grandfather probably thought he'd be blamed if Wallace knew he had one of the dragons," Riley said. "It makes sense."

"You still have the box, don't you, Father?" David asked. "I saw it a long time ago. It wasn't in the basement when Mrs. Chen started the fire, was it?"

Wallace hesitated for a long moment. "We kept the records of our transactions in the box. I had removed it to my house for safekeeping."

"So you have my grandfather's dragon and the box." Riley picked up the other dragon from the coffee table. "I think it's time we put the pieces back together again."

An hour later they were gathered together in the dining room of the Hathaway mansion with one more member of the family in attendance, Victoria. Paige's mother was furious at all that had transpired outside of her presence and had made that quite clear to Paige when the motley group, as Victoria referred to them, had descended on the mansion. But no one was paying much attention to Victoria. There were now three pieces on the mahogany table, the two matching dragons and a long narrow box with an ornate lock.

"We should do it together," Paige said, motioning for Alyssa and Riley to come forward. "I believe we three were meant to put the pieces back together."

"I agree," Riley said, handing Alyssa the dragon that had been kept in her grandparents' apartment for so many years. Then he picked up the one belonging to his grandfather.

Paige picked up the box and held it out to them. She felt a shiver of excitement run down her spine as the box seemed to grow warmer in her hands. She could almost hear voices from the past, or was it music? For somewhere in her mind she could hear the distinct sound of a distant flute.

Riley and Alyssa moved forward, joining their dragons together. With Paige's help, they inserted the back joint of each dragon into the box. Their eyes met at the same moment the lock turned, and the lid snapped open.

Paige reached for the several pieces of paper that were inside the box, but Wallace grabbed the papers from her hand. Before anyone could move, he had pulled a lighter from his pocket and set the papers to flame, the evidence burning quickly.

"Damn, you're good," Riley said, not making it sound like a compliment. "No one will ever know the extent of your thievery."

"Or your grandfather's involvement," Wallace said. "We did this together."

"He is right," Lee said. "We made our choice a long time ago. It was wrong. We were all cursed because of it, but now it is over."

"Not quite," Riley said. "These pieces are going back to China, to be restored to the National Palace Museum." He paused. "You agree with that, don't you, Paige?"

She looked at her family standing across from her, waiting, watching. She couldn't remember when she'd had their attention before. And it was time to stand up, to take control as her grandfather had told her to do.

"Yes," she said. "The pieces will be returned, to the museum as soon as possible. My father will make sure of that, won't you, Dad?"

"It would be my honor," David replied.

"But--" Wallace sputtered.

"Don't try to stop us, Grandfather," Paige said. "It's the right thing to do, and we're going to do it.

"And just how do you think you're going to do it?" Wallace asked David. "Where are you going to say you got the set?"

"He's going to say," Victoria interrupted, "that the House of Hathaway in association with their friends, the Chen family and the Delaney family, discovered a rare and previously lost piece of Chinese art that is now being returned to its rightful place."

Her mother was so smart, reading the situation quickly and coming up with a solution that would turn the three men from thieves into heroes. Everyone in the room seemed dumbstruck by her suggestion. But who could argue? Each family wanted to protect their own.

"Shouldn't they have to pay for what they did?" Alyssa asked finally.

"Everyone has paid in his own way," David replied. "My father lost his wife, his daughter, and his granddaughter. Your grandfather suffered the shame of knowing that his wife had burned down the store. Your grandmother suffered horrible burns on her arms. Your mother lived a life of shame and dishonor, from which you suffered as well."

"And my grandfather lost his daughter to drugs," Riley continued. "He also lost his mind and can't even remember his name, much less what he did fifty years ago. Mr. Hathaway is right. Everyone has paid a price for what was done." He paused. "Now, knowing that we've all agreed on what has to happen, I want to ensure it actually does happen. I think we should have the pieces put into a secure vault until they can be transported back to China."

"I'll make sure of that," Victoria said. "But first we'll put them on display in the upcoming Hathaway exhibit at the Asian Art Museum." Her eyes lit up at the thought. "You'll all be given due credit, of course. I'm a genius with a press release. Just ask anyone. I'd better make some calls."

"She's really something, your mother," Riley said to Paige as the group began to disperse.

"Yes, she is. I guess it's finally over." She couldn't help wondering where they would go from here now that they no longer had a dragon to chase.

"Not quite. I need to fill in my grandmother."

"Give her my love," Paige said. She watched him walk out the door with a heavy heart. Would she ever see him again?

"My family and I are leaving now," Alyssa said, coming up to Paige. "It's almost the new year. I think it's going to be a good one."

"I do, too. By the way, how do you feel about a new job?"

"What do you mean?"

"The House of Hathaway could certainly use another Hathaway."

"But I'm not a Hathaway."

"Aren't you?”

"Really? Can you do that? Hire me on without asking anyone?"

Paige smiled. "As a matter of fact, I can. You see, I'm the Hathaway heir. Only, I just recently discovered that I'm not the only one. And if I have to run that damn store one day, so do you. Of course, we'll have to get my mother out of it first."

"She's not going to want me there."

"No," Paige agreed. "But it's about time she realized that she's not the only woman in this family who gets what she wants. I want you in the store, and in my life. You're my sister. And I can't wait to get to know you."

Alyssa threw her arms around Paige and gave her a hug that Paige gladly returned. Out of this entire mess had come a new, wonderful relationship with a woman she could call a sister.

"I have to go," Alyssa said. "I have a man to meet."

"Ben?"

"I'd like to ring in the new year with him." She paused. "Maybe you and Riley should do the same thing."

"He's already gone."

"So go find him. You want him, too, don't you?"

She did. But this time he would have to come to her.

Paige entered her apartment just before midnight, exhausted from the night's events. All she wanted was a hot bath, a glass of wine, and bed. Two out of three were waiting for her in her bedroom. She smiled in pure delight. Riley had come to her. Granted, he was asleep, but it was the thought that counted.

She sat down on the side of the bed and put her hand on his chest. He stirred ever so slightly as she leaned over and put her mouth to his. She knew the moment he awoke, the moment he gave his heart to hers in one long, tender, passionate kiss.

He cupped her face when she tried to pull away and kissed her again as if he wanted to make sure she'd gotten the message the first time.

"Beautiful Paige," he murmured as he released her. "What took you so long?"

"I didn't know you would be waiting. How did you get in here?"

"I know a little bit about locks. And you need a better security system. In fact, I can think of a lot of things you need."

"Anything in particular -- or should I say anyone?"

"Me," he replied with a grin.

"What about you? What do you need?"

"You, Paige."

"I want a long-term commitment."

"How long term?" he asked warily.

"Marriage, children, pets, a house of my own, furniture I choose, a garden."

"Whoa. Time out."

"What's the matter? Scared?"

"Terrified," he admitted.

"Okay, then, we'll start out slow. How about a real date involving dinner, maybe a little dancing, some champagne, rose petals on satin sheets?"

"Now you're talking. When can we go?"

"Any time you want."

"Paige," he said more seriously, "I don't know if I have it in me to be the kind of man you want and deserve. I don't want to disappoint you."

"You couldn't do that, Riley. And while I do hope for everything I said before, what I really want is you, on whatever terms you can give me. The truth is I'd rather have a few days with you than a lifetime with someone else. You've set me free, brought out a side of me I didn't know I had. I'll never be the same again."

"You've done the same thing for me." He pulled her hand to his heart. "I thought this had broken a long time ago. But you brought it back to life."

"I'm glad. We ended up on the same side after all,"

she said.

"Yes. Both our grandfathers were thieves. And Alyssa's, too. So much for protecting our families' names."

"Let's just hope our generation can turn things around."

"We will." He paused. "Are we going to have to wait for our romantic date to... you know?"

"I think so. You should have to work for it this time."

"Paige," he groaned, "you're going to kill me."

"You better believe it. Starting now," she said with a wicked smile.

"I thought you just said--"

"It's a woman's prerogative to change her mind. Besides, we haven't made love in this bed yet." She leaned over to kiss him, but he put a finger against her lips.

"Uh, Paige."

"What now?"

"I just remembered. I don't have my wallet."

"You have to start driving with your driver's license, Riley."

"I don't suppose you have another copy of the Odyssey laying around?" he asked hopefully.

"Unfortunately, no, and I hate to admit it, but this bed has seen about as much action as the one in my parents' house. I haven't brought a guy here in a long time. I don't think I have anything."

"That's all right. We have the rest of our lives to make love to each other."

"I like the sound of that."

"So do I," he admitted.

"Do you trust me, Riley, really trust me?"

"Yes, I do. Let me show you how much." He tossed

her back on the pillows, his hands slipping under her sweater.

"This feels more like lust," she teased.

"Now it's your turn to trust me. There are a lot of things we can do without a condom."

"Show me."

"I intend to." He paused, gazing into her eyes. "You're an amazing woman."

"And you're an amazing man. By the way, when we get married -- and I know we will," she added with a smile of her own, "I'm taking your name. I think I'm going to be a better McAllister than a Hathaway."

"I just want you, Paige. I don't care what your name is."

"I love you, Riley."

"I love you, too," he whispered, sealing his words with a lingering kiss.

THE END

Keep on reading for an excerpt from

SILENT RUN

EXCERPT – SILENT RUN

Sanders Brothers - Book One

Prologue

Large raindrops streamed against her windshield as she sped along the dark, narrow highway north of Los Angeles. She'd been traveling for over an hour along the wild and beautiful Pacific coastline. She'd passed the busy beach cities of Venice and Santa Monica, the celebrity-studded hills of Malibu and Santa Barbara. Thank God it was a big state. She could start over again, find a safe place to stay, but she had to get there first.

The pair of headlights in her rearview mirror drew closer with each passing mile. Her nerves began to tighten, and goose bumps rose along her arms and the back of her neck. She'd been running too long not to recognize danger. But where had the car come from? She'd been so sure that no one had followed her out of LA. After sixty miles of constantly checking her rearview mirror she'd begun to relax, but now the fear came rushing back.

It was too dark to see the car behind her, but there was something about the speed with which it was approaching that made her nervous. She pressed her foot down harder on the gas, clinging to the wheel as gale-force winds blowing in off the ocean rocketed through the car, making the driving even more treacherous.

A few miles later the road veered inland. She looked for a place to exit. Finally she saw a sign for an upcoming turnoff heading into the Santa Ynez Mountains. Maybe with a few twists and turns she could lose the car on her tail, and if her imagination were simply playing tricks on her, the car behind her would just continue down the road.

The exit came up fast. She took the turn on two wheels. Five minutes later the pair of headlights was once again directly behind her. There was no mistake: He was coming after her.

She had to get away from him. Adrenaline raced through her bloodstream, giving her courage and strength. She was so tired of running for her life, but she couldn't quit now. She'd probably made a huge mistake leaving the main highway. There was no traffic on this two-lane road. If he caught her now there would be no one to come to her rescue.

The gap between their cars lessened. He was so close she could see the silhouette of a man in her rearview mirror. He was bearing down on her.

She took the next turn too sharply, her tires sliding on

the slick, wet pavement.

Sudden lights coming from the opposite direction blinded her. She hit the brakes hard. The car skidded out of control. She flew across the road, crashed through a wooden barrier, and hurtled down a steep embankment. Rocks splintered the windshield as she threw up her hands in protest and prayer.

When the impact finally came it was crushing, the pain intense. It was too much. All she wanted to do was to sink into oblivion. It was over. She was finished.

But some voice deep inside her screamed at her to stay awake, because if she wasn't dead yet, she soon would be.

Chapter One

The blackness in her mind began to lessen. There was a light behind her eyelids that beckoned and called to her. She was afraid to answer that call, terrified to open her eyes. Maybe it was the white light people talked about, the one to follow when you were dead. But she wasn't dead, was she?

It was just a nightmare, she told herself. She was dreaming; she'd wake up in a minute. But something was wrong. Her bed didn't feel right. The mattress was hard beneath her back. There were odd bells going off in her head. She smelled antiseptic and chlorine bleach. A siren wailed in the distance. Someone was talking to her, a man.

Her stomach clenched with inexplicable fear as she felt a strong hand on her shoulder. Her eyes flew open, and she blinked rapidly, the scene before her confusing.

She wasn't home in her bedroom, as she'd expected. A man in a long white coat stood next to the bed. He appeared to be in his fifties, with salt-and-pepper hair, dark eyes, and a serious expression. He held a clipboard in one hand. A stethoscope hung around his neck, and a pair of glasses rested on his long, narrow nose. Next to him stood a short, plump brunette dressed in blue scrubs, offering a compassionate, encouraging smile that seemed to match the name on her name tag, Rosie.

What was going on? Where was she?

"You're awake," the doctor said, a brisk note in his voice, a gleam of satisfaction in his eyes. "That's good. We were getting concerned about you. You've been unconscious for hours."

Unconscious? She gazed down the length of her body, suddenly aware of the thin blue gown, the hospital identification band on her wrist, the IV strapped to her left arm. And pain—there was pain... in her head, her right wrist, and her knees. Her right cheek throbbed. She raised a hand to her temple and was surprised to encounter a bandage. What on earth had happened to her?

"You were in an automobile accident last night," the doctor told her. "You have some injuries, but you're going to be all right. You're at St. Mary's Hospital just outside of Los Olivos in Santa Barbara County. I'm Dr. Carmichael. Do you understand what I'm saying?"

She shook her head, his brisk words jumbling up in her brain, making little to no sense. "Am I dreaming?" she whispered.

"You're not dreaming, but you do have a head injury. It's not unusual to be confused," the doctor replied. He offered her a small, practiced smile that was edged with impatience. "Now, do you feel up to a few questions? Why don't we start with your name?"

She opened her mouth to reply, thinking that was an easy question, until nothing came to mind. Her brain was blank. What was her name? She had to have one. Everyone did. What on earth was wrong with her? She gave a helpless shake of her head. "I'm... I'm not sure," she murmured, shocked by the realization.

The doctor frowned, his gaze narrowing on her face. "You don't remember your name? What about your address, or where you're from?"

She bit down on her bottom lip, straining to think of the right answers. Numbers danced in her head, but no streets, no cities, no states. A wave of terror rushed through her. She had to be dreaming—lost in a nightmare. She wanted to run, to scream, to wake herself up, but she couldn't do any of those things.

"You don't know, do you?" the nurse interjected.

"I... I should know. Why don't I know? What's wrong with me? Why can't I remember my name, where I'm from? What's going on?" Her voice rose with each desperate question.

"Your brain suffered a traumatic injury," Dr. Carmichael explained. "It may take some time for you to feel completely back to normal. It's probably nothing to worry about. You just need to rest, let the swelling go down."

His words were meant to be reassuring, but anxiety ran like fire through her veins. She struggled to remember something about herself. Glancing down at her hands, she saw the light pink, somewhat chipped polish on her fingernails and wondered how it could be that her own fingers didn't look familiar to her. She wore no rings, no jewelry, not even a watch. Her skin was pale, her arms thin. But she had no idea what her face looked like.

"A mirror," she said abruptly. "Could someone get me a mirror?"

Dr. Carmichael and Rosie exchanged a brief glance, and then he nodded to the nurse, who quickly left the room. "You need to try to stay calm," he said as he jotted something down on his clipboard. "Getting upset won't do you any good."

"I don't know my name. I don't know what I look like." Hysteria bubbled in her throat, and panic made her want to jump out of bed and run... but to where, she had no idea. She tried to breathe through the rush of adrenaline. If this were a nightmare, eventually she'd wake up. If it wasn't... well, then she'd have to figure out what to do next. In the meantime she had to calm down. She had to think.

The doctor said she'd had an accident. Like the car crash in her dream? Was it possible that had been real and not a dream?

Glancing toward the clock, she saw that it was seven thirty. At least she knew how to read the time. "Is it night or morning?" Her gaze traveled to the window, but the heavy blue curtain was drawn, making it impossible for her to see outside.

"It's morning," the doctor replied. "You were brought in around nine o'clock last night."

Almost ten hours ago. So much time had passed. "Do you know what happened to me?"

"I'm afraid I don't know the details, but from what I understand, you were in a serious car accident."

Before she could ask another question, the nurse returned to the room and handed her a small compact mirror.

She opened the compact with shaky fingers, almost afraid of what she would see. She stared at her face for a long minute. Her eyes were light blue, framed by thick black lashes. Her hair was a dull dark brown, long, tangled, and curly, dropping past her shoulders. There were dark circles under her eyes, as well as purple bruises that were accentuated by the pallor of her skin. A white bandage was taped across her temple. Multiple tiny cuts covered her cheekbones. Her face was thin, drawn. She looked like a ghost. Even her eyes were haunted by shadows.

"Oh, God," she whispered, feeling as if she were looking at a complete stranger. Who was she?

"The cuts will heal," the nurse said. "Don't worry. You'll have your pretty face back before you know it."

It wasn't the bruises on her face that filled her heart with terror; it was the fact that she didn't recognize anything about herself. She felt absolutely no connection to the woman in the mirror. She slammed the compact shut, afraid to look any longer. Her pulse raced, and her heart beat in triple time as the reality of her situation sank in. She felt completely vulnerable, and she wanted to run and hide until she figured everything out. She would have jumped out of bed if Dr. Carmichael hadn't put his hand on her shoulder, perhaps sensing her desperation.

"You're going to be all right," he said firmly, meeting her gaze. "The answers will come. Don't push too hard. Just rest and let your body recuperate from the trauma."

"What if the answers don't come?" she whispered. "What if I'm like this forever?"

He frowned, unable to hide the concern in his eyes. "Let's take it one step at a time. There's a deputy from the sheriff's office down the hall. He'd like to speak to you."

A police officer wanted to talk to her? That didn't sound good. She swallowed back another lump of fear. "Why? Why does he want to talk to me?"

"Something to do with your accident. I'll let him know you're awake."

As the doctor left the room, Rosie stepped forward. "Can I get you anything—water, juice, an extra blanket? The mornings are still so cold. I can't wait until April. I don't know about you, but I'm tired of the rain. I'm ready for the sun to come out."

That meant it was March, the end of a long, cold winter, spring on the nearby horizon. Images ran through her mind of windy afternoons, flowers beginning to bloom, someone flying a kite, a beautiful red-and-gold kite that tangled in the branches of a tall tree. The laughter of a young girl filled her head—was it her laughter or someone else's? She saw two other girls and a boy running across the grass. She wanted to catch up to them, but they were too far away, and then they were gone, leaving her with nothing but a disturbing sense of loss and a thick curtain of blackness in her head.

Why couldn't she remember? Why had her brain locked her out of her own life?

"What day is it?" she asked, determined to gather as many details as she possibly could.

"It's Thursday, March twenty-second," Rosie replied with another sympathetic smile.

"Thursday," she murmured, feeling relieved to have a new fact to file away, even if it was something as inconsequential as the day of the week.

"Try not to worry. You'll be back to normal before you know it," Rosie added.

"I don't even know what normal is. Where are my things?" she asked abruptly, looking for more answers. Maybe if she had something of her own to hold in her hand, everything would come back to her.

Rosie tipped her head toward a neat pile of clothes on a nearby chair. "That's what you were wearing when they brought you in. You didn't have a purse with you, nor were you wearing any jewelry."

"Could you hand me my clothes, please? "

"Sure. They're a bit bloodied," Rosie said, as she gathered up the clothes and laid them on the bed. "I'll check on you in a while. Just push the call button if you need anything."

She stared at the pair of blue jeans, which were ripped at the knees, the light blue camisole top, the navy sweater, and the gray jacket dotted with dark spots of blood or dirt, she wasn't sure which. Glancing across the room she saw a pair of Nike tennis shoes on the floor. They looked worn-out, as if she'd done a lot of running in them.

Another memory flashed in her brain. She could almost feel herself running, the wind in her hair, her heart pounding, the breath tight in her chest. But she wasn't out for a jog. She wasn't dressed right. She was wearing a heavy coat, a dress, and high stiletto heels. She tried to hang on to the image floating vaguely in her head, but it disappeared as quickly as it had come. She supposed she should feel grateful she'd remembered something, but the teasing bit only frustrated her more.

She dug her hands into the pockets of her jeans and jacket, searching for some clue as to who she was, but there was nothing there. She was about to put the jacket aside when she noticed an odd lump in the inner back lining. She ran her fingers across the material, surprised to find a flap covering a hidden zipper. She pulled on the zipper and felt inside, shocked when she pulled out a wad of twenty-dollar bills. There had to be at least fifteen hundred dollars. Why on earth had she stashed so much cash in her jacket? Obviously she'd taken great care to hide it, as someone would have had to examine the jacket carefully in order to find the money. Whoever had undressed her had not discovered the cash.

A knock came at her door, and she hurriedly stuffed the money back into her jacket and set it on the end of her bed just seconds before a uniformed police officer entered the room. Her pulse jumped at the sight of him, and it wasn't with relief but with fear. Her instincts were screaming at her to be cautious, that he could be trouble.

The officer was on the stocky side, with a military haircut, and appeared to be in his mid-forties. His forehead was lined, his skin a ruddy red and weatherbeaten, his gaze extremely serious.

"I'm Tom Manning," he said briskly. "I'm a deputy with the county sheriff's department. I'm investigating your car accident."

"Okay," she said warily. "I should tell you that I don't remember what happened. In fact, I don't remember anything about myself."

"Yeah, the doc says you have some kind of amnesia."

His words were filled with suspicion, and skepticism ran through his dark eyes. Why was he suspicious? What reason could she possibly have for pretending not to remember? Had something bad occurred during the accident? Had she done something wrong? Had someone else been hurt? Her stomach turned over at the thought.

"Can you tell me what happened?" she said, almost afraid to ask.

"Your car went off the side of the road in the Santa Ynez Mountains, not far from San Marcos Pass. You plunged down a steep embankment and landed in a ravine about two hundred yards from the road. Fortunately, you ran into a tree."

"Fortunately?" she echoed.

"Otherwise you would have ended up in a boulder-filled, high-running creek," he told her. "The front end of your Honda Civic was smashed, and the windshield was shattered."

Which explained the cuts and bruises on her face.

"You're a very lucky woman," the deputy added.

"Who found me?" she asked.

"A witness saw your car go over the side and called nine-one-one. Does any of this sound familiar?"

The part about going off the side of the road sounded a lot like the dream she'd been having. "I'm not sure."

"Were you alone in the car?"

His question surprised her. "I think so." She thought back to her dream. Had she been alone in the car? She didn't remember anyone else. "If I wasn't alone, wouldn't that other person be here at the hospital?" she asked.

"The back door of your car was open. There was a child's car seat strapped in the middle of the backseat, a bottle half-filled with milk, and this shoe." Officer Manning held up a clear plastic bag through which she could see a shoe so small it would fit into the palm of her hand. Her heart began to race. She had the sudden urge to call for a time-out, to make him leave before he said something else, something terrifying, something to do with that shoe. "Oh, God. Stop. I can't do this."

"I'm sorry, but I need to know. Do you have a baby?" he asked. "Was your child with you in the car?"

END OF EXCERPT